Sandie B

The Angel at No.33

By Polly Williams

The Rise and Fall Of A Yummy Mummy
A Bad Bride's Tale
A Good Girl Comes Undone
How To Be Married
It Happened One Summer
The Angel At No. 33

The Angel at No.33

POLLY WILLIAMS

headline
review

First published in 2011
by HEADLINE REVIEW
An imprint of HEADLINE PUBLISHING GROUP

1

Cataloguing in Publication Data is available from the British Library

ISBN 978 0 7553 5886 1 (Hardback)
ISBN 978 0 7553 5926 4 (Trade paperback)

Typeset in Sabon by Avon DataSet Ltd,
Bidford-on-Avon, Warwickshire

Printed and bound by CPI Group (UK) Ltd, Croydon, CR0 4YY

Headline's policy is to use papers that are natural, renewable and
recyclable products and made from wood grown in sustainable forests.
The logging and manufacturing processes are expected to conform to the
environmental regulations of the country of origin.

HEADLINE PUBLISHING GROUP
An Hachette UK Company
338 Euston Road
London NW1 3BH

www.headline.co.uk
www.hachette.co.uk

To Ben, with love

Acknowledgements

A big thank you to Imogen Taylor, Jane Morpeth, Caitlin Raynor, Jo Liddiard, Vicky Cowell and everyone at Headline, my agent Lizzy Kremer, Katina Doyle, Andrea Chase, Julia Williams, and, as always, Ben, Oscar, Jago and Alice.

One

So I get run over by a bus and I am wearing my worst knickers. Yellow knickers the size of the O2. I lie there in Regent Street, skirt hitched up around my waist like one of those binge drinkers you see on the news. As a crowd clusters, I pan back from the indignity of that crumpled body, fast, shakily, until the figure recedes to a lump on the road, surrounded by a circus of flashing lights. Still you could have seen those knickers from space.

Am I dead? Not sure actually. Don't *feel* dead. Maybe it's that I don't feel dead in the way that an old person doesn't feel old. Or I have a phantom self, much like an amputee has a phantom limb. Either way, totally weird. I am a christened non-believer who never goes to church apart from midnight Mass at Christmas – soft spot for carols and candles – but I don't believe. Not in that stuff. I believe in a bit of yoga (lapsed) and the healing power of cold white wine of an evening (unlapsed). But I don't believe in heaven. I don't believe in ghosts. Or angels.

And yet.

I am at my own funeral. Look up. I am here, near the

rafters, where pigeons poo and virulent woodworm has set in, unbeknown to the gay rev. (Colin. He would be called Colin.) There is a drone of shuffling damp shoes on cold dry stone. It's my Facebook page sprung to life. Heads down, frowning, they walk solemnly through the church's heavy wooden doors. They all look at least ten years older than their profile photographs, ashen-faced, wearing charcoal and black and sunglasses, like an army of glum fashionistas. Some I haven't seen in the flesh for years – can't quite believe my ex Chris Adderson has the nerve to show up after screwing Sara, also here, shameless – and I watch as they sing, cry and, yes, yawn. (True to form, Danny Brixham taps on his BlackBerry during the prayer.)

Among the throng I spot the tight cluster of my Muswell Hill friends, neighbours, school mums, the people who've populated my daily life since I had Freddie and moved out to the 'burbs, the people who make up my favourite coffee circuit in the world. Yep, there's Tash, cutting a dash in black with red shoes. (Red shoes at a funeral? Me neither.) Lydia, the loudest sobber in church – there's always one, and if you knew Lydia you'd know it absolutely would have to be her. And Suze, dear old Suze with her wild blonde 'fro, twitching her speech notes, raring to go. She loves public speaking of any kind (entirely wasted on the PTA, should be running a small nation) and I can see she has written reams of absolute tosh about my role in the school community, the volunteering that she's repeatedly bamboozled and guilt-tripped me into at the school gates: cake sales, international evenings, Christmas fairs, let's-make-bunting parties, the 5K I ran in a red polka dot fifties ballgown for the twin school in Bolivia.

2

Standing in the same block, directly in front of them, is my poor darling family. Mum, broken. Dad, disbelieving. Mad aunt Pat, looking like she's rather enjoying the drama, certainly the opportunity to wear what looks like a giant Oreo cookie on her head. And then there's my little sister, Mary. If ever anyone needed a bit of privacy. Poor sis. And my best mate Jenny, just behind her, who looks like she's been breakfasting on crystal meth and has put her make-up on in the dark. There is so much I want to say to my dearest Jenny, not least that she always used to say that I'd be late for my own funeral. (Wrong!)

Funeral. That means I'm really dead, doesn't it? I'm presuming someone's actually checked my pulse. Fuck. What if they haven't? What if there's been some terrible error?

Ollie's handsome face says that something awful has happened. His eyes are puffy, slitty, unlit windows. He is cloaked in a cold blue aura like a surgical overall. While Freddie . . . No, I can't go there. My darling, beautiful little Freddie.

Whenever I think about either of them living even one minute longer without me I hear a whistling sound, a terrible roar, like a vicious wind howling across a featureless moor, and it fills me with darkness.

There are no words.

Five days ago I was alive enough to get riled by the way Ollie stacked the plates in the dishwasher. Alive enough to worry about the six pounds I'd put on over Christmas and vow to start the Dukan diet. Alive enough to make a new year's resolution, assuming I'd make one the year after that, and the year after that, and the year after that, and . . .

OK, let's rewind. Forget my funeral, here's how the curtain fell.

Five days ago

It's only a damp Tuesday night, but after the hungover drear of New Year's Day I am really quite keen to get out of the house, to see someone who isn't my immediate family. But I am late. I am always bloody late. This time I've lost a boot, and this is slowing my progress out of the house. My husband is not helping.

'You love me how much out of ten?' Ollie asks, sitting on the bottom step of the stairs, head resting on his knees, watching me with those heavy-lidded black eyes of his. They are the eyes of a young Italian lover, even though he's not that young, nor Italian. He's originally from Wigan.

'Nine and a half.'

'When we first met it was eleven.'

'That was before we shared a bathroom.' I hop down the hall on my solo boot. Daft Punk blasts. 'Turn it down, Ol, seriously. Where the hell is my other boot?'

Ollie shrugs, pulls Freddie on to his lap. 'We have means of stopping Mummy going out in sexy boots, don't we, Freddie?' Ollie and Freddie. Their faces repeat the same handsome features in a different colour palette. They look at each other and grin an identical Brady-patented grin.

'Ollie, I haven't seen Jenny in yonks!'

'Must be at least twenty-four hours.'

'Not since Christmas, actually.'

'Sweetheart, it's January the sixth.'

I ignore him and start pulling things out of the wicker basket in the hall: gloves, trapper hats, fleecy wellie warmers, umbrellas, remnants of Christmas wrapping paper that survived my new year cleaning purge. Ping Pong, north London's least affectionate tabby, pounces on a glove and kills it, shaking her head from side to side with the offending item in her jaws. 'How can a boot just disappear into thin air? How is this *possible*?'

'Mummy's boot has made a break for it.' Ollie laughs and nuzzles his nose into Freddie's brush of blond hair. 'It's passed through the portal into that world of lost things never to be found again.'

'Like Doctor Who,' Freddie nods gravely.

'Like my sunglasses. Did you ever find those flash snowboarding glasses that your sis gave me for Christmas, Soph?'

I give him an exasperated look – he is constantly losing things, which is why I suspect him of playing a key role in the disappearance of the boot – and hop into the living room. 'No, I didn't.'

'What's for our dinner?'

Annoyed by this assumption – albeit correct – that I am in charge of all things fridge, cupboard and supermarket, I say nothing and bend down to look beneath our grey velvet sofa, the underworld where Lego bricks and hair balls breed.

'Soph? I'm marvin'. What's for supper?'

'Last night's lentil and hock soup.'

'Aww. Can't we have fish and chips?' asks Freddie. Ollie winks at him. And I know that they will have fish and chips, probably with one of those artery-fuzzing battered sausages and one of those pickled eggs that looks like a rude body part preserved in a jar.

'AHA!' Lost object found. I grab a plastic segment of Hot Wheels track, prod the boot determinedly into my reach and tug it on. My foot collides with something hard and sharp. A Transformer. I zip the boot up and it feels tight, too tight, like the waistline of my skinny jeans which have also miraculously shrunk. I know that my legs have been stuffed like Christmas stockings with brandy cream, champagne truffles and mince pies. I know that some long, hard weeks of denial lie ahead of me and this is depressing. I hate dieting. It's not in my nature. I'd like more of everything: more food, sex, sleep, shoes, and more time. Why am I always running out of time?

My phone beeps.

It's a text from Jenny. She's in the new tapas bar on Beak Street, where we've only got a table because swanky London is still drinking mulled wine beside log fires in bolt holes in the Cotswolds. 'Pitying look from waiter. Where r u?'

'On way!' I fib back, yanking on a shaggy black fake fur coat. (Like to think it gives me a slutty Hollywood glamour. Ollie says it makes me look like a giant goatee and is only acceptable if I go nudie underneath.) Freddie sinks back against Ollie's chest, drinking me in, studying me intently, as he always does when I'm dressed up, as if I'm morphing into someone who isn't just his mum.

'You've dropped something, Soph. Behind you,' says Ollie.

I bend down. Nothing. 'What?'

'Just wanted to see what you looked like when you bent over.' Ollie grins. It's his filthy rock star grin.

'Ollie!' I roll my eyes, enjoying that after all this time my bottom still rocks his world. I blow them puff-puff kisses like the movie star I was certain I'd be when I was a kid, before I got booted out of the Saturday club aged fifteen for snogging my drama teacher. 'Boys, be good.'

'What time you back, beautiful?'

'Won't be late.' I step out of the warm hug of number thirty-three into the exhilarating possibilities of the London night. 'Love you,' I call over my shoulder, as I always do, but meaning it all the same.

Forward three hours. Jenny and I are at the tapas place, second bottle of red wine almost finished. I can no longer feel the blister on my left pinkie toe caused by those damn boots – is it possible to put weight on one's toes? – and the evening is beginning to fray pleasantly at the edges. I am probably talking too much because I've spent too long brooding on things over Christmas and am feeling the need to unburden myself, dropping my sticky, undigested gripes on to the restaurant table like the remains of the figgy pudding in my fridge.

'Do you want the hard, bitter January truth?' Jenny is refusing to indulge me.

I peek out at her from between my fingers. 'If you must.'

'Most people would kill for your problems.' Satisfied by this decree, Jenny slumps back into her wooden chair as the waiter uncorks another bottle of wine and pours it into our lipstick-smudged glasses. 'And . . .' she says, waggling her finger, '. . . most women would kill for a man like Ollie, and you know it, Soph.'

'They would change their mind once they'd tried living with him for longer than it takes to finish a *Mad Men* box set.'

She laughs, looks at me fondly. Her eyes are pink rimmed because she's pissed. We're both pissed. 'You're a hard woman, Sophie Brady.'

'Nocturnal, totally unpractical. He's less domesticated than Freddie.'

She gives me a sharp look.

'Yeah, yeah. Obviously I wouldn't have him any other way.'

'So the problem is . . . ?'

'No problem. It's just rubbishy life stuff.' I sip my wine, not really tasting it now. It's got to that stage of the night. 'Not something to be *solved*, Jenny. Not everything can be solved. Life is not a sudoku puzzle.'

'Hmm,' she says, unconvinced. Jenny is an optimistic sceptical pragmatist. She believes there is a global conspiracy to make us all worry too much so that we buy newspapers and insurance and comfort products 'like Babybel cheese, the world's weirdest food'. Her words, not mine. I like Babybel. The colour of that red wax is the same as the lippy I wear every day, naked without it.

'If you've been with someone since you were twenty-two and . . . Oh, I don't know. I'm sure it's the same for him. He only ever got to have two other girlfriends before I came along. We were both so YOUNG! And now we've been together longer than Blair was in government. Or Thatcher.'

I sluice my wine around the glass. I think as I do this that I'll never get tired of seeing red wine stain the sides of a glass pink. Simple pleasures. 'The truth is, and God, I'd never say this to Ollie, so swear on your life not to repeat this, but I miss how it used to be, Jen, you know, in the early days. It's sad knowing that I will never feel that adrenaliney lust rush thing again. That, you know,' I assume a bad cockney accent, 'me and Ollie is for keeps, like.'

'That's actually a far sweeter sentiment than you realise, Soph.' Jenny looks a bit wistful.

I feel bad for having what everyone wants and not being grateful enough. I've brought us down. I must bring us up again. 'But what about the *grrr*?'

'The what?'

I growl again. 'The *grrr*. Come 'ere! That feeling.'

Jenny laughs. A couple on the adjacent table who don't look like they have much *grrr* going on pretend they're not listening in. The woman's feet curl around her chair legs. She frowns.

'Overrated.' Jenny's eyes dance. I love the way her eyes dance. She's one of those rare women who looks prettier drunk, loosened up a little.

'I think it's just that I'd like to feel that *grrr* one more time before . . .' I slam my hands on the table. Jenny is glazing over. 'Sorry! I'll shut up. Clearly I'm going through some kind of horribly clichéd mid-life crisis. It's boring and I apologise.'

'Don't apologise,' she laughs. 'Just tell me when it peaks. Because we've not even started, Soph.'

'Actually, I think it might have peaked already.'

'When?' she laughs.

'Sainsbury's, this afternoon.' I gulp back some wine, warming to my theme. 'You know those self-serving tills that never work and you always end up having to wait for a real live human being to come and unlock the damn thing because it malfunctions if you use your own bag? "Unidentified object in the bagging area!" Fuck, I hate them. I hate supermarkets. And no, I don't have a Nectar card. No, I don't *want* a Nectar card!'

'Don't be poncy.'

'The day I get a supermarket loyalty card it's all over, Jenny.' I gulp back more wine. 'See, a clear case of mid-life crisis.'

Jenny leans back in her chair and studies me in that scrutinising way of hers. 'You're not old enough for a mid-life crisis, Soph. You have to be *forty*. You're thirty-five.' Jenny is very exact. She has an ordered walk-in wardrobe of a mind. Mine is more like an overstuffed knicker drawer.

'I could die when I am seventy and that would make me mid-life exactly.' (Posthumous note: no discernible shiver of irony felt at the time.) I scoop a spoonful of crème caramel into my mouth and its sweetness is like a kiss.

'Women don't die at seventy any more. We die at eighty-two or something.' Jenny breaks into the crust of the chocolate torte with the edge of her spoon, releasing a river of sweet goo. It looks better than my crème caramel. 'The blokes go first.'

'Just as well. Ollie would confuse the laundry rack with his zimmerframe and hang underpants on it.'

'This is amazing. Taste?'

I reach across the table and attack her pudding with my spoon. (Calories don't count if they belong to someone else.) It *is* better than my pudding. 'But isn't the really tragic thing that we'll be too old to enjoy our freedom when we finally get it?'

'No! I'm looking forward to us being old.'

I try to imagine us old, like proper old. It's hard. We've been young forever. I still buy polka dot tights at Topshop. Last year I rolled around in the mud at Glastonbury, naked.

'I don't want to be one of those exhausting women who try to stay thirtysomething forever. I want to wear different shades of beige and write letters of complaint about bad language to the BBC. I'll feel cheated otherwise.'

'Why is it you always order the better pudding, Jenny?'

'I just go for the most calorific option. Simple tactic.' She wipes her mouth with her napkin. It takes off the last bit of her pink lipstick. She looks about ten without make-up, like a frighteningly intelligent schoolgirl with her pretty soft baby face, wide blue eyes, and permanent frown of studied comprehension. Jenny is my only girlfriend who tackles the weekend newspapers before the magazine supplements. She devours all the big, heavy books you're meant to read, rather than the fun ones. She actually finished *Wolf Hall*! That said, Jenny knows all the lyrics to Dolly Parton's back catalogue, too. 'I intend to eat more puddings all year,' she adds cheerfully. 'My new year's resolution is not to beat myself up for being over ten stone. I've thought about it, and I've come to the conclusion that I'd rather eat pudding than be skinny.'

'Me too, me too.' I reach across for another spoonful.

11

'Fat, happy and gobby.'

I pick up my wine glass with a camp flourish. 'My new year's resolution was not to drink in January.'

Jenny raises her glass and we giggle.

'Fat faces age bloody well, you know,' I reflect.

'True, true.'

'The brilliant thing is, fat people don't have to choose between their face and their ass. They say, I'll have both please! Like in a restaurant.'

'Good point.' Jenny licks her spoon. 'And you know what, Soph? When we're old, like proper old, we will eat pudding for every meal because . . . who gives a toss?'

'All the men will be dead, anyway. And all the skinnies will have died of carb deficiency.' I rest my chin on my hand and reflect on the happy gluttony awaiting me. 'For the record, Jenny, when I'm old I'm going to wear one of those see-through plastic headscarves to keep the rain off my blowdried bouff. And I'll be rocking those orthopedic shoes with padded soles. I've always fancied some of those.'

'We can go on cruises together. I've always wanted to go on a cruise, one of those really cheesy ones with a songstress in red sequins on a white grand piano belting out Shirley Bassey.'

'Me too! Me too!' I raise my glass. It wobbles in my hand. 'We can cruise to the Galapagos. I've always wanted to go to the Galapagos.'

'To see turtles and those giant spooky stones.'

'That's Easter Island, div.'

'OK, Easter Island, too.'

'And St Barts. I will dreadlock my pubes and smoke

psychotropic skunk on the beach, because hell, why not?'

'Shall we do Vegas, too? We could gamble our pensions.'

'Fuck yeah.'

We sit in easy silence for a few moments, scraping the last smears of sweetness off the pudding plates, enjoying the crushed happy hubbub of the restaurant and being away from the dog end of the Christmas holidays. We devour the remains of the breadbasket and chortle childishly when a waiter drops a tray beside us in a slapstick manner. The tea light is at the end of its wax, smoking and spluttering a salty blue. It is in this happy drunken blur that I decide this is the moment to bring the subject up. 'Dare I ask, Jenny?'

Something flickers across her eyes. She doesn't want me to ask. 'The answer's no.'

I lean sloppily over the table, warming my hands on the dying tea light. 'But I thought you were going to have the Big Conversation?'

'It shrank. It became a conversation about the best way to cook the rack of lamb,' she says briskly, looking away from me into the restaurant.

'I guess you've got to set a wedding date at some point,' I say carefully. 'I mean, you don't want to end up walking down the aisle in your seventies looking like Vivienne Westwood.'

She doesn't laugh like she's meant to. Instead she sniffs. 'It's perfectly normal to be engaged for one year.'

'I was joking, Jenny.' This is my cue to tell her. My mouth opens then closes. Nothing comes out. I can talk absolute nonsense until my larynx bleeds, but I can't talk about this. Best friends, no secrets? True. But I don't want to ruin our supper, or worse. Anyway, I'm probably too pissed. Yes, yes, too pissed. So I promise myself that I'll call round to her flat next week, during the day, while Sam's out, and we'll have coffee and passion fruit cheesecake and we'll talk then. She loves cheesecake. The cheesecake will help.

She looks at me, narrows her eyes. 'I know you don't approve of him, Soph.'

'That's not true.'

Silence. We both know that the conversation has hit a protrusion, like a speed bump in the road. We do the same thing, look away from each other and around the restaurant, smiling hazily, women who've drunk too much and know each other well enough to drop the topic before we start whacking each other over the head with our handbags. Some diners are beginning to leave now, picking up bills, bustling to the loo, while the late-night crowd, flushed from a theatre or bar, take their tables and over order tapas.

A waiter asks us if we want to order anything else, like he wants us to leave. I glance at my watch. 'Where has the evening gone? I feel like I only got here five minutes ago. I should get home.'

Jenny looks disappointed. 'But we haven't dissected Sarah's affair yet.'

'I know, nor Maxine's new teeth. They file the real teeth to Shane McGowan pegs before they put veneers on. Isn't that totally gross?'

'I've heard that the veneers drop off all the time. Imagine, you'd never want to bite into an apple again.'

Giggles snort through my nose. 'Do you remember when my hair extension blew off on Primrose Hill and landed on

David Walliams's labradoodle?' I don't know why I suddenly remember this, but I can see it vividly. That gorgeous gusty day on top of Primrose Hill, the whole of London before us, Freddie, a baby then, sitting on the picnic blanket, squashing strawberries into his mouth with his fist. A lifetime ago, literally.

'And the dog humped the bouff!'

I catch the time again on the oversized watch face of the woman sitting adjacent to us. It really is getting late.

Jenny catches me looking. She knows what I am thinking. 'Isn't it bad karma to leave so much wine?' She draws a finger down the bottle's label. 'Good wine, too.'

'It would be a bit studenty to ask to take it home, wouldn't it?'

'It would, Soph. Yes.'

'It does seem rather a shame.'

'And you *were* late, Sophie. Had you been on time then we would have finished the bottle by now.'

'Excellent point. What do you suggest then?'

Jenny fills our glasses. 'Rude not to.'

'I hold you fully responsible, Jenny.' I hiccup. 'And I want you to know that I will put all the blame on you when Ollie's on my case about me coming home rat-arsed.'

She raises her glass. 'Yes, I take full responsibility. That is what unmarried friends are for, isn't it? To get their married friends off the hook with their husbands.'

When we finally leave the restaurant it is raining outside, hard rain that comes at you at an angle. It is icy cold, threatening sleet. The street is splashy and full of people who've drunk too much, have not got an umbrella, and want to get home; people like us, desperately trying to get a cab. We give up trying to find one on Beak Street and walk towards the promising river of traffic on Regent Street, the leather soles of my boots skiddy on the wet pavement. Occupied cab after occupied cab zooms by, some maddeningly clicking their lights off just as they pass, others commandeered by new groups of revellers filtering in from Great Marlborough Street and Fouberts Place, nicking cabs that are rightfully ours seeing as we've waited for years already. A newly stolen cab throws a wash of dirty puddle over our feet.

'This is rubbish, Jenny. Time to get a dodgy cab.'

'Mini cab drivers all look like criminal photofits.'

'I'm not doing the flippin' Tube at this time.'

'Yay!' Jenny grabs my hand. 'Ye of little faith. Look. There's one. Just behind that bus.'

We watch as a yellow light, a warm, happy smudge in the wet darkness, moves towards us, slowly getting brighter.

'Right,' I say, jaw set, arm outstretched. 'Watch this. I'm going to get this cab if it kills me.'

Two

The coffin was white, decorated with a trembling bunch of marshmallow pink lilies. To Jenny it seemed too small, pitifully insubstantial. The idea that Sophie's body – beautiful, funny, larger than life Sophie – was inside, dead five days, cold as clay, was almost unbelievable. She squeezed Sam's hand harder, feeling the stiff rim of his shirt cuff push into her wrist.

A sob echoed around the overcrowded church. Each time this happened, which was frequently – every four or five breaths, she'd counted – Jenny's teeth ground together and her fillings twanged. Not knowing where to look, she kept her gaze on the forlorn figure of Ollie standing in the front pew. He had a new stoop in his coathanger shoulders and his face was full of shadows, even in the flat bright daylight. It was as if all his energy had pooled into his left hand, the hand knitted tightly to Freddie's. No wonder. Freddie looked so heartbreakingly tiny, shrunk to Lilliputian proportions by the soar of the stained glass windows and the yawning width of the church.

Ollie and Freddie, the two great loves of Sophie's life,

were flanked by Ollie's formidable-looking mother, Vicki, and, holding Freddie's other hand, Soph's mother, Sally, slighter than ever, all angles and elbows in a black skirt suit, the lone black feather on her hat shaking. Mike, Soph's dad, had one arm belted tight around her shoulder – squishing the jacket's shoulder pad up oddly – his other around Sophie's sister, Mary. Poor Mary, whose normally pretty face was puffy as a mushroom from crying and given a strange pallor by light streaming through a yellow pane of glass.

She had no doubt that they must wish it were her, Jenny, who'd stepped out in front of the bus instead of their beautiful daughter. She wasn't a mother, a wife, didn't and would never burn as brightly as Sophie. If she could have taken her place she would. But it had all happened in an instant. A hand outstretched, a slip of sole, a knuckle crunch of metal and bone. She could still see Sophie lying in the road. The image was imprinted in her brain forever, like a bright light bulb after you close your eyes.

'Deal.' That was her word. And it kept coming back to haunt her. She'd selfishly cajoled Sophie into drinking more wine when she should have realised that Sophie was a mother, that they weren't twentysomethings any more. Sophie had responsibilities: most women their age did. She was the oddity, needily trying to squeeze more out of her friend, unable to let go. If she'd let her return home earlier then it wouldn't have been raining and the road wouldn't have been slippy and that particular bus wouldn't have been on Regent Street, it would have been somewhere else on its route. And so would they.

As requested by the rev – Colin, she thought how much

Sophie would appreciate the fact he was called Colin – she held up the photocopied hymn sheet. Sophie's beautiful face was stamped at the top, so that it resembled a press release. The paper shook and the ink smudged beneath her sweating fingers. Could she sing? She was amazed that song was coming out of her mouth, not screams. 'Jerusalem'. She and Soph had sung this many times over the years at weddings. Some couples had worked out, others hadn't. None of them were ever as glamorous and besotted as Ollie and Sophie. Had been. Oh God. The hymn sheet shook harder in her hand. So, so wrong. She looked up at the sweeping church rafters, eyes prickling with tears. Sophie, where are you? Please stop being dead. It's not big and it's not funny. No one's bloody laughing.

All she wanted to do was lie down in bed with a pillow over her head and listen to Sophie's answer machine message over and over – 'Soph's phone, don't you dare hang up before leaving a message!' – and pretend none of this was happening.

'You alright, babes?' whispered Sam, looking down at her from his six-foot height.

She nodded, mouth dry. She could sing but not speak. Which did not bode well for her speech. (Unless she sang it?) The service continued, painfully slowly. It was like Sophie's wedding, she thought, but in reverse.

Oh God, eulogies. She was nowhere near ready. She needed another six months of prep. Sophie's sister Mary was the first to go. Never lifting her swollen eyes from her notes, she attempted some anecdotes about Sophie as a child – how she'd once found a kitten in the street that she'd named Sock and, fearing that her father wouldn't allow her to keep it, had nurtured Sock in her knicker drawer for three days on milk-sodden digestive biscuits before anyone realised he was there – and then tried to articulate what a wonderful mother she had been. At that point Mary's voice crumpled like a brown paper bag and she had to be led back to her pew.

Not her yet. Not her yet. She had a few minutes to pull herself together. Come on, Jenny.

A new speaker started to walk purposefully down the aisle. She checked the service notes. Suze. Suze Silver. She vaguely remembered Sophie mentioning her name. A school mum? Yes, she was pretty sure she was a school mum. Suze. Long on the z.

Suze had a rubbery face beneath an extraordinary helmet of frizzy hair, oddly fascinating in its extreme of unflattery. (How could she still notice unflattering hair even in the depths of grief? What was *wrong* with her?) Suze tilted her chin upwards, revealing a large mole resembling a squashed raisin beneath her jaw, and started to speak, her thunderous voice submitting the congregation into still, respectful silence like an evangelical pastor's. She rhapsodised about Sophie's contribution to school life and the community, her volunteering, her cake baking, her quiz night organising, the fact that she was the most glamorous mother at the school gates. How the other mothers used to joke that she never wore the same shoes twice. Then, minutes later, the frizzy orator had finished. Colin was looking at her expectantly, one bushy eyebrow raised.

'Sure you're up to it?' Sam looked doubtful.

Jenny started the long walk to the podium, her hard-soled

shoes clattering unpleasantly on the stone floor. Her new black trousers, bought in haste online for the occasion, dug into her hips as she walked. They were a size too small, she realised – she was a fourteen, not a twelve, kidding nobody – and frumpy in their bland formality, like a campaigning regional MP's. She wished she'd worn something more flamboyant in homage. Sophie would have worn black and leopard print, a vintage fifties full-skirted suit. Something like that. The walk went on forever, the trousers shifting around her waist with every step, so by the time she finally stood up on the podium, raised her eyes to the congregation, the zipper was twisted and pulled up inside her crotch. Camel hoof. Great. Sophie would be laughing.

All eyes were on her now. The tension in the church was a pulse. She could hear it. Tick, tick, tick. Like an electric fence.

Notes. She just needed to read her notes and she'd be fine. But the handwriting swam before her. She gulped, refocused. The words she'd written and practised reading aloud to Sam over the porridge she couldn't eat that morning suddenly seemed wrong, written about someone who wasn't Sophie. She looked up helplessly at the rows and rows of expectant, flushed, strained faces, then quickly down again. Sweat dripped down her nose and splodged onto the paper. I'm going to fuck up. I'm going to fuck up explosively.

The pause stretched, taut, painful, like a doctor pulling a stitch from a wound. She glanced at Sam. His face was knotted with embarrassment. She looked at Ollie and his wounded black eyes surprised her by their softness. He was the one person who should hate her and didn't.

21

'I've written these notes,' she began, taking courage from Ollie. If he could be brave, so could she. The microphone amplified her voice. She didn't sound like her. She sounded like Margot Leadbetter. 'And they're all about what a wonderful person Sophie...' She couldn't say 'was'. She couldn't. 'But you all know that. That's why this church is crammed. So I'm going to go off-piste with this. Please bear with me.' Sam was biting his fist now, shaking his head and looking at her like she'd completely lost the plot. 'I was the last person to see Sophie alive.' A collective intake of breath. 'And for this I am hugely privileged. We had fun that night, the night she died. Apart from anything, Soph, my oldest, dearest friend, was the best laugh. And she found humour in the blackest places – she'd find it here today.' Ollie cracked a small, surprised smile. The rest of the congregation looked stony-faced, like she'd said something terrible. 'And that night, she was more alive than most of us will ever be. She was one of those people, full of... light and dazzle, the central point in any room. And she had the rudest, loudest laugh. We used to call it The Honk.' She choked up then. Her mouth made an involuntary pop-pop noise, as if her heart was exploding like space candy on her tongue. It was unimaginable that she'd never hear The Honk again. 'Whenever I think of Sophie I think of Sophie dancing. She loved to dance and she never gave a sh—' She caught herself. '... monkey's what anyone thought. She didn't have hang-ups like the rest of us. In fact she loved people looking at her. Which I guess brings me to...' She paused, suddenly unsure what to say next. '... *hats*! Sophie loved hats, especially vintage ones with plumes. And swirly skirted dresses. Sequins and shoes. She was the high priestess of shoes.' There was a ripple of laughter, a sense of people finally relaxing. 'Sophie could get away with anything because she was beautiful, but also because she was happy. She made happiness glamorous. And it was her family who made her so very happy, so secure in who she was.' Ollie was wiping away tears on the sleeve of a crumpled black jacket. 'She was madly in love with Ollie. And Freddie . . .' Freddie was staring down at the floor, as if willing himself to disappear. 'Freddie made her just the proudest mother on earth.' Her voice broke. She sniffed, collected herself. 'I guess all I want to say is that I will miss Sophie forever. As a girlfriend, as a human being, she is totally irreplaceable.' She looked down at her unused notes, a wave of doubt crashing down on her. What on earth was she thinking? Wrap, wrap! 'That's it, um, thanks.'

As she began the excruciating walk back to her pew, eyes boring into her navy Marks and Spencer shirt, Neil Young's 'Harvest Moon' started to crackle through the church's ancient speakers. Rows of people – the friends, the cousins, the exes, Freddie's teacher, Sophie's hairdresser, her cleaner, the music industry friends of Ollie's, all the people who'd ever known and loved Sophie, for to know her was to love her, Jenny realised, wishing she'd said that too – dissolved into tears. Jenny wondered how many of them recognised the song. It was Sophie and Ollie's first dance at their wedding reception. Sucking the tears down her throat, she joined the mass shuffle to the graveyard. The light was yellowy and dark clouds were boiling over the steeple of the church. The air smelled of rain.

'Why did you change your speech at the last minute?' asked Sam.

'Was it rubbish?'

Sam pulled her towards his dark blue suit. His second best suit. 'No, your speech was . . .' He hesitated. 'Sweet, really sweet, Jenny. Don't worry about it.'

She fisted her hands deep in her jacket pockets. All she wanted to do was go home, pour herself a humungous glass of wine and phone Sophie. That was what she always did after a bad day. And this was the baddest of days. She turned to Sam and saw him being pulled into the crowd by Seb, the bisexual gardener with the gold tooth who Sophie had recommended for their flower boxes. Without Sam sandwiched next to her, she felt exposed, watched, the last person to have seen Sophie alive, the bad influence. She wished she could scoot away like the other guests, sink back into the north London streets, into her altered life. She checked her watch. Not long now. The burial in Highgate cemetery was to be just a small family affair, thank goodness. She didn't have the stomach for it. Her job was to take Freddie back to Ollie's and make him supper. She was glad she had a job, a use. Yes, she must find Freddie. Where was he? Peering over the obfuscating hats and feather fascinators in the crowd, she noticed a woman ploughing determinedly towards her. 'Jenny!'

She froze. It was the woman being eaten by her own hair.

'Suze Silver.' An extended purple-gloved hand. The handshake crunched Jenny's fingers. 'I've heard so much about you.'

'You have?' she said, taken aback.

'From Sophie,' Suze explained.

She felt the heat rise on her cheeks. 'Yes, of course.'

Suze moved closer, conspiratorially, biscuit breath on Jenny's face. 'You were brave speaking off the cuff like that, really brave.'

'Thanks.' She smiled back, not knowing what to say. Sophie's death had left a smouldering gap in her conversation. Yet it was all anyone wanted to talk about.

Suze persevered. 'You must feel terrible. Being there.' She paused, giving Jenny the space to fill in the gory details. 'Seeing the accident and everything,' she added when no details were forthcoming.

Jenny looked away. She could still see Sophie's body in the road. Hear the crunch and thump.

'Look, sorry, any time you want to talk.'

'Thank you.' I don't want to talk. I don't want to talk to you, she thought. And I don't like your purple gloves.

'And if you don't mind, I may get in contact anyway.'

'Yeah?' Perhaps she could climb up and over Suze's hill of hair and flee over the shoulders of the crowds.

'Ollie will need all the help he can get now, won't he?'

'Yes, yes, he will.' She smiled, feeling a stab of guilt for her earlier irritation. Suze was clearly a nice, practically minded woman. She was Sophie's friend. Making a renewed effort, she riffled in her handbag and found a curly-edged business card. 'Here's my number.'

Suze looked down at the white card – 'Jenny Vale, copy editor' – with a glint of triumph. 'Brill!'

Jenny sidled away, faking an obligation somewhere else.

Before she could get very far, Ollie touched her lightly on

the arm. 'Hey, Jenny.' His voice was barely audible.

'I'm sorry, I'm just so sorry, Ollie.' The dark grey cloud had engulfed the steeple. It started to rain suddenly, pinprick-sore against the raw skin around her eyes.

He glanced at his watch. 'We're going to . . .' He hesitated for an eternity. He couldn't say 'bury'. She took his hand because it felt like the right thing to do. But once she had it she didn't know what to do with it. '. . . go to the cemetery now.'

'I'll take Freddie back.'

They stood for a moment, transfixed by the back of Freddie's tousled blond head, neither of them moving, not wanting to take him away from his mother's body. And she was still holding Ollie's hand. She needed to drop it.

'Jenny, there's something I need to ask you.'

'Yes?' She had a bad feeling about what he was about to say next. She dropped his hand.

He fixed her with sleepless baggy eyes. 'Did Sophie talk about us, about me and her, our marriage, the night she died?'

The bad feeling got badder. What could she say? If she told him the truth he might take the words of Sophie in a drunken, restless mood and hold them against his heart forever. And she'd promised Sophie she wouldn't repeat them.

'I need to know if—'

Colin the rev interrupted them. 'Ollie,' he whispered, a ringed pink hand on the sleeve of Ollie's black wool suit. 'It is time.'

Three

I can't bring myself to peek inside the coffin. Not going to be a good look, is it? So I leave my beloved family scattering chocolatey Highgate soil into the hole, soak away past the graves of George Eliot and Henry Moore, the gothic avenues of tombs, the guarding stone angels, through the damp, dark, ivy-cloaked trees of Highgate Cemetery into the January air, filling the empty cavities between grave and home like water. I follow Jenny as she drives back to number thirty-three in her little yellow Mini, with Freddie in the back seat, staring out of the window, puzzled, silent. I follow them through the grey front door – *hours* of my short life I wasted locating that exact shade of cloud grey – past the surprisingly tidy hall. Clearly, mother-in-law has been busy and her grey felt slippers sit neatly, incongruously, beside my old knitted moccasin boots. I skirt along the stripped pine floor and into our kitchen, always my favourite room, with its wooden units that nearly bankrupted us, the red Kitchen Aid cake mixer, the big range oven, the Dualit toaster, things I loved so much in a way that Ollie never understood, but being Ollie indulged anyway because he'd do pretty much anything to make me happy. Ping Pong hisses as I pass and bolts out through the cat flap. Charming. Missed you too.

After the cold and damp of the church, the smell of Jenny burning fishfingers is immensely comforting. (Jenny has many talents but cooking is not one of them. She would happily survive on Marmite toast, Minstrels and pre-cut packaged carrot sticks.) Freddie eats it all up, which makes me curdle with maternal pleasure. It's good to know that he's not lost his appetite, that nature's hardwired imperative for his six-year-old body to run and eat and grow overrides his grief. After some warmed rice pudding topped with half a jar of honey on top – Freddie tells her that's how much I used to put on, the monkey – they curl up together on the velvet sofa. Freddie's lids slowly shut as Jenny reads *Tintin in Tibet*, her Captain Haddock voice a dead ringer for Billy Connolly. While he sleeps, Jenny cries, stroking his unbrushed mop of curls. I move closer to them, not wanting to frighten her, hoping that somehow, if I wish it hard enough, I will radiate some heat, something that will comfort them, let them know that I am here.

Ollie and the grannies come back. Jenny does her big bright smile thing that she always does when she's trying to pretend she's not been crying, and fools nobody. Freddie doesn't want her to go. She hesitates, unsure of the protocol, not wanting to disappoint Freddie, not wanting to intrude. Granny Vicki crushes Freddie to that bosom – it's the Thames flood barrier of bosoms – and Jenny leaves for the flat she shares with Sam in Camden.

I become the dust in the shadows, only brightening again as a button moon rises above the slate rooftops and London's insomniac skyline glows acid orange. Restless to be back where I belong, I feather down the hall, shaken by the tectonic rumble of my mother-in-law snoring in the spare bedroom, sinus problems having taken a turn for the worse.

It's midnight. I want to get back to my side of the bed, the side nearest the bathroom, because ever since I had Freddie I've needed to go in the night. (No, didn't do my pelvic floors. Does anyone?) My side of the bed is oddly empty. Odd because I normally go to bed before Ollie, who is prone to watching MTV with a beer in his hand late into the night. But nothing's normal now, is it? Everything is the same but different, like one of those pictures in Freddie's puzzle books where you have to spot things that are wrong, like the dog with five legs, the lady with a teapot poking out of her handbag.

Ollie is not sleeping like he usually does either, like a hibernating grizzly, but is twisting and turning, ruching up the bed sheets – the same bed sheets that we slept on together last week – asleep but talking indecipherably, then sitting bolt upright, flicking the light on, getting up, walking to the kitchen, pouring himself a large whisky, downing it, then staggering through to Freddie's room, crawling under the pirate duvet, and with Freddie stirring slightly in his arms, finally falling asleep. I hover a few inches above them, rising and falling on the valleys of their warm breath like a bird.

The night is over in a millisecond. Dawn breaks, Ollie breaks wind, Freddie unfurls from sleep in his green pyjamas like a new shoot, and Vicki starts bustling around the kitchen, beginning, I kid you not, to reorganise my spice cupboard.

29

Nothing is sacred.

Hours shuffle like cards. Suddenly it's Monday. Ollie doesn't look like he's slept at all. He can't be arsed to shower, and when I get near him, laminating his body as close as I can, he smells of scalp and skin and sweat. He's been sweating a lot even though it's cold. It's as if he's carried a stash of drugs through Dubai customs in the sole of his trainer. He needs to shave, but doesn't. He attempts to pack Vicki off to the local supermarket while he gets Freddie ready for school. But she won't budge. She's fussing. No, Ollie mumbles. He wants to do this himself, he's got to be able to do it himself. Finally, Vicki takes the sledgehammer hint and is successfully banished to buy a pint of milk. Ollie rummages through the kitchen cupboards, looking for Freddie's lunchbox. It's on the shelf above the sink, as it always is, but, maddeningly, he looks everywhere but there. He curses, gives up. He puts two Penguin bars in an old Tesco bag – two? – alongside one of Jenny's cold burned fishfingers, which he wraps in cellophane – impressed by the cellophane bit – and a Marmite sandwich made from bread that has outlived me. He does not brush Freddie's hair, which sticks out like wings. And he does not notice that Freddie is wearing his Superman pyjama top beneath his grey school shirt. Freddie has been trying to wear this top to school for at least a year.

Ollie, one of the greediest men alive, forgets to feed himself and, more cataclysmically, forgets to feed the mightily disgruntled Ping Pong. He can't find the school bag, which is on a hook in the utility cupboard, the same hook it's been hung on for the last two years.

I'm beginning to realise how much I did. How much I micromanaged our lives. And I'm worrying about how Ollie is going to cope. Because there is the domesticated man. And there's Ollie. This is a man who once watered a houseplant for a year before realising it was plastic. This is a man who only last week put washing powder tablets in the tumble dryer. Yes, Ollie is a brilliant music producer. His brain can organise an infinite variation of bars and chords and breaks. But it cannot compute how many pints of milk a family of three drink in a week. (Five.)

Ollie and Freddie finally leave for school, hands knotted together. How much I want to slip my hands into that tight little knot. How much I want to run my fingers through Freddie's hair and feel his hot boy's neck. How I want to yank Ollie back to his full height, to stop that gorgeous body collapsing in on itself like a wonky old deckchair. He is normally so reassuringly solid – wide shouldered, barrel chested, male and bulky like a hunk of roughly hewn oak – but day by day he looks whittled down. His twisted-fit Levis are slipping down his hips. His face is newly angular, unshaven and angry, his jaw is jutting because his teeth are constantly clenched. He reminds me of how he used to look in his twenties when he'd spent too many sleepless weekends on the coke that made him so elated then so utterly miserable, before his 'angel of Harpenden', as he used to call me back then, rescued him and made him drink Chablis instead. But I can't rescue him now. It seems I'm merely watching them rather than watching over them, more CCTV than celestial being.

At the school gates there's a throng of mothers, milling

with muted excitement as if waiting for sale doors to fling open. Freddie and Ollie walk down the street towards them. The hushed talking stops immediately. They part to make room for his passing, buggies are swiftly jerked out of his way, fevered looks are exchanged. Eyes fill with tears.

My husband, the Pope!

Ollie blanks them, walking determinedly towards the cheerful red door of class 2B to the left of the playground, the furthest class from the gate, and therefore the one with the longest public parade. The crowd's ventriloquist whispers sound like distant storms at sea. The mothers discuss protocol beneath their breath. There is no consensus and a few are now breaking ranks and gamely stepping forward to smile sympathetically at Freddie – he looks down, hates being singled out at the best of times – and offer condolences to Ollie, who scuffs his trainer against the painted yellow lines on the concrete playground like a schoolboy. Resisting the urge to hug Freddie – he is still mine, still someone else's child – the women reach instead for Ollie, patting his arm or hand maternally, or, rather less maternally in Tash's case, the small of his back, near the waistband of his jeans. Even those who are tearful and tongue-tied want to touch Ollie, as if they need to know what a bereaved dad actually feels like. Perhaps touching one makes them believe it won't happen to them, too. I guess we've all wondered: having children makes you ponder your mortality, ghoulishly hypothesise the what ifs. Funny thing is that before this happened, I did that too, idly, indulgently, comfortable that things like this didn't happen to people like us.

The school bell rings. There is a twitch in Ollie's lower lip now, barely perceptible but a sign to me, who knows that lower lip as well as I know my own, that he is fighting tears.

If Ollie cries now I swear someone will try to breastfeed him.

Mrs Simpson, Freddie's teacher, greets them at class 2B's door. She is professional and kind and does not make a fuss – much to Ollie and Freddie's obvious relief – and takes Freddie's hand and leads him inside his old classroom, which, I hope, will be mercifully the same as it always was, unlike everything else in his life. The door closes. Ollie stands there for a moment, facing the shut door, lost, his face blank like a man who has woken up and no longer has the first clue who he is. Then his features reconfigure and he takes a deep breath, walks back to the tall iron school gates, his black eyes drilling into the ground.

This is not a good enough defence. Oh no. Without Freddie to shield him, Ollie is open season. Some of the women have been waiting for him to return: I know their migratory patterns and I know that normally they would have flocked to Starbucks by now. Instead, they're hovering by the gate. Suze. Tash. Lydia. Liz. Usual suspects.

'Is there anything, anything at all we can do to help?' implores Suze. Her giant breasts quiver in the deep V of her gaping blue blouse as if they are domed conductors for the group's electric pent-up emotion.

Ollie shakes his head and tries to smile. 'No. Thanks.' He starts to walk away.

Lydia bars him with her Ugg boot. 'Washing?'

'Washing?' repeats Ollie, puzzled.

'Would you like us to do your washing, Ollie?' Lydia

speaks slowly as if addressing a small child, even though Ollie towers over her fairy frame.

'Washing,' he repeats as if it were something he hadn't ever considered before, and probably hasn't. 'My mother . . .'

'Or shopping?' Liz agitates her foot on her son's blue scooter.

'I . . . I . . .' Ollie is a man of few words, but is never normally lost for them. He stares blankly at the scooter.

'Would Freddie like to sleep over?' Tash jumps into his hesitation, stepping closer so that he can smell the perfume caught within the soft pelt of her white fake fur stole. (Even I can smell the perfume and I'm near the school hall guttering.)

A lemony sun breaks through the cloud. Ollie's pupils shrink to pencil points. In the last three weeks he's spent a lot of time alone in the dark, like a miner. His olive skin is pale and flaky. 'I'm trying to keep Freddie close. Just at the moment.'

'As normal as possible. Of course, of course,' gushes Tash apologetically. 'But if you ever need me to take Freddie to school, when, er, you go back to work.' She blushes, wondering if she's said the wrong thing. 'Not that I want to . . .'

I feel for him. Normally at this juncture I'd read the signs, swoop into the conversation and pluck him out, the sunny, social one to counterbalance his Heathcliffian northern tendencies. 'Thanks. That would be great,' he mumbles, giving them what they want, waiting to be released.

Tash looks around at the other women with unmistakable triumph.

Ollie digs his hands into his jeans pockets, attempts to walk away again.

Not so fast, buster! 'You *will* let us know, won't you?' says Suze. She's somehow standing in front of him without anyone sure how she got there. It's social kung fu. 'If you need anything, Ollie, anything at all? Just pick up the phone. You've got my number, haven't you? Let me write it out for you just in case. Oh, bollocks. Anyone got a pen?'

Ollie grunts, like he always grunts when he begins to feel obligated. Ollie is one of the world's kindest men, the best of men, but he hates obligation. He likes to think he can be selfish if he wants to. It's an adolescent thing that lots of wives of music producers have to contend with. Most of the time his main selfishness, apart from nicking my moisturiser and refusing to cook, manifests itself merely in putting on headphones and sinking into his music, annoying but not up there in the great pantheon of male selfishness, clearly. I complained about this in the past but now wish I hadn't, firstly because I knew about his anti-social solipsistic tendencies from the beginning – I'd wake up in bed to find him wearing these big fat headphones over his long hair and I thought it quite the sexiest thing ever, like Paula on the bed with Michael Hutchence – and also because the flaw, if it is a flaw, is just Ollie. I should have realised I'd have been bored to tears with the man I often complained he wasn't: the domesticated, fully socialised, Muswell Hill thirty-something dad behind the cake stall. Why did I not tell him more often that I loved him just as he was?

Like secrets, words that are left unsaid get buried with you.

Four

'Firecracker.' Sam rolled off Jenny with a skin-prising squelch. 'I needed that.'

Jenny flopped back into the slightly sinister microclimate of their Tempur mattress. She did not feel like a firecracker. Since Sophie had died – three weeks, three days, eight hours ago – sex didn't work, not for her at any rate. Sometimes she wondered if she'd ever orgasm again. Part of her hoped she wouldn't. Sophie couldn't. Why should she? She'd grown a giant retro bush. She'd stopped shaving under her arms. Yes, she was morphing into the world's unsexiest creature. And she didn't give a toss.

She just wished her heart would stop slamming, that's all. It was a frantic tattoo. She'd ditched coffee after one pm, forced herself to bathe in candlelight before bed – setting fire to a tinderstick loofa in the process – but still her heart jumped about inside her chest like someone who'd snorted a kilo of amphetamine and was prancing about on a speaker in a nightclub.

Sam yawned, releasing a mist of morning breath. Inside his mouth his tonsils looked pink and animate, like they might have an opinion. They probably did. Later, she knew that he'd brush his tongue. He was the only person she'd ever met who brushed his tongue. She watched him fiddle with his omnipresent iPhone; Mumford and Sons poured out from a hidden speaker in the bedpost. The flat was full of hidden speakers. Music suddenly blasting out of cabinets and walls and baths like raucous ghosts, making her jump. It was a boy's flat, home to families of remote controls, gleaming with hard, aeronautical steel surfaces, smelling of freshly ground coffee. It was like waking up in Business Class every morning.

He trailed a finger down her shoulder. 'Shall we ambulate down to the greasy spoon?' He didn't look up, back on the phone again. Tap tap tap. 'I need transfats.'

'No, I'm taking Freddie out, remember.' She smiled as brightly as she could manage, trying to look normal. But nothing was normal. Sophie being alive was normal.

'You've got to find a way of moving on,' that's what Sam kept saying. But, damn, move on *where?* For the last fifteen years of her life she and Sophie had been on the same train, Sophie sitting beside her, her favourite apple-green boxy handbag on her lap, shopping bags at her feet, body tilted towards Jenny at an angle so that their shoulders touched and she'd get a mouthful of Sophie's luscious long dark hair which always tasted of expensive honey-scented shampoo. Even a train journey with Sophie was a hoot. She was one of those women who would cheerfully chat loudly and unself-consciously in a crowded carriage about anything, gossip, politics, the shoes of the woman down the carriage, the headlines on the man opposite's newspaper, and sex. Sophie loved talking about sex. ('OK. Sex in a tent. Boris Johnson or David Cameron? No, no, no! You have to choose one, you *have* to, Jenny. My God, you're blushing! You've thought about this before, haven't you? I reckon you're a Boris bonker. Fess up. No, I'm not going to shush.') What she wouldn't do now for just one more journey from Oxford Circus to King's Cross with Sophie. One more gossip. One more chat. There were so many things they still had to say.

Sam looked up and eyed her with a mixture of wariness and concern. 'You alright, babes?'

She snapped back to the bedroom, to the present. 'Fine!'

Sam started doing one of the morning stretches that Big Eric, his trainer, had taught him last month for an extortionate sum, something weird and painful-looking involving his arm being bent back over his shoulder and a fair amount of clicking. 'Stiff as a corpse this morning,' he muttered through the exertion. 'I told Big Eric no more fucking weights. Masochist.'

Wishing he hadn't said corpse, she watched his arms bulge. They'd certainly got bigger. Secretly she preferred them as they were before, sinewy but strong, the way he was meant to be. Funnily enough, out of all of his handsome frame it was his head she loved best, the only thing he couldn't work out in the gym. His head was like Bruce Willis's, closely shaved to hide the spreading bald patch, symmetrical, satisfying, like a slightly furry pet. She liked to place her palm across it and feel its heat. And she liked that it flowed seamlessy into his smooth, unusual face without the interruption of hair. Sam's good looks were architectural, vulpine. He had a face that could have been designed by Norman Foster.

She'd noticed him instantly at the small book launch in a Marylebone bookshop all those years ago. He'd been smartly dressed, swaggery – red socks! – not the usual publishing type, no surprise when she discovered he wasn't. She'd felt the burn of those bright blue eyes following her around the room. Shyness had prevented her returning that confrontational gaze. Of course she'd had no idea at the time that this shyness would be misinterpreted as hard-to-get hauteur. That he'd see getting into her pants as the ultimate challenge. (She would have said yes please if he'd asked politely.) Sam loved a challenge. He liked his women 'slightly difficult, chewy like hard toffee,' he'd once said, qualifying it with, 'it was only afterwards I discovered you were more like fudge.' That had made her laugh. He used to make her laugh a lot.

Sam released his biceps and lay heavily back on to the bed, his jaw cracking as he yawned. 'Robocop, I am not.'

'You've been working late all week.' She meant this nicely but it came out wrong, more like an accusation. This kept happening, words coming out wrong.

He looked up at her sharply. 'It's good that I'm this busy, bloody brilliant in the current climate.'

'I know, I know.' Had she made Sam defensive about his career? That hadn't been her intention. He'd once dreamed of being a human rights lawyer and had grown up to be a divorce lawyer. This was what happened to most people in life, a gradual distillation of intent. One had to be pragmatic. She'd once dreamed of being a gardener, and she was a copy editor. How did that happen? Well, the rent happened.

London happened. Her 'career' happened while she was thinking about other things. Like nights out with the girls in karaoke bars in town. Chris. Tim. Sam. Chelsea Flower Show. Her highlights. Her waxing schedule. How to avoid going home for lunch every Sunday. Dolly at Wembley Arena. The demanding full-time vocation of being Sophie's best friend. Her love of books.

So she dotted the i's and crossed the t's and realigned paragraphs. She was good at it. Although sometimes it felt like her pastime was copy editing and her real job was trying to get her printer to work. Her specialism, her passion, although she would take on anything, were the kind of sumptuous gardening-and-home books that few bought, less read. She'd always loved detail, the ant-like march of letters across a page, the excitement of undressing a manuscript from its large padded envelope. But she'd made some embarrassing mistakes recently. Only last week she'd failed to spot that a manuscript had three chapter fives. If there were a disacknowledgements section for people who'd made the production of the book infinitely more difficult, she'd take pride of place.

'Let's go somewhere fancy soon. I don't know, Barcelona? Rome? Business is good, all good, babes,' Sam added, rubbing a hand along her thigh.

She smiled. 'As long as you're not one of the divorcing couples.'

'As long as you're not the husband. Some of the payouts. Woo-wee!' He whistled, stared up at the ceiling. 'It's a miracle anyone gets married.'

The elephant in the room swished its tail. She remembered

Sophie asking her about the wedding date that fateful night. Pushing the conversation out of her head, she quickly sat up and slipped her feet into the sheepskin slippers. She didn't want to think about that.

'Interesting look,' he smiled, glancing down.

'Oh!' She'd put the slippers on the wrong feet. Yesterday she'd gone out to buy a newspaper with her jumper inside out. How she missed her old brain, her tidy, organised, optimistic brain. Where had it gone? It was as if someone had crept in the night Sophie died and emptied all her boxes, books and files all over the floor, like a demented ex-employee sabotaging the boss's office.

'Chuck over the lighter. Thanks, darling.'

She handed him the bullet-cold weight of the Zippo and gazed out of the window at the poised row of grubby Georgian houses on the opposite side of the Camden street. They looked different since Sophie had died, in a way she couldn't quite put her finger on. She felt the faint vibration of a Silverlink train, heard its rumble, then the deaf bloke's telly next door. Again, these familiar noises now sounded foreign, like something outside a hotel window the first morning in a new city.

Sam exhaled a curl of smoke. 'Where you taking Freddie?'

'Thinking zoo, but it's a bit arctic, isn't it?' The freezing sky was the colour of an old man's baggy Y-fronts. 'I remember being dragged to the zoo as a child when it was like this. The only thing you get to see are llamas and rare breed pigs.'

'Nothing wrong with a rare breed. Preferably between two slices of bread with a dollop of ketchup.'

41

She bit down on her bottom lip; she had developed a permanent dent like the pothole Camden Council wouldn't mend outside the flat. 'Why don't you come?'

'Don't do zoos, babes.'

Sam didn't do north of Watford or easyJet or rubber-soled shoes. The zoo thing was a new one. 'Huh?'

'The sight of animals in cages freaks me out.'

'You know you really should have become an animal rights lawyer.' It was meant to be a joke, but he shot her a dark look over his coffee cup. 'Aquarium?'

'A tank is a cage.'

'So is a flat. Oh, go on, darling. Come.'

He shook his head, serious suddenly. 'You know what I'm like with kids, Jen. I never know what to say at the best of times. Let alone . . .'

'Forget it.'

'Why don't I take you for lunch first?' he said, trying to appease for refusing to play zoos with Freddie. 'Then I can drive you up to Muswell Hill.'

'Thanks, but I'm having lunch with Ollie first.'

Sam's face clouded. He ground out the cigarette with a long stub and got out of bed. Led Zeppelin's 'Whole Lotta Love' started to crash out of the speakers. He turned it up and mouthed along to it.

'What?'

'You've spent more time with Ollie than you have with me recently.'

'Come on, Sam.' She shook her head at the futility of explanation. They'd been here before. 'He's no good on his own. I owe it to Soph to be there now.'

He rolled his eyes. 'You make it all sound like a country and western track. Sweetheart, Ollie's a *man*. He just needs the space to drink himself into oblivion and shag himself stupid.'

'Sam!' She felt everything tense between them again. It had been building over the last few weeks. Like an electrical storm about to break.

'You can't make it better, Jenny, don't you get it?' His voice was higher now, that odd pitch he used when he was angry but tried to hide it. 'You can't bring Sophie back.' He took her hand, pressed the tips of her fingertips to his soft morning mouth. They would smell of cigarettes all day.

'Sophie would have looked out for you had I died,' she said gently.

He made a scoffing noise in the back of his throat.

She yanked her hand away. Rage was starting to build in perfect synchronicity with Jimmy Page's guitar solo. 'Did you even *like* Sophie, Sam?'

He visibly started, paling beneath his smooth skin. 'What are you saying?'

'You don't seem that affected, that's all. It's like everything is the same as it was.'

'What do you want me to do, wear a T-shirt?'

No, grief had made neither of them better people. It was almost banal, this bickering. That constant feeling that something was lost. Her keys? Her phone? She'd scrabble around in her handbag before realising that the lost thing was Sophie.

'She was a beautiful woman who died too young. But she wasn't my wife, Jenny. I'm not going to pretend my life is decimated by her dying.' Sam pulled on his white underpants, rearranged his balls. 'I refuse to emote on call.'

'I'm not asking you to emote, I'm asking you . . . to . . . to give a bit more of a shit, that's all!'

He looked at her in disbelief. 'You think I don't give a shit? Bloody hell. You really don't know me at all, do you, Jenny?'

At Sam's persuasion – 'exercise is a mood enhancer!' – she'd gone to a punishing class of Legs, Bums and Tums with a Leo Sayer lookalikey instructor who'd shouted, 'Hey, you at the back with the hair!' when she could go no further with the star jumps that were making her tits ache. (And what was wrong with her hair? Pots and bloody kettles.) Hamstrings singing with pain, ears ringing with Girls Aloud, she'd reversed badly out of the gym parking space beneath the gaze of three sniggering hoodies who asked her if she was The Stig, and now here she was, still a bit BOish, sitting in a snarl of traffic en route to Muswell Hill, London's tightly packed heart now behind her, pulsing beneath its grey layer of grimy snow.

She wondered if Ollie's mother, Vicki, would be at Ollie's today, and hoped not. Sophie used to call her 'Joan Collins's long lost sister from Basingstoke'. Still, rather Joan Collins's long lost sister than Soph's poor mum, Sally, who was a sodden tangle of tears, hurt and neediness. She'd called Jenny every night last week wanting to go over the fateful evening in detail. What had Sophie drunk? Eaten? What had they talked about? As she spoke her pain was audible, like nails scraping a blackboard. A mother's pain, no lessened by her daughter's age. Sophie may as well have been five.

Stopping at traffic lights, Jenny glanced about her and exhaled the tension of crowded inner London.

Trees. That was the first things she noticed about Muswell Hill. All the trees, skeletal now but in summer shivers of green, then wider roads, lots of white people, and a lovely view. From different points in the neighbourhood you could see the whole of London spread out below you like a meal on a plate. Jenny pulled up outside Ollie's house. A typical suburban Edwardian house, it had a fashionable circus-style number thirty-three transfer on the upper window pane, a soft grey door, a recycling box alarmingly full of empty wine bottles and beer cans next to the pathway, and a broken scooter that Haringey Council refused to dispose of. The blinds were shut and the frosted front path unscuffed by footprints. She knocked, and waited for a few minutes before Freddie opened the front door, wearing his Superman pyjamas and clutching a battered stack of Match Attax cards.

'Hey, Freddie!' She hugged him, sniffed his hair. It didn't smell how it usually smelled, fresh and boyish, like wind and soil. No, he smelled sockish today, and his angelic curls were matted at the back. 'You alright?' Stupid question.

'Yes thank you.' Freddie smiled politely, as Sophie had taught him, but he didn't maintain eye contact for long. She wondered if the horrible truth – that his mother wasn't coming back – had dawned yet. A notably slimmed down Ping Pong curled around his ankles and mewed pitifully.

Inside the hall it was chaotic, more so than last week.

Not just mess, but layers of mess, stratified. Monday's mess on Tuesday's, and so on. Boots everywhere, like fallen soldiers. An empty chip tray nestled inside Freddie's bicycle helmet. It was as if Sophie's death had frozen everything in situ like petrifying volcanic mud. The television was on in the living room, tuned to a Sky menu. The potted palm in front of the bay window was drooping pathetically, its leaves curling and yellowing at the edges. A duvet was balled into the corner of the velvet sofa. It didn't contain Ollie. 'Where's Daddy, sweetheart?'

'Kitchen,' said Freddie, matter of factly.

She put her hand lightly on his soft cheek, still as adorably convex as a baby's, but he shrugged it off and ran upstairs.

Ollie, or a man who vaguely resembled Ollie, was hunched pathetically beneath the huge Sex Pistols' 'No Future' print in the kitchen, staring at a small, crumpled sheet of white paper. He was wearing the same black jeans he'd been in last time she saw him, as well as the same navy cashmere jumper with the giant hole in the left elbow. 'Ollie?'

He looked up with puffy eyes and tried to smile. 'Hey, Jenny.' His voice rasped, like that of a forty-a-day smoker. She swore he had peppercorns of grey on his temples where he didn't have them a week ago. She wanted to put her arms around him and hug him close, but still felt as if she didn't quite have permission, or the familiarity. The truth was, she'd actually always felt quite shy around Ollie – he was too good-looking – and she had only known him through the prism of Sophie. Sophie had been her best friend. Ollie had been Sophie's husband. If they'd divorced – always the test – she'd have been in the Sophie camp. And now, here they were, thrust together in the most unlikely of circumstances.

'You've got a starter beard.'

He ran his fingers through it. 'Bit Bin Laden?'

'No, sort of Jim Morrisonish.'

'Riders on the storm.'

A pop cultural reference, a good sign! He was functioning. Feeling a wave of relief, she smiled properly for the first time that day. She liked it at number thirty-three. Apart from anything else, her misery paled against his and this made her feel like the sane one. 'Any grannies in the house?'

'Sent Mum home.'

'Really?'

'Don't worry. She's still phoning every couple of hours. Like a speaking clock.' He pushed the bit of white paper up beneath his fingernail and put on a woman's voice. 'It's four o'clock, Oliver. Have you got dressed yet? Have you cancelled Sophie's bank accounts? It's five o'clock, Oliver, has Freddie had his tea? Have you spoken to the lawyers? When is the case coming to court? And on and on.' He shook his head. 'Bless her. She's driving me nuts.'

'Er, I guess there's a lot of stuff to sort out.' She could only imagine.

'We die and do you know what we leave behind?' Ollie kicked back in his chair angrily. 'Admin. We leave admin. Fucking great.'

'Maybe it's too soon to send your mum home, Ol,' she said, wondering when she'd slipped into calling him Ol rather than Ollie and whether this was weirdly overfamiliar. Sophie had called him Ol. 'How about Soph's sister? Would—'

'I need to do this on my own.' Eerie medieval chanting music started to pour out of the kitchen speakers. It reminded her of churches and crypts. No, it was not going to help. He needed Emmylou Harris.

He glanced at her, reading her mind. 'It's this or replaying Sophie's voice on the answer machine.'

A déjà vu suddenly hit her with such force she stepped backwards. Two years ago. A dark winter's afternoon. Walking up the path of number thirty-three, hearing music, loud music, soft, smooth, old soul. The lights were on in the house, the curtains open, and she saw Sophie and Ollie clutching each other, dancing around the living room, oblivious to anything but themselves, his arm tight around her waist, her eyes fixed hungrily on his face. Like Taylor and Burton, she'd thought. Shocked by the erotic intensity and not wanting to intrude, she'd turned right round and walked twice around the block, realising that she'd never danced like that with anyone. From that to this. It was pitiful. 'You can't be alone,' she said quietly. 'Not right now.'

'I'm not alone. I've got Fred.' He looked out of the window, eyes focused on something invisible in the middle distance. 'It was airless in the house with everyone here, Jenny, all of us choking on grief. Believe me, this is easier.' He shook his head. 'A few days ago, I had this energy surge and ran about sorting everything out, phoning the idiots at Orange, calling her building society, some twat at London

48

Transport, and feeling almost positive, even though that sounds mad, and then . . . I . . . I just crashed.'

'Oh, Ollie.' This big, wonderful chunk of a man as vulnerable as a little boy, it wasn't right. But he'd get through this. He had to. She was going to make sure of it.

'It keeps going round and round my head. If you'd both left the restaurant thirty seconds earlier . . . If you'd got a cab . . .' His face crumpled. 'The what ifs of it all make me want to rip my skin off. Fuck. Fuck. I can't explain.' He looked up at her desperately. 'I can't *be*, Jenny. I can't just be any more. Tell me how. Please.'

She leaned towards him then, needing to be close to him. He smelled different from Sam. Saltier. She recognised the smell from Sophie, who'd always smelled slightly of Ollie in the way other people smelled of their houses.

'I don't want to be here, Jen,' he said so quietly she could barely hear him.

'Don't even say that, Ollie. Freddie needs you.' She noticed that there was a Coco Pop trapped in his beard.

His eyes darkened. 'I need him more. And I hate that. It should be the other way round.'

'I think you're holding up well, Ollie. I do, really.' Should she tell him about the Coco Pop?

'Every day I wake up knowing not only that she's gone but that I've got to face another day missing her. Then I spend the whole day waiting for her to come back, expecting her to be late.'

The medieval monks started chanting more incessantly, the same Latin words, over and over.

'Ollie, bereavement is a process.' She wished desperately

49

that she could offer less trite words of comfort. 'It's not always going to feel like this.'

He snorted. 'You believe that, do you?'

'Yes, yes, I do. I have to.' It just hadn't happened yet. And in a weird way, part of her didn't want it to happen. Her grief was all she had left of Sophie. She wondered if Ollie felt the same. Or were there different types of grief, Jenny wondered. Different strains and hybrids. So that the grief of a mother who'd lost a child was fundamentally different to the pain of losing a friend or wife. Or was everyone stuck in the same long, dark tunnel, maybe just in different places, some closer to the light than others?

Ollie rolled himself a cigarette, licking the paper with the efficiency of someone who did it all the time, rather than someone who had supposedly stopped smoking years ago, when Sophie was pregnant with Freddie. The blue-grey smoke curled out of his mouth, over his beard, and into the room like a spirit. 'I woke up yesterday and I swear I couldn't remember what she looked like. The past is fading, Jen.'

Jenny bit her lip, trying not to cry. Hopeless. She'd come here to comfort Ollie. She didn't want him comforting her. She had to be strong. Strong and organised and helpful.

'No one else was there, you see. It was our world, the two of us. She was the witness. Now it's gone. All fucking gone.'

I was there, thought Jenny. I saw it. I saw you two fall in love. I saw how happy you made Sophie. You two were the yardstick by which I measured every relationship, *my* relationship. You two were the real deal. She saw them dancing again, on their private stage, the look in Ollie's eyes as he gazed at Sophie, a gaze of wonderment and ball-busting lust.

Freddie barrelled into the room. 'Hungry.'

'Are you? Um . . .' Ollie scratched his head, as if trying to make sense of the meaning of the word. 'Fancy some toast?'

'We had that already today. Daddy, you have something in your beard. Yuck.' He picked out the Coco Pop and flicked it to the floor.

Ollie walked over to the fridge, opened it and surveyed it blankly. A stale cheesy smell wafted into the kitchen.

'I'll pop out to the deli,' she said. Now this *was* something practical she could do. Something maternal. 'You've got a nice one, haven't you, up on the high street?'

'Can you get some chocolate cake?' Freddie asked.

'Sure. Whatever you fancy.' She winked at Ollie. 'Chocolate cake for breakfast, lunch and dinner.'

Freddie pulled on Ollie's hand. 'Can I watch *Deadly 60*?'

Ollie shook his head. 'Too much telly already, Fred.'

'*Strictly*?'

Jenny smiled. 'You like *Strictly*, Freddie?'

'Freddie loves *Strictly*,' grinned Ollie. 'Soph got him into it. She had it all ramped up on the Sky Plus.' He looked down at the floor. 'It's still there. He watches it over and over.'

'I wish I was allowed to watch *Strictly*. Sam won't let me,' she whispered to Freddie. 'You and I must have a secret *Strictly* sesh together, Freddie.'

A smile lit up Freddie's face. 'Now?'

'Not right now, Fred,' said Ollie quickly. 'I'm talking to Jenny.'

'Daddy . . .'

'Oh, OK, *Deadly 60*.' Freddie ran out of the room before Ollie had a chance to change his mind. Ollie rolled his eyes. 'Can't refuse him anything.'

'Totally understandable.'

'He's my little warrior. He doesn't deserve this shit.' Ollie took one more pull on his cigarette and stubbed it out, half-smoked. He looked out of the window. A cream puff of snow was settling on the sill, airy and solid at the same time. Like love, Jenny suddenly thought. Like how true love is meant to be. Like Soph and Ollie. 'How has Freddie been?'

'Nightmares.' Ollie rested his square jaw in his hands. She noticed a crescent of grime beneath his fingernails. 'Although he's better when he sleeps in my bed. He dreamed of Ben Ten last night. Progress?'

'Definitely progress.' Jenny tried to stop her eyes filling by blinking really fast. She could cope with most things, just not the idea of Freddie losing his mother. 'And the counselling?'

'Nice lady, says he's doing OK. Well mothered, she says,' raising his eyebrows at the irony. 'It helps.'

'Well fathered, too.'

Ollie turned to her, black eyes blazing. 'Jenny, he thinks that Sophie is still *here* in some way. That she talks to him. That she's in the room.'

Jenny felt the hairs prickle on the back of her neck. 'I sometimes feel Sophie is still here,' she confessed quietly. She'd never tell Sam that. Sam would tell her to get a grip. 'Do you?'

Silence. He looked at her long and hard before speaking. 'Yes.'

She felt a wave of relief. It wasn't just her. 'Do you talk to her?'

'Doesn't talk back,' was all he said, turning to face the window despondently. The sky was a cushioney blue above the rooftops now, framing the crow wing black of his shoulder-length hair. 'But the bond between her and Freddie was so close, so . . . so umbilical that maybe she can connect with him.' He shook his head, closing his eyes again. 'I'm going back to the studio Monday.'

It took a moment to sink in. 'Already?'

'I need to do something.' Ollie started rolling another cigarette. 'Anyway, there's no one else who's going to do it.'

'What about Freddie's pick-up times and stuff?' Jenny didn't really know what childcare was involved, but she'd heard Sophie talk about it often enough, the endless deadlines. It had always struck her as an enormously complicated business requiring military planning. The reason that Sophie hadn't been able to go back to work was because Ollie worked such erratic and long hours, sometimes not leaving the studio until late evening. How on earth would Ollie, not the most practical of men, fill her shoes?

'Don't worry, Jenny. I'll sort it.'

'I'll help you all I can. Happy to take him swimming, whatever. I mean I'd love to, if you want me to,' she stuttered, suddenly worried that she might be intruding. 'I wish I could do more, Ollie. I wish I lived closer.'

Ollie got up, walked slowly to the fridge and pulled out a beer.

Should she say anything about the drinking? No, no, she shouldn't. Not now. Let it go. 'Is there anything I can help you with today? Like now, as I'm here? I feel like I should be doing something.'

He snapped the can and looked at her sharply. 'Maybe you can explain that list on the table.'

'Sorry?' She started at the change in the tone of his voice.

'That piece of paper on the table.'

She bent forward, peering at the crumpled square of paper, Sophie's large, rounded writing. 'What is it? A to-do list.' She smiled. 'Sophie was queen of the to-do list.'

Sophie used to say that without her to-do lists she'd be the most disorganised mother in the world. Jenny never believed this. Sophie had always had a knack for the domestic. Although she was often late – she made being late glamorous rather than just annoying – she always knew where she was going, where she needed to be. She didn't forget stuff. Like smear tests, or her grandmother's birthday. She organised and decorated any environment she was in for more than ten minutes, whether that was a tent – Sophie camped with battery-powered fairy lights – or her room at university, which had boasted non-dead orchids, sidelights dangerously draped with Indian silks, black and white framed photographs, and a dressing table with little white china lidded pots for cotton wool, all of which had seemed impossibly chic at the time. Jenny had taken her own make-up off with wet toilet paper and the only decoration on her walls consisted of her lecture timetables.

Jenny smoothed the paper with the edge of her hand and began to read.

1. Ollie dentist.
2. Buy fish oils.
3. Thank Suze for play date thingy.
4. Guttering!
5. Cake stall year two next Friday – bake?
6. Roots.
7. MOT.
8. Lobotomy.
9. Speak to Jenny about *it* ☹

'Speak to Jenny about *it*?' She frowned, puzzled. Why the glum smiley? 'No, no idea, sorry.'

He frowned. 'The lobotomy. She says lobotomy. Was she so bloody bored with her life, Jenny?'

'No!'

'She was frustrated. I hate that.' He twisted his hands together. They were hands that she'd seen dance along piano keyboards at parties involving mojitos and an improvised rendition of 'Benny and the Jets' in happier times. Today, for some reason, they looked broken.

'Look, Sophie had a good brain on her.' She tried to sound calm and composed and rational but inside she was panicking. She remembered the question in the churchyard, a question, thankfully, he'd not asked again. She felt it looming. 'She was one of those women who could have done anything. But she chose her family. That was what she wanted. You. Freddie. This. Exactly this. She was so happy, really happy. You two had what everyone wants, Ollie. I knew her, Ollie. I knew her better than anyone. And I know she loved you and her life here more than anything.'

He leaned against the fridge and magnets scattered on to the floor. 'I just keep looking for . . . for proof.'

'Proof of what?'

'I don't know. Something. Something . . .' he said, his voice drifting off, making the hairs on Jenny's arms prickle.

Zoo trip postponed, she closed the door of number thirty-three with some relief and strode off purposefully towards Muswell Hill Broadway in search of a deli, freshly fallen snow squeaking under her feet. She wondered again what it was that Sophie had wanted to talk to her about. Why the glum smiley? It must have been something bad. Something important for her to underline it. How incredibly frustrating that now she'd never know.

The Broadway was all as it was, the armada of expensive baby buggies, the glittering shop fronts selling knitted toys and organic beauty creams, the steaming lattes and cinnamon cakes. One second she was finding the familiarity of the street comforting, the next she was winded by loss. She realised there was no one else she could meander along a high street with in the way she did with Sophie. And for this reason, just one reason among millions of others, she'd miss her forever.

Sophie had loved shopping for its own sake. She'd loved a bargain. In their twenties they'd spent many weekends meandering around Camden market, Portobello or Brick Lane. She was a collaborative shopper, as happy to find something for Jenny as she was for herself. She adored buying presents, spending money. Her eyes would glow with pleasure as she handed over a wodge of notes or a credit card, whereas spending made Jenny anxious; she'd been brought up to think she should save, and had been the proud owner of a Post Office account that had earned about two pence a year interest since she was a small child. And while browsing with Sophie was always fun, it sometimes got out of hand. Sophie made her buy things she didn't often wear. Sparkly things. And there was that time she'd got trapped in a dress. Sophie being Sophie had insisted she try on a vintage creation – by an acclaimed designer she'd never heard of – with a strange twisty cut and smocking in a frighteningly cool shop with unfeasibly thin shop assistants. The dress, despite its age, was completely unaffordable, and, in Jenny's uninformed opinion, hugely unflattering. It was also impossible to escape from. It took two shop assistants and twenty-three minutes to free her. Sophie had officially peed herself laughing.

Things had changed when Freddie reached school age and Sophie and Ollie had, bafflingly at the time, left the gritty grooviness of Kensal Rise and settled in the suburbs, muttering darkly about schools. How could a good school compensate for not having a Tube station? She didn't get it. After that it had become harder to meet up, especially in recent times. Their lunches would no longer spill into the afternoon with the same abandon. There was always the school run, play dates, football lessons, and a seemingly endless list of deadlines and responsibilities, none of which involved ingesting Bloody Marys or getting trapped in dresses. Having given up work at the small event organiser that demanded such long hours, Sophie no longer earned her own money and felt that she wasn't justified in spending Ollie's on the utterly frivolous, although of course the odd splurge still went under the radar, and Sophie was quite happy to throw money at furniture, as well as endless 'finds' on eBay.

Relying on her husband's income had struck Jenny as an uncomfortable dynamic. How she'd hate to have to rely on Sam's. But Sophie, of course, took it in her breezy stride. She still had funds from her single working years to fall back on, as well as friends with discounts in the fashion industry, and an eye that could whip up showstopping outfits from the most unlikely sartorial components: *Doctor Who* scarves bought second-hand from the school Christmas fair, holey jeans exposing a tanned knee, a furry gilet from Topshop and Ollie's The The tour T-shirt from the early nineties. She once accessorised her yellow gingham bikini with a boa made of slimy seaweed on a beach in Cornwall. Needless to say she looked amazing.

Jenny pushed open the heavy glass doors of the deli into a fog of noise and smell and warmth – frothing milk machines, the hushed gossiping of huddled mothers, the smell of cake, coffee and suede boots dampened by the snow – and pushed her way past the buggies to the salad and deli dishes behind the counter. Having glimpsed the interior of Ollie's fridge – beer and milk – she placed a generous order of food with the pretty girl behind the counter.

'Jenny?' said a voice behind her. 'It is Jenny, isn't it?'

She turned. A swathe of pink sweater was emerging from the back of the queue, a frizzy halo of blond hair held back in the jaws of two enormous tortoiseshell plastic hairclips.

'Suze?' It was the woman who'd done the speech before her at the funeral. The booming voice. That hair.

'You look totally different out of your funeral outfit!' Suze lunged forward. It was a full-on kiss on the cheek, tea-wet and followed up with a hug so that Jenny found herself spluttering into the bobbly cerise sweater. As she did so she came eye to eye with a startled ginger-haired baby strapped to Suze's back in a sling.

'Here, Lucas!' Suze yanked a fluff-haired blond toddler back by the strap of his denim dungarees. 'Stay here or no muffin.' The toddler looked outraged.

'Wow! How amazing to meet like this,' said Jenny, weakly. 'How are you?'

Suze rolled her eyes. 'Don't ask. You know what it's like with young kids. I feel as though I'm losing control of the monkey cage at the zoo.'

Monkey? Zoo? What on earth was she talking about? She kept having this problem, not getting stuff. Like everything was happening under water.

'Night feeding problems,' explained Suze, reading her lack of comprehension. 'The reason I look seventy-five.'

Jenny smiled, nodding politely, not wanting to encourage further expounding of Suze's tiredness. She'd noticed this a lot about people with kids: they spent hours talking about tiredness. The Eskimos' dozens of words for snow had nothing on a mother's vocabulary for tiredness.

'Don't look at your mama like that!' She smiled and squeezed toddler Lucas's cheek. He muttered something ungracious about the muffin and ramped up the cross look. Suze turned to her. 'How old are yours?'

'I don't have any kids myself. I'm just up here seeing Ollie and Freddie,' she said quickly, feeling like she should explain herself. After all, what the hell was she doing in Muswell Hill if she *didn't* have kids? She wished the girl behind the counter could be a bit more slapdash and shove the food into the brown cardboard boxes so she could leave now.

'Ah.' Suze's eyes narrowed. 'Ollie. How *is* Ollie?'

'Well . . .' Jenny hesitated, not wanting to gossip about Ollie behind his back, but not wanting to gloss over the situation either. 'Could be better, obviously.'

'Poor, poor man. Well, at least he's got his mum living with him. Thank God for mothers, eh?'

'She's gone back home actually. I think he wanted a bit of space.'

'Oh, has she?' Suze's face brightened. She lowered her voice conspiratorially. 'Between you and me, Jenny, I've tried to help out a few times in the last few weeks and I've always found the mother a bit of a, well, a bit of a brick wall to be perfectly honest. She doesn't seem to want anyone else getting too close.' She shook her head, as if trying to stop herself saying more. 'So how's Ollie coping *alone*?' She drew out the words slowly, as if hinting at the comprehensive length of answer she expected in reply.

'Well . . .'

'As Tash suspected.' Suze shook her frizz. 'She had a peek through the letterbox on Tuesday and said the hall looked like a festival site.'

'He's not that domestic at the best of times,' Jenny said.

'And as soon as he goes back to work . . .'

'Next week. He's going back next week.'

'Next week! Blimey,' Suze exclaimed, oblivious to the surge of lunchtime diners trying to get past her to the till.

She grabbed the sleeve of Jenny's coat urgently. 'This is fate, you know, me and you meeting like this. Fate!'

'Er, fate?' She didn't like the idea of fate any more. It had pulled some nasty tricks.

'I actually went to phone you last week, but of course I'd lost your number.' Suze slapped her temple hard with the side of her hand. 'I changed handbags and . . . oh, I won't bore you with the details.'

Jenny smiled politely. Alarm bells started to ring.

'It is time, Jenny,' Suze announced as her baby regurgitated something on to her shoulder.

She had absolutely no idea what Suze was talking about. 'Time for what, sorry?'

'Sophie's girls to come together.' She rubbed at the milk stain on her shoulder with a wet wipe that she'd plucked from her handbag. 'I've always said we need a Help Ollie committee and, you know what?' she said determinedly. 'We're going to start it!'

Suze obviously didn't realise that of all the people most likely to start a support group with a bunch of women she didn't know, she, Jenny, would be at the bottom of the list. She even found the idea of a book group kind of excruciating, hen nights only under severe duress. She had never, ever been a girlie pack animal.

'Lucas!' Suze hissed as her son stuck a finger into the golden disc of carrot cake on the counter. 'That was your *third* warning. You are now out of warnings.' She blew her fringe up off her forehead in exaggerated exasperation.

The girl behind the counter finally finished the food boxes. 'Well, I really must be getting back to Ollie's . . .'

Suze grabbed her arm again. It was a vice-like grip. Jenny felt a surge of sympathy for the disobedient Lucas. 'How are you fixed Wednesday morning next week?'

'Um, working, I'm afraid.'

'The afternoon?'

'Working too. Sorry.'

'Thursday?'

Jenny shook her head before she even considered whether she was free or not.

'Sorry, I'm hounding you.' Suze's face fell, and without her big smile it looked saggy and defeated and Jenny felt sorry for her. 'I'll let you get on.'

She was hardly running the treasury. She could take *one* morning off if she wanted to. What if it was a genuine help to Ollie? 'Actually, you know what, Suze? I'll work it out somehow. I'll come on Thursday.'

'Fan-bloody-tastic!' Suze dug into her handbag and pulled out a baby yoga leaflet, scrawled her address on the back of it with a red biro, and thrust it into Jenny's hand. 'I can't believe I've finally got Jenny Vale, the real life Jenny Vale, coming to my house.'

'Right,' she said, bemused.

Suze winked. 'Sophie always spoke so warmly about you, Jenny.'

Jenny felt a glow inside. 'Did she?'

'Although you were a figure of much intrigue, let me tell you. Her clever copy editor friend with the complicated—' Suze suddenly stopped and flushed from neck to hairline, as if she'd caught herself just in time.

Five

Nothing like dying to give you a sense of perspective. The strange thing is that from up here, a few centimetres below the bathroom ceiling, engulfed in Matey steam – I've been watching over Freddie while he has a bath, willing him to wash behind his ears; he hasn't – I've realised that certain universal truths passed unnoticed while I was alive. I was so busy living that I forgot to think about the things I'd miss when I was dead, which is kind of understandable once you think about it. Like that famous Damien Hirst shark in the tank of formaldehyde, 'The Physical Impossibility of Death in the Mind of Someone Living'. I always liked that shark. I used to joke that I'd get Ping Pong preserved like that and call it, 'The Physical Impossibility of Ollie Remembering to Feed the Cat'. Ha!

Anyway, first, the obvious stuff. Family and friends are the most precious things in the world. But you know what? I knew that. (*You* know that. Sorry.) I can honestly say, hand on the place my heart used to be, that I was never someone who took either for granted while blood was pumping pink around my veins. Every time Freddie kissed me it gave me a little bloom of pleasure. I'd watch other women watching Ollie at a party, everyone wanting more of him than he ever gave – so elliptical, my rock 'n' roll Darcy – knowing that I was the one going home with him, the one who got to talk to him for hours late at night, roll around the bed with him, read him stories from newspapers that made him laugh, the Ted Hughes poems he loved, placate him with kisses when I'd accidentally deleted *Spooks* from Sky Plus and filled up all the recording space with Kirstie Allsopp vehicles. And I got to see them both asleep – there but not there, dangling on the edge of dreams – Ollie the most handsome man asleep, Freddie, just the most delicious boy who ever fell to earth. I always used to wonder if I filmed Freddie and speeded that film up whether you'd actually get to see him growing, like one of those wildlife documentary tricks. I guess you would: he's grown five millimetres since I died.

I even watched Jenny sleep once, not that I ever told her because she'd get embarrassed about it, being Jenny. It was the time I forced her to come to Bestival by stealthily buying her a ticket and a sleeping bag. (Brief character note here: Jenny is *not* a festival type of person. She thinks the 'all together now, one love' vibe is distinctly phoney, whereas I've always been a bit of a sucker for it. She'd much rather visit a stately home with sculpted hedges and a tea garden.) We were sharing a leaking tent, lying side by side in our damp sleeping bags, having already lost one phone (hers), one brand new North Face anorak (mine) and, on account of getting hopelessly lost on the festival site, missed all the acts we had gone to see, which I assured her was par for the course. Anyway, I'd been struck by how pretty Jenny looked asleep, not blank pretty like conventionally pretty women, but thoughtful, like someone who had drifted off over the pages of an engrossing book. She is far prettier and far smarter than she imagines. I've told her this lots of times – not enough, I realise now – but she never believed me. Self-doubt. She blames her parents. Personally, I blame Sam.

Anyway, to get back to Damien Hirst's fancy shark . . . I made a list this morning while waiting for Ollie to wake up and feed poor old neglected Ping Pong. (Needless to say the concern isn't mutual. He still hisses every time I pass.) OK, the list. I do like a list.

A few random things I wish I'd realised before the bus hit:

- I would spend twenty-two of my thirty-five years of life counting calories. That's a lot of unnecessary maths.
- I would only ever wear one quarter of my wardrobe. That's a lot of unnecessary clothes.
- I should have had more sex. You can't have sex when you're dead.
- Rare is the friend who inhabits both your single life and is still there when your kid starts school. (Step forward Jenny.) Most disappear into the vortex somewhere between the 'we must meet up soon, LOL' email and the Facebook friend confirmation.
- One-third of the people we invited to our wedding seven years ago we haven't seen since. (Apart from my funeral, but that doesn't count.)
- That it is OK to imagine marriage will be like New York City and discover that it's more like Brussels. It

65

does not mean that something is wrong, or that you are doomed to divorce. It just means you've hopped on a different plane.

- Turbulence isn't going to bring the plane down.
- The guy sitting next to you on the Northern Line, the one with the rucksack and the frenzied darting eyes, is not a terrorist. He's just been dumped by his girlfriend.
- That every phase passes. The baby stops teething. The tantrums become sulks. The darling baby bootees will no longer fit. He will learn to spell 'because'. (This said, not sure Ollie will ever remember to put the recycling out on a Wednesday night.)
- You can have too many tea lights.
- That I did drink too much. That those glasses were not one unit, they were three. But they didn't kill me in the end.
- That I sunbathed too much. It gave me laughter lines. But it didn't kill me in the end. I never did get round to having my moles photographed either.
- No life is too short to stuff a mushroom. Stuffing the mushroom is one of the nice bits. It's washing up the baking tray afterwards that's to be avoided.
- No one will notice if you don't bake a cake for the school cake sale unless you apologise profusely.
- Revision: only Suze will notice.
- If you harbour a secret from your friend and you agonise whether to tell them and are almost on the verge of telling them when you get knocked down by a bus, it means the secret is irretrievable. It's like dropping a laptop in the bath.

Six

It was hardly a blood-soaked favela. It was leafy. It was lovely. It was the kind of street where children chalked hopscotch on the pavement and people hung dropped gloves on the neighbour's hedging. So why was the 'Four by four free zone' sticker on Suze's living room window making her so bloody anxious? Suze's text message yesterday afternoon – 'Bake cake guys!' – hadn't helped either. Who were the 'guys'? And baking? *Baking!* Jenny hadn't baked since home economics. What did it mean that she was mid-thirties and childless and had never baked so much as a scone? Jesus. It must mean something. Panicked, she'd bought a cake from a posh bakery, a wholemeal apple cake that looked like it would take at least six months to digest, and could in fact double up as a bulletproof vest if sewn artfully into a puffa jacket. In order to take the pretence to the next logical level, she would decant it from its white cardboard box into a cake tin. But she didn't own a cake tin . . . Of course she didn't. Why the hell would she own a cake tin?

She glanced at her watch and groaned. Yes, once again she'd done her crap shtick of arriving unfashionably early.

(She was the only person in London for whom the traffic lights were consistently green and the Tube rarely delayed, as if the great traffic controller in the sky had marked her out for some kind of loser's social experiment.) She waited a few moments, took a deep breath of the pleasant wood-smoke smelling air and pressed the bell. Three shrunken 'Happy Birthday' balloons hung from string on the door knocker bounced jauntily in the wind.

A heavy plodding, then the cherry-red front door was flung wide. Suze beamed at her, a vision in an orange batik blouse with that wedge of hair and, mystifyingly, a round, wet circle on the front of her blouse the size of a two-pence piece. 'You didn't flake!'

'No.' She tried her best not to be offended that Suze had her down as a flaker, and tried even harder not to look at the bizarre stain on Suze's blouse which appeared to be spreading like ink on blotting paper.

Suze pulled the stained blouse away from her bosom and flapped it. 'Sorry. Feeding baba.'

Jenny blushed. Of course! She hovered uncertainly, wiping her sweaty palms on her navy pressed trousers. Apart from the fact she'd lost all social skills since Sophie died, it felt odd meeting Sophie's friends without her, as if she'd turned into one of those traitorous people you introduce to a friend, who then goes on to invite them to dinner without you. Stepping into the yeasty heat, the house reminded her of Sophie's but on a far messier, less cool scale. There was a jumbled row of wellington boots in tiny sizes pushed up along the hall wall, like the entrance to a classroom. Next to them, children's scooters, five, six, covered in stickers and elastic bands. Toy cars, a one-eyed doll and a bumper pack of recycled loo rolls were heaped at the bottom of the stairs.

The hall walls were painted a cheerful apple green and stamped with children's pictures – collaged topographies made from glued lentils and milk bottle tops – and endless family portraits of kids on rainy beaches wrapped in towelling ponchos, blown up too large on canvases so that they'd gone all blurry. There was a smell too, yes, unmistakable, a smell of cakes actually baking. And just as unmistakable, an undernote of urine.

She followed the swinging slab of Suze's bottom down the hall and tried to identify the orange blob stuck to her back jeans pocket – satsuma segment? lone nacho? As they entered the kitchen, a large 'Keep Calm and Carry On' poster bore down bossily from the wall.

'Ladies,' said Suze. She stepped aside to reveal her catch. 'I bring you the famous Jenny Vale!'

'Lovely to meet you all,' she managed, relieved to find only three women sitting round the table, not a terrifying team of mumsnetters. She'd feared an Amazonian tribe in Breton stripes and ballet pumps, heatedly discussing cyber-bullying tactics for getting pram parks outside Space NK.

'Hello!' the voices chimed back. A boiling kettle clicked somewhere. It reminded her of a long-forgotten sound from her own childhood and something in her relaxed a little.

'Take a pew,' said Suze, pushing the face-eating frizz away. No wonder. 'How do you take your tea, Jenny? Builders'?'

'Lovely. Milk. No sugar, thanks.' She sat down on the nearest chair, not realising that there was a gaping hole in the wicker of the seat. She perched on the edge of its hard frame, grateful for her well-upholstered sitbones. 'So this is Soph's other life,' she said, speaking her own thoughts.

'Yep, welcome to our world.' Suze dunked a teabag in a Union Jack mug of boiling water with her pen-scribbled fingers.

Their world – Sophie's world – certainly looked different to hers. Everything was on a different scale. The kitchen made her and Sam's kitchen seem like a tiny, clinical laboratory. The wooden island was *actually* the size of a small island. Whereas her and Sam's black granite worktops gleamed with lack of use, here the scratched worktops were stained, piled with paper, crayons, glittery pipe cleaners, dirty baby bottles, and there was an orange nappy bag, clearly heavily loaded, sitting right next to a fruit bowl. Saucepan handles protruded out of overstuffed drawers. So much kitchen equipment, so industrial. And the fridge! Forget four by four carbon emissions, surely this fridge alone was like having a huge cow farting vast quantities of methane round the clock.

'I'm Liz. My daughter is in Freddie's class,' said a woman with a smattering of caramel freckles and a cropped pixie haircut, the tips of which were dyed bright red, like they'd been air dried in ketchup. She was breastfeeding a child that looked too old to be breastfed, ruching up one side of an old T-shirt that said 'Talentless but connected' and exposing a blue-veined breast that resembled one of the root vegetables in the Abel and Cole organic box under the table. Although wary of anyone who wore slogan T-shirts, let alone someone in a slogan T-shirt with a boob hanging out, there was something genuine in her smile that Jenny immediately warmed to. 'I remember Soph mentioning you,' she said, only half sure she was right.

The truth was that Sophie hadn't told her much about her mum friends, or her community life. It wasn't until her funeral that Jenny had realised how important it had been to her, or quite how many mum friends there actually were. Seeing them sitting around the table like this, with the easy, slightly competitive edge of sisters, they all seemed so tight. She couldn't help but wonder why she had never been invited into this world before. Had Sophie really thought her socially inflexible?

'Tash,' said another woman in one of those posh croaky north London accents that had always made Jenny feel provincial. She leaned across the table and offered a slim, tanned hand bejewelled with large silver rings set with enormous coloured stones.

Tash was so beautiful it was hard to look at her directly. She had a swishy curtain of liquorice black hair, feline grey eyes and full lips – Soph would have called them 'blowjob lips' – slightly parted, as if she was blowing out air discreetly. (Jenny had read that this was a trick used by Nigella Lawson to look hot in photo shoots, and had once tried it herself, only to free a strand of spinach from a tooth and send it across the room at high velocity.)

Tash swished one leg over the other. It was a long, lean leg, shod in a lovely Cuban-heeled boot, the kind of boot with just the right height of heel that Jenny was always looking for but could never find. 'My son, Ludo, he's in Freddie's class, too. We're the cult of 2Bers, I'm afraid.'

Cult? What was 2B? Or was it, to be? 2B or not to be.

'Lydia. Call me Lyds.' The woman opposite waved like a little girl, fingers starfished. She was petite and milktop blonde with delicate pointy features, the kind of fairy woman Jenny imagined might blow away in the wind unless weighted down by a big expensive handbag. A pudgy girl peppered in alarming red spots sat, in startling contrast to her mother's fragile beauty, on her knee. 'And this is wee Flora.'

'Hello wee Flora.' Do not stare at medieval skin condition. Do not mention medieval skin condition.

'I must ask you immediately, Jenny,' said Lydia as her daughter jumped off her knee and pegged it out of the kitchen. She stared at the roll of flesh swelling over Jenny's ungenerous waistband. 'You're not preggers, are you?'

The shock of the question rocked her back into the hole in the seat. 'Er, no,' she said, extracting herself and feeling embarrassed. 'Not. Definitely not.' She sucked her tummy in.

'Jenny,' said Liz quietly, sweetly coming to her aid. 'Flora, Lydia's little girl, she's got chicken pox.'

'Oh, *right*!' Perhaps she wasn't so fat she looked like she should be in a birthing pool. 'I've had chicken pox. Really, don't worry about it.'

'Swap chairs?' whispered Liz kindly.

'No, I'm fine, thanks.' Actually her bum was beginning to ache.

'I thought your speech at the funeral was so lovely,' said Liz, placing her baby/teenager down on the floor, where it promptly toddled off towards a kitchen cupboard door and started disembowelling it of pans. 'Soph would have appreciated it.'

'Thanks. Thanks so much,' said Jenny gratefully, relaxing a little. Perhaps the meeting wouldn't be so bad after all. They weren't so different. They were all friends of Sophie's. All women.

'It was spot on.' Tash smiled, flashing a broad, perfectly even row of tiny white teeth. 'You know what? It's so nice to meet someone from Soph's pre-mum life, putting all the bits of the jigsaw together. From what I remember Soph saying, you two go back a long way?'

'Yeah, we shared student digs in the first year of uni.' Something tightened in her throat again, remembering the early days. How she'd been mesmerised by Sophie, the loud, garrulous beauty. How honoured she'd been to be her friend. 'Manchester uni. We were in the same house. She made me cheese on toast that first night.'

'She was always good on cheese, wasn't she?' smiled Liz, running her hands through her red hair. 'Every time I went round to hers for dinner I'd leave with a certain nagging doubt that the lump of supermarket Cheddar sweating in my fridge drawer didn't quite cut it.'

Jenny remembered the sight of Ollie's pitiful fridge. She doubted it even contained cracked Cheddar. She sat up straighter, reminding herself why she was here. This was not about her. It was about Ollie and Freddie. She must put her reservations aside and remember this. It was time for her to step up. What was she scared of?

'So did you meet your husband at uni too?' asked Lydia curiously.

'No.' Jenny coughed, remembering Suze's comment in the deli about her having a complicated . . . well, love life, surely? They'd obviously muddled her up with someone far more interesting. 'We're not married.'

Suze looked at the blue stone ring on her finger and winked. 'Engaged, I see.'

'What does he do?' asked Tash, sipping her tea nonchalantly, like this question was a perfectly acceptable line of enquiry when you'd known someone ten minutes.

Jenny had always disliked the 'What does he do?' question. On principle. (Were people their jobs?) But also because . . . 'He's a lawyer,' she said quietly, trying to wrap the subject up quickly.

'Ooh,' Tash said. 'What kind of lawyer?'

She braced herself, feeling her shoulders rise towards her ears. 'Divorce lawyer.'

'A divorce lawyer!' Tash brightened.

'Oh my God, that's just *so* romantic.' Lydia closed her eyes. 'Despite everything he knows about the statistics.'

'I should take his number,' muttered Tash, digging into the large mouth of her vast handbag. 'I could do with a new lawyer. May I?'

She was too awed by Tash's self-assured beauty to say no.

'Ladies, shall we start the meeting proper?' Suze sat down heavily on the chair next to Jenny's, knees cracking. 'We'll have tonnes of time to get to know one another in the next few weeks.'

Tonnes of time? So this wasn't a one-off meeting? Jenny's stomach clenched.

'Okey dokey.' Suze rummaged busily for a pen in a pile of school homework. Pen located, she spoke officiously.

'Thanks for coming here on this freezing afternoon.' She smiled at Jenny and angled her pen towards her. 'Especially you, Jenny, taking a day off work.'

Tash coughed.

'And you, of course, Tash. And Liz. Sorry, Tash, I'd forgotten you'd gone back to work,' said Suze quickly.

'Three days a week,' said Tash, examining her nails, which were painted a shade of taupe that Jenny guessed must be fashionable. It would never occur to Jenny in a million years to paint her nails taupe. 'Toby's alimony saw to that,' she muttered.

Liz raised an eyebrow. There was a moment of awkwardness.

'Right,' said Suze briskly, pushing the wilful wall of hair away from her face again. 'I don't think anyone will disagree with me when I say that Ollie and Freddie need help right now. And I'm talking proper, controlled, organised help. Don't you think, Jenny?'

They all turned to face her. Feeling spotlit, her right eyelid twitched. What had she got herself into? 'Yes, yes, absolutely.'

'And we're going to step in. We're going to do what Sophie would have done for us.'

'Abso-bloody-lutely!' exclaimed Liz.

'Too right,' said Lydia, licking icing off her fingertips. 'I mean, have you seen the mess in Ollie's house, Jenny?'

'Soph actually did her own cleaning, you see,' said Liz. 'Domestic goddess.'

'Why not hire him a cleaner?' said Jenny.

'A cleaner!' Suze scribbled furiously in her notebook. 'Ace idea, Jenny. There's that Brazilian who works at number seven who's meant to be great. I wouldn't inflict mine on anyone. Too la-di-dah to do toilets. And I'm too bloody liberal to make her.'

'But not liberal enough not to care,' added Liz wryly.

Suze ignored this. 'Now, shall we tell Jenny our concerns?'

'Freddie was sent home from school last week for being too tired. Apparently he fell asleep on a crash mat during PE,' Lydia said, her fine-boned face wimpling into a frown. 'I don't think he has a proper bedtime any more.'

What was a proper bedtime for a six-year-old boy? Jenny had no idea. 'Right,' she said, hoping she sounded like she knew what she might be talking about.

'And Lola's mum told me he's got lice,' winced Suze.

'Oh God, not again,' Lydia groaned, dropping her head into her hands. 'My whole life is infested with bloody lice. Flora's head was hopping for weeks last year. I treat it, they come back. I reckon that school has developed some super hybrid of lice, a master race.'

'Nazi lice!' said Liz. 'Ve 'ave vays of making you itch.'

'Leave it to me,' said Jenny, feeling her own head itch. She seemed to remember some carcinogenic potion from her own childhood that could nuke an army of locusts.

Suze made a big red tick in her notebook. 'Anything else, ladies?'

Liz rested her face in her hands. 'Ollie's listening to weirdy churchy music, Jenny. All the time. It makes Leonard Cohen sound like the Beach Boys. I worry it's going to make him depressed; well, obviously he's depressed. But *more* depressed. It would make me totally suicidal.'

'And dare we mention the beard?' ventured Suze.

'Oh I do like the beard,' smiled Tash dreamily.

'Me too,' sighed Lydia. 'It's kind of . . . biblical. He looks like Jesus.'

'Lydia,' groaned Liz.

'Unhygienic,' decided Suze. 'It's like having pubic hair on your chin. I've never understood beards.'

Not as unhygienic as leaving a nappy bag next to the fruit bowl, she wanted to point out. 'I don't think we can get involved in every aspect of his life.'

Suddenly there was a loud sniff. Jenny turned towards Lydia and saw that her eyes were full of tears. She waited for someone to do or say something sympathetic, but no one did. Should she say something? Or was it some kind of winter hay fever?

'What about food, Jenny?' said Suze.

'Food?' Jenny said blankly. She had no idea how to run Sophie's domestic life. She, Jenny, didn't have a domestic life. She had Sam and takeaways and meals out. For the first time ever she wondered if Sophie had secretly thought her best friend's life a tad tragic.

'Do you think we need to hatch a supper strategy?' Suze reached for a homemade chocolate chip biscuit the size of a saucer, as if just the mention of food had wetted her appetite.

'Er, sorry, what's a supper strategy?'

'It's America's new tactic for smoking out members of Al Qaeda from caves,' deadpanned Liz, and Jenny laughed.

Suze rolled her eyes, unamused. 'It's a home delivery service of *meals*, Jenny.'

'Hey, that's a great idea. I think he'd really appreciate that. I do.'

'Do you?' beamed Suze, delighted to have Jenny's approval. She glanced over at Tash with a look that was not unlike triumph. 'Then a supper strategy we shall arrange.'

'Lasagne!' Tash slapped the table. She was going to better Suze if it killed her. 'Men love lasagne. I make a mean lasagne.'

'One of my specialities too, actually,' said Suze, scribbling 'lasagne!!!' in her notes.

There was another loud sniff from Lydia. She dabbed at her small nose with a tissue.

'Are you OK?' Jenny asked, unable to ignore it any longer.

'Lydia's *very* emotional, Jenny, heart on her sleeve,' Suze explained blithely. 'Now let's talk about . . .'

'Hopeless,' sniffed Lydia, shaking her head. 'Hopeless sop, I am. I could only listen to the first couple of lines of your speech. I was in pieces, *pieces*, wasn't I, Liz?'

'You were, Lydia,' Liz reassured tersely, with the minutest flicker of an eye roll.

'How could someone as beautiful as Sophie *die*?' Lydia sobbed more freely now. Liz reached for her hand and gave it a patronising pat. 'Freddie, motherless at six. How can a child ever recover?'

'Deep breath, Lyds. Deep breath. We've all been where you are now,' said Suze. 'I think we owe it to Ollie and Freddie to be strong, don't we, Jenny?'

'We do,' Jenny said. The others must have hearts of stone to let Lydia sob like this. 'But it's OK to cry, too. No point in bottling it up.' She'd had to run out of Legs, Bums and Tums only yesterday because Destiny's Child's 'Survivor' came on and it would always remind her of Sophie doing her bootie shake thing in her kitchen. 'Or it spurts out sideways.'

'You're right, you're so right, Jenny.' Lydia smiled at her appreciatively.

'Could we not set up a charity?' Tash wondered, pushing the conversation forward.

'Hmm?' Suze asked Jenny.

'I'm not sure,' said Jenny. A charity? For whom?'

'We could do the London marathon!'

'A cake sale?'

'A naked calendar.'

A naked calendar! Jesus. 'Don't mean to rain on your parade, but I don't think it's money that . . .'

'Jenny's right.' Liz frowned. 'Oh, it feels awful talking about these things. But he earns a fair bit, doesn't he?'

Jenny nodded. 'I guess so. He's one of those producers that you and I may not have heard about, but he's very well respected in his field.'

'Has he ever worked with Take That?' asked Lydia, brightening.

She shook her head. 'Doubt it. It's advertising, film stuff, you know.'

'Oh.' Lydia's face fell. 'I totally love Take That. Thank *fuck* Robbie's back!'

There was an ear-splitting yelp from the sitting room, the sound of something heavy and airborne landing. Lydia jumped up and flew out the kitchen. 'Flora!'

Liz shrugged, like she'd heard it all before. Another blood-curdling yell.

'Ludo?' Liz turned to Tash.

'Sounds like it.' Tash got up wearily from her seat. 'Sorry, ladies, better go and umpire.'

'She's not joking either,' muttered Suze, the moment Tash left the room. 'Ludo's a bloody nightmare. I'd better go and check he's not swinging baba around by his toenails.'

As soon as they were all safely out of the kitchen, Liz filled up Jenny's mug with tea. Her mouth twitched with a smile. 'You don't have to say anything, Jenny.'

She laughed, feeling a rush of warmth towards Liz. Yes, she liked Liz best. She liked the fact that she dyed her hair ketchup red. Personally, she'd never have the balls. For the hair. Or that T-shirt.

'It's like a little wagon circle, isn't it? I'm afraid we must come across as right little interfering Stepford busybodies.'

'Not at all! I had no idea Sophie had this network.' The niggling feeling that she'd been shut out from parts of Sophie's life came back to her. 'It's brilliant.'

'Well, she told us lots about you,' said Liz kindly.

What exactly *had* Sophie told them about her? She thought of the list that Ollie had shown her. 'Talk to Jenny about *it*.' About what? What 'it'? Perhaps these women knew what 'it' was. Perhaps if she hung out with them they'd tell her. 'I hardly know my neighbours. There's so much neighbourly motivation here. It's amazing, really.'

'Ah, a lot of local women will become *extremely* motivated where Ollie is concerned, I suspect.' Liz put her mug to her cheek and winked. Jenny noticed how her pea-green eyes clashed with the red of her hair, in a good way.

'What do you mean?'

'He's the sexiest dad at the school by a few trillion miles. Everyone's always fancied the pants off him. Dark, devoted and moody.' She closed her eyes in a mock swoon. 'And a musician.'

'You're joking? He's just lost his wife.'

'*Exactly.*'

She put her hand over her mouth. 'Blimey. It had never occurred to me that . . .'

'He's a wonderful father, handsome, successful, clearly capable of love and commitment, and, heartbreakingly, *tantalisingly*, in need of rescue.'

'But aren't this lot coupled up?'

Liz glanced at the kitchen door, checking no one was coming through it. 'Loosely,' she said in a hushed voice. 'Tash divorced last year, although there's a Polish builder, otherwise known as Marko The Wildebeest. Lydia is married to some city guy whom she never sees. Suze . . . well, Suze's motivation is probably purer, she loves being needed and even the PTA cannot channel all her energies, but then again you never know. And there are many, many others, waiting in the sidelines, believe me.'

Jenny threw her candour back at her. 'And you?'

Something sad and wordless passed across Liz's face. 'I loved Soph,' she shrugged simply, sweetly. 'That's all.' And Jenny believed her.

'All good! All good!' Suze burst back into the kitchen, carrying the marsupial ginger baby that Jenny remembered meeting in the deli. She was accompanied by a pong of poo, and as she bounced the baby on her knee the smell got stronger. 'So, Help Ollie project is full steam ahead, eh?'

81

'Let's go for it.'

'Brill. I'll sort out rotas and stuff from the Muzzy Hill end . . .'

'I wish I could do more . . .' She needed to come clean about her own general uselessness. 'I'm a bit in the dark where kids and stuff are concerned, to be honest. I'm probably the least useful person, much as I want to help.'

'Oh, you don't understand, do you?' said Suze. 'We *need* you involved in this. We really do. In fact you are crucial to the operation.'

'I am?' She hadn't been crucial to anything or anybody for months, maybe never.

'Completely,' insisted Suze.

'Why?'

'You know Ollie better than any of us,' said Liz, taking a sip of her tea. 'We need someone in the group who can speak for him.'

'I can't possibly speak for him.'

'Look, someone has to,' said Liz. 'Our job is to organise his domestic life over these coming weeks. Your job is to stay close to him, so that he's got one woman by his side, a woman who is not his mother, or sister-in-law, a woman who doesn't *want* anything from him.' She gave Jenny a meaningful look. 'A safe place. You know what I'm saying?'

Jenny nodded. The ginger baby reached across for her gold bracelet. His fingers felt silky soft against the skin of her wrist. She studied the top of his scabby cradle-capped head and felt a wave of tenderness for his unphotogenic qualities.

'The fact is,' said Suze, trying to hold the wriggling baby

82

still, 'you knew Sophie better than anyone, didn't you?'

She nodded, but a little voice in her head had begun to wonder. There were clearly whole parts of Sophie's life that she didn't know anything about at all.

Seven

Curious goings on in north London, let me tell you.

Three days ago, I nudged my non-atomic self – take that Stephen Hawking and suck on it – through the muddy cat flap of Suze's house and gripped on to the tail end of a conversation between Jenny and Liz as it writhed about the room like a barracuda. Something about the local women *fancying* my husband! I'm barely dead, for Pete's sake. Bravissimo are still sending me catalogues. I've still got five hundred free mobile minutes left.

But then people do keep surprising me. They are far weirder than I ever realised. Get this.

Two days ago I watched as Jenny sat in her bedroom, bolt upright, absolutely still, like one of those keeno yoga devotees, as the clock ticked and the room fell into darkness. My mother kept ringing on her telephone. Once, twice, three times over the course of a couple of hours. She didn't answer. Sam came back from work and found her in the dark, still sitting upright, tears pouring down her cheeks. He asked her what was for supper. She didn't reply. And yesterday I found her making what looked suspiciously like a collage. Jenny crafting! I swear she was actually cutting out bits of paper and sticking things down with the ever useless Pritt Stick – winding the damn thing up, down, trying to pick off the old crust of glue on the top that stops it being a glue and makes it a smearer of white snotty gloop. No, she's not her usual self at all. I'm so relieved that Sam is The Wedding Date Shirker. Jenny needs time to paddle around in her sadness before she makes any big decisions about her future, or is let loose anywhere near a bridal department without me.

Meanwhile, in deepest Essex, my sister is channelling all her tears into repeat viewings of *Bridges Of Madison County*. Further south, Dad is spending hours and hours in his shed, constructing the world's most complex hammock frame. He's never wanted a hammock before. Is it something to do with its cradle aspect? Perhaps he needs to be soothed to sleep. Actually suspect he's retreating to the shed to escape Mum, who is still desperately sad. Poor, poor Mum, cloaked in an aura so cold and crunchy it looks like she's been breaded in ice in a dodgy overactive freezer compartment.

As for Ollie? Right now my poor love is under siege. He is staring at the five foil-covered packages that line our kitchen table like crude homemade IUDs. The doorbell rings. He flinches.

'Shall I get it, Dad?' whispers Freddie, running up behind him, Chupa Chup a conker in his cheek.

Ollie pulls at his beard. He looks like a shipwrecked pirate. 'No, it could be . . .'

Freddie pulls a face. 'Not more lasagne?'

The doorbell rings again. Ollie raises his finger to his lips. 'Shhh. Don't make a sound.'

They wait there together in silence, hiding from the enemy. The doorbell rings again. They wait some more. Finally, the sound of receding footsteps on the path outside. Freddie crouches down by the front door and peeks through the letterbox. 'Daddy, there's something on the step.'

'Shit,' mutters Ollie, running his hands through his greasy hair. He walks down the hall, stepping over numerous wooden balls – they've been using the hall as a bowling alley – opens the door, glancing uneasily from side to side as if there might be a hidden sniper lurking on the other side of the cherry tree, grabs the Pyrex dish and slams the door shut behind him. He puts the dish next to the others and wearily reads the note on the top. 'OK, Freddie, we've got a new one here. And this one is from Tash, Ludo's mummy. That makes it her second in three days. This one is, er, bolognese sauce.' He looks perplexed. 'Goes well with the custard pudding, she says. What custard pudding? Oh right. Here.' He peels foil off another package.

Freddie makes a gagging noise and puts his fingers down his throat.

'Got any ideas, Fred?'

'Yes.'

'What?'

'Ping Pong.'

'Freddie, my son, your mind is dark.' He raises his hand into a high five. 'You are a genius.'

Freddie grins. It's almost a proper beam. Like he used to do all the time. I'm amazed that he can still smile like this, awed at how resilient he is. He opens the back door. 'Here, Ping Pong, here, pussy, pussy! Dinner time.'

Later, as the evening falls harder and colder – icicles are hanging like frozen tears from the windowpanes by nine pm – I curl into Ollie's old black Converse trainers. They are contained and safe and smell reassuringly of Ollie. I don't want to smell his aftershave, or the washing liquid on his clothes, or his dry skin shampoo. I want the meaty essence of him, the expelled bodily odours, the flakes of skin, the hot stink of his maleness. I'd actually hang out in his armpit if I could, but I fear this might make him itch.

It's nine-thirty now. Ping Pong's paw prints polka across the snow on the deck. There are bald patches on our little scrap of lawn where Freddie and Ollie have scooped up snowballs in cold red hands and tossed them at each other. In the right-hand corner of the garden, beneath the plum tree that bears the world's tartest, most inedible plums, there is a snowman, a muddy parsnip for a nose, his eyes withered conkers carefully kept by Freddie the previous autumn. Although the house is a tip it is warm – a veritable sauna in the trainer, actually. Ollie has lit a homely fire in the sitting room fireplace. Making fires is the one domestic thing Ollie's always been good at, having enough of a Ray Mears whiff about it to appeal to him, unlike cleaning the roasting pan. (You never see Ray Mears washing up his wild fungi cooking pans in the woods, do you? Bet he's got some poor assistant doing that. Bet she's female.)

They are sitting beside the fire now, Freddie curled inside Ollie's knees, resting his head against his chest, listening to the thumpity thump of his heart, the exact same position I used to snuggle into on winter nights. Freddie's lids are beginning to droop. Ollie strokes the soft curls off his forehead with the plane of his palm. The fire spits and crackles. Its heat gives their faces a healthy glow and hides the puddles of grief beneath Ollie's eyes. They look too beautiful for words. And I wonder why I was ever, ever restless in those last few months of my life? What was I hankering after exactly, if not this? Jenny was right. Isn't she always right? About other people's lives at least.

Thing is, how the hell was I to know that I'd end up as road kill on Regent Street? If one's demise could be predicted more accurately – 'You're unlikely to last much past Christmas, make it a good one, Mrs Brady' – then at least I could have *planned*. Made an imminent to-do list. A memory box. I would have left Ollie final instructions – a domestic kick-the-bucket list – with relevant phone numbers and information. (Remember my mother's birthday. Take Freddie to the dentist every six months. Do not leave woollens out because of moths. Feed. The. Cat.) And, more than this, much more than this, I would have had a chance to appreciate what I had. Take stock of my lovely life. What's that quote, 'I had such a lovely life, if only I'd realised it sooner'. Dorothy Parker? Anyway, I like to think I would have been able to face my expiration with some grace, although I realise there's a chance I would have panicked and refused to accept the fact I was dying, like poor Aunt Linda, and spent all my money on an alternative medicine clinic in Austria and massage and vitamin injections.

Did I have an alternative destiny? Was there some small seed of fate buried within my body that I didn't know about, a lump in the breast too small for detection? A furring of the left aorta? An unknown yet lethal genetic predisposition embedded in my helix of DNA set to activate aged fifty-five like a bomb in the hold of a plane? I guess we all carry the seeds of our death within us. Then you're hit by a bus. And those seeds are blown to the wind like a dandelion clock. It's a fucker, it really is. I realise that nothing else in my life was a fucker now, even though I thought so at the time. Not the fact that I couldn't conceive a second child. Not the fact that I didn't become a film star. Or never found the perfect boot. No, being hit by a bus is the fucker of all fuckers, end of.

You know the truth? The horrible grave-chilly truth? I feel robbed. I feel robbed of my beautiful child, the sock and honey smell of him, the concavity of his flexible back, his focus as he makes a Lego spaceship, that pink wet tongue curling out of the corner of his mouth with absolute concentration. I feel robbed of his laughter and love, of watching him grow up. And I also feel robbed of the man I fell in love with, the man I'd watched for three years at university, shy of his looks and his cool kid reticence, the man who kissed me in a field one cool summer dawn in Somerset and made my heart corkscrew with happiness.

I even feel robbed of my flipping wrinkles! I never ended up looking like my mother. Or my grandmother, a grandmother who lived in near perfect health to the age of ninety-seven then fell asleep into her cream of mushroom soup one afternoon and didn't wake up again. I will never be able to say, 'It was better in my day,' or marvel at how no one can remember what an iPhone was. No, I am forever a twenty-first-century thirtysomething, like one of those photographs of women in the forties who died during the war and can only ever be remembered with set curls and red lips. Vintage.

'Was it fun playing at Ludo's earlier?' Ollie asks, interrupting my thoughts before they get gloomier.

'Ludo's dad has gone,' Freddie replies deadpan, cat's cradling an elastic band between his fingers.

'No, he doesn't live there any more, Fred,' replies Ollie softly. 'He lives in another house.'

(FYI, with the old au pair, Astrid.)

'But he still sees Ludo,' Ollie reassures.

Freddie ponders this for a moment, his eyes wide, processing. 'I think that's better than being in heaven. I wish Mummy just lived in another house.'

So do I, my love. So do I.

They sit there watching the flames of the fire leap blue and orange. I desperately want to curl up beside them, run my fingers along the coiled ridges of their earlobes. Surely my love must conduct itself to them somehow? Love can't just expire. It's not got a pulse. Therefore it cannot die.

Freddie looks thoughtful. 'If you emailed Mummy on your computer what would happen?'

'Nothing, Fred.'

'Have you tried?'

He hesitates. 'Yeah. I did once.' He looks down, embarrassed. 'Didn't get a reply. The account is closed now anyway.'

'What about the thingy on the computer when you get the face like it's a telly?'

'Skype?'

Freddie nods. 'The one we use to talk to Granny sometimes.'

Ollie's eyes are filling. The lump in his throat is rising up his neck. He's trying really hard. 'She's not there either, Freddie.'

'But she's somewhere!' Freddie shouts. 'I *know* she is.'

Ollie takes Freddie's face in his hands and holds it. 'She is somewhere. And she loves you. She loves you so much. But she is not on the earth, not like you and me.'

It's a valiant attempt. How would I explain it?

'Like an angel? A superhero?'

'An angel.'

Look, no wings!

Freddie clenches his jaw. 'It's still not fair.'

'It's not fair. It's absolutely not fair.'

'Why did the bus driver not die? Why Mummy?'

Ollie's face darkens. 'The bus driver dying would not bring Mummy back, would it?'

'No,' acknowledges Freddie with heartbreaking forgiveness. I hope he holds on to this gift as he gets older, my sweet soulful boy.

'It was an accident.'

Freddie looks unsatisfied. 'But . . .'

'Bad things sometimes happen to people. Not very often. But they do.'

'Like when Granny lost her purse in Sainsbury's.'

'Worse stuff.'

'Like what happened to Mummy?'

'You can be in the wrong place at the wrong time.'

'Like Jenny,' he nods more thoughtfully.

Ollie laughs. 'What do you mean?'

'Jenny looks like she's in the wrong place sometimes.'

Out of the mouths of babes.

'You mean she looks sad?' says Ollie, concerned now.

Freddie nods.

'I think she just misses your mummy, Fred.'

He spreads his hands in front of the fire and warms them like toast. 'Why doesn't someone kiss Jenny better?'

Ha! God, I love this boy.

Ollie smiles softly. 'I'm sure Sam kisses her better.'

Freddie considers this for a moment, wrinkles his nose in distaste. 'I'd rather Sam got run over than Jenny.'

Me too! Bring on the no. 23!

'Look, Freddie. It's not an either or thing. Sam's not about to get run over. Nor is Jenny.' He bends down and talks close to his ear. 'Jen's here for you.'

'Like you?'

'Like me.' Ollie strokes Freddie's cheek. 'I'm not going anywhere, Freddie.'

'Promise?'

He gives a military salute. 'Scout's honour.'

Freddie still looks worried. 'So it's just us two now?'

'Just us two. We'll make Mummy proud.'

And *how* proud!

Freddie's forehead knits. There is something bothering him. 'I won't get another mummy?'

The room vibrates. I freeze on the mantelpiece.

'Ludo says he now has two mummies,' Freddie continues. 'One at home. One with his dad. He doesn't like it. I don't think I'd like it either.'

'It does sound kind of complicated.' A muscle in Ollie's jaw twitches.

He's skirting it! He's not saying there won't be another mummy.

'Anyway, I don't need another mummy. Jenny can take me swimming.'

'Fred, no one will ever replace your mummy. I will always love her, and you, more than anyone else in the whole world.'

That's better. Almost.

'Universe?' says Freddie.

'Galaxy.'

'Cool,' says Freddie, leaning his head back on Ollie's shoulder, satisfied at last. Within seconds he is asleep.

Eight

'I want a date, Jen,' Sam said as he walked into the flat, shaking glittering blobs of rain off his suit on to the polished hardwood surfaces and clamping shut his black golf umbrella.

'Good idea.' Jenny pushed away her manuscript, happy to be disturbed and finish work for the day. 'Wouldn't mind going to that new place in The Stables. I'm totally starving and there's no food here, sorry. I've been on the phone to Soph's mum for *hours* . . .'

He dumped his briefcase. 'Please turn off that crap.'

'What crap?'

'The music.'

'It's Lonnie Donegan!'

'Jenny.' He pulled off his tie, striding over the beige Conran rug in the manner of a romantic hero stalking across windswept moors. 'I'm talking about a date for the wedding.'

'Wedding?' Jenny froze. Better turn off Lonnie.

'Or have you forgotten that we are engaged?'

'No!' It was just that compared to the death of Sophie, it,

like everything else in the universe, had begun to feel almost insignificant, abstract, a date in the diary that wouldn't happen for a while and could comfortably be ignored in the meantime.

Hurt flickered over his rain-wet face. 'Curb your enthusiasm.'

She stood up, slipped her arms around his waist. 'Oh, Sam, I'm sorry. I'm a little stunned, that's all. We've been engaged for so long and . . .' She kissed him. 'After all this time. Why now?'

'Death. It focuses the mind, no?' He stroked her hair off her face. 'We've got one life. Let's seize it, babes.'

A random, weird thought jumped up in her head: I don't believe him. I don't believe that's why he wants to marry me right now. She pushed the upstart thought away. They'd been getting on so badly. This must be his way of trying to make things right.

He put his hand on her jaw, turned her head to face him, regain her attention. 'Life goes on, right babe?'

She nodded but couldn't help noting that actually it was death that went on and on and on. Not life.

'Don't cry. I'm not worth it.'

She laughed, wiped the rogue tear away. 'I don't want you to marry me to *save* me, Sam. I don't need saving. I just need . . .' She hesitated. What did she need? 'I think I just need time.'

'How much more?' His voice had an edge to it now. 'We've been engaged for ages.'

Part of her couldn't believe they were having the conversation at all. So long she'd craved a date, prodded him gently for it, wanted to prove to Sophie, to her parents, that the wedding would happen and she wasn't Waity Jenny. And now? Well, she still felt funereal.

'I'd like to do it as soon as possible.'

'As soon as possible?'

'In the summer.'

'Next year?'

'This year.'

'But . . . but that's not long.'

'What's stopping us?'

'Well, nothing I guess.' She dug her nails into her palm.

'You look worried.'

'I'm not worried.' She was worried. 'We're not ready, though. I haven't got a dress. We haven't decided on the venue . . .'

'Well you can get a dress easily enough, can't you? And I always assumed we'd just bang up a marquee in my folks' garden.'

'Yes, yes of course.' That was logical enough. Her own parents lived in a bungalow built in 1982 with far-reaching views of a chicken farm. His family home was Georgian, enormous, garden like a deer park. What did it matter that she'd failed to enjoy so many Sunday lunches in that house? No, it didn't matter at all.

'I'm reading hesitancy, baby.'

'It's just . . . there's so much to do. And I'm really up to my neck in this Help Ollie thing right now. It's taking up a lot of time and . . .'

'Mum will help with all the organising.' Sam's features tightened. 'Anyway, you need to get the Muswell Hill ladies to do the donkey work. It shouldn't fall to you. You're just the . . . the consultant.'

'Hardly!' It was now six weeks since that first meeting. They'd had a meeting once a week since, and countless phone calls and emails. Sam already said he wanted her to scale it back. Funnily enough she was discovering that she didn't want to scale it back. That despite her initial doubts she was enjoying being involved. She woke up thinking about what Ollie and Freddie needed, thinking up ways that might make them happier. If nothing else, Help Ollie had given her a reason to crawl out from under the duvet in the morning. In a way, and it was hard to accept given the morbidity of their task, it was kind of fun too, what with the other women, the collective sense of purpose. And by getting to know Sophie's friends – the life she'd hidden away up there in N10 – Jenny felt she was getting to know another side of Sophie too. And this was important. It meant that in some small way she was still alive. That the story wasn't totally over.

'The wedding will be lovely,' he said softly. 'It'll make you feel better.'

She tried to imagine it. The white dress. The flowers. The confetti. And it made her cry. Oh God, she was turning into Lydia.

'Don't cry,' he said softly. 'What is it?'

'A wedding without Sophie.'

'Hey, come on.' He hugged her.

'She would have been matron of honour and now she won't.'

Sam held her by the shoulders. 'You can ask someone else.'

'No, if she can't do it then no one can. I can't replace her. It would be like pretending I still have a best friend and I don't.'

'You might change your mind nearer the time.'

'I won't.'

'No, you won't, will you?' He sighed, let go of her shoulders and walked over to the fridge to retrieve a beer. 'There must be something you can do to get over this.' He looked thoughtful, frothed the beer into a glass. 'A shrink? Do you think you should see a shrink?'

'Actually I'd like to talk to Ollie.' Sam's forehead knitted. She chose her words more carefully. How to explain that without Sophie around to give her blessing, she needed Ollie's? 'Just let him know, I mean, so he's the first to know. I think that would make a difference.'

'For fuck's sake, Jenny.' He squeezed the bridge of his nose with his fingers. 'This is about *us*. It's got nothing to do with Ollie.'

Nine

Something should have stopped them reaching the altar. That something should have been me. Unfortunately I spent my last meeting with Jenny talking about tooth veneers and Nectar cards. These were not meant to be my last blimmin' words. They really were not. And now he's only gone and set a wedding date.

A few things happened, you see. With Sam. Sam and me. Some were little things. Unsaid. Others existed only as suspicions and hunches. Others . . . well, there were other things too. I'm not proud of them.

A party, two years ago. It was Wendy Law's thirty-fifth. Tufnell Park, north London. It was a hot, sticky summer's night. Too hot for shoes or long hair. Sweaty and grimy, the streets of London pulsed in the heat. Music poured from open windows. People fainted on the Tube. Dealers cruised the noisy streets in their convertibles, stereos blaring. It looked like the pavement on Brecknock Road was melting. And in a little walled patio garden off that road we celebrated Wendy's new Sapphic epiphany – she'd fallen madly, deliriously in love with a maths teacher called Penny. We all had. Penny was totally delicious, super smart, and the dream lesbo lover for any woman. Wendy had never been happier. Their coupling was startling and sexy and satisfyingly ruffled her retard ex who had treated her appallingly. We were all dancing madly outside, old early nineties tunes. Arms in the air. Like you just don't care. That sort of thing. The music whooshed me right back to the time before Freddie was born and I was wild and free and wore red Kickers. I felt sexy for the first time in months. Not like someone who had emptied her boobs of their bounce with excessive lactation or who had a zipper of stitches linking my vagina with my anus. In short, I felt hot, sexy and twenty-five again.

By two am a hardcore of inebriated thirtysomethings were dancing wildly. I had the beginnings of what would become a Mount Vesuvius blister on the ball of my left foot, the neighbours were complaining and the police had been called. In other words, it was a rockin' party. Even Jenny was dancing with an abandon I hadn't seen before. After months of crap singleton dates with men who were allergic to oral sex – not making this up – she'd settled in with Sam, who was a walking, talking cunnilingus-loving vindication that the crap date purgatory had all been worth it. He was the upbeat end to a woman's magazine article. The twist at the end of a rom com. Apart from fancying the pants off him, Jenny saw the idealistic, good man beneath the lawyer's crisp suit, the soft heart beneath the laddish wit. We all did. We thought Sam was great.

We'd done quite a lot of hanging out, me, Ollie, Sam and Jenny. A day trip to Whitstable. Dinners at number thirty-three. A remarkably debauched New Year's Eve involving absinthe and lobster. While Ollie and Sam weren't exactly bosom buddies – Ollie is not the most social animal, he'd happily see no one other than his family and his music studio – they got on pretty well, in the tolerant buddyish manner of men who are thrust together because of the closeness of their other halves.

I didn't plan to need the loo at the same time as Sam. It just happened that our bladders synchronised. We left Ollie and Jenny dancing to Kylie while we queued outside the endlessly locked bathroom door. I say queued. Actually we were trying to outdo each other in bad taste seventies rock. Journey! Jefferson Airplane! Kenny Loggins! It was funny, really funny, as things tend to be in the early morning, pissed, after the babysitter had texted to say, 'don't rush back, all fine'. I remember snorting with laughter, howling out the lyrics at the top of my voice. Then suddenly, without warning, it wasn't funny. His hand was on my bottom. It took a moment to register. Yes, his hand was definitely on my bottom and it wasn't moving. I wiggled it off and made a joke of it, telling him that he was drunk and should go and sober up somewhere and keep his paws to himself. I even tried to think of a seventies rock lyric that would sum it up nicely and make light of the accidental hand, but couldn't. Mostly I couldn't because he was looking into my eyes, I mean really looking, like he'd lost something in them. Then he said coolly, 'I'm not in the least bit drunk, Sophie.'

'Oh.' I laughed, adjusted the waistband of my big white hula hula skirt. I was still frisky, restless for the dance floor, for dancing motherhood away, just for the night. I hopped from one heel to the other. 'Have I got canapé on my tooth or something?'

He was staring really hard now. It felt like I was being sucked into those pale blue eyes, like a little wooden boat pulled towards a giant hungry whirlpool.

'What?' I said, uncomfortable now, wishing the girl in the loo would get on with it and signal that the wait was almost over by flushing the chain.

He smiled, a knowing smile. Like he could read what I was feeling, knew how helpless I was to escape. 'I know you're the kind of woman who likes to be looked at, Sophie, so I'm looking at you.'

'Right,' I said, recognising the weirdness through my drunkenness. We shouldn't be talking like this. Something funny was going down.

'You are so very beautiful, Sophie,' he said in a way that was so disarmingly sincere that it froze me to the spot.

'Thanks,' I said quietly, glancing around me in case someone was watching, or Jenny was coming towards us. There was no one. Yes, I should have said 'Fuck off' at this precise point, but it's hard when a man is looking at you like that and you're pissed and you're not quite sure what's going on. Shamefully, I was a little bit flattered too. For a moment I was not a stay-at-home mother from Muswell Hill. I was Sophie Matilda Brady, man magnet. Like I used to be. Sophie superstar.

'You feel it?' And his eyes flashed filthy.

'Feel what?'

'You know what I mean.'

'I don't,' I said, knowing exactly what he meant, feeling

my own body start to tingle with the most appalling arousal. Honestly, up until this point I'd never felt an attraction to Sam before. It had never occurred to me that he might even be sexy. He was Jenny's boyfriend. That was that. I didn't go there. But now, suddenly, he was someone else too. Someone apart from Jenny, someone who existed in my space, in this private erotic moment, with me, just me, not me as someone's wife, or mother, or neighbour, but me as I used to be when I was young and single and could walk into any street and bring traffic to a screeching halt.

'Sophie . . .' He reached out to me, his hand firm on my waist. I flitted away from him in one move like a dancer. The toilet door opened, a woman came out, and I ran in. I shut the door firmly behind me. It was to prove much harder to shut out Sam from my head.

I should have told Jenny, shouldn't I? But I felt horribly guilty and decided to put it down to a blip of high spirits, a drunken conversation late at night in a sexy, charged atmosphere. And Jenny was so happy at that time. She had her hands in the air. She was mouthing the words to 'Start Me Up'. Was it worth ruining her happiness for a blip? Was it worth telling Ollie then trying to stop him socking Sam in the jaw? No. It wasn't. So I told no one and hoped that Jenny and Sam's relationship would run its course sooner rather than later.

I never expected it to last, you see. After that, why would I? The guy had ants in his pants. A cock that wanted walkabout.

The secret was a burden. It was also slightly thrilling. He messed around in my head in that sexy puréed area between sleep and waking, at the edge of my thoughts, at the edge of my vision. After that I would notice him looking at me over dinner, his eyes always on my mouth. And I'd feel a jolt when his hands brushed against mine, which they seemed to do frequently, and I'd glance up to see if Jenny had noticed. She never appeared to – maybe she chose not to. And I tried not to flirt, I really did, but it's always come so naturally to me, I'm afraid. It's like breathing. Given the opportunity, why would a woman not want to flex her coquettish muscle? It's fun. Not everything in life is fun. Flirting is.

Then it stopped being fun. It got more intense. In my head. I realised that to stop it in its tracks I had to reel away from Sam. I started making excuses. Excuses to get out of days out, picnics, foursome suppers. I put it all down to my busy family life, the school, the neighbourhood community. And I kept Jenny and Sam as separate as I could from my Muswell Hill social life. Those two worlds had to be kept apart, you see. I didn't want to exclude Jenny, but because Jenny came with Sam, I had no choice.

I comforted myself with the knowledge that it would only be a temporary measure.

I gave their relationship another six months, max. I figured that a guy who'd hit on his girlfriend's best friend was bound to hit on someone else, too. It was only a matter of time before he did, and another woman exposed him. But six months passed and nothing happened that ruffled Jenny, nothing that she knew about at any rate. A year passed and the relationship was going from strength to strength. When he proposed to Jenny, I must have given the world's most hollow congratulatory whoop. After that I made a real effort to try and forget what happened at that party. Either that or I had to say something. But what? She was engaged to him. She'd developed this bouncy new walk, like she had little foam wedges in the soles of her shoes, and her eyes shone. The time was never right. And oh God, maybe there was a teeny part of me that was jealous. I don't feel good about that. I really don't.

But Sam was evasive when it came to setting a date, and I, along with the rest of Jenny's friends, began to suspect that it might never happen. Nobly, I even encouraged Jenny to demand a wedding date because I knew that this would push Sam away, that he was that type of man. You know the ones: the more you demand, the less committed they are. I thought that if they didn't get married then I wouldn't have to tell her about the party. Or the other things. She would be saved.

I was wrong.

Ten

'Hey, Ol.' Jenny quickly assessed his mental state. Not looking too good actually. He was wearing grubby tracksuit bottoms, an old Rolling Stones tour T-shirt, and around his shoulders, a pink cashmere scarf. Without thinking, she reached out to hug him. He sank his head against her shoulder and they stood like that for a few moments in silence. It struck her how they never would have done this when Sophie was alive, that somehow the boundaries between what had been a hands-off relationship between a wife's best friend and her husband were blurring slightly.

'First a beard, now cross dressing,' he mumbled, shaking his greasy black hair out of his eyes. 'Come in.'

She walked into number thirty-three. 'I wasn't going to say anything.'

'It's Soph's.'

'I kind of guessed that.'

'Sorry for emotionally blackmailing you round.'

'It wasn't emotional blackmail.'

'If you don't come over immediately I might do something silly. Throw myself off the trampoline.'

She laughed.

'I was being a drama queen. Sorry.'

'You're allowed to be.' The truth was she had been hugely worried about him – he'd sounded so down, monosyllabically depressed – and had grabbed the car keys after that phone conversation and run to the car like a mad woman. She was hugely relieved to see him, smiling grimly, wearing pink.

'Worse, there's no tea.' He kissed her on the cheek. 'Kettle's blown.' She followed him into the kitchen. 'Put it on without any water. Went upstairs.'

'At least you didn't go out.'

'At least I didn't put it on then kill myself. The paintwork would have been completely destroyed. Soph would have been mad.'

'She would. Thanks to this kitchen I know the Farrow and Ball paint chart like I used to know the periodic table. Hours she took to get the exact right shade of white, sorry, "string".' She checked out the soot mark on the ceiling, unplugged the kettle from its socket and made a mental note to order one from Amazon. There was a mountain of empty beer cans piled in the recycling box. Oh well, as long as he was eating. She opened the fridge door to assess the food situation. The shelves were crammed with enough foil-covered Pyrex dishes to keep him alive for weeks. It whiffed, not fresh. 'Have you not been eating this food, Ollie?'

He fiddled with the fringing on Sophie's scarf. 'Kind of lost my appetite.'

'Some liquid nourishment here, I see.'

'Ah, that's Tash. She restocks the fridge with beer every few days.'

'Does she?' Well, that was *not* on the Help Ollie agenda. 'Alcohol's a depressant, Ollie,' she said, wishing she didn't sound so disapproving. 'It's not going to help.'

Ollie's smile was a flare in the darkness. 'Thank you, Mother.'

She winced. 'Sorry.'

'If you could let the ladies know about the lasagne invasion. It's been going on for weeks. Tell them I surrender. I can take no more. Can it stop now, please?'

'I will report back and request retreat. Ollie . . .' She wanted to tell him about the wedding. She'd already put it off on two other occasions, she wasn't sure why. It never seemed the right time. And she felt nervous about it. She just couldn't shift the feeling that getting married was a bit like getting pissed and doing the conga on Sophie's gravestone.

'Thanks, Jen, for dropping everything.' He frowned and suddenly looked a hundred years older than he had five minutes ago. Just as handsome though, funnily enough. Not fair the way men could look hot when suffering, while even beautiful women ended up looking like Gillian Taylforth caught up in an *EastEnders* abortion plot.

'Sometimes, being alone, especially when Freddie's at school, my head goes to funny places and I just want to be with someone who knew Sophie like I knew her. You're the only one. I feel connected to her through you.'

Jenny busily cleared a pile of out-of-date newspapers off a kitchen chair, trying to hide an unexpected flush of pleasure. 'You can always call me. Whatever time of day, you know that.' She cleared her throat, hesitated. 'Ollie, I need to tell you something.' She took a deep breath. 'Sam wants us to get married this summer.'

Ollie's face did not change. It was a study in non-plussedness.

'I just wanted to let you know first,' she gabbled, feeling silly now. 'Sophie was going to be matron of honour, and I know it will be, er, difficult for you. But I'd love you to be there. If you can face it.'

He smiled, finally. 'Of course I will, you doughnut. Jenny Vale married . . .' He tried the words on for size. 'About bloody time.' He hugged her and their faces were suddenly too close. She backed away, feeling oddly deflated. 'Do you think Freddie would like to be page boy?'

'Ask him.' He reached out and touched her arm lightly. 'Now can I ask *you* something?'

'About the wedding?' She knew he'd find it difficult. Poor Ollie.

'No. I was going through Soph's things.'

'Oh, right.' She blushed.

'Every time I open our wardrobe a tiny, irrational part of me hopes that she'll be in there. That they're not just dresses.' His eyes shadowed gypsy-black. Had they always been this black? 'I thought I wanted to keep them but now I think that as long as they're there . . . it's like a fucking kick in the face every morning. I can't explain it. Would you sort through them, maybe find them another home?'

'Of course!'

'Just pick out . . . oh, you know. You choose. I've haven't really got the foggiest about fashion, but if you could keep special things for Freddie.'

'To be honest, Ollie, I'll probably end up saving Freddie a tonne of Primark. I've not been blessed with an innate sense of style, as you can probably tell.'

'You scrub up alright, Jenny.'

Mortified, wondering if he thought that she was angling for a compliment, or worse, comparing herself to Sophie, she felt the heat rise in her cheeks once more. 'And, er, what do you want me to do with the other stuff?'

Ollie's face darkened. She couldn't read it. He looked, as he had done numerous times in the last few weeks, like a totally different man to the one she'd known when Sophie was alive. It was as if Sophie's death had deleted a version of him and someone else was emerging, changing the structure of his face, making it harder and rougher, older. 'Oxfam. The mum mafia, I don't know. It makes no difference to me. It's just stuff. They're not going to bring her back, are they?'

He was wrong. For when Jenny slid back the white wardrobe doors, there she was, a whole clutch of Sophies from different years, different parties, shreds of her in the print of leopard spot, in the fluff of a rabbit skin collar, the tilt of a cowboy hat. There was Sophie's peacock feather dress, the one she used to wear to weddings, when she'd invariably be late, falling through the church doors noisily, turning every head, seeking out Jenny. She remembered how they would stand there wedged together. 'Do you reckon it will outlast the wedding list electricals?' Sophie would joke, and they'd both giggle silently until Sophie completely lost it and did The Honk and everyone would turn and glare at them.

Ah, here was the seventies-style caramel silk blouse that

she'd worn on their shopping trip to Westfield a couple of months before she died. That was the time Sophie had bought some yellow heels from Topshop and frog-marched a reluctant Jenny to the tills to buy a navy sequin shift dress – 'Not age appropriate!' Jenny had protested – that now sat unworn in her own wardrobe, like a glamorous relic from a different, sparklier life.

The long cable knit cream cardie that Sophie used to wear effortlessly to the park with Freddie. (Sophie did knitwear, Jenny wore jumpers.)

Some dresses, unworn, a couple with price tags still attached. There was also a series of more basic dresses and trousers in a Parisian palette of black and grey and navy, the background hum to the times they'd met for coffee, walks in the park, a stolen morning matinee; Sophie's habit of interrupting Jenny's day of editing by luring her for noodles at Wagamama, flour-free lemon cakes at Gails, or 'a quick mosey' around Ikea. 'Not to buy. Just to see.' They would invariably come home laden with white picture frames, pink plant pots and enough tea light votives to light up north London.

Jenny touched the sleeve of a red vintage dress gingerly, half expecting it to vaporise at her touch like a ghost. This was one of Sophie's favourites, with a sexy slit up the side that showed off her lovely shapely legs. She lifted the sleeve to her nose and sniffed. And there she was again. Sophie's perfume: floral, sexily old fashioned, the perfume of a 1950s sex bomb. She wondered how many times Ollie had done the same thing, sucked in the very essence of her. She quickly let go of the sleeve, feeling voyeuristic.

Two piles. The peacock dress would be kept. The jersey dresses would go. The vintage prom dress would be kept. The cashmere sweaters would go. The hats would be kept. So would her wedding dress, obviously, she decided, closing the lid on the white box in which she'd discovered it carefully folded in white tissue paper. The shoes would be redistributed among the mums. Or was that morbid? On she went, tearfully picking apart Sophie's wardrobe, trying her best to discriminate between the clothes that were somehow intrinsically Sophie, or valuable, and those that weren't. It was hard. Sophie could transform from school run mum to pop wife to fashion bunny with a swish of a scarf. How on earth would she, Jenny, who hadn't a clue what was Pucci and what Primark unless she studied the label, decide which item was more significant?

She couldn't help but wonder what anyone would make of her wardrobe if she died. Would anyone really get sentimental about her Gap jeans, Wallis shift dresses, repeat-buy navy sweaters and rack of white shirts? No, she would leave nothing of note behind. An explosion of T-shirts. A pile of books. Although she did have a very good collection of classic country and western. Perhaps she would be buried with Dolly's *Greatest Hits*, like a Pharaoh queen with her jewels.

She opened a drawer of Sophie's dresser. What was this? About a trillion sizes too big. Oh, she realised with sadness, Sophie's old maternitywear. She frowned, puzzled. It didn't make sense. Why had Soph kept it? Sophie had told her repeatedly that the baby thing was all over. That she had tried for a baby with no luck for a couple of years after

Freddie was born and had decided to forget about it and end the monthly disappointment – she couldn't face the hormonal cyclone of IVF. Jenny crushed the clothes to her face. Poor, poor Soph. So she'd never given up hope, after all. Wishing Sophie had confided in her about this, she folded the clothes carefully and respectfully. Clearly you never knew anyone until you'd emptied their chest of drawers.

Soph's knickers. She hesitated. It felt like a violation of privacy. But Ollie had asked her, hadn't he? It would be far worse for him to do this job. Anyway, she could imagine Soph up there in some pillowy heaven laughing her socks off at her friend's prudery. She wouldn't give a toss. When they'd first shared a house at university, a red brick hunk of crumbling and frequently burgled Victoriana in Fallowfield, Soph would pad around in a pair of knickers after a shower, hair wet, conical breasts bobbing, looking for a hairdryer, while Jenny, who'd grown up in a household where long, maroon-coloured terry dressing gowns always hid naked flesh – she hadn't seen her own mother in the nude since she was a toddler – did her very best not to appear shocked and bourgeois.

Some of Soph's smalls were reassuringly normal, the failsafe multi-pack style from M&S that reminded her of the big yellow ones Soph had worn the night she'd died. But there was also a decidedly slinky contingent, balled neatly to one side of the drawer, obviously *not* designed for practical purposes. Two pairs were actually crotchless! She blushed, trying to push the image of Sophie and Ollie having sex out of her head, knowing that she wouldn't be able to meet Ollie's eyes later if she didn't.

Problem was, Soph and Ollie were one of those couples who it was hard *not* to imagine having sex. They'd had nuclear chemistry. It had been embarrassing to be in the same room as them sometimes. In the early days they never stopped touching each other, a hand on a bottom, a hand on a knee, a brush of a fingertip against Sophie's lips. Jenny remembered the holiday they'd all gone on together not so long ago: Sophie and Ollie's bedroom had been next door to hers and Sam's and it had been a thin, brickless partition. They'd heard everything. She stuffed the knickers into the bin bag briskly, pushing the memory and its animal acoustics from her mind.

Relieved to have finished the underwear, she started on the dresser's lower drawers. Parrot-green kaftans. A beach sarong. A lilac silk dressing gown in a silk bag. And what was this? Something hard and small wedged at the very back of the drawer, stuffed beneath the polka dot drawer liner. She stuck her hand in and pulled it out. It was a small dark wood box inlaid with pretty white shell. Puzzling.

She opened the box carefully, unable to rein in her curiosity. Oooh, letters. A stack of them, folded neatly. She caught glimpses of handwriting, biro doodles, and others that were simply typed. 'My beautiful Sophie . . .' Love letters! Oh God! Startled and guilty, she snapped shut the box and shoved it back into its hiding place beneath the drawer liner. 'Sorry, Soph,' she said, looking up at the ceiling. 'You dark horse.'

Eleven

Absolutely would have paid good money to see Jenny sorting my smalls, but I returned to number thirty-three just as she was dropping the black bag into the wheelie bin. 'Goodbye, Soph's smalls,' I heard her mutter under her breath, making the critical error of releasing the wheelie bin lid before stepping out of the way so that it crashed down upon her head. Sorting a dead friend's knickers is beyond the call of duty, isn't it? Still, I do wish she'd protested more when Ollie suggested giving my things away. Take my smalls! Just not my Acne Pistol boots! I'm not sure I want anyone else to have any of my beloved clothes actually. Well, maybe my sister, Mary, although she hates anything that doesn't come box-fresh from Marks and Spencer so may be slightly grossed out by dead sis's vintage. And I wouldn't mind Jenny taking a few prize pickings, even though she's bound to put the dry clean on a forty degree cycle.

Just not Tash.

Too late. It's eight pm now, three weeks later, Suze's house. It's steamy with the smell of pesto and marinating nappy bags, the windows misted with condensation from

London's endless Narnia winter. The Help Ollie squad are sitting in Suze's dark red living room facing off the pile of my clothes on the wooden Indian coffee table, trying not to look scared. Only Tash is eyeing them like a wolf might a small, succulent baby sheep grazing away from its mother. Her fingers twitch at her sides. Her Achilles heel is stretched, poised to dart forward. The others are less sure, sitting upright on the cat-clawed sofas and drinking wine too quickly. Liz fiddles with her hair. Jenny bites her nails. Suze rises a couple of inches on her seat as she clenches her buttocks to repress wind. Tense times.

'Well *one* of us has to go first, ladies.' Tash lurches towards the coffee table, yanks my Jaeger leopard print skirt out of the pile and flaps it out in front of her. 'Come on, let's not stand on ceremony.'

Suze takes a deep breath, pulls out a pale blue silk blouse with a pussy bow at the side and holds it away from her body, eyeing it suspiciously, lest it leap up and love bite her neck.

'That'll look great on you,' says Tash with a smirk, knowing perfectly well it'll transform Suze into a member of the WI.

'You think so?' Suze struggles to push that frizzy foam-wedge of hair through the neck hole. (Suze should sell her locks as mattress filler. Ultimate bounce! No springs necessary!) Tash comes to her aid, yanking it firmly down over her head, releasing a storm of static that makes Suze's hair spark. They're both sweating from the exertion.

'It doesn't seem right, does it?' Liz whispers to Jenny, who is sat next to her on the sofa, sheltering behind a vase full of splayed bare twigs.

'The blouse?'

'No, this.' She pulls a long face, glancing over at Suze. 'And yeah, the blouse looks a bit rubbish, too. How on earth is she going to get *out* of it?'

'Dunno. I got trapped in a dress once,' says Jenny, looking pained. 'It was horrible.'

Lydia leans towards Jenny on the other side and whispers, 'Talking of dresses. I've been wondering, what happened to Sophie's wedding dress?'

Jenny grimaces. 'Saved for Freddie.'

(Thank you, Jenny. It's now folded like a lily at night. I loved that dress.)

'Oh God!' Lydia fans herself with a copy of *Homes and Gardens* and a litter of leaflets shower on to the floor. 'Don't. It's going to set me off.'

Tash and Suze walk over with their new bits. They eye Lydia's emotional magazine-fanning warily. Jenny too, I see, has learned to ignore her. Lydia sniffs loudly. I have no idea how such a phlegmatic builder's sniff can come out of such a teeny woman.

'Come on, Lyds,' says Suze impatiently, eyeing the fallen leaflets scattered over her stripy rug with irritation. 'Let's not get all morbid. Again.'

'But it *is* morbid.'

'It's what Ollie wanted,' says Tash quickly, smoothing down one of my white shirts over her architectural hipbones approvingly. 'It really is.'

Jenny suddenly slams down her wine glass on the coffee table, leaps to her feet and starts bundling up the clothes in her arms like a mad woman at a jumble sale. 'Lydia's right.

It's too weird. Shall we just give the rest to Oxfam and be done with it?'

'Good idea,' Liz says with a puff of relief, reaching over to fill up her wine glass. 'Take all the stuff away, Jenny.'

'Oh, but what about these boots?' Tash pulls on one of my black Acne Pistol ankle boots determinedly. Damn. It fits her. 'They're too good for Oxfam.'

'Oooh. Nice boots.' Lydia sits up straight, morbidity forgotten. 'What size?'

'My size.' Tash knocks her heels together like Dorothy.

I retreat to the corner of the room and crouch down on the dusty edge of Suze's framed Matisse repro print. *My* Acne boots. Mine.

When I wake from my celestial sulk the clothes have been bundled out of sight by Jenny and the tight atmosphere has loosened, like the stitching on the blouse when Suze finally struggled out of it, blinking and sweating like someone emerging after years trapped in a small, dark cave. The wine has wound them all down now too. Good old wine. There's a reflective, dreamy air. Liz is looking sleepy; she was up changing children's bed sheets in the small hours last night. Tash is still admiring the boots. Lydia is lying out on the sofa, hair spilling prettily over frayed turquoise cushions, looking more cheerful. 'Ollie and Sophie are forever the perfect couple.' She sighs noisily, expelling more air than is strictly necessary to create drama. 'They'll never split up now. Isn't that *wonderful*?'

Jeez. Never thought of it like that. Guess there's an upside.

'I read somewhere that couples actually know less about each other the longer they stay together.' Suze reaches for a mini pizza. Observational note here. Every time I see Suze she's reaching for food. She's put on at least a stone since I died. It's actually kind of touching: I grieved so much I piled on fourteen pounds! 'We assume we know everything so we stop asking,' she says thoughtfully. 'They're spared that indignity at least.'

'Nor will they become one of those couples who sit in a restaurant trying to think of something to say that isn't about the children,' Liz adds.

Ha! You think we were never there? Everyone sits at that table at some point in their marriage. It's the one at the back, near the toilets. Bad service.

'Nor will she get to that point when she thinks nothing of farting loudly while pouring out his Cheerios in the morning,' adds Suze, mouth full of Parma ham parcel.

Deafening silence.

Lydia's mouth drops open, exposing a hidden brace. 'You don't?'

'What?'

'Break wind in front of the hubby like that?'

Suze blushes. It pulsates across her giant pale facescape like the northern lights. 'Well . . .'

She does!

'At least Sophie won't have to face him running off with some prepubescent,' snarls Tash, pushing back her cuticles forcefully with a cocktail stick. 'Not that he would, of course,' she quickly corrects. 'Ollie's one of the good ones.'

'Let's hope he gets to taste all that with someone else,'

observes Liz, as they sit contemplating the farts and other indignities that Ollie and I have mercifully escaped. 'He's only in his thirties.'

'Thirty-six.' There is a new look on Tash's face, one I've never seen before. 'Too young to be alone forever,' she mutters darkly. 'Far too young.'

'Too red blooded,' adds Lyds, constructively.

OK, I'm now rather wishing I hadn't broadcast the fact he was a needs-it-once-a-day man to them all on numerous drunken occasions.

'Interesting, isn't it?' says Tash, eyes flashing. 'A thirty-six-year-old widower is Mr Eligible, whereas a thirty-six-year-old female divorcee is second-hand goods.'

'You're not second-hand goods!' groans Liz. 'Jesus, Tash. You sound like one of those bitter fat blokes who sit on a bar stool moaning about women because they haven't got laid since they were fifteen.'

'Thanks, Liz!' Tash laughs, despite her offence. 'OK, let's put it another way, and be horribly honest, who's hotter, a thirty-six-year-old widower or a thirty-six-year-old widow?'

'Are we talking Angelina Jolie?' asks Lydia thoughtfully, twirling hair around her finger. 'Because if we're talking—'

'No, Lydia. We are not talking Angelina Jolie. I'm talking normal. Not loaded either. Because I'm sure I'd have more interest if I *were* loaded, not that I'm talking about myself . . .'

'Absolutely not,' says Liz mischievously.

'No, I'm talking about widows.' Tash is warming up, getting impassioned now. 'I mean, would we be saying that such and such widow was too horny to be single for long? I don't *think* so! It's as if women are expected to throw their sexual selves on their husband's funeral pyre in some kind of hara-kiri!'

Good point! I'm with you on this one, Tash.

'*A-hem*.' Jenny is shifting in her seat, uncomfortable at the turn in the conversation. Clearly, she doesn't want to dwell on the sexual habits of widowers. I suspect she'll protect Ollie's chastity for years out of loyalty to me, like a formidable Victorian aunt. 'Shall we have a quick rundown on the Help Ollie campaign? It's getting kind of late. I've got to get back.'

Everyone agrees with faintly disguised embarrassment. Parma ham parcels are put back on plates half-eaten. Wine glasses are planted back on their bamboo coasters. It's serious again.

'I can report that the Supper Strategy is working well, Jenny,' says Suze, doing one of her officious councillor coughs.

'Without lasagne?' says Jenny.

'Ottolenghi baked aubergines,' says Tash, tapping something on to her iPhone. 'With pomegranate.'

Oh Jeez. When will they realise that Ollie is a steak and chips and peas man? Put the pomegranate away!

Suze clears her throat. 'Let me report back some gaps in his groceries.' She consults her pad. 'He's out of Hoover bags, English breakfast tea and cat food. Who's in charge of placing Ollie's Ocado delivery?'

Liz puts up her hand sheepishly.

'If you could add those to the next order . . .'

'Yes, sir.' Liz winks at Jenny.

I like that wink. I like it that Liz and Jenny are becoming friends. I really do.

'Now have you checked out the Facebook Sophie Brady RIP site yet, Jenny?' Suze asks, tapping her pen on her knee.

Tell you what, *I* have. I have lain on top of the wifi cloud – feels like sitting on an ant heap in case you're wondering, itchy with info – and read some of it. Embarrassing and touching is all I'll say. ('Brave'? Reckless more like. 'Clever'? Failed my Maths GCSE. Twice.) I wanted to correct them, like on Wikipedia, but couldn't.

'There are seventy-five messages in the online book of condolences so far,' continues Suze. 'I hope we'll triple that number in a week. Make sure you let all your friends know. I'm going to photocopy a note and put it in year two's book bags.'

'Life is so fucking unfair!' blurts Lydia suddenly, making everyone jump. 'Why didn't someone in a crap marriage die? Why take someone as loved as Sophie? *Why?*'

Oh Lord, the woman's going to blow. Someone do something.

'Let's take heart from the fact that Ollie could be doing so much worse,' says Liz calmly. 'Looking on the bright side, well, he's not had a breakdown.'

She didn't see him lying naked on the bathroom floor with my pink pashmina over his head last week.

'I can't even begin to imagine how George would cope without me,' Lydia sniffs. 'Flora would be whipped away by Social Services.'

'Mine would all have to survive on cat food,' observes Liz. 'Probably improve their diet considerably.'

'And that's why Help Ollie is *so* important,' interrupts

Suze, clutching her notebook to her pulsating bosom. 'It's about the community rallying around and looking after their own. The Big Society! This is *it*, ladies! We are the rocks against which Ollie can crash. And if he falls, we will catch him.'

Blimey. Who knew lasagnes could achieve so much?

'Hear, hear!' Tash raises her glass. The room is soupy with feeling.

'We will be there for him until he's feeling better,' Suze declares, in orator mode again. 'Or until . . .'

'He can't take any more?' Liz says, exchanging looks with Jenny. The corners of their mouths twitch with repressed laughter.

'*No*, Liz,' says Suze crossly. 'I mean until . . .'

The room crackles with anticipation. There is a collective intake of breath. I freeze.

'. . . Ollie meets someone else.' Suze picks something out of her teeth with the edge of her fingernail. 'Don't look like that, Jenny, it can only be a matter of time. Now, anyone for a nice fat green olive?'

Twelve

1. *She* – name tbc – must be kind, clever, selfless, and adoring of Ollie and Freddie.
2. She must like cats.
3. She must like six-year-old boys. Lego. Farts caught in cupped hands in the bath. *Toy Story, 1, 2, 3,* on loop every Saturday morning. Football. Jenny. Cleaning sticky yellow wee off the loo seat. Not necessarily in that order.
4. She must not spoil Freddie, only when the moment dictates it, like if he's crying or missing me. She needs to intuitively know when to make the distinction.
5. She must understand I will always be Freddie's mummy and the love of Ollie's life. That's the deal, love.
6. She must be beautiful but not as beautiful as Ollie thought I was.
7. She can't be skinnier than me. Or have better boobs. She can't be the kind of woman who won't eat cake.
8. She must satisfy Ollie in bed, obviously, but not in the way I did. She must be a different kind of lover, so he

can't make comparisons, and not give competitive forget-the-first-wife blowjobs.

9. She is allowed to have her own children with Ollie, but she must treasure Freddie as the first-born.

10. She must not ever change the living room curtains that I had hand-printed at great expense for a sum so eye watering I never even disclosed it to Ollie. Nor redecorate the sitting room. Ditto.

Editor's note: Does this exclude ninety-nine per cent of women in London? Good!

Thirteen

The letters thumped into her head as if posted through a letterbox, making her reverse into the parking space with a loud screech. This happened all the time. She'd forget about them. Then, randomly, the letters would be all she could think about and she'd get a tight feeling in her chest, like she couldn't breathe properly. Did Sophie have something to hide from Ollie? A lover? A past that neither she nor Ollie knew about? And why did she care so much? Yes, she hated the fact that Sophie might have kept secrets from her. But she also needed to believe that Jenny and Ollie's marriage had been perfect. Perfection protected the past, kept the boundaries between them all defined, unassailable.

She turned the engine off and rested her forehead on the steering wheel, still so deep in thought that she did two double takes before registering the woman outside her flat. Yes, there was a woman standing outside her front door, staring up at the flat, transfixed, like it was Madonna's house or something. She was wearing a sequinned beret that sparkled silver in the sun. Under the beret her long, dark hair fanned in the wind, up and out, in an Annie Hall kind of way. There was something about that hair and general demeanour that reminded her of someone. Who? And why was she staring at the house? Sensing she was being scrutinised, the woman glanced over at Jenny, but the strands of her long, blowy fringe prevented Jenny getting a proper glimpse of her face. She walked hurriedly away, until with a flash of sun-hit sequins the woman turned the corner.

Not expecting Sam to be back from work so early, she jumped when she heard a cough. He didn't turn to look at her. He was giving her the freeze-out. She'd feared one when she'd left the voicemail. 'So you're going to Muswell Hill tonight?' He reached for his cigarette box, tapped a fag out and lit it. 'Again.'

She smiled cheerily – no point trying to talk him round when he was in the mother of all grumps – and tried coffee to make the peace. Sam could always drink coffee late in the day. Rarely did anything keep him awake at night: death, divorce, Lavazza, nothing touched the sides. They sat at the breakfast bar in silence, feet dangling from the chrome bar seats. She plunged the cafetière too quickly. It spurted up over the sides and she felt his irritation at her clumsiness. She mopped up the coffee from the counter top with a tea towel and wished they had kitchen roll, like a good old Muswell Hill household. But Sam refused to have kitchen roll in their flat on account of it being sinisterly suburban and ruining the sleek lines of the Bulthaup kitchen.

'Look, I'm sorry, Sam. It's just . . .'

He looked at her with a more forgiving weariness. 'I

know, I know. Sorry. I suppose I should be pleased you're no longer sobbing under your duvet.'

Had she really done that? The aftermath of Sophie's death had passed in a blur. It was now April. Only four months? She couldn't remember how she'd spent her days now, or how she'd got through it. Perhaps things were a little bit better, she realised for the first time. The days somehow had more meaning.

He ground out his cigarette half-smoked in the ashtray. 'It's just that Ollie's all you talk about, him and Freddie.' He gave her a dry half-smile. 'Oh sorry, darling. Do I sound like a heartless tosser?'

'No, my love, you sound jealous.'

She expected him to laugh – she was joking! – but Sam's blue eyes blazed. 'Maybe I am.'

She spluttered on her coffee. 'Sorry?'

'I feel like you've been stolen from me by Muswell Hill, Jenny. And I flipping well hate Muswell Hill.'

'Come on,' she laughed, flattered, struck by an image of a leafy avenue swallowing her whole. 'What's Muswell Hill got to do with anything?'

'It just winds me up.'

She sighed. 'Everything winds you up, Sam.'

'No. Only certain things. Phoney things.'

'What's phoney about Muswell Hill?'

'It's smug. It's stultifyingly middle class. It pretends to be in London, but it's in zone one hundred and three or something. It's not even got a Tube.'

'Actually you can walk to East Finchley Tube in ten minutes.'

'Yeah, if you're Usain Bolt.' He stroked the rim of his coffee cup with a finger. He had the cleanest nails she'd ever seen outside a beauty salon.

'Have you ever actually been there, Sam?'

'Course not. Don't need to visit Baghdad to have an opinion on it, do I?'

'You're being very touchy.'

'You've gone to the other side.'

'Yes, it's bloody dangerous in the 'burbs, Sam. Haven't you heard of that new drug, *cake*?'

A smile flickered over his mouth. He was beginning to enjoy himself. 'Those women *plot*, Jenny. From what you've told me you're all plotting.'

Jenny laughed, relieved that they were connecting again. 'We're not plotting!'

'You're like the witches of Eastwick.'

'It's the Help Ollie committee, nothing more, nothing less.'

'God help the poor bastard.' He pondered her for a moment. 'What exactly *are* you lot doing?'

'Sorting out Ollie's childcare arrangements, cooking for him, offering practical help,' she said, fearing it sounded too woolly. 'We've organised a rota of meals to be made and delivered by local mothers, as well as after school care for Freddie on the days Ollie can't leave work early. Er, that sort of thing.' She hopped down from her bar stool – a high wire act, never easy, she hated the damn things – and put her arms around Sam's waist, slipping them beneath his shirt to his gym-crunched belly. 'Why don't you come? To the meeting?'

Sam pulled away from her. 'Like the reverse psychology, Jenny. No thanks. I've got the small matter of a wedding to organise. In case you've forgotten we're getting married in August.'

'I know, sorry.' Jenny sighed. She should be doing more wedding stuff, and she felt bad that it was falling so heavily on Sam's shoulders. Leaning against the window frame, she pulled back the heavy beige linen curtains. On the pavement opposite the house, studenty types were engaging in a self-conscious drug deal. A noisy group of young girls, an arm-in-arm mesh of shaggy furs, leopard prints and heels, were tripping past on the way to a night out, their laughs exploding like fireworks in the cold night air, making Jenny miss Sophie with a raw pang, like when something sweet touches a sensitised tooth too close to the root. The gaggle of girls turned the corner. Apart from a tramp plucking aimlessly at a two-stringed ukulele, the street emptied. She pressed her hands against the cold glass, feeling like she was looking for someone. It took a few moments to realise who that someone was. The woman. The woman, she realised with a nauseous flip of the stomach, who looked uncannily like Sophie.

Fourteen

Secrets, all relationships have them, don't they? The little things we choose not to know about each other, stuffed somewhere we can't see, like clothes that we can't bring ourselves to throw away but will never wear again in that zippy nylon bag under the bed.

Sliding between houses, I get little glimpses of my friends discreetly building slivers of secrets into the fabric of their day.

Take Lydia, for example. She did not accidentally miss that contraceptive pill. She picked up the blister pack last Tuesday from the bathroom cabinet, stared at it for a few moments then, without popping one out, put the pack back in the cabinet. Did she mention this to George? Of course not! Did she hump George that night? Of course she did! She ambushed him in a pink teddy nightgown with pom poms that flicked off her thighs.

Take Liz. When she got the Facebook message from Riley, the big love of her life – the screwy, intense, creative one who'd dumped her cruelly before she met her husband Martin – telling her that he still thought about her every day, how did she respond? Did she write back telling him that she was happily married with kids and asking him not to contact her again? No, she did not. She sat staring at the screen, biting her nails, before finally writing back, 'I don't know what to say,' and thus leaving the door wide open for him to respond, 'Say you feel the same.' She hasn't responded to that message yet. But she has gone through her ancient photo album and spent twenty minutes gazing at an old photograph of her and Riley on a beach in Ibiza, their eyes sparkling, their bodies baked gold, limbs entwined. If I'd done the same thing she'd have slapped me. I mean, how can Martin and motherhood possibly compete? It's like comparing the tummy you had at seventeen with the one that settles around your middle at forty after two babies and a nightly Sancerre habit.

Tash lies to Marko The Wildebeest, her Polish builder, all the time. I guess the point here is that their tryst wouldn't last another two minutes if either of them told the truth. (That she is bored and horny and he is well hung, disposable, and married.) They have a little ritual, you see. He knocks three times on her door. The first question is always, 'Anything need doing, baby?' Marko is super cheesy. He bursts through the front door with thrusting pectorals, Freak Brothers hair flying, pumping with testosterone, like a soft metal star running on to the stage into a shower of airborne lager cans. He actually says, 'Huh!' Then he shags her hard against the wall. A few thrusts and he's done, pummelling Tash to the peak. Afterwards he always says, 'You love me, baby?' Tash always laughs and says, 'Of course.' Bullshit. My dear, she doesn't give a damn.

And as for Jenny and Sam. Well, things are getting a lot stickier there, let me tell you. The wedding date has piled on the pressure at a time when Jenny clearly can't cope with it. And it's not just that. Jenny seems different, like there's something bothering her when she should be happily anticipating her long-awaited wedding. There ain't no joy, man. Yes, her best mate's dead. That's probably not lifting the mood, granted. But it's more than that. There's a twitchiness about her that's developed in the last few weeks, a restlessness, some kind of inner struggle. Yes, *something* has been internalised, sucked in like a breath. For once I haven't the foggiest.

And Sam? Well, he's no stranger to secrets. There I was thinking that maybe, just maybe, he wants a date for the wedding because he is finally appreciating what he's got. But what the hell was last night all about then? Who was the woman he was speaking to so intensely at his front door while Jenny was punishing her quads in Legs, Bums and Tums? She didn't look like a Jehovah's Witness to me. They don't do that skirt length. She wasn't selling tea towels either. But she did look like she meant business.

Fifteen

Jenny unclasped her tan satchel and pulled out her creation with fumbling fingers. She so wanted them to like it. It had taken hours. She had a sore thumb from using the crap kitchen scissors. She'd applied the Pritt Stick to her mouth, thinking it was lip salve. No, she hadn't got a D in her art GCSE for nothing. 'Sorry it's taken so long, Freddie. Your mummy fills a lot of pages.'

Ollie smiled at her reassuringly and she felt a little less nervous.

Freddie grabbed it. The green holographic cover threw shards of light against his smooth cheek. There was a photograph of him and Sophie on the cover, above which she'd written 'The Mummy Memory Book' in her best swirly handwriting in gold pen. He pulled his finger down over it slowly.

'There are boxes, little boxes for you to fill in,' she explained, heart in her mouth, watching his reaction, willing him to like it.

'So it's like homework?' Freddie looked up apprehensively.

Jenny laughed. 'No, not at all,' she said, kneeling down

to his level. 'You just write in it if you want to. Like your favourite holiday with Mummy. Mummy's favourite TV programme . . .'

'I like the photos best,' said Freddie decisively, pointing to one of Sophie wrapped in a huge yellow towel on the beach, as if trying to absorb the essence of her through his fingers. He flipped the pages and smiled at the old photographs. Soph's mum had given Jenny a hoard to use: infant Sophie sitting on the beach, all doughy thighs, curly toes and sandy red spade; a young Sophie toasting dampers – a flour and water paste – on a stick in front of a bonfire. Jenny had picked through lots of photos of bonfires actually, the leaping and furious kind that she had never been allowed to build in her own childhood on account of health and safety and the fact that it was a waste of good firewood. She remembered how entranced she'd always been by Sophie's tales of family camping trips to the woods – Jenny's own mother was 'allergic to camping' because she swelled up like a whoopee cushion when bitten by midges – and crabbing and sunbathing. It always seemed to be summer in Sophie's childhood.

Jenny's own childhood summers were about fluorescent ice pops from the freezer in the garage, cardigans and picnics on shingle beaches aborted because of the rain. They weren't well documented either. Jenny's parents had never got to grips with the 'new fangled' camera they'd bought in 1974, and there was a gap of two years when the camera had broken and not been replaced when absolutely no milestone of hers was recorded.

As a reaction against her own parents' lack of enthusiasm

for posterity, when she went to university she made a real point of photographing as much as she could. This meant that she had a huge mine of memories, so many pictures of Sophie laughing, head thrown back, all her teeth showing, that funny little chip on her left canine, the result of cava-liering down the stairs on a teenage boyfriend's skateboard aged fifteen. No wonder everyone fell in love with her.

At university their photographs and memories had become even more collaborative, twisted together like tights spinning in a washing machine. Flashbacks rushed through Jenny's head like a speeded-up silent film: old jokes, fake tan disasters, favourite bands, losing then finding each other at parties, scrawled messages exchanged silently during dull lectures, singing along to Happy Mondays' 'Step On' at the tops of their voices in Soph's crappy old Renault Clio, holiday scrapes involving too much alcohol and too much sun, bad drugs, bad sex, good sex, one night stands, shocking home hair dye kits, unrequited love, swapped essay notes, shared lip glosses, pregnancy scares, fertility scares, period pains, the joy of dancing all night and watching the sun come up over a cornfield in the morning and knowing that they'd be friends forever, whatever. Back then the worst thing that could ever happen was getting dumped by some-body you thought you were in love with. (They'd invariably be fully recovered within three weeks.) Life was about possibilities. Now it just seemed to be about consequences.

She jumped, yanked back from the flashcards of her past. Out of the blue Ollie put a hand on her lower back, in the gap where her T-shirt had ridden up. 'Thank you, Jen. The book's amazing.'

Her skin fizzed beneath his palm. Horrified by the idea that he'd somehow sense this, she leapt away from his hand as if stung. He looked at her curiously – a look she hadn't seen before, registering something – and she blushed fiercely, feeling transparent and caught out.

'Look at that one, Daddy.' Freddie laughed and pointed to a picture of Jenny and Sophie as students – 'Mummy At College' – before the Halloween ball. Jenny was dressed as a pumpkin, Sophie a far more glamorous witch of the wild west with black and white stripy tights and a billowing black cape.

'Have you seen the one of you and Mummy at the zoo last year?' She flicked through to one of her favourites, still flustered and midsummer hot. 'Ah, there's Mummy and Daddy getting married.'

Sophie wore a vintage dress, the skirt bouncing out from her hips fifties-style, a tiara wound from ivy and white flowers on her head, a flower behind her ear. She looked like a naughty rock and roll wood nymph.

Ollie pointed to a dumpy-looking figure in a blast of Monsoon cerise. 'And there's our Jenny.'

She glanced up at him and smiled. Again, there was a funny look in his eye. It felt as if something had passed between them, some silent collective recognition that this was the photographic evidence of how they used to be when things were . . . different.

She was much relieved when he finally went back to the studio, leaving her babysitting. The house felt different without him, reassuringly Sophie's space once more, safer, girlier, less complicated territory. She gave Freddie a bath, admiring his lovely lean boy's body, and feeling a fresh twist of sadness that Sophie would not see his shoulders widen, his legs grow long and hairy, his chin develop angles. She tucked him up in bed, next to the uncuddlable beeping Buzz Lightyear toy that he so adored, and read him Roald Dahl's *The Twits*. 'Just one more page,' he begged, until the last page. She stooped down to turn off his light. 'Night, night, sweetheart.'

'But . . .'

'It's really late now.'

'Tell me about Mummy. Or I won't sleep. Daddy always tells me about Mummy before I go to sleep.'

She hesitated. 'Does he? OK. Well, um, Mummy was . . . well, she just wasn't like most people, Fred.' She sank back down on his bed again, feeling a maternal buzz of contentment when Freddie nestled his head against her shoulder. Is this how Sophie must have felt every night? She'd played it down, but God, she'd had so much to lose, so much more than her. The injustice that it was Sophie who'd died, rather than her much more dispensable self, hit her hard again. There was no justice.

'And?'

'Well, Mummy was funnier than most people, and cleverer and very beautiful.' Freddie didn't look too impressed. He expected better. 'She could also be a bit silly, couldn't she?'

Freddie brightened. 'I remember her being silly.'

'Do you? And do you remember how she loved to laugh? Silly practical jokes. And parties, especially if they involved fancy dress, like in the Mummy book.' She'd wondered if all the stories about Sophie were suitable for Freddie, as so many of the best ones happened in their twenties and involved copious amounts of cheap white wine. Oh well, one day he'd be old enough to understand. 'Given half the chance I think she would have worn fancy dress every day.'

Freddie grinned. 'She made me a pirate outfit with a sword holder and everything. I was the best pirate at Josh's party. I won a huge lollipop that cracked my baby tooth.'

'That sounds worth cracking a tooth for. I'd like to see that outfit someday.' She paused for a moment, remembering. Sophie dancing. Always dancing. Sophie bursting out of dressing rooms in mad red dresses. Sophie playing cards, raising them flirtatiously over her face like a veil. 'She was also a very good card player, did you know that?'

Freddie shook his head. 'I always used to beat her at Snap.'

'That's because you're very clever too. She could thrash Daddy at poker. And she was excellent at chess.'

'I'm learning to play chess at school.'

'She would be very pleased about that.'

'I want to learn chess so I can beat Joe. He's in my class. I don't like him.'

Who was this Joe? She bit down on her bearlike protective rage, suspecting an outburst would not be helpful. 'Why don't you like Joe?'

Freddie shrugged, clammed up. 'Dunno.'

She remembered how Sophie used to tell her that extracting any information about school from Freddie was like trying to get his Buzz Lightyear to engage in conversation about Middle Eastern politics. 'If you keep practising, you will beat Joe at chess. That will feel good.'

'Yeah.' He pressed his head harder on to her shoulder. 'Tell me more things about Mummy.'

'Ah, let me see.' There was so much stuff about Soph it was almost impossible to pick one thing. 'She had a very sweet tooth.'

'So her tooth tasted of sweets?'

Jenny laughed. 'No, a sweet tooth means you like cakes and sweet things. If we were in a café and I ordered a cake she'd always want the cake I ordered too. Mummy was a cake monster. Almost as bad as me.'

Freddie giggled.

'And you know what, Freddie? You know how Mummy was so good at making cakes?'

'Chocolate crispy cakes. We made them with cornflakes. We stirred in melty chocolate. I wasn't allowed to lick the bowl until afterwards.'

'Yummy! But do you know the funny thing? Before she had you she couldn't cook *anything*. Well, she could make toast and boiled eggs and maybe pasta. But after she had you she learned to cook. She learned so much. And she became one of the best cooks I know.'

He smiled. 'Because of me?'

'Because of you.'

She peered down and saw that Freddie's eyes were beginning to shut. 'You made her happier than anything, Freddie.'

'I miss her,' his voice choked.

'I know, sweetie. She knows too.' Atheism be damned. This boy needed to believe. 'And she's watching over you.'

'Oh, I know *that*,' he said, as if she'd stated the bleeding obvious. 'She talks to me all the time.'

She thought of the conversations that she and Sophie hadn't had, and the conversations that they could have had – *should* have had – about Soph's desire for another baby. Those letters.

He twisted Buzz Lightyear's arms upwards. 'Does she talk to you too?'

'No,' she said sadly. 'She speaks to you because you're special.'

Sixteen

This place, whatever it is, this world that runs parallel to yours, is a bit like one of those hardcore Austrian spas where you pay thousands to eat nothing and float around white rooms feeling hungry and helpless. Just without the enemas. It makes me long for simple, sensual things. A crashing Atlantic wave. A warm wind on my face as I cycle. The first bite of a Magnum on a slippery hot day. A cup of sugared tea. God, I'd love a cuppa.

My craving is not helped by the fact that everywhere I turn there are kettles. There are currently four kettles – four! – on the kitchen counter. Three are gifts from mothers at the school: Lydia, Tash, and Posh Brigid with the IVF twins in year four. The nicest kettle is from Jenny, of course. (She knows I'm not the kind of woman who'd ever let a white plastic Russell Hobbs anywhere near my work surface.) Still, no one needs four kettles.

You can't take them with you. I can tell you that for sure. Death is for minimalists.

It's ten am, Saturday morning. Ollie is staring at the kettles, rubbing his fingers anxiously through those stiff black hairs exploding from his chin. I know from the exact angle of the arrow between his eyebrows that the kettles are upsetting him. That the kettles are making him feel obligated to the givers of the kettles – the gift of a kettle will almost certainly require the offer of a cup of tea to the giver of the kettle. It is like the flowers that he had to vase, easier if they didn't arrive in the first place.

No, Ollie is not a sociable beast, nor is he a tea fan. He likes his caffeine, and his social life, condensed into an adrenaliney gulp. The exhaustion of the English breakfast teabags in the tin is therefore nothing to do with him and everything to do with the endless roll of – mostly female – visitors. That's what we English women do when someone dies. Drink tea. And shop. Incidentally, Lydia's Johnlewis.com habit is spiralling out of control. How much Joseph and Joseph kitchenware does one household actually need? It won't bring me back, hon.

Ollie drums his fingers on the wooden work surface – rotting since it is now left to puddle with water – waiting for Freddie. And where is Freddie? Freddie is swimming. Drumroll . . . with Jenny!

A word on this extraordinary event: Jenny hates swimming. More than this she hates swimming in municipal pools. She hates the changing rooms with their wet verruca-y tiles, the lack of privacy. She hates exposing her body to the indignities of a swimsuit. And she hates getting her hair wet. (FYI, chlorine makes her highlights go green.) So imagine my shock when a few minutes ago I spread out through the filter vents into the lukewarm urinated water of the local pool. There was Jenny standing upside down, her hair whipping around her like Beyoncé's against a wind machine, her navy swimsuit – Speedo, only Jenny would wear Speedo, as if it were Basingstoke, 1985 – gaping at the top, those fantastic bristols dropping towards her chin, only her pale chunky feet stamping above the surface, like a drunk synchronised swimmer. A couple of feet away, swinging on a metal ladder, wearing his red goggles, was Freddie, howling with laughter. And I realised then that Jenny will do anything, absolutely anything, to make Freddie happy, even if it involves standing upside down in a pissy municipal swimming pool on a Saturday morning when she could be in bed with Sam. And I love her completely for that. Feeling reassured and not wanting Freddie to pick up on my distracting wavelength – am wondering if he is in fact sensitive to my presence and has a hardwired mum-sensor – I shot back through the vent, deep into the labyrinth of heaters and pipes in the pool room, then, passing like a small cloudette of chlorine-scented vapour back over the streets of north London, I came home. And here I am.

As time goes on – can you believe I've been dead for over four months now? – I'm getting more confident about leaving the house and getting out and about, like a person learning to live with a new disability. My disability is that I don't exist – quite a handicap when you think of it. And I really don't like being invisible. There are no second glances. No whistling builders. I can't help but wonder if this is what old age would have been like.

On the plus side, there are no fares up here. No queues. No sticking an Oyster card into a machine and the machine not being able to read it and dozens of people behind you clicking their tongues. (Whenever I see that now I want to swoop down and yell, 'One day you'll be DEAD!' in their ears, just to see if it makes them jump the turnstiles. Really, what's the worst the London Transport police can throw at you?)

Sometimes I can get to a place miles away in the time it takes a live human to inhale and exhale their coffee breath: I'm a Japanese high-speed train of a spirit. Other times I just cannot move, I'm leaves on the line. It's as if I'm falling asleep, or zoning out, or whatever you call sleep when you're in my state – dead to the world? – and when I come to hours later, sometimes days later, I am filled with a terrible fear that something might have happened to Freddie and Ollie while I wasn't watching over them. But, thank goodness, it never does. It won't strike twice, will it?

Ollie is walking upstairs now, one hand on the banister, the other dug deep into his pocket. He's always got his fisted hands thrust into his pockets these days, giving him the air of a moody teenager. I follow softly behind him, like a whisper of breath against the iron filing black hairs on the back of his neck. With every step, his body releases a tiny whiff and I gorge on it, swilling his essence round and round inside of me, like a sommelier a fine wine. It is never enough.

He walks into our bedroom, slumps on the blue velvet throw and drops his head into his hands. I curl around his shoulder blades like a feather boa and feel the rise and fall of his bones. He sits like that for some time, head in hands, listening to the sounds out of the window. A car revving. Birds. Someone calling their dog. He flicks through photos on his iPhone. Me in different settings – leafy parks, Cornish beaches, coming down a slide in Kew Gardens, Freddie on my knee, naked in bed eating an almond croissant – and he stops at the naked one, which I think was taken in the summer because I've got strap marks. Then he clicks off his phone, gets up and walks to the dresser. For one awful moment I wonder if he's going to rummage through my drawers and find the letters. But he doesn't. He opens his sock drawer, that unfathomable cargo hold of mismatched socks. And he pulls out . . .

My knickers! Lordy. The palest pink Agent Provocateur knickers he bought me for Christmas last year, the ones with the little red ribbon ties at the hip. How did they escape Jenny's knicker cull?

Ollie always did love these knickers. They are the kind of knickers that proved their worth by the rapidity with which they were removed. I can barely watch as Ollie takes the knickers and buries his nose in them. He falls on to the bed, knickers still covering his mouth and nose, red ribbon tickling his chin. And then . . . Oh God. He unzips his flies, shoves his hand down his jeans, grabs his erection and starts to move his arm.

O-K. Weird now. I sink back into the wall. He has always had a high sex drive. And sex is life, so I don't know why I'm shocked. Perhaps it's because the sight of Ollie masturbating reminds me of everything I have lost and will never know again: his pumping heart against my breast bone, his soft groan, the salty stickiness dripping down my thigh.

Doorbell! It's like a scream in the softly panting silence. Once, twice. Ollie curses and starts hopping downstairs, one sock on, the other in his hand. Flushed and sleepy – he's a post-coital dozer – he is shoving his shirt into the back of his jeans, lolloping down the stairs, two at a time. He trips over Ping Pong who is regurgitating a Garibaldi biscuit on to the sisal matting.

Tash is standing in the doorway. *Tash!* Wearing red lipstick.

Now, call me paranoid, but I have never seen Tash wear red lipstick. She is not a red lipstick woman. She wears soft pinks and taupes. She is from the Bobby Brown school of discreet make-up, not a *'woo!'* Mac girl. Things have changed.

Tash beams. She is holding a heavy white plastic bag that pulls on her palm. 'Beer.'

'Ah, brilliant.' He stands there for a moment, as if trying to remember what social convention dictates he say next. She doesn't budge. She is waiting. 'Er, come in,' mumbles Ollie.

Tash steps over the threshold and hands him the bag of cold beers.

He smiles. 'You don't need to keep doing this, Tash.'

Tash waves her hand. 'It's the least I can do.' She glances around, taking in the details, looking for signs of not coping. 'Where's Freddie?'

'Jenny's taken him swimming.'

Tash grins. They are alone!

'Would you like a cup of tea? I have a range of water-boiling appliances in which to make it.'

Tash puts her hand across her mouth and laughs like a little girl. 'I wasn't the only one to buy you a kettle?'

'Nope.' He goes into the kitchen, bag of beers in one hand, old sock in the other. 'But thanks anyway.'

'Looking tidy in here,' notes Tash approvingly, sitting down at the kitchen table and resting her bosom on its surface for support, which has the effect of pushing up her cleavage and making it spill out over the top of her blue denim shirt like a rising loaf of bread. As I have settled directly above her on the smoke alarm, I get an eyeful.

Ollie throws his spare post-masturbatory sock on the work surface then begins to open all the cupboard doors, looking for biscuits. He's clearly had practice at this tea game, knowing that all women would rather have a biscuit with their tea than not, even if they don't realise it until it's winking at them from a saucer.

'Jammy Dodger?'

Tash is not a Jammy Dodger type of woman. She is a Ryvita woman. She takes the Jammy Dodger.

Ollie glances at the clock and sighs. 'I guess it is too early to have a beer.'

Yes, far too early.

'Never too early,' grins Tash. 'It's the weekend. I'll join you.'

He grabs a beer from the bag, puts the rest in the fridge, sloshes it frothing into two glasses. Then he sits opposite Tash. He stares. No, he cannot fail to notice how beautiful she is, can he? No man could. Nor can he help but notice that cleavage. He's always been a boobs man.

'How *are* you?' she asks, in that way that suggests he can confide in her, even if he can't other people.

I'm starting to prickle now. I mean, I like Tash. I *did* like Tash. We were thrown together at the school gate in reception and her son Ludo gets on well with Freddie, which I'm grateful for as Ludo's one of those slightly thuggish testosterone-y boys you don't want to get on the wrong side of. And Tash has been so helpful since I died. *But* . . . she's not the kind of friend I'd have if I didn't have Freddie. She's one of those fun but intense women who always leave you slightly drained. Her conversation is urgent, dramatic, especially if it involves her, which it usually does. And you know the telling thing about her? The screensaver on her phone is not a photo of Ludo. It is a photo of herself in a white vest, laughing, holding a tennis racket, like something from *Sports Illustrated*. What mother has a photograph of herself rather than her child on her phone screensaver?

Ollie's eyes dart to her cleavage and away. She squeezes her arms together. His eyes are sucked back again. She's waiting for an answer to her question.

'Up and down,' says Ollie, trying not to look at her tits.

'Tell me about it.' Tash bends down to stroke Ping Pong under the chin. She looks up and fixes him with an eyelash fluttery stare. 'Oh, Ol. Are you not able to find pleasure in *anything*?'

Ollie reddens. He was wanking less than ten minutes ago. 'Um . . .'

Tash grins. And it's like she *knows*. She's sniffed out the fug of sex. I want to shout down at her that it was *my* knickers he was bringing himself on, not her boobs. Put the bazookas away, woman! Save them for Marko The Wildebeest.

'I've been busy. So much stuff to do . . .' he drifts off, as if he is thinking of court cases and compensation claims and all that other stuff that his brain is so not able to deal with right now. 'Thank you for having Freddie after school. It's helped a lot.'

'God, anytime!' She rolls her eyes. And it's then that I realise that she's wearing false eyelashes. Falsies! At eleven o'clock on a Saturday morning. I'm willing a false lash to drop off and stick on the end of her nose like a giant nostril hair. 'Freddie's been a pleasure. A civilising influence on Ludo. You wouldn't know that his mum . . .' She stops herself.

Wouldn't you? Something tightens inside of me.

'That's good. I guess that's good.' Ollie is studying her face in that quietly intense way he's perfected, his eyes feeling their way across her features like a blind man's fingers on Braille.

'Ollie . . .'

There is something about her tone of voice that unnerves me. It is quiet and intimate. It is a voice that I have never heard her use before. It is certainly not a voice that she would ever have used to address my husband while I was alive.

'I know it must be hard, so hard on your own. If ever you need . . .' She looks up at him from beneath the falsies, ' . . . female company.'

Female company! She's been spending far too much time with corny Poles. I am shaking with indignation. The little red light on the smoke alarm starts to beep on and off very quickly. Ollie looks puzzled, then something passes over his face and I know that he knows what Tash is referring to.

'Dinner. A comedy night . . . something that might cheer you up.' She stares at her hands, clearly disappointed that he hasn't jumped.

The more indignant I get the faster the light on the smoke

150

alarm flickers, as if it's picked up some kind of energy. Or perhaps I really am so incensed I'm actually smoking.

'Thanks.' He shifts his feet under the chair, fingers the edge of the newspaper on the table. The air in the room is beginning to vibrate like a plucked guitar string.

'It's just that, you know . . .' She speaks very quietly. 'I've been on my own since divorcing Toby. I know what it's like. That's all. I know what it's like.'

You have no idea! I want to shout but can't. The light on the smoke alarm blinks even faster.

'Not that I'm equating what I've been through with what you've been through,' she corrects quickly. 'Not at all.'

'Fucking smoke alarm.' Ollie suddenly stands up, walks across to Tash's side of the table, stands on a chair and reaches up towards me on the ceiling, his T-shirt lifting up at the front as he stretches, showing a sliver of adorably hairy brown belly. He presses the reset button and it stops misbehaving. He steps off the chair, but before he has a proper chance to launch himself out of her orbit, Tash throws her arms at Ollie's waist, lassoing him like a bison. She rests her blow-dry against his belly as Ollie stands there helplessly. 'Oh, Ollie, you poor love.'

And it is only then that I see something that hits me harder than the no. 23.

Tash is wearing my Acne Pistol ankle boots.

The smoke alarm starts to wail then. Tash and Ollie leap apart.

Seventeen

Jenny couldn't shake the feeling she was being followed. She'd first noticed the white Fiat, one of those cutesy bubble-shaped ones, near the woods. It had been on her bumper all the way back from Highgate. It was that woman again. The woman who looked like Sophie who was hanging outside of the flat that evening last month. She was sure of it. Again, a stupid, irrational part of her wondered if it really were Soph – admittedly somewhat plastically altered – come to tell her that she'd staged her own death. If only she could stop the car and ask the woman questions that only Sophie would know the answer to. (Q: 'In what year and where did I end up in A&E because of dry Martini poisoning?' A: '1996. St Mary's, Paddington.' Q: 'What was the name of the man I was violently sick on while snogging?' A: 'Chris Butterworth, outside Haçienda, Manchester, '92.' Q: 'What is my favourite sexual position?' A: 'Head in the pillow, bum in the air.' Blimey, hadn't done that in a while.) And yes, she would ask Sophie about the love letters, too.

Checking her mirror again, she was relieved to see that

the car had gone and she rationalised that there were hundreds of Londoners who might drive from Muswell Hill to Camden at any hour of any day. She was being paranoid.

When she got back home Sam was spread out in the living room with a newspaper, cigarette dangling from his lips. He didn't look up. 'How was the lunch with Soph's mum and sister, babes?'

'Sad. Sweet. Kind of funny.' She smiled, happy to find him in such a good mood. He'd been unpredictable and irritable in the last few days. And he'd been listening to Radiohead, never a good sign.

He looked doubtful. 'Funny?'

'We laughed a lot about things she did. Freddie was writing it all down in his Mummy Memory Book. Bless.' She smiled and shrugged. 'I guess it hit home how much everyone loved her.'

'She was indeed much loved.' And for a moment he looked soft and vulnerable and almost unbearably pained.

'I wish you'd been there, Sam.'

He blew out a smoke ring, puffed away the sadness from his features. 'You know I'd just be this eejit in the corner saying the wrong thing.'

'No, you wouldn't,' she said, feeling sorry for him. He really did struggle to express his emotions. She was sure he'd feel so much better if he let them romp a bit more freely. 'Honestly. Ollie would have appreciated some grown-up male company.'

'Next time, eh?'

Was Sam avoiding Ollie? It did look like that. Or perhaps he couldn't face up to death full stop. Some people were like that. Her phone started ringing, interrupting her thoughts. She pulled it out of her handbag, glanced at the interface and pinged it to voicemail. 'Sorry, Tash again.'

He brightened. 'Tash Wright?'

'Yes. Er, how do you know her surname?'

He blew out a thick rope of smoke. 'Didn't I tell you she phoned me last week?'

'Really?' she said, forgetting for a moment that she'd given Tash Sam's number weeks ago. 'She wanted advice?'

He rolled his eyes. 'Yeah, asked The Questions.'

She knew all about The Questions. Since Sam's friends had hit their forties there had been many discreet enquiries about divorce. Tash was probably after a bit of free legal advice in the same way she'd been after a free pair of ankle boots.

'She can gas for England that one. It's a small world, as it turns out . . .' He stopped and took a lug on his cigarette, frowning. Something was bothering him.

'What?'

He shook his head. 'Just a couple of people we both know. Knows Seb Lewis at Pulson Partners. Small world. Actually, she knows his sister.'

'Oh, right,' she said, not relishing the coincidence. Sam was one of those people who appeared to be five rather than six degrees separated from everyone else. Especially women. 'Sam, it's really weird,' she said, changing the subject and sitting down next to him on a scratchy wicker floor cushion. 'I had a funny feeling that I was being followed in my car on the way back from lunch.' Spoken out loud it sounded even more monstrously silly.

He looked up, startled. 'Followed? By whom?'

'Some woman. On my bumper all the way back from Muswell Hill to Camden.' She rubbed her temples, trying to rub some sense into her head. 'I don't know. I just noticed her, that's all.'

'Woman?' Something unreadable passed across Sam's eyes. He smiled. 'Perhaps one of Ollie's new acolytes wants you taken out. It's a murky world, the world of the new widower.'

'Yeah,' she laughed, resting her head against his knee, suddenly grateful that she had him. That she was not on her own. Like Ollie.

After dinner they had sex. Jenny faked an orgasm. It was the first time she'd faked with Sam. As she'd hoped, he promptly rolled over, satisfied, and fell asleep. Needless to say, she couldn't sleep. Her brain was like the bluebottle she could hear banging itself between the double glazing. So when her phone bleeped at two am it was a relief to find that she was not the only person awake. She turned on her side to read the text.

'U up?'

Her heart quickened. She thumbed back a reply, keeping one eye on the sleeping form of Sam, who was snoring now. 'U OK?'

'Blk dogs. Can't sleep.'

'Nor me.'

She sank back into the bed, heart pounding, clasping the phone, willing Ollie to text back. After ten minutes he still hadn't. Her mind started to gallop. Was he in a bad way? What if he did something silly? No, that was stupid. Then again, anything could happen. He was so up and down. And she wasn't sleeping anyway. And there would be no traffic at this time. Sam wouldn't even notice she'd gone, would he?

She drove north in record time. The moon was low and heavy in the sky, tarnished silver, and London's empty streets unfolded before her like a computer game. She didn't ring Ollie's doorbell for fear of waking Freddie. Nor did she need to as Ollie must have seen her shadow through the glass, opening the door immediately. He pulled her towards him, sinking his chin on to her shoulder, where it wedged in the fleshy bit.

He stank of booze.

Even in the half-light she could see he looked terrible, piratical. Then she wondered what she herself must look like, no make-up, bed hair, and Sam's old jumper that she'd thrown on in the blur of the bedroom. 'I'll make a cup of tea,' she said, sounding uncannily like her mother in times of crisis.

Ollie stumbled into the kitchen in the clattery, noisy manner of a drunk man trying to be quiet.

'Stop drinking, Ol,' she said, pouring water into the kettle. 'You've got to stop it. It's not helping.'

He scoffed. 'It's helping me.'

'No, it's not.' She leaned back against the cool brick wall. It broke her heart to see him like this.

'I want her, Jenny. I want her back.'

'I know,' she replied softly, unearthing two cleanish cups from the cupboard, wishing she hadn't admonished him for drinking. She'd love a stiff drink herself.

'I can't stand this,' he growled with sudden, startling ferocity. 'I can't stand . . . the days . . . the nights. How long do I have to fucking wait?'

'What for, Ol?' she asked softly.

His gypsy eyes flashed. 'How long do I have to wait before I have sex again, Jenny?'

Sex! The question danced provocatively on the delicate boundaries that protect friend from friend's husband. She could feel the heat rise on her cheeks. '*Well . . .*'

'I've embarrassed you, sorry.' He shook his head, despairing of himself, then looked up and grinned wolfishly in a way that made something in her stomach fizz. 'I promise I haven't lured you round here to have a pop.'

'Don't be stupid. I know that.' Did she? Yes, yes, she did. Of course she did.

'It's just sometimes my . . . mind boils over.'

'I guess it must be very hard.' *Hard!* Why had she said that? She blushed furiously again and fumbled in the cupboard for a teabag. Her clumsiness activated an avalanche of takeaway ketchup sachets on to her head.

'I think I might have just had an offer actually.'

The boiling water splashed over the sides of the cup all over the work surface. 'Really? God. Who?'

He looked at her deadpan, raised an eyebrow. 'Tash.'

'*Tash!*' Oh no. She crushed her hand to her mouth in horror. 'You didn't . . .'

He looked sheepish. 'No. But part of me wanted to.'

'Right. Right.' She didn't know what to do with herself. She wanted to stick her fingers in her ears. Tra-la-la-la. But then again . . . *Tash!* Outrageous! Tash would never appreciate Ollie. She'd never understand him. She'd . . . she'd use him. And worse. How dare she?

He slumped back against the wall. 'And now I feel like a piece of shit.'

'I'm sure this is all normal stuff,' she said briskly, wondering about the box of letters. Had he found it? Is that why he was thinking about other women? Had something in them given him the green light to seek alternative sexual gratification? No, no, her mind was playing tricks on her.

'You think so?'

'Well, it's a *bit* soon,' she managed, her voice high and squeaky. She despised herself at that moment for not giving him her blessing. That was clearly what he wanted. She was the closest he got to Sophie and he was using her as a conduit to get permission to have sex. Damn. Why couldn't she give it? That would be the humane response.

'When is not soon, Jenny?' he growled from behind his fringe.

'I just don't know, Ollie.' The full force of the late hour hit her all at once. She was totally exhausted. She must get home. She wished she'd never come over here so late. What if Sam woke up and found the bed empty? What was she thinking being here in the small hours?

'You think I'm a fucker for even mentioning it, don't you?'

'No!' Yes.

He sank his head to the table in despair then. Appalled, blaming herself for her inappropriate prudery, she stroked his arm, unable to hug him as she normally would in case he suspected she was doing a Tash too. He looked up, eyes ink black in the early morning gloom. 'I don't want to be alone, Jenny. I want to love and be loved.' He dropped his head into his hands. 'Oh fuck, now I sound like a James Blunt lyric.'

'For what it's worth I think you're doing brilliantly,' she stuttered. He must think her so priggish, so deeply uncool. 'You will meet someone else eventually, in time, of course you will.'

'I can't fucking stand that idea,' he spat out.

'But you just said . . .'

'I know. Both are true.'

'Tea.'

He pushed the tea away from him as if the sight of it revolted him. 'That's the head fuck.'

'You've got to think of Freddie, that's all.' She put her cup down. 'Stating the obvious, sorry.' The atmosphere in the kitchen tightened. She really must get back. It was a stupid idea coming here. 'Look, it's late. I better go.' She did up the buttons on her coat with clumsy fingers. Her head was messy all of a sudden, all whooshes and hisses, a tangle of contradictory thoughts. And then there was that strange curdling, excited feeling in her stomach that she couldn't explain.

He put a hand upon her arm. 'I see Sophie in you, Jenny.'

Words clumped in her throat. The silence of the house started to pound around them.

'You two were so tight it's almost like a little bit of her has brushed off on you.' He hesitated. 'Or maybe it's the other way round.'

She didn't want to be compared to Sophie. No woman would. 'I better get back.'

He studied her intensely. 'You're spending too much time up here, aren't you? Sam pissed off yet?'

She bit her lower lip hard, fighting tears, suddenly feeling immensely gullible for having driven through the night to be with Ollie, imagining she was so important when all he wanted was permission to shag Tash. It was embarrassing. She was embarrassing. 'If I'm crowding you out, I'm sorry.'

He stroked feather light fingers across her cheek. 'Jenny, Jenny. You're not crowding me out.' She was paralysed by his touch, the slight rasp to his fingertips. 'I'm so pleased you exist, you've no idea how pleased I am that you exist.'

The curdling feeling in her stomach became something else, a tugging in her lower body, something so tidal, so powerful, that it stole her breath away. Suddenly it felt like anything might happen.

'Daddy,' a little voice whimpered from the landing. They both jumped. 'I've wet the bed.'

Eighteen

Is it just me or might Jenny be going ever so slightly crackers?

She keeps twitching the curtains of her flat, staring out at the street like an actress in an ITV domestic crime drama. Who is she looking for exactly? And why on earth did she wake up at five am this morning and bellow, 'Don't touch the box!', scaring the living daylights out of Sam, and me too, quite frankly. Sam had to shake her to make her calm down and bring her back to wakeful sanity. And did I mention that she has still done absolutely nothing, *nothing* about her wedding dress? She has not even bought her wedding shoes! She's only got three months to find the shoes, and it takes her two years to choose a flip flop. Her roots are three inches long too, slightly green. Dolly Parton would be appalled. Although I do not think that marrying Sam is the best idea in the world – could in fact be the worst – if she is going to do it she better do it properly.

No, she's not herself. Really not. Picture this. Earlier Sam popped out and brought her back a bunch of daffs, which was sweet, give him that. Jenny barely seemed to notice them. She stuffed them into a vase, snapping their stems and making the petals fall off. Inconsequential? I think not! This is a woman who has a photograph of her favourite tree (wild cherry) above her desk, who collected cactuses rather than Barbies as a child, and occasionally sings Dolly's 'Jolene' to her pet bonsai tree.

It's evening now, eight pm. And she's still looking a tad deranged. Sam is cooking dinner. She tells him she's going to change and disappears off to the bedroom. Is she changing into something slinky? Is she hell! She has put on flannel pyjamas and, Jesus wept, knitted bed socks. Jenny, have I taught you nothing? The bed socks are purple. Purple! No woman under seventy who is in charge of her own marbles and wardrobe wears purple bed socks.

She emerges without a hint of shame. Sam glares at the bed socks as if they are a personal affront, which of course they are. If socks could talk, these would be saying, 'You're not getting laid tonight.'

She stares dreamily out of the window from her parrot perch on the bar stool while Sam stirs prawns and noodles around the gleaming wok and tells her about his client who is fighting his wife for custody of the Aga. She smiles like she's pretending that she's listening. He tells her that his mum has invited them for lunch on Sunday and that she is making beef Wellington and trifle and could Jenny bring the cheese? Nothing too French and stinky. That there's a Tube strike on Monday. That the TV licence needs renewing. That Berlin is the hottest city right now and they should go for a weekender, shouldn't they? Jenny nods, not meeting his eye, suddenly looking stricken. She cannot manage more than a few noodles and does that gulpy thing when you're trying to eat and not cry at the same time. It never works. The throat's not wide enough. You've got to do one or the other. I'm not sure if Sam's noticed or not.

Then he has to notice. As he swerves towards the table, glossy Patisserie Valerie tarte tatin balanced precariously on his palm, she starts to cry. Is it the tarte tatin? Sam asks. Not. Is it Sophie? Sam asks. Jenny says maybe, but she doesn't know. Sam looks irritated. Men hate this kind of answer. They'd rather women wouldn't cry in the first place, and if they do cry they like to have the reason hoisted like a flag on a ship so that they can offer a practical solution and move the issue on so it doesn't ruin their supper. Unwisely he suggests that she goes shopping for her wedding dress tomorrow. This will cheer her up, won't it?

Oh dear, this will not! Jenny drops her head into her hands and sobs a goddamn river.

Sam puts his arm around her shoulder. She rests her head against his belly, and frowns.

I watch the evening slide uneasily around them. Telly noise. Wine. A bubble bath. Jenny's head held too long beneath the froth of bubbles so that she emerges gasping for breath. They're in bed now. And she's still wearing those damn bed socks. Undeterred, Sam puts a hand on her hip, turns her towards him. He slips his other hand between her legs.

I shouldn't be watching. But it's kind of compelling watching your friend having sex. You know you shouldn't look but you do. I'm a little shocked. I'd have thought Jenny would be a bit more of a live wire actually – she used to be. But her body is very still as he makes love to her.

He's doing the jiggy finger between her legs now, cradles the back of her head in his hand, tells her she's sexy. He enters her with two small ricochet movements. Pummelling faster now, eyes shut. She's looking over his left shoulder. Her lashes are wet, half-closed. And it's then that I see it. That look.

That, unless I'm much mistaken, is the look of a woman making love to a man and thinking of someone else.

Nineteen

This is beyond a joke. Tash is back in my boots again. You'd never know that she had twenty-one pairs back at her house in transparent plastic storage boxes, and that's not including her multi-coloured Hunter welly collection. She wore my boots when she shagged Marko The Wildebeest against the bathroom wall last week too, leaving a slick of Frizz Ease on the Farrow and Ball. And she had the gall to wear them to the school gate this morning. It's not just me. Other mothers are noticing too, these dead wife's shoes, that everyone commented on when I bought them – they were the hot boots of the season, featured in every magazine – and much lusted after.

Posh Brigid is staring, looking puzzled, the collection box for the school playground fund frozen in her hands. Now this is something. Brigid wouldn't notice if she went out of the house with a bra on her head. She wafts through life trailing children – she has five, looks like she's had none – and is so posh that she is a second cousin three times removed to Prince Philip, and sometimes in the summer doesn't bother to wear shoes at all. While Emily, a key PTA orator, bossily manning the cake stall, is talking to Tash's boots rather than her face and thoughtlessly handing a child cupcakes rather than the requested flapjacks. Tash curls her right foot self-consciously behind her left.

I tried to tell her earlier while skimming over the dust-free edges of her wardrobe doors. I really did. But all I could do was ruffle the air molecules. I keep forgetting that I cannot speak, that the words just roll back and forth, cold and hard on my icy tongue like frozen peas. And why was I on her wardrobe doors, you ask? Spying. That's what.

Come on, she's a 34D and two genes short of Katy Perry! Plus, she's looking after Freddie two afternoons a week, which gives her an inside advantage. While there appears to be nothing I can actually do to stop the military march of her seduction other than activate smoke alarms – of all the paranormal powers to have, honestly – I still feel that it is my duty as a dead wife and mother to fully investigate her suitability for the post of shagging my lonely heartbroken husband. Let alone replacing me, which is, I'm beginning to suspect, her end game.

So that's why I've been on Tash's trail all week, waiting for her to slip up. As yet she has not fully incriminated herself. She has not attended an STD clinic or shown any signs of an addiction to cocaine or Calpol Night. There was a wobbly a couple of days ago when a gym-bulked plumber lingered for an unnecessarily long time around her sink's U bend, and Tash girlishly twiddled a tendril of dark hair around her finger then sucked it, letting down all of woman-kind who try their damnedest to speak in gruff, matter of fact tones to builders so that they're not overcharged. But the inappropriate divorcee sex didn't actually happen. Tash is no fool. She's not about to waste her erotic energies on a plumber. Not when a recently liberated music producer is living a few metres from her house.

I'm not stupid. I can see, objectively speaking, that Tash is hot. If one was to go there – too late for me now – she is one of those women you could almost imagine getting it on with. There's nothing yuck about her. No hairy chin. Nothing that suggests feminine hygiene issues. She's as lickable as a lollipop.

And she has another ace up that draped Vanessa Bruno sleeve: Ludo. Ludo, her improbably named son (should be called Battleships or Twister), is notorious as a right pain in the arse. The oldest and tallest in his year, he has become more dominating and difficult since Tash and Toby divorced, someone who has to be invited to parties because of the fear of repercussions in the playground if you don't, like a third world tyrant invited to a UN convention. But the funny thing is he has been a good friend to Freddie in the last few months. He used to ignore Freddie. He didn't notice him in the same way he wouldn't notice a scab on his knee or a toddler in the path of his football. But now Ludo and Freddie appear to have forged an unlikely bond. They certainly look an odd couple. Ludo, tall, cleft jawed and daft looking; Freddie, the small-for-his-height beauty who looks like he might have dropped off the ceiling of the Sistine Chapel. In the playground when the other children play 'don't step on the bogie', Ludo will make sure that no one pushes Freddie at the bogie on the playground floor. Maybe it's because they have both lost a parent from the household in different ways – one to divorce, the other death – but he's become Freddie's unlikely protector.

Sometimes I imagine them getting together. Tash and Ollie, not Ludo and Freddie. The two single parents. The two boys. There's a symmetry to it, a ready made family for Ollie, the child that I couldn't conceive emerging straight from the wrapping, skipping the sleepless nights stage, flat-packed into boyhood.

So what's my problem? This is my problem. Looking over my stone-cold shoulder back to my life, I have a new clarity when it comes to friendships. The group of friends that I hung out with on a regular basis are beginning to separate like oils and vinegar in the French dressing jar. They have formed three distinct groups.

1. Proper old friends. Like Jenny. Friends who'd stand upside down in a swimming pool for Freddie while their highlights go green. Friends who know your failings and think they're really amusing. Friends who will never say you look tired even if you haven't slept in years. Friends who genuinely think you look better at thirty-five than when they knew you at eighteen. Those kind of friends.

2. Circumstantial friends. Like Suze. Or Liz. Really Nice Women who I was grateful to be befriended by at the school gate when I felt like Johnny-no-mates in Freddie's reception year. The type of friend who surprises you by *being* your friend. Some of these circumstantial friends were on the path to becoming proper blood sister friends. Like Liz. I think I just needed to live through

one more excruciating PTA fundraising disco with her and we would have been friends for life.

3.   Friends you don't particularly like. Tash falls into this category. Funnily enough the FYDPL is usually a God-I-totally-love-this-person when you first get to know them. They're funny and glamorous and have an interesting life story and proper signed art on the walls rather than prints. They make your old friends seem dowdy and irrelevant. It's like a crush. Then, gradually, you become aware of a sinking feeling when you're scheduled to see them. You know that you'll emerge from that cappuccino drained. Your hair will feel frizzier. You will feel poorer and fatter. Did I mention that Tash falls into this category? Tash falls into this category.

Anyway, back to my ankle boots. Off they go again. Click clack. They've dropped Ludo off at the classroom, where the moment her back is turned he swings his school bag hard against little Rex's eczema-raw knees. She is back at the school gate now, looking around for somebody. Ollie, I suspect. But, unbeknownst to her, Ollie has made a quick getaway and is dashing up the stairs to the school office to deliver the cheque for Freddie's school lunches which is four months late. Tash hovers, then gives up and starts click clacking back to her house, checking her phone repeatedly and texting as she walks.

I'm through the letterbox and into her house before she is, watching from the banister as she fiddles in her cavernous black handbag for her door keys. She opens the door and freezes. Suddenly she is looking right at me. She pales. Like she's seen a ghost. (Ha!) For one strange moment I wonder if I've been spotted. Although being invisible to everyone but Tash would be like some kind of paranormal sick joke. But no, no, she's looking away now, flurrying through to her kitchen to make herself a coffee. The moment's passed.

I settle to watch.

Only now do I understand why womankind designed net curtains. In the space of five minutes, Tash, beautiful fragrant Tash, sitting at her Conran oak table on her £300-a-pop Eames Eiffel chair – her house is full of famous designer chairs – farts loudly, goes for a pee, doesn't wash her hands, and takes a bite out of a lump of Parmesan in the fridge. She then switches on her iPad and spends five minutes updating her status on Facebook and Twitter – 'Natasha is having an existential bed linen crisis' – another ten idling Johnlewis. com's virtual aisles looking at duvet sets, not buying any-thing. Another eight minutes is spent in ASOS's accessories section. She puts a gold-plated chain bracelet – £77 – in her basket but doesn't check out. She eats some seeds from a jar. One more fart. (Seeds, huh?) She spends the next seventeen minutes of her precious life ordering new socks and pyjamas for Ludo from Marks and Spencer's website, but she can't remember her password, cocking up the order. Cursing, she spends another seven minutes on email. She goes there to find the new password sent by Marks and Spencer and gets diverted by a sensational email from Brigid regarding the infamous psycho mother in year two who thinks the no-nut policy is an infringement of her son's human right to have peanut butter sandwiches in his packed lunch and is picketing the school gate with leaflets. Her coffee machine whirs noisily and spits up a coffee, which she throws back into her open pelican throat, chased by a packed lunch fruit bar. She moves a basketful of washing from washing machine to tumble dryer, skim reads the Angelina and Brad story in *Grazia*, then, bloody hell, it's eleven o clock!

Where does the time go, eh? Well, I tell you what, it goes like that.

My ankle boots are tripping up the sisal stair carpeting now. Tash is looking at her watch, like she needs to be somewhere soon. She gets changed. Off come the jeans. She fingers a Spanx half-slip and decides against it. (She doesn't need it. This woman does so much Pilates her pelvic floor muscles could shoot golf balls into the next postcode.) On goes a short black skirt and grey tights. She zips up some conker brown knee-high riding boots, tongs her dark hair with her GHDs, squirts some Chanel no. 5 behind her ears and slicks on some pale pink lipstick. Dressed to kill. Or thrill. On a Thursday morning. Where the hell is she going? Interesting.

I don't float home as planned but follow her instead, always a few feet behind like a long summer shadow, down the wet tree-lined streets towards East Finchley Tube. She gets on, crosses her legs, assesses the carriage quickly for loons and settles into her newspaper, flicking past the news straight to the horoscopes. The Northern Line belches and rattles to Tottenham Court Road. She gets out, smoothing her hair with her fingers and swivelling her skirt around on her waist so that it's centred properly again and checks her watch.

Goodge Street. Backstreets. Roadworks. Small, dark Italian café. She looks nervous sitting at the front of the café, near the window, unable to stay still. She reapplies her lipstick using a little gold hand mirror.

Curiouser and curiouser.

The lipstick is snapped back, shoved into her bag. She is watching someone out of the window now, expression changing.

He's pushing open the glass door, striding across the café's tiles in his dark suit before I notice him.

Tash leaps up from her seat, napkin falling to the floor. There is a moment of awkwardness while they decide whether to shake hands or kiss each other on the cheek. They kiss each other on the cheek.

Sam sits down, smiles, tugs at his shirt cuffs. 'It's good to put a face to the voice at last.'

Tash looks a little embarrassed, to her credit.

'Thanks so much for meeting me like this. I know it must seem a little odd.'

'No, not at all. I was in town this lunchtime anyway.' She leans forward, resting her face on the cradle of her hands. 'So?'

'I'll cut to the chase.' He sighs. 'Someone's causing me a bit of trouble.'

She looks puzzled, her tongue licking her bottom lip. 'Sorry. I don't understand.'

'Dominique.' He drags his fingers down his strained face.

She looks at him blankly. 'Dominique? Who's . . .'

'Seb Lewis's sister. You remember Seb, our mutual friend?'

'Oh.' She still looks like she doesn't get it. Neither do I.

'Dominique. Right.' Her expression changes. Something's dawning. 'Didn't you two once . . .'

'Look, I know how this looks,' he says quickly. 'I need to ask you a favour.'

'Sorry, but . . .'

His blue eyes flash electric as he smiles his most charming smile. 'Natasha, there's no such thing as totally free legal advice.'

Twenty

Three weeks later and Ollie's words were still spinning around Jenny's head like fairground horses: 'I'm so pleased you exist, you've no idea how pleased I am that you exist.' Every morning she had to shoot those horses down, one by one, reminding herself of her own inherent absurdity, her disloyalty, the sheer vileness of her own brain. What was going on with her feelings towards Ollie? How on earth could she escape them? Jesus. She needed distance, quick.

Actually, what she needed was a plan.

The next day, she stepped over the huddle of marinating nappy bags in Suze's hall with a new sense of purpose. Yes, it was a bloody good plan, if she said so herself.

Suze pressed a glass of wine into her hand as she sat down on a wicker chair, before she had a chance to draw breath. 'Sophie's RIP Facebook page now has eight hundred and forty-five condolences, can you believe it?'

'That's a lot of friends she never met.'

Liz laughed loudly. 'One of them was in her yoga class but had never actually spoken to her. Hey, they stretched hamstrings together.'

'Those that stretch together stay together,' muttered Tash, picking some icing off a slice of cake and pushing it to the side of her plate as if it might be radioactive.

'Ladies, I have an idea,' said Jenny brightly.

'Hit us with it, Jenny,' said Suze, looking at her while pouring water out of a bright blue jug.

They all turned to face her.

Jenny took a deep breath. 'An au pair.' She looked around at the blank faces. There was a terrible silence. Liz coughed and looked down at the table. Er, why weren't they hailing her genius? 'Let's hire an au pair for Ollie.'

'You are fucking *joking*?' hissed Tash, murderously.

Jenny glanced at Liz appealingly. Help! What was going on?

'The thing is . . .' began Liz, face contorting in a way that suggested Jenny had made some steaming faux pas.

'Since when was some gold-digging freaking eighteen-year-old Ukrainian wearing street market lingerie moving in to a widower's house a sensible idea?' spat Tash.

What on earth was going on here?

'I can name you two marriages that have been atomised by au pairs,' Lydia said quietly, making a funny half-nod towards Tash and trying to tell Jenny something with her widening eyes.

'*Three!*' corrected Tash.

'The Sebolds.' Suze shook out some chocolate flakes from a silver sprinkler into her palm and licked them off. 'Alec had an affair with her for three months while Lily was pregnant. The Wintersons. Actually, that was a manny. Do mannies count?'

'And *me*, Jenny.' Tash spoke with a snarl. 'My husband ran off with my au pair.'

Jenny crushed her hands over her mouth. 'Oh, I'm so sorry. I had no idea.'

'No, of course you didn't,' said Liz kindly, putting her hand lightly on Jenny's arm. 'Look, an au pair for Ollie is not a bad idea, not at all. Let's look at this with fresh eyes shall we, ladies? What happened to you, Tash, it's awful but we can't presume all au pairs are the same, can we?'

'I don't see why not,' muttered Tash.

'How about we make sure the au pair's got buck teeth and weighs thirteen stone?' said Jenny brightly. Suze stiffened and slammed the sprinkler hard down on the work surface, sending a puff of chocolate into the air. Did Suze weigh thirteen stone? Oops.

'It makes no difference,' said Liz. 'Astrid had such bad teeth it looked like she'd eaten a brick.'

'Can I just say?' said Lydia, putting up her hand. 'What's wrong with Operation Ollie, Jenny? *We* can do all the stuff the au pair does.'

'Yes, we can,' said Jenny carefully. 'It's just that Help Ollie can't go on forever.'

'Well, I don't see why not,' said Lydia, affronted.

'An au pair will give him more autonomy,' Jenny said. 'And that's a good thing, isn't it?' It would also mean that she could put some distance between herself and number thirty-three and stop these weird . . . feelings.

'Let me digest, let me digest . . .' Suze pulled at the long sleeves of her purple mohair sweater, so that her fingers poked out the loose stitch like finger puppets, and riffled them back and forth anxiously along her lower lip. 'OK, let's consider the possibility that Jenny is right.'

'Don't tell me you're saying our services are no longer needed, too?' Tash pushed her glass away and glared at Suze, as if she'd defected traitorously to the other side.

'Come on, Tash, he's probably sick of the sight of us,' said Liz. 'We've become helpful through sheer persistence and he's had enough. We've become the Helpful Friend that everyone dreads.'

Jenny laughed. 'It's not that.'

'He did end up with four kettles.' Liz caught Jenny's eye and they both tried not to laugh. 'Three babysitters all turning up on the same Saturday night. When the poor guy didn't actually want to go out anyway.'

Tash sat up very straight. 'Is this all because Lydia let herself into his house last week to do his recycling?' She glared at Lydia.

'You didn't?' laughed Jenny.

'Can I take this opportunity to say, Lydia, that you're welcome to do my recycling anytime,' Liz interrupted. 'Quite welcome.'

'I thought he'd appreciate it.' Lydia shrank back into the floppy rollneck of her grey cashmere sweater sulkily. 'Sorry for breathing.'

'You wouldn't fuss about like that for your own husband,' muttered Tash, crossing her arms over her chest.

Lydia covered her mouth with her hand. 'You know the funny thing is I probably wouldn't. That's food for thought, isn't it?'

They sat in musing silence for a few moments, the sound of children fighting in the background.

'Onwards and upwards!' said Suze, reverting to her officious meeting voice. She looked around the table. 'It's been fun, in a weird way, hasn't it, girls? But maybe it is time to move things on.'

Tash bristled.

'Let's vote. Hands up for an au pair.'

Liz raised her hand slowly. Suze followed suit. 'Sorry,' said Jenny to Tash, as she put her hand up too. 'Not personal.' But she couldn't help get a little kick of triumph out of it all the same.

'OK, three in favour of an au pair. Two not. An au pair it is!' Suze refilled everyone's glass. 'Anyway, I don't know about you but I need to refocus my energies on my own family. Right now I've got a mother-in-law threatening to move into the shed at the bottom of the garden. And a seven-year-old child who can't spell his middle name.'

'It is Zebedee,' Liz pointed out.

Suze ignored her. 'I actually sent Chris packing to the pub tonight so that we could have this meeting. He didn't want to go. And you know what? I feel shitty about that now. I keep neglecting my *own* husband because of Ollie. Not that it's Ollie's fault,' she added. Following it with the requisite, 'Poor Ollie.'

'You've done so much, Suze,' said Jenny warmly, sensing the downward shift in mood. 'I know Ollie really, really appreciates it.'

Lydia's eyes were filling with tears. She sniffed and stood up, pulling her handbag over her shoulder. 'George didn't really want me to go out tonight either. And maybe I've been pouring all my energies into . . .' Her voice broke and she trailed off. 'I need to reassess my priorities, too.'

The oven pinged. Suze leapt up, slid a tray of charred mini pizzas out of her range cooker. Cursing as she burned her fingers, she picked up three of them and threw them into some kitchen roll, which she handed to Lydia with too much force. 'I insist.'

Lydia accepted the smoking offering reluctantly. 'Keep me posted,' she said.

'Jesus Christ. It's like she's got some irrigation system going on in her tear ducts,' Tash muttered, as the front door closed behind Lydia. 'Is she *ever* going to stop crying?'

'Troubles with George,' said Suze knowingly. 'That's what that's about.'

'They're not happy?' Jenny asked, thinking not of Lydia but Sophie suddenly.

Liz swallowed a mini pizza whole. 'Come on, is anyone happy?'

Jenny was taken aback by the question. It was a dangerous question. No, she wasn't happy. But Sophie had died. How could she be happy?

'Don't all stare at me like that. I mean happy in the way we *thought* we'd be happy when we were young, you know, imagining being married and grown up.' Liz stared searchingly into the plate of charred pizza as if it somehow held the answer. 'Most mere mortals don't get Soph and Ollie's marriage. That soulmate thing they had. Most of us meet our soulmates in our twenties and the relationship implodes in a bloody combustion of sex and insecurity and clashing levels of timing and commitment.' She shrugged. 'My experience anyway.'

'Sure as hell didn't imagine I'd be divorced by the age of thirty-five.' Tash let out a short, shrill laugh. 'What about you, Suze?'

'Happy?' Suze stopped lowering a string of mozzarella cheese into her open mouth like a worm. 'I don't really have time to wonder if I'm happy or not to be honest.'

'That answers that question then.'

'Actually, Liz, I think I *am* pretty happy,' said Suze. 'I mean, life's not what I thought it'd be, but then you have no idea what having kids is going to be like before you do it, do you?'

Jenny became aware of Tash staring at her. She could feel the question coming and wished she could duck out of it with a 'no comment'. She waited. And it came.

'What about you, Jenny? I mean, if I'm marriage, The Sequel, you're still at the trailer stage, yeah?' Jenny thought there was something about the way she asked the question that made it seem craftily rhetorical.

'Glued to your seat. Eating popcorn,' added Tash.

Jenny laughed. 'Oh no, I hate people who munch popcorn in cinemas. I discreetly suck lumps of chocolate.'

'Sounds like a women's mag question,' smiled Liz. 'Are you a muncher or a sucker?'

'You have a *filthy* mind, Liz Wilson.' Suze turned to Jenny with an intent look on her face. 'Do you ever wish you'd settled earlier, Jenny? Like Sophie.'

'No. I feel like I'm only grown up enough to make the right decision now.'

'I'm not sure falling in love has anything to do with being grown up,' said Liz with just a barely detectable note of weariness.

Suze patted Jenny on the hand, leaving a smudge of grease on her skin. 'Well, I hope you have a marriage like Sophie's.'

Jenny smiled ruefully, knowing that she wouldn't have a marriage like Sophie's. No one had a marriage like Sophie's.

'They had the perfect marriage, didn't they? That's the tragedy of it all.'

'They had their problems just like everyone else,' said Jenny, and immediately regretted it. Why had she said that? The letters. It was that damn box of letters again. She wished she could forget them. She wished she'd never found them.

The women swivelled to look at Jenny, the evening newly energised by a shudder of schadenfreude.

'What do you mean, Jenny?' Tash asked. 'They weren't having problems, were they?'

'No, not really,' she said quickly, feeling guilty that she'd betrayed Sophie's confidence. 'Just that they were like any couple in a way, well, a pretty gilded version admittedly.'

'I always did wonder why Sophie never had another child,' said Tash. She exchanged a knowing glance with Lydia.

Jenny remembered the maternitywear carefully folded in the drawer. To disclose this would be an even greater betrayal. She kept her mouth closed.

'A shame. It would be easier for Freddie if he had a sibling.' Liz looked wistful. 'Poor little Freddie.'

'He might still get one!' blurted Tash, with rather too much enthusiasm for Jenny's liking. 'Ollie could have more kids. Why not?'

'Whoa! One step at a time. The guy has not even thought about dating yet, has he, Jenny?' said Liz.

Jenny bit her lip. 'No,' she lied. She couldn't bring herself to admit even the gist of their conversation the other night. His words would be misinterpreted. She must protect him from himself. From the predators. From Tash.

'Hold your horses!' Suze grabbed Jenny's sleeve. 'Has the time come for us to introduce him to other women, do we think?'

'No!' protested Jenny.

'Nothing serious, Jenny,' Suze said, eyeing her with obvious amusement. 'Just someone to have dinner with?'

Tash sat up very straight and sniffed. 'That's not necessary. I'm his dinner partner.'

Liz kicked Jenny under the table.

'Well, you know, just the odd dinner.' Tash's eyes glittered. She couldn't keep the smile down. 'Why is everyone staring at me like that? We're both on our own, it's natural.'

Twenty-one

It was a cool, sunny Saturday morning and the scent of white freesias in the window box puffed pleasantly through the café's open window. Coffee. Pastries. Newspaper. Laptop. Bedhead hair. They looked how they used to look before Soph died, Jenny thought, a happy couple, freshly woken in each other's sleep-dozy arms, easy in each other's company. It would only be the most acute observer who'd notice how their silences went on a little longer than they used to, the fewer times their hands touched, the way Jenny no longer took a casual bite of Sam's pain au chocolat.

'Hired yet?' Sam looked up from his newspaper, his eyes tracking the pert behind of a pretty young black waitress.

'I may as well have advertised for a nanny for a newly single Brad Pitt.' She'd been worried that every au pair would check the 'no father-only households' box, but instead she'd had dozens of replies from all over the world: Australian, Bulgarian, Irish, Congolese, Thai, Swedish, and, yes, Ukrainian. Seventeen, nineteen, twenty-one years old. Reams of bubbly CVs with thousands of exclamation marks, badly lit photos and declarations of being 'hard working!' and 'loving children!' and 'no job too small!!!'

Sam gestured to his mouth, meaning she'd got cappuccino froth on her upper lip. 'I advise you to just pick the prettiest, Jenny,' he said, looking down at the sports pages. 'Seriously, cheer Ollie up a bit.' He shook out his paper. 'I know what I'd want in an au pair.'

'Charming. Actually, Sam, the main priority is Freddie. It's got to be somebody who'll bond with Freddie.'

Sam laughed, stole the last remaining bit of croissant off her plate, dunked it in the small pot of jam. 'You tell yourself that, Jenny, darling.'

She rolled her eyes. 'Not every man is as Neanderthal as you, Sam.'

'Ah, you're so wrong.'

Three coffees later, Jenny had a shortlist. Out had gone the ones who couldn't spell at all – they had to spell better than Freddie, that was the benchmark – and out went the ones with dodgy blanks on their CVs, or dodgy jobs – 'after college I worked as a masseuse' – or unnerving hobbies such as 'dog breeding and rifle shooting' or, rather ominously, no photos. And at Sam's insistence out went the really plain or fat girls. This made Jenny feel mean because she was sure they were perfectly nice, nicer in fact than the prettier girls, and had she been sitting alone in the café – as she should have been, if she'd planned the exercise properly – she would have picked a plainer one.

Sam craned to the side, watching over her shoulder. This meant that she had to let a few more beauties through the net. Only when he went to the toilet did she get a chance to do a stealthy cull of the sexiest girls.

Finally, a list of five. All nice, bouncy, wholesome girls. Attractive, yes, but none showing cleavage in their headshots.

'Done?' Sam stirred another sugar into his coffee. He always rotated the teaspoon in the cup five times. 'Can we reclaim our Saturday now?'

'Yep. I'll email them later.' She shut the laptop with relief. She was closing one chapter of her life and moving on to the next, moving away from number thirty-three. The pretty waitress took away the dirty plates and Sam did that silent bill-scribbling motion with his hands, despite the fact that she was close enough to talk to.

She knew better than to say anything. Sam enjoyed lording it over waitresses. Like he enjoyed being worldlier than her. It was all part of a power dynamic that pleased him in quite a boyishly endearing way. When they'd first got together he'd had to show her how to get the fish off its bone with the back of a knife: she'd previously got around this by ordering a fillet. He was the kind of man who'd order braised offal whenever the opportunity arose. She'd always preferred a chicken breast done simply, and no, of course she'd never eat the skin. He thought this hilarious.

Sam's phoned beeped. He looked at the message and his expression changed. 'Completely forgot to tell you, babes, and I better tell you now in case she mentions it . . .' He looked a little flustered. 'I met Tash for lunch last week.'

'What?' Jenny stared at him, puzzled. 'Tash? Muzzy Hill Tash?' First a phone call. Now lunch.

He leaned back in his chair, dangled his hand out of the open window. 'She called again, wanted free advice, and I was just round the corner from her so, you know, we grabbed a sandwich.'

'Why didn't you say anything last week?'

'Sorry. It's crap of me. Been mental.'

'But I saw Tash round at Suze's the other night. She didn't say anything either.' It didn't make sense.

'She didn't?'

'No, she didn't.'

He smoothed his palm over his shaven head and sighed. 'I guess she's embarrassed, poor thing.'

An indignant snort noise tunnelled out of her nostrils. 'She never struck me as the embarrassed type.'

'People do find divorce embarrassing, Jenny,' he said, putting on his soft, talking to the client voice. 'They see it as a personal failure. That's pretty much universal.'

'Suppose.'

He leaned forward and kissed her lightly on the mouth. 'Not us. We'll be one of the happy ones.'

Was he right? Yes, of course he was. She smiled. 'We will.'

'In August you are going to send me berserk with happiness.'

She laughed. The sun moved, throwing a shawl of heat against her back. The early June air was drenched with the smell of freesias. And Sam's eyes matched the strip of sky above the Camden rooftops perfectly. In a funny way, she realised, Sam confessing to a meeting with Tash confirmed something fundamental about him to her. Something good. Reassuring. No, Sam wasn't perfect, but at least he was honest. She'd take honest and flawed over perfect and shifty every time. Yes, perhaps Sam did have a bit of a wandering eye, but at least he didn't do it behind her back. At least she knew who she was marrying. She'd forgotten how great Sam was. He was great. He was so great! No, she wouldn't have him any other way. She'd been spending too much time with Ollie, and it had confused her. Yes, that was it. She reached over to kiss Sam, harder this time, a proper snog. For the first time ever they clashed noses.

Twenty-two

Her name is Cecille. (Long on the 'eeeel'.) She is standing outside the front door of number thirty-three, pulling at the straps of the black fabric holdall that is digging into her long Gallic neck, giving her love bites. Twenty, apparently, looks no more than sixteen. Her hair is brown and wavy and youth-glossy in the sunshine. She's wearing no make-up, which is reassuring. But she doesn't need it, which is less so. She has olive skin, a full moon face that is beautiful from the nose up – eyes like chocolate buttons, improbable eyelashes, and very round cheekbones – and plain from the big nose down to the mouth with the chipped front tooth and slightly zitty chin. I'm also pleased to report that there is nothing particularly chic about her. She is wearing the universal uniform of the French square – pressed straight jeans, pink buttoned-up shirt, navy sweater and loafers – which is sweet rather than sexy. A London teen would eat her for breakfast.

Yes, I can see why Jenny plumped for Cecille. She comes from a large provincial family – four siblings, all brothers, all younger than her – from the Poitou-Charentes region in the west of France. Her father is a garage mechanic, her mother a housewife. She also comes with a stack of glowing references and a place on one of those evening courses to learn finance. What's not to like? Only the fact that she is attractive and French and twenty. Hey ho.

Ollie opens the door and stares at her, surprised, as if he is expecting someone else. Jenny scrutinises her from behind his shoulder. She nudges him. Ollie smiles, coughs and says, 'Can I take your bag?'

Cecille flushes, silent. Has she forgotten her English? Perhaps she assumed all British men were a hybrid of Mr Bean and Prince Philip. 'Thank you,' she says, recovering herself. Wowzer! That French accent. That's sex appeal without even trying.

'Hello, Cecille!' Jenny says, stepping forward. 'How was your flight from La Rochelle?'

'Good, thank you.' Cecille smiles nervously, glances at Ollie again.

Jenny guides Cecille through the hall, brushing past Ollie. They both flinch at the touch. Something ripples the air. Have I missed a row between these two or something? Things feel kind of crackly.

'Something to eat, Cecille?' asks Ollie a little brusquely. He's nervous. He always sounds brusque when he's nervous.

'No thank you, Mr Brady.'

'Ollie, seriously. Call me Ollie.'

Colour rouges her cheeks, like the brightening of a flower at dawn. She is prettier than the photograph she sent in. Clever girl.

'Freddie!' Ollie bellows up the stairs. 'Cecille is here. Come and say hi.' They all stare expectantly, smiling fixedly up the stairs, at the reason she's here. No Freddie appears.

'Freddie!' Ollie calls again.

It becomes clear that Freddie has not appeared because Freddie does not want to appear. There is a click of minor embarrassment. Jenny makes a 'kids, huh' face and runs upstairs to coax him down.

Forward-wind forty-five minutes and Freddie has forgiven Cecille for arriving on his doorstep and not being me. Cecille is sitting cross-legged on the sitting room floor making a Lego spaceship: it's the way to my boy's heart.

Jenny's phone beeps incessantly. I thread myself through the zipper and into her handbag to check the messages. Suze: 'Friend or foe?' Liz: 'Report back immediately.' Tash: 'Hot?' Lydia: 'Tash having minor breakdown.'

Jenny and Ollie go through to the kitchen. The cleaner has done an extra shift in anticipation of Cecille's arrival. There is the smell of pasta pesto that Ollie's made for lunch. There are yellow tulips on the table. Fresh linen in the spare bedroom.

'She seems lovely. Shall I leave you to it now?' whispers Jenny, looking like she's itching to leave.

He grabs her arm. 'Don't go, not yet. What the hell will we talk about?'

'Flaubert. Derrida?'

'Now I'm really scared.'

'Ollie, she will be into MTV and Gaga. Talk about that.'

Ollie groans. 'Oh God.'

Good. The air is loosening a bit between them now. 'Just get her cooking. She says she can cook. And she's French. All French people can cook.'

'Lasagne?'

Jenny smiles properly for the first time since she arrived at number thirty-three.

He puts a hand over his mouth. 'Oh no! What have I done?'

'Shhh. Just remember that you will no longer have to rely on Lydia doing your recycling or Suze's bake-offs or Tash's after school club. You'll be free to go out in the evenings. You've got a babysitter on call,' says Jenny.

'I don't want to go out.'

She pulls her bag briskly over her shoulder. 'Well, you might do one day.'

Ollie looks doubtful and fingers his beard.

'Suze is going to invite you to some soirees very soon. Prepare yourself.'

'Haven't I suffered enough?'

She laughs, checks her watch. 'I better get back.'

'Thanks for sorting this out, Jenny.'

'It was nothing,' she lies. There is a moment's hesitation when she looks like she might be about to kiss him goodbye. But she doesn't.

Twenty-three

A week later, Jenny is dutifully back at number thirty-three, having dropped Freddie home from swimming. I observe her, noting the tiredness under her eyes, pink from the pool, the little twitch in the centre of her pretty, full bottom lip. She looks nervy watching Ollie and Freddie kicking a ball around the garden, fidgeting, crossed-legged, tapping her fingers on the deck. I wonder if it's something to do with this Dominique business. Does she know? I suspect not. Sam can be discreet as a spook when he has to be.

Jenny stands up, brushes down her denim shorts and tells Ollie she's going to the toilet. But it seems she is not going to the toilet! No, she is walking past the toilet without so much as a tinkle, eyes furtive, a woman on a mission. She's creeping along the landing now. Ah! What's this? She is going into Ollie's bedroom. How odd. Glancing from side to side as if scared of being disturbed, she is padding across the sheepskin rug. Crouching now, she's pulling open a drawer of the chest, her fingertips leaving damp spots on the wood. She's yanking the jumpers out of the way, frantically pulling them out and dropping them on the floor so that Cecille's

192

ordered neatness is destroyed and they're left sprawling, arms open, like old skins. Her hands are patting the bottom of the drawer like a blind woman. She is pulling up the lining paper.

Oh no! Oh God. I get it now. I shrivel to a black dot.

Jenny sits back on her feet, shakes her head. 'Gone?' she says out loud through the hand crushed against her mouth. 'Fuck. Fuck. Fuck.'

Gone? *Where?* And how the hell does Jenny know the letters were there in the first place? I hear soft, almost-silent footsteps, the crush of the carpet fibres under a bare foot.

'Jenny?' Suddenly Cecille is standing in the doorway, glaring. 'What are you doing?'

Jenny leaps back from the drawers, mortified, mouth opening and closing. 'I . . . I . . .'

Cecille frowns. 'Why have you taken out all the clothes?'

Jenny's cheeks are on fire. 'I was looking for something.' She looks down at her twisting hands.

'In the drawers?'

'Yes.'

'What?'

'Er, something private.'

'Private?' Something flashes across Cecille's face. As she is standing and Jenny is crouching she's looking down on Jenny, literally and in other ways too.

'Sorry, sorry.' Jenny starts shoving the clothes back in the drawer manically.

'I'll do it,' Cecille says, squatting down beside her, giving Jenny a fearsome sidelong glance. 'I know how Ollie likes it.'

Twenty-four

Light puddled through the trees to the green floor of Highgate cemetery. It was a lovely day, the sun custard-yellow, the sky blue, the kind of day that would have made Sophie grin impishly and declare herself 'horny as an old goat'. She'd have worn one of her glamorous wide-brimmed hats today, Jenny imagined, the Joan Collins-style one with the leopard print sash. And she would smell slightly sweaty, sexy hot skin, rather than anything BOish. She'd be bare legged, of course. Sophie would do a bare leg in any temperature over freezing. Unlike herself who liked a good opaque. She was wearing opaques today in fact. Navy. 60 denier. The tights were making her hot. She could smell her armpits when she raised her arms from her sides.

She wedged the round box of pink champagne truffles close to the head of the gravestone. Happy thirty-sixth birthday, Soph, she muttered silently, squeezing her eyes shut and trying to commune, just in case Soph could hear her. I love you so much, Soph. I miss you so much. I wish you were going to get old with me. We never did get to go on a cheesy cruise and sing along to Shirley Bassey impersonators, or sit on a beach smoking skunk and getting obese on chocolate torte and growing our pubic hair long and wild like Indian Sadhus. You know what? I don't even mind you haunting me – if that is you – and following me in your white Fiat. Although why the Fiat? I think you're more a convertible Mini lady. I just wish you'd show yourself and tell me . . . well, so many things. Not least how to colour block. I'm so bored by navy. You always told me I'd get bored with navy and black. You were right about that. You were right about so many things. Although you were wrong about Sam, who has finally set a date for a wedding I'd sell my own mother for you to be at. I haven't got the dress, of course. How can I buy a wedding dress without you to lash me into the dressing room and pull them over my head? And by the way, Sophie, the box full of letters wasn't there. I tried to protect you in case you'd done something stupid that you never told me about – tsk, tsk – and find those letters before Ollie did, but the box wasn't there. And yes, OK, maybe I was being a little bit nosy, too. Whatever happened to no secrets, Soph? Whatever happened to *us*?

She waited for some kind of answer. But there was nothing but a stirring of the breeze and a small white fluttering butterfly. Feeling a little silly now, she squatted down, waiting for Freddie and Ollie to catch up, relishing her small moment of peace with the silence of Sophie. There were few people around in the cemetery today, but it felt fine being alone here, she decided. She'd never had herself down as a grave lover. But she'd fallen in love with this cemetery, a little idyll in London. There were so many graves – over 52,000, she'd read – and so many effigies – angels, dogs, gods – but it felt magical rather than morbid, stepping out of the noise and grit of north London into another world, a secret ghostly garden. There were many worse places to end up.

The scrabble of small feet. And Freddie was there, panting at her side. He stood a few feet from the grave, uncertainly, gripping his bunch of white flowers tightly.

'I've put my chocolates there,' smiled Jenny, reading his apprehension, trying to coax him forward.

'Happy birthday, Mummy,' he said quietly, putting the flowers on the grave and then leaping back to avoid being grabbed by a ghost. He reached for Jenny's hand. His felt hot, tight and small in hers. She squeezed it, feeling a rare sense of peace and a warm fuzzy feeling that wasn't unlike happiness. Absurd, considering. She was pleased that she'd agreed to come to the cemetery today. She'd made excuses when Ollie first asked, not wanting to intrude, wanting to maintain some distance. But then she thought about it for all of two seconds and knew that if she didn't go and visit with Ollie and Freddie on Sophie's birthday, she'd regret it forever. She'd been at every one of Sophie's birthdays since she was twenty.

It barely seemed like yesterday that she, Sam, Ollie and Soph had celebrated Sophie's thirty-fifth. They'd gone to Odette's in Primrose Hill, got hammered and eaten scallops and then propped up the bar until late, trying not to rubberneck Jude Law sitting at an adjacent table, their discretion failing spectacularly. Sophie had been in a particularly loud, silly mood. She'd put the pink flower from the table vase behind her ear and stabbed herself in the foot with her own stiletto, drawing blood. Ollie gave her a fireman's lift to the taxi, making Jude Law smile.

Ollie appeared, carrying a bunch of yellow roses. She stood back respectfully as he kissed the gravestone. 'Happy birthday, darling,' he muttered, and the love in his voice seemed to vibrate in the warm spring air. Then he put a hand gently on Jenny's shoulder and they stood there together in silence, a column of sunshine breaking through the thick canopy, united in missing her. It wasn't like she was part of the family or anything. And yet today, for some odd reason, more than ever before, she felt she was.

'Can I see the grave with the sleeping dog on it now?' Freddie pulled away from them and hurtled down the path.

Ollie stared at the gravestone, his face unreadable, lost in private thoughts. 'Gone five months.'

'I can't believe it either.'

'Sometimes I can't remember what she looks like, Jenny.' He turned to her and his eyes were very dark, all pupil. 'I have to get out photos. Other times it's like she just popped out to get some milk. And it's like I'm waiting for her to come home. I still get bits of her, Jen. Every day some crappy catalogue drops on the mat.' He smiled. 'It's like the car's braked but all this stuff from the roof box is still flying forward.'

She laughed.

'Oh, Sophie,' he said, shaking his head again, as if still disbelieving that she could have done anything so stupid as step out in front of a bus on Regent Street.

'Should I give you a minute?'

'No,' he said firmly, turning to look at her, his face alive and motile again, as if snapping back from the past to the present. 'I've hardly seen you since Cecille arrived.' His eyes were shadowed by their brows in the sunlight, making them hard to read. 'Have I pissed you off in some way?'

'No.' Mortified that he should think that. 'Not at all.'

'What then?'

'Nothing, Ollie.' She shuffled her feet under his long, hot gaze. This wasn't the time. 'I'll check in on Freddie.' She turned to walk through the shrub-shaded path, sat down beside the loyal stone dog, worrying that she'd ballsed the trip up in some indefinable way. 'You alright, Freddie?'

He looked solemn, stroked the dog's cold ears. 'Don't like it here, Jenny.'

'Why don't you like it?'

'Makes Daddy sad. I don't like Daddy sad.'

'Oh, Freddie. You are such a sweet, kind boy.' She kissed him on his warm forehead and they sat in silence for a few moments, watching a large glossy black beetle lumber its way over the sticks and bubbles of moss and leaves on the ground. 'Daddy won't always be sad, you know.'

Freddie said nothing and stared glumly ahead.

'He'll always love Mummy but he won't always be sad.'

'Good.' He prodded the beetle gently with a stick. 'Sad is boring.'

'I guess it is.' But if sad was so boring, why was she beginning to find this in some weird, black way the most exciting time of her life? In some way she didn't quite understand she'd never felt more alive. Not able to compute the contradiction, she closed her eyes, pressed her fingers hard into the lids. God, it was all so fucked up.

'You don't come over so much any more,' said Freddie.

'You've got Cecille now,' she said, twisting with guilt. Freddie was the last person in the world she wanted to upset.

'Will you still come and visit us when you get married?'

'You bet!' Jenny pulled him towards her in a hug and glanced up at Ollie, who was sitting now on the grave, arms locked around his knees, staring into the shaded tangle of trees, a silhouette against the gravestone. Would there ever be a time he wouldn't be framed by that gravestone, she wondered.

'I'm worried about the wedding.'

'Oh no! Worried? Why, Fred?'

'Ludo says I'm going to look really silly and that he was a page boy once and had to wear a sailor's suit,' he said solemnly.

Jenny laughed. 'No sailor's suit, promise. You can wear what you want.'

He grinned. 'I can wear my Superman T-shirt?'

She hesitated. Oh, to hell with Sam's mother. 'Yeah. You can wear what you want.'

He slumped against her, leaning into her body. 'Will there be dancing? Like *Strictly*?'

'Definitely.'

Freddie kicked out his feet in his khaki Crocs. 'And will I be allowed to have fun?'

Jenny was puzzled. 'You're always allowed to have fun.'

'I feel like I'm not allowed to have fun.'

'Who said that? Did Cecille say that?' She wasn't sure about Cecille now. Not now that Cecille had something over her. And she would never forget that piercing look she gave her beside the chest of drawers. Yes, she should have gone for Magda, that pale, studious one with the specs.

'No.' He shrugged. 'It's just that I feel bad when I'm happy because Mummy is dead and that means I shouldn't be happy.'

'Oh, Fred. You mustn't feel bad for being happy. Mummy always wanted you to be happy, didn't she?' She pulled him towards her tighter. 'She'd be so proud of you being happy.'

Freddie was breathing noisily and Jenny could tell that he was trying not to cry.

She pointed at the ground. 'Hey, look, that beetle's carrying a leaf now. Ninja beetle.'

They watched the beetle with its leafy burden scurry into a hole in the soil. 'Daddy doesn't like Sam,' he said matter of factly, not looking up.

'Sorry?' Jenny couldn't quite believe what he'd said. The hairs on her arms prickled.

'Daddy doesn't like Sam.'

'I'm sure he does, Freddie.'

'I know that he doesn't.' He picked a large white flower and rolled the stem between his fingers.

She glanced up sharply at Ollie, a dark figure in his battered Barbour. Surely Freddie was wrong? But then why had he said it?

As if sensing her gaze, Ollie stood up and walked towards them, brushing flakes of green moss off his trousers. 'Pizza?'

Freddie jumped up. 'Pizza!'

They retraced their steps through the sun-dappled avenues of tombs in silence. A man in green overalls passed them with a wheelbarrow full of small chunks of broken stone.

He stopped. 'Ah, you mustn't pick the flowers, lad,' he said, looking at the plucked flower in Freddie's hand.

'Sorry.' Freddie looked down at his offending hand, bit his lip. He hated being told off by strangers.

'Eh, it's alright.' The gardener looked at Jenny and winked. 'You just make sure you give it to your pretty mum, eh?'

In her horror she stepped backwards, the heel of her shoe catching on the crumbling stonework of Edward Ebenezer Stewart's final resting place. Her ankle turned and she slipped and dropped her handbag. The tableau froze: her on the old grave; Tampax and phone and chewing gum rolling out of her bag; a sharp pain in her ankle. She shut her eyes, wishing that the grave would open up and she could just sink into its dank depths until the awful moment passed. This not being an option, she scrambled to her feet, noting with renewed mortification that Freddie had picked up the Tampax and was examining it carefully as if it were a rare albino beetle. She snatched it off him, shoved it back into her handbag.

'You alright, love?' asked the gardener, smirking.

'Fine!' She carried on walking, knees stinging. Freddie ran on ahead of them now. 'God, I'm sorry,' she said stiffly, mortified, unable to look at Ollie.

Ollie stopped. 'Jenny. You don't need to apologise for anything.' He put his hands firmly on her shoulders, demanding that she look at him. She shyly met his gaze and saw that his lovely dark eyes were creased with repressed laughter. Clearly, he found the idea that she might get mistaken for his wife hilariously funny.

She was a joke.

Twenty-five

I'm getting restless. The house is swelling with the unseasonal heat. I can hear minute cracks spidering inside the bricks, Muswell Hill's clay soil beneath the foundations contracting, hardening, threatening number thirty-three with subsidence problems. Freddie is outdoors a lot now, stretching, strengthening those skinny, bendy limbs, jumping, naked but for his white pants, ya-ya-yahooing, throwing himself off the trampoline so that he's a flying, wild-haired angel cut out of north London's paddling-pool-blue sky.

Cecille is watching Freddie, enjoying him, laughing, her river of brown hair sheeny in the sunlight. She is wearing a denim mini skirt that shows off her slim brown legs. It did not travel over from France with her and it bears the Topshop label, like so many of her new purchases. The French square's pressed navy sweater hasn't made an appearance for a while, I realise. She slings her weight lazily to one hip, a feline sexuality about her I've never noticed before. She yawns, tired because she and Ollie were up last night until one in the morning drinking beers in the garden, beneath the warm black sky and the stars sharp as cookie cutters. Yeah, OK, I'm jealous.

So I catch a thermal down the hill, buffeting over the cool air that hangs above the black still spots of Hampstead ponds, through the nitrate fug of Camden to check in on Jenny. Well, Sam actually. I'm still trying to get to the bottom of this Dominique business that's been rumbling for weeks. Who the hell is she? And what's she got to do with *Tash*, of all bloody people? Jenny's wedding date is rushing towards us all. I need to find out.

Jenny needs to find out, even if she doesn't know it yet.

I enter through the open balcony window of Sam and Jenny's flat. Bingo! Jenny isn't at home. Sam is. But who is this powdering her nose in the marble bathroom? Oh damn, his mother, Penelope, the battleaxe from Sussex with the overactive salivary glands. She spits when she talks and little strings of saliva link her upper and lower teeth when she smiles, like a brace. She creates a dust bowl of perfume wherever she goes. She should only be allowed in well-ventilated areas.

'Her phone's still on answer?' Penelope says tersely, applying a layer of powder to her face, thick as pollen. 'Surely she knows I'm here to discuss the floral arrangements.'

Sam pushes up his shirt sleeve and glances at his Rolex. 'Give her a minute, Mum. She's probably just caught in traffic.'

'I'm not even going to ask where she is, Sam,' Penelope sniffs. Which is her way of asking.

'She's not in Muswell Hill actually. She's having her roots done.'

'Thank goodness.' She laughs shrilly. 'Not like her.'

What a cow! I think we can safely declare Penelope to be the mother-in-law from hell.

'We're going to a party tonight.'

Penelope sits down at the kitchen table, spreading her hands on the table top so that the veins pop out like pipes. She examines her manicure in loaded silence. 'That's nice.'

'What?' says Sam.

'Nothing.'

'Come on, Mum. I know that face.'

'I'm concerned about Jenny. Very concerned, Sammy.' She spits a fine coat of drizzle over her son's hand. 'She's not playing ball on the wedding. Everyone's waiting for her to get back to them. And it's not like she's not had offers of help. Did I tell you that Penny Ridgemont's daughter has offered to give her a free make-up session? She's waiting for a yay or a nay, too.' She shakes her head. 'It just looks like bad manners, I'm afraid.'

'I'll talk to her,' Sam says wearily.

Penelope gives him one of those scrutinising looks that only mothers can give. 'Is everything OK between you, darling?'

'Yes, yes, of course.' He is a man who could lie to anyone, including his mother.

'It's just . . .' Penelope looks down at her hands.

'What?' He slams down his coffee cup. 'What, Mum?' He turns the tables nimbly, so that his disloyalty is now hers.

'I feel you should both be more excited, that's all,' she says, picking her words carefully, like the flowers in her front garden. 'I remember when me and your father got married, gosh, I was hopelessly beside myself, I really was!'

She swivels her gold wedding band around her fat pink finger. She's going to get buried with that ring. 'And your sister. Pip was like one of those gypsy brides, wasn't she? You know the ones on telly.'

'Jenny's best friend has just died, Mum.'

'It was some time ago now.'

'Try telling her that.'

They sit in silence for a few moments. The traffic hoots outside. There is the rhythmic drum of a police chopper, flying above the houses. 'I thought the point of having the wedding this summer was to start a new chapter?' She won't let this go.

'It is.' He looks down at the table, as though he can't look his mother in the eye either.

'The funny thing is, Sam, Jenny doesn't look like a woman about to get married. She looks . . .' Penelope hesitates. 'I don't know, fevered.'

Sam throws back his shaven head and laughs. '*Fevered!*' He drops his head in his hands and lets out a mock groan. 'Mum, please. This is not a period drama.'

'Skittish, not happy, not sad, not bereaved even! Not like I was when poor Mark got tongue cancer. I couldn't get out of bed for two weeks. I lost sixteen pounds. That was the only upside,' she reflects, sipping tea.

'Mum, will you please just leave it?' There's a growl to his voice now that shakes the air particles in the room like a maraca. He gets up, walks to the window and looks down the street. His eyes flicker and focus in recognition of someone or something below.

I swoop over to the curtain rail.

Ah, Jenny's back! Getting out of the car, glancing around, up the street, down the street, like she's seeking someone. Looking, yes, *fevered*! Oh dear. I want to sound out a warning. Mother-in-law's here! Don't look like a mentalist. Stop the divving around. Approach with caution. But all I can do is madly wave my non-atomic arms in frustration. I am the world's most useless guardian angel.

What the hell is the point of *me*?

Twenty-six

Jenny glanced behind her one last time. No, no sign of Sophie's hubcapped celestial chariot, whatever it was. Was she imagining stuff? Had she lost it, like Sam said? The thing was, she'd come out of the hairdresser, jittery on coffee and *Hello!* magazine, and was walking down the street to her car, sharply aware of the pins in her ill-advised wedding rehearsal Sarah Palin up do – the overbearing stylist had insisted – when something had caught her eye. She'd turned. It was a woman walking quickly away, her beige trench coat flapping open in the wind like a tent, a mass of glossy brown hair piled up on her head. A gash of red scarf. She got into her car – and yes, it *was* a white Fiat – slammed the door and revved off, starving Jenny of any proper scrutiny of her face. But she was pretty damn sure it was the same woman. The same woman who'd turned up at her flat all that time ago, the one who looked like Sophie. How could she forget her?

More importantly, how the hell could she forget that Penelope was coming over? And now she was late, for once. Standing on the doorstep of her flat, she checked her iPhone, which had turned itself on to silent as it so often did in her handbag, and saw she'd had four missed calls from Sam. Anxiety bubbled in her tummy like gas. She knew she was in for another earful from Sam. And silences that could kill from Penelope.

She would fail as a potential daughter-in-law before she'd even opened her mouth. What with her Sarah Palin hair. Her pimply chin. The insomnia bagging around her eyes, the bad dreams that had bugged her ever since visiting the grave on Sophie's birthday. The same ones over and over, like an endlessly repeated mini series. The most popular was the one when she spilled red wine on her bridal dress then on closer inspection realised it wasn't wine but blood and that she'd got her period early and Sophie had to run off to find Tampax but couldn't because all the shops were shut because they were in the country and shops were never open in the country and so the vicar had to ask the congregation, 'Is there a Tampax in the house?' And the day and the dress were ruined. After that dream, the following day would always pass in a blur. As though she was wearing a pair of glasses that weren't the right prescription.

The wedding was beginning to feel like a reptile bought from a pet shop that had grown bigger and fiercer than its owners could cope with, and unmanageably hungry. She'd said that she'd prefer a simple, small ceremony, but kept getting shouted down by Sam's family, who had forked out a small fortune. Now her own parents, who could ill afford it but didn't like to feel they weren't stepping up to the high water mark set by Penelope, had felt compelled to donate seven thousand pounds of their savings. It left her feeling guilty and beholden and anxious. And, no, she still hadn't bought the dress.

Penelope would be bound to ask about the dress today. It would be top of her bullet-points. And to prove to Penelope that she had actually *tried* to find a dress and wasn't a complete timewaster, she'd have to relive last week's shopping trip with her mother, which had ended with a tense coffee and a stale Eccles cake in John Lewis's fourth floor café and her mother saying she was 'the world's fussiest bride'.

Everyone said that when you saw the right dress you *knew* it was The One. But they all just looked like shockingly overpriced bits of fabric to her. She had yet to find the dress. And the dress had yet to find her.

As she fumbled for her keys it started to rain lightly. She stopped for a moment, resting her hands on her knees, thankful that she wasn't being watched and that she could snatch this one moment to realign herself, catch her breath before Penelope, before the party.

Something caught her eye. She looked up through the bead curtain of rain. There was someone at the window of her flat, waving. It was Sophie! Clear as day, standing in the frame of her sitting room window, her dark hair tumbling over her shoulders, waving manically! She stumbled backwards, wobbly with joy. But then, slowly, heartbreakingly, the arm disappeared and all she could see was Penelope's stern, frowning face looking over the mountain range of her bosom. Get a grip, she told herself. Dead people did not wave from windows. Nor did they drive Fiats. Get a grip.

Twenty-seven

Forget knock knock knocking on heaven's door, I would just like to know if I am on the waiting list, thanks all the same. I can pinpoint the moment it all began – collision between big bus and big pants – but I have no idea when it will end. And don't all things end, eventually? Blair. Bootleg jeans. Teething. Youth. Isn't that the lesson we don't want to learn?

Don't get me wrong, I'm in no hurry to leave. Not when Freddie and Ollie are still here. It's just that it's exhausting not being able to make my presence known to anyone but terrified household pets. Ah, the restless ghost of Sophie Brady. Wooo!

It's so frustrating not being able to alter the course of events, only to see them. Like Jenny's wedding. She's about to marry a toad and I can do fuck all to stop it. I can't discover Sam's secrets. I couldn't even be Rentaghost.

People have existential crises about the point of life. (Is this it? Well, no actually, it ain't.) But I'm in crisis about the point of being dead. It's not like I've got wiser and more spiritual. In fact, worryingly, the opposite appears to be happening. I'm getting pettier, more irritable. Yes, more like a live human in fact. Let me list the ways.

- Cecille rolls Ollie's socks into balls and lines them all up in his drawer like a plot of small cabbages, or rather, *petit choux*. I used to just put them in a pile on the dresser. This really irritates me.

- Cecille irons his underpants. Not even I ironed the grunderpants. Beyond the call of duty. More than pisses me off, obviously. She has even ironed him underpants for Suze's party. Does she think he's going to pole dance or something?

- Worse – could there be worse? Yes there can! – Cecille also irons her own knickers. No woman of twenty irons their knickers. And it's *not* career appropriate to iron your frilly smalls – not for Cecille, M&S multi-packs – while your boss and his son are sitting a few feet away on the sofa watching the footie on telly.

- The new dolphin tattoo on Cecille's left buttock. Couldn't help but be rather pleased when it got infected. See how lacking in Buddha-like compassion I am?

- The way she pretends to *'adore'* Ollie's favourite Hugh Fearnley Whittingstall's nettle ale – come on, you're French, fooling no one, love – and sits on the back step sipping it, sunlight threaded in her hair, gazing at Ollie as if she were Vanessa Paradis and he Johnny Depp.

- The question of my secret letter stash is eating away at me. I still have no idea where they are, which is very worrying. Cecille, mistress of the drawers, is chief suspect. If she does have them, has she any idea that she is custodian of a bomb that threatens to shatter lives like windows?

Twenty-eight

Jenny manoeuvred her Sarah Palin up do out of the orbit of a particularly unflattering down lighter and surveyed Suze's party, still disbelieving that she'd actually dragged Sam up here, despite the showdown with his mother earlier that day. There were twenty, thirty people in the living room, she guessed, clutching large wine glasses or small bottles of beer, laughing, shouting over each other shouting, their tongues working within their cheeks to extricate bits of Suze's sticky cocktail sausages from between their teeth. They seemed to meld into a certain type that she'd become familiar with on her visits to the neighbourhood: women in their thirties and forties, nicely dressed, media-ish, tired-looking, a few pregnant; fortysomething men with superfluous body hair. Yes, she definitely recognised some of the individual faces. The man in the suit and the Trilby, the self-conscious twiddle of moustache. The lady with the white-blond Gaga bouff. It took a moment for her to realise that she recognised them from Sophie's funeral all those months ago.

Snitches of conversation slid about the room. 'How is your new nanny working out?' 'No, honestly, thanks, I'm on the wagon. Total torture.' 'I know I shouldn't say this but she looks fabulous on the chemo. She's lost a tonne of weight, hasn't she?' 'She only gives you the time of day if she thinks you might be able to offer her eldest a work placement, I wouldn't worry about it.' 'I hear you've got gay guinea pigs, too? Let's throw a gay guinea pig disco!' She felt like an outsider.

'No Ollie, then?' whispered Sam into her ear. 'If he's a no show I predict a riot.'

Jenny swallowed hard. Ollie was late. He wouldn't come. No, he wouldn't. It was probably better like that. What with Sam being so chippy about him.

'Ow. What the . . .' He stepped away from a large urn of twigs, one of which was pokering him in the backside.

'It's a twig, Sam. They're ornamental. You can't be angry with a twig.'

'Jenny!' Suze's hair suddenly engulfed her, teased into an even greater fro for the occasion. 'It's good to have you back in the 'hood, lady!'

Jenny kissed her warmly on both cheeks. It was surprisingly good to see her again. She realised she'd missed them all. 'Suze, this is Sam.' She glanced at Sam nervously, daring him to behave. 'Sam, Suze.'

'Ooh, the divorce lawyer!' Suze giggled, poking Sam in the ribs. 'I'd better keep you away from my husband. Don't want him getting any tips, eh.'

Sam shot Jenny a hard WTF look over his wine glass.

Suze swayed on her high wooden-heeled clogs. 'Oh, I'm sorry,' she hiccupped. 'It must be like being a doctor and having people ask you questions about their gall bladder all night.'

'Ha!' Sam said with a gritted smile.

'Jenny's been a real star these last few months,' Suze continued, oblivious. She put a hand on the sleeve of Sam's crisp blue shirt, dusting it with canapé crumbs. 'We wouldn't have been able to run the Help Ollie committee without her.'

'Oh, rubbish,' said Jenny quickly. 'You're the one who put in all the donkey work, Suze.'

Suze looked satisfied at this, not being sober enough to feign modesty.

Sam brushed the crumbs off the sleeve of his shirt with a subtle flick of his hand. 'So Ollie's survived. The operation's over?'

'*Well,* the last few weeks have certainly been a bit quieter because of . . .' Suze hesitated as if she couldn't quite bear to say her name. '. . . Cecille.'

'The precocious French girl?' Sam brightened, looking around the room. 'Is she here?'

Suze laughed. 'No, Sam. Hopefully, she's going to be babysitting tonight.' She leaned towards Jenny. 'Now, hon, have you heard the latest on Cecille?'

Jenny shook her head. Something knotted in her stomach. Thinking about Cecille gave her a feeling much like bad indigestion.

'Our little *fille* has changed,' said Suze cryptically. 'Let me tell you.'

'Like how?' asked Jenny, fearing she was going to like this conversation less and less as it went on.

Sam raised an eyebrow. 'Go on.'

'Remember those sweet little sweaters and loafers she used to wear?' Suze paused for effect. 'Gone! She now wears mini skirts. Little T-shirts.' She pulled her silk blouse tight across her breasts to illustrate the point. Sam spluttered into his drink. 'There are even reports of a *tattoo*!'

'A tattoo!' Oh God. She had a vision of a terrifying *Maman* appearing at her door armed with a rolling pin to fish out her darling *fille*.

'There are also rumours of her going out and coming back rat-arsed.'

'Aren't French girls meant to sip half a glass of wine over a three-hour meal?' said Sam archly. 'I do like the sound of this Cecille, Jenny. You picked the right one after all.'

Jenny ignored him.

Suddenly Lydia popped out of the crush of partygoers like a cork. 'Hi! I'm Lydia.' She stuck her small, diamond-encrusted hand towards Sam.

'Delighted,' said Sam, shaking her hand. 'Another Help Ollie foot soldier?'

'Absolutely.' Lydia beamed. Jenny noticed how her neat breasts were contoured candidly by her pale pink pussy bow blouse. She noticed Sam noticing them too. It hit her that she, Jenny, would never wear pale pink. Only women who thought they were pretty wore pale pink.

'Jenny!' Liz was striding over now, legs kicking out of a green silk dress that contrasted with the punkish red tips of her hair. She reminded Jenny of a firework.

Jenny hugged her warmly. 'Love the dress.'

'Love the hair!'

Jenny patted the Sarah Palin up do. 'Can we not mention it, Liz? Misunderstanding in the salon.'

'Ah, one of those. I like it though.' Liz laughed, eyes

switching from hair to Sam. 'And you must be Sam? So we get you up to Muzzy Hill at last. We were all beginning to wonder if you even existed.'

Sam eyed Liz with obvious wariness, circumspect of any woman who dyed her hair a colour that wasn't pretending to be natural for the obvious benefit of the male gaze. 'Great minds, Liz. For all I knew the whole Help Ollie thing could have been one huge conceit cooked up by Jenny, and she was up here having a rendezvous with a mysterious lover,' he deadpanned.

Jenny tensed. Is that what he really thought? There was something hard in those blue eyes that suggested he wasn't entirely joking.

'So now you see,' said Liz, unruffled. 'It's quite the den of iniquity. Have you found the lover?'

'Oh, I will,' he smiled, giving Jenny a mock steely glance that made the hairs on her arms stand to attention.

Liz glanced quickly at Jenny as if to check her reaction, sensing the tension. 'You never know, Sam, you may end up moving here yet.'

Thank goodness Liz was more than a match for Sam at his most laconic. She wanted Sam to understand that he couldn't just write these mothers off as bovine suburbanites. That he'd got them all wrong.

'Oh, God, it'd be totally wonderful to have Jenny up here,' gushed Suze, slouching towards Sam drunkenly. 'Do you really think you might . . .'

'Hate to disappoint you, ladies,' Sam corrected, shooting the idea dead in its tracks and edging back from Suze's 'fro. 'More chance of us moving to Mogadishu.'

'That's what they all say,' said Liz, eyeing him somewhat combatively from behind her wine glass. She nudged Jenny gently in the ribs. 'Then you have kids.'

Sam looked away into the party. 'Guys, you're really selling it to me.'

Jenny felt a wave of indignation. Why couldn't he just play along? Why did he have to be so . . . so bloody *superior* all the time? She'd had to socialise with some of the dullest human beings on the planet at some of his friends' parties. She'd never complained. She'd smiled, she'd laughed, she'd done what partners are *supposed* to do.

'Oh. My. God. Congratulations!' squeaked Lydia, seizing the mention of kids as the logical entrée to the next step of conversation. 'How are the wedding plans? Tell us everything. I am a wedding fiend. Love it, love it, love it!'

Jenny studied the floor, remembering the awful conversation they'd had with Penelope this afternoon about her wedding dress, or lack of one.

'Coming along, coming along nicely,' said Sam, lifting himself off his toes for a moment in the manner of a TV policeman. 'Yeah, cool.'

Jenny felt relieved. She didn't want to wash their dirty linen in public either. 'Fine,' was all she added.

Lydia grabbed Jenny's hand. 'The dress!' She lowered her voice to a stagey whisper. 'Have you found the dress? Close your ears, Sam! Close your ears!'

'Yeah, well, almost.'

Sam shot her a dark look.

'Well, I want to be the *first* to know when you do.' She let out a loud, wine-fumed sigh. 'This is all *so* romantic,

Sam. None of us can quite get over it.' Her eyes started watering ominously.

Oh no, thought Jenny, looking helplessly at Liz. They both knew what the other was thinking. She's going to cry. Make her stop!

'Right,' said Sam, his eyes wandering around the room over Lydia's shoulder while somehow still keeping her as the focus of his attention. It was a look he'd perfected at industry dos, he'd once explained to Jenny, where over-shoulder-scanning was necessary if one wasn't to expire of boredom before ten pm. She wished he'd bloody well stop it.

'But a wedding between a divorce lawyer and a copy editor,' Suze grinned, pushing the 'fro off her face with her wine glass. 'I'll be looking out for the spelling mistakes in the order of service. And speeches lifted from the Net that might infringe copyright law.'

Sam laughed, properly now, the beer having finally loosened him. Jenny noticed his eyes alight on someone or something in the crowd. He shuffled his body, widened his chest, moved his legs further apart like compass points. Following his sight line over Lydia's shoulder, Jenny saw Tash trailing through the crowds in a long gauzy leopard print dress with a neckline cut so far south it should come with its own passport, liquorice hair swooshing around her shoulders, tanned legs appearing in tantalising slivers through the slit in her dress. To Jenny, used to the little black high street dress and smudged-mascara-behind-specs look of her publishing parties, Tash's glamour was alien and dazzlingly retro –

'Hey, Jenny,' said Tash, almost bashful, as if unable to

decide on how much to give away by her greeting. Yes, thought Jenny, actually I *do* know you had lunch with my fiancé. You should have mentioned it.

'Hello.' Sam became aware of the others studying him, waiting for an explanation as to why an introduction wasn't necessary. 'We've met,' he said, matter of factly.

'*Really?*' exclaimed Suze, frowning, trying to work out how this extraordinary detail had escaped her. 'You've met? You and Tash?'

'We've met,' Tash confirmed breezily, kissing Sam on the cheek. Jenny stiffened.

'So how's it all going, Natasha?' Sam asked in a business-like manner, designed to quell the palpable waves of intrigue radiating from Suze, Lydia and Liz.

It didn't quell anything. He'd called her Natasha. Most interesting.

'Can I thank you for lending me your clever legal-head fiancé, Jenny?' said Tash, resting her hand lightly on her arm.

'Anytime,' said Jenny, not intending to sound so clipped. She suddenly wished she'd worn something racier, rather than the navy Reiss shift. Sophie would have got her to wear the sequin dress. Or something with a slit. Yes, she would buy a dress with a slit.

Tash surveyed the room and frowned. 'No Ollie then?'

'Not yet, no,' said Liz. 'Sadly.'

'Told you he wouldn't come.'

'Give him time, give him time,' slurred Suze.

'Cecille's probably grounded him,' quipped Liz.

'Ladies, ladies.' A man appeared dressed in high-waisted

jeans and a black blazer. He put his arms around Lydia's waist. 'This is my husband, George,' said Lydia wearyingly, as if referring to a pesky child who should be in bed. 'George, this is the wonderful Jenny. Soph's best mate. And Sam, her fiancé.'

George nodded, displaying a shop front of bad dentistry. 'Good to put faces to the names at last.' He turned to Suze. 'Trust you're not getting Lydia waywardly drunk again? You must bust your annual alcohol units each time you meet to debate who's going to feed Ollie's cat.'

'*George!*' hissed Lydia, giving him a sharp look. 'Sorry, ladies.'

'Evidently you lot need to find yourself a new widower and fast,' quipped Sam. George roared with laughter, making his belly shake above his brown leather belt.

'So cynical, Sam,' purred Tash, looking at him indulgently. 'Even for a lawyer.'

George turned to Sam. 'You realise, don't you . . .' There was a moment of awkwardness when it became clear that George had forgotten his name already.

'Sam,' Sam said, picking up on it. 'Jenny's sidekick.'

'. . . that we have no hope of competing with a young, handsome widower.'

Sam grinned, clearly warming to the bumptious George. 'I do realise this, George, yes.'

Jenny frowned. She hoped Sam wasn't going to run with this one – he enjoyed running with anything with the whiff of bad taste. He could be a liability at a party.

'How can you two joke so lightly about something so tragic?' blurted Lydia, all her anger directed at her husband.

There was a moment's uncomfortable silence in which everyone cleared their throats. 'Well you gotta laugh or cry, eh?' George said, putting an arm over Lydia's shoulder. 'I know what Sophie would have preferred.'

Lydia shrugged the arm off, picked half a bottle of wine off the sideboard and sloppily poured herself a glass so that it spilled over the sides and on to the wooden floor.

'Easy, sweetheart,' George muttered under his breath.

'It's a fucking party,' Lydia replied through teeth so close she looked like a ventriloquist. 'Piss off.'

George switched his attention from his wife to Sam. 'I haven't seen you around, mate. Are you a member of the class of 2B mafia? Do you have kids at the school, too?'

'No, no kids,' said Sam with a tight smile.

Jenny looked away. Why was she finding it harder and harder trying to imagine them with kids? Sam bottle feeding the baby, changing its nappy, the muddy wellie boots and scooters in their pristine hall. No, impossible to visualise.

'But they're getting married this summer,' said Suze, as if to explain the improbable scenario of her guests being childless. 'The patter of tiny feet can't be far off.'

'I fully recommend just the one,' George said.

Lydia shot him a gladiatorial glare. Clearly she didn't see the joke.

'No more?' smiled Suze, not picking up on the hissing signals of impending marital implosion. 'Go on, just one more, Lydia.'

'I would,' said Lydia murderously, in a voice so low it was barely audible. 'George isn't so keen.'

'I'm too old for this game. We've been tired since 2004, haven't we, Lyds?' said George affectionately.

'God, that's nothing. I've been tired since 2003,' said Liz cheerfully, gulping back her wine. 'You get used to it after a while. It becomes the norm. In fact I think I'd feel weird if I wasn't tired.'

'True, true. It's a question of surrender. You know what? I realised the other day that I hadn't actually bought a CD since I had my first,' marvelled Suze, as if this was something to be proud of. 'I've never downloaded anything from iTunes. And, excuse me, but what the hell is an *app*? Is it a new erogenous zone?' She howled with laughter. 'Check out the app on me.'

Jenny could sense Sam stiffen. Poor Sam. The evening was turning out exactly as he'd feared. She felt a wave of affection and sympathy for him. A fish out of water, what on earth was she thinking, dragging him up here?

Tash glanced at her watch. 'I wonder if I should call Ollie?'

'No need! Look!' Suze let out a joyful yelp, grabbed Jenny's arm and pointed to a shadow behind the bay window. 'I told you he wouldn't flake it!'

Twenty-nine

I escort Ollie to Suze's front door, what remains of me wound tight around his left wrist like a watchstrap, as needy and nervous as a mother taking her son to a first play date. This is the first party he's been to since I died. Dead proud, I am.

If I'd been widowed I'd have a face like Keith Richards sucking a hornet, but Ollie's just slimmer and hairier and greyer. Nothing diminishes his cuteness. Tonight he's wearing the shoes I bought him for his birthday last year, chunky brogue boots hiding an endearing odd match of socks. His white (ironed) boxers peek over the top of his belted jeans when he bends over to tie a loose lace. He's still got the world's sexist ass.

The door blasts open. It is Posh Brigid, barefoot in a fluoro lime green dress. She is squealing. 'Ollie!' She thrusts his head down on her glitter-dusted décolletage. Then, gripping his hand as if he were a little boy who might just run off in the other direction if she didn't, she pulls Ollie into the thrum of the party.

Inside the house we hit a bank of alcohol fumes. A scrum

of noise – voices, glasses, music – bashes about the room. Then Ollie is spotted. There's an immediate deathly hush.

Panic streaks across Ollie's dark, beautiful eyes. Spotting Jenny and Suze he staggers through the crowds towards them, leaving a disappointed open-mouthed Brigid in his wake. As he moves through the party, the crowds part. A laying on of hands. Men reach out to touch his arm lightly in a supportive brotherly way, while women go straight for the exposed flesh, fingers or cheek.

Ollie finally arrives at his destination. Sam claps him on the back. He does it with too much force. Sam gabbles a sheepish apology for not visiting and Ollie tells him not to worry about it. Apology and forgiveness out of the way, Sam hands Ollie a beer. Ollie drinks. He finishes the beer in minutes, doing his best to appear cheerful, as if cheerfulness itself is a defence against those who will ask any question just to sample the pitch of grief's rawest notes.

I use the opportunity of being this close to Sam to try and read him. I buzz around his smooth, shaven head. I peek down into the glacial-blue eyes but see nothing but a small white ring of what could be a cholesterol deposit. He is looking at Tash. He is not looking at Jenny. Has he not actually noticed how damn gorgeous Jenny looks tonight?

Her hair is lovely. I like it piled like that. Those green cone heels rock. The navy dress is, well, navy – should have worn the sequin one! – but she looks so very pretty, even if there is a microscopic muscle on her left eyelid flickering in spasm.

I shift my attention to my beloved. He's on white wine now, always a bad idea. And he gets more moody-looking with every refill. Is he really ready for his first party? Suddenly not sure now, not sure at all. I'm worried.

Someone else is drinking too much as well, I see. Lydia. Swaying beneath a potted palm like a woman on an inflatable boat, she is staring at Ollie so intensely that even Ollie has noticed. Just as well George is in the kitchen debating whether Steve Coogan is funnier than Stewart Lee with a drunk Danish man wearing a Trilby.

Oh no, here comes dear old George, looking for the wife. His belly arrives ahead of him, bumping into people obliviously, like someone carrying a rucksack on a crowded Tube.

'You OK?' He slides his hand around Lydia's slim waist.

She steps aside and the hand slips down to the small of her back, then off.

'What's the matter?'

Lydia sways on her heels. 'Nuffink.'

'You must be dead tired from Flora waking up last night.' He strokes her cheek. 'Darling, she's got to learn to take herself to the toilet. You can't be getting up night after night.'

'It's not that.' Her bleary eyes are still focused on one person and one person alone and it's not her husband. George follows her gaze.

'Why are you staring like that?' Insecurity makes George's voice higher than normal. A muscle clenches in his jaw.

Lydia continues staring with what can only be described as *longing* at Ollie, who is chatting to Tash and Jenny now and refusing the figs wrapped in Parma ham. He's never going to be a canapé kind of man.

'You're drunk, Lyds.'

'Oh God, like who cares?'

'And you're being kind of embarrassing.'

'Yeah? And you're being ridiculous.'

Wonder if in fact he is being ridiculous. Wondering if Lydia is at least thinking of elbowing her way on to Ollie's new wife list, ignoring the minor impediment of being married already.

'Lydia, stop fucking staring at Ollie!' George is cuckold red now.

Lydia shrugs, as if she doesn't give a shit. And she doesn't. Yes, she's really drunk. Fear this cannot end prettily.

'What's this about?'

'You're boring, George. Please stop going on.'

'Or is it so obvious that I've refused to see it?'

She turns round fiercely. 'What's so flipping obvious, George? That Ollie has made me *think*, think hard about things that matter.' Her pale pink pussy bow blouse trembles.

'Now you sound totally adolescent.'

'We have one life, George. *One!*'

He snorts. 'It's taken you this long to work it out?'

'Our relationship. It could be the only one we'll ever know! It could be . . . be . . . this then death! I thought my life would be . . .' She wrings her hands together. '. . . bigger somehow.'

George sighs wearily. 'Do you think you'll ever reach your limit for drama and self-obsession, Lydia?'

Lydia's bottom lip wobbles and I feel sorry for both of them. I think of all the times I've seen Lydia and George at parties or PTA meetings and outside the school gates, and how I've always thought they were an odd couple but a happy one, and that it is nice when two different people come together to prove to the world that you don't have to be samey – me and Ollie are a bit samey – to have a good marriage. Has my dying not only smashed a hole in my own family, but punched small holes in the glasshouses of other people's marriages too?

With a loud sniff Lydia turns on her gold heel and storms towards the toilet, leaving a bewildered George standing with his hands fisted at his sides in impotent fury, trying to look like nothing has happened.

Everyone at the party knows that something has happened, of course. Tash and Liz's eyebrows are question marks. Ribs are elbowed.

When Lydia emerges from the toilet she is tear-streak-free, pink lippy on. The pussy bow has been smartly rearranged. She smiles at George, a cold, hard smile that doesn't crease her eyes, but refuses to talk to him and the party continues apace. When George takes a call on his mobile then announces that Flora has been sick and he's going to go back to take over from the babysitter, a cross stitch of knowing looks threads across the party. The main show over, I settle on to Suze's mantelpiece, sliding between the wedding pictures and children's piano certificates, thoroughly exhausted. I am no longer the life and soul of the party.

Ever gone to a party and not drunk while those around you get plastered? Being dead is a bit like that. Being dead at a party is even more like that. I try not to dwell on the aching sadness that *I* am not on Ollie's arm, or fall into the memory trap of Parties Past. Like the warehouse party in Hoxton in 1995 when we actually got stuck in the building's industrial lift for two hours, and when the thing finally juddered to the top floor we were caught on the job by a whooping huddle of partygoers. Or the dinner parties we threw when we lived in Peckham, when the words dinner party seemed so ironic and hilarious and everyone put on their most glam seventies Halston-style dresses from Oxfam and the only thing I knew how to make was chicken curry with Pataks paste. Or indeed our wedding party, where I shook and whirled my dress to our very own hired Elvis while my girlfriends clapped me in a circle and I felt like the luckiest woman alive. Anyway, that stuff.

The party crackle rises and falls around me. The alcohol fumes get stronger and stronger, the body heat turns the air pink, and there is a smell of BO that can no longer be masked by Suze's scented candles. So I take a mini break around the house to get some air. After gliding upstairs on a thermal of body heat, I gaze longingly at Suze's children asleep angelically in their beds. They make me pine for Freddie. Quibble the hamster freezes with fear as I pass. He is so still I worry that I've brought on cardiac arrest, then, thankfully, he scuttles back into his hay nest. I have a good nose around Suze's bedroom. (A Rampant Rabbit in Suze's sock drawer! Suze, who knew?) I am touched by the fact that she and Chris sleep on two pillows embroidered, albeit slightly cheesily, with the word LOVE and their names. And it makes me realise how the unsexiest couples can be the ones most happily humping away. There is a certain majesty in a solid middle-aged marriage, no? We value youth and passion, but perhaps it's here, among the grey pubes and middle-aged spread and loose pelvic floors, that the real romance exists, having been tested to the point of exhaustion.

Moving on. Into the bathroom. Posh Brigid is texting somebody while sitting on the loo. Even though there is a sign saying 'only loo paper please!' she flushes her Tampax down the toilet. The woman after her – Sara, upholsterer to the stars, once did three pink PVC chairs for Meg Mathews – riffles through Suze's bathroom cabinet and borrows Suze's mascara. (Brave. Suze's family is blighted by recurrent conjunctivitis.) Another woman borrows her deodorant. (Rather her than me.) And Adam Cross from number thirty-five is sick in the toilet, leaving the tap running to hide the noise of the retching while another woman waits impatiently outside, crossing her legs tightly.

Out through the fan in the bathroom window, sliding between its blades like someone in a revolving door. Outside the fresh air is cool, luxurious, like a waterfall frothing down a rock. There is the peaty smell of barbecues. The social smokers puff away, united by a feeling of contraband naughtiness. When they come back into the party they carry the tang of tobacco in their hair. As everyone gets drunker, the sensible school gossip burns away and is replaced by the hot fumes of bawdiness, bad jokes, drunken confessions of how they voted Tory for the first time in the last election, and crushes on tennis coaches and other parents. And, of course, outrageous flirtation.

Suze has unbuttoned her blouse so that her Grand Canyon cleavage is on show. Every time she laughs it undulates. (Middle-aged romance or not, kind of wishing I didn't know

229

about the Rabbit now. Not sure I will see her in the same light ever again.) Pete from four doors down has a hand on the romper-suit-clad bottom of the hot New Zealand single mum, Zara. Someone has found the courage to skin up a spliff in the kitchen. Tash is zig-zagging round the party making An Impression: she is one of those women for whom a good time means feeling like the hottest female at the party. Fear I might once have been a *little* like this myself.

Jenny and Ollie are locked in deep conversation, which is hard to make out over the rolling noise of the party. She is wearing her intense listening face, head cocked at an angle, saying very little. She's one of the few people who genuinely want to hear what you say, as opposed to those people who are merely looking for an opportunity to slide their views into the gaps in the conversation.

Oh, what's happening? Jenny is looking down at the floor. She is shifting from foot to foot. She looks sad all of a sudden. Ollie is putting down his drink on the fireplace, picking up his jacket to leave.

Suze spots the dissent immediately and strides over so purposefully her cheeks wobble like jellies. 'You're not going?'

'Yeah, going to call it a night, Suze,' he says.

'Very wise. I'd make your escape now before she pins you to the sofa with a cocktail stick,' says Liz.

Ollie slips on his jacket. 'Thanks. It's been great.'

'Has it *really*?' Suze wants more. She wants more juice, more reaffirmation of her own social ability to lift the grief-struck widower from the tear-sodden depths of his misery.

Ollie just wants out. He's the kind of person who would rather slip away without saying goodbye at the best of times.

There is movement in the hall. Suze swivels, eyes widening. 'You're not going too, are you, Lydia?'

Lydia is in her white fake fur bolero, still swaying. 'George has gone already. I'll walk back with Ollie.'

'He'll have to carry you at this rate,' says Jenny, looking none too pleased at this idea.

Lydia hiccups. Then, suddenly, out of nowhere, Tash is galloping towards them, a fluttering vision in silk leopard print, breathing heavily through her nose like a horse. 'But I thought *we* were walking back together later, Lydia?'

'Oh, sorry, Tash,' Lydia says, not sounding sorry at all. She hiccups again. 'I need to check on Flora.'

'Well, maybe I should call it a night, too.'

Suze grabs Tash around the waist. 'You are not going anywhere, lady! It's only eleven-thirty. It's socially unacceptable to leave a party before midnight.'

'But . . .'

'And, missy, I know that Ludo is at his dad's, so you haven't got the babysitter excuse either.'

Check mate. Tash is stuck. She doesn't look happy about it.

Outside a soupy summer fog is licking the pavements clean. Lydia slips her arm through Ollie's and leans against him. Seeing them walking together like that, two dark figures in the mythic romance of summer mist, I splutter like a redundant old lawn mower. They look pretty together, no denying it, Lydia all fluffy and bundled up, a babe in the woods in that bolero; Ollie's hair long and damp with fog, his walk drunken and laid back, his boots dragging on the slippery pavement like a cowboy's.

I must stop.

This is Lydia we're talking about, sweet little Lydia. Lydia, who learned how to make lasagne especially for Ollie. Lydia, who sobbed throughout my funeral and still cries herself to sleep about me. Lydia, who has spent three hundred pounds on bereavement kitchenware. I cannot blame her when she leans her body more and more to the left. When she rests her blond head against Ollie's shoulder. When she tells him he is 'a total inspiration'. Can I?

We get to the door of number thirty-three. Lydia lives about two hundred yards away. They hesitate. Ollie says to Lydia, 'I'll walk you to your door.'

'Can't I come in?'

'Come in?'

'Yes. I'd kill for a quick cup of tea. If I go home I'll wake up George.'

'Oh, right.'

Right!

They walk down the paved path, and as they walk, Lydia moves closer and closer to him, as if she wants to dive into him like a sleeping bag. By the time his key is in the lock the toe of her boot is scuffing against the heel of his, her hand on his back. He turns the key, knocks the door fully open with his knee. They are in the hall. They don't get any further.

Lydia starts to sob.

'Lydia?' he says, aghast.

'I'm so sorry, Ollie, crying like this.'

'What is it, Lydia?' The tenderness of his voice fills me with longing. He always was the world's best shoulder to cry on.

'George.'

Ollie frowns. His face is full of shadow. His unease taps out a rhythm through his foot.

'It's gone wrong, Ollie. Wrong between me and George.'

'What's happened?'

'It sounds weird . . .'

'Go on.'

She takes a deep, wobbly breath. 'He doesn't love me like how you loved Sophie. And now I've realised it I can't unrealise it and it's completely doing my head in.'

There is a whirring silence. A smile twitches at the corners of Ollie's mouth, like he's trying not to laugh. 'Hey, you just need to sleep it off. Let's get you home, honey, come on.'

'No. I'm going to pull myself together and we're going to have that cup of tea,' Lydia says firmly. She lets go of his arm and staggers into the kitchen, tripping over Freddie's football boots that he's left in the middle of the hall. When they are both in the kitchen she closes the door behind her, leans against it and giggles coquettishly. 'Don't want to wake Freddie.'

It takes Ollie four minutes to find the teabags.

'Sit next to me.' She pats the chair next to hers.

Ollie sits obediently. The tea is forgotten.

For a moment Lydia appears relatively normal and sober. 'I can't bear this any longer.' She starts to cry.

'Oh, Lydia, don't cry.'

'I could leave him.' Her head falls against Ollie's shoulder.

'All marriages are hilly.'

'Yours wasn't.'

Ollie pulls at his beard. For the first time, I really don't know what he's thinking.

'Men like you know how to love a woman properly.'

Ollie laughs then, really laughs, like this is the funniest thing he's heard in years.

Lydia stops laughing abruptly. The lids of her eyes lower. 'I'd leave George for you, Ollie.'

Ollie starts away from her. There's a terrible silence. The little red light on the smoke alarm is beginning to flash. 'You've had a lot to drink. Come on, sweetheart, I'll take you home.'

Lydia wipes the tears from her eyes. 'I wouldn't expect to take Sophie's place, I really wouldn't . . .'

Ollie's eyes are filling with tears now. And I don't know whether this is because he fancies Lydia or because he misses me or because he hasn't held a woman in his arms for so long. He puts one finger very softly on Lydia's mouth. 'Shush.'

I didn't expect this. The finger on the lips thing. I didn't expect it at all.

Oh fuck. It's going to happen. It is going to happen. Lydia tilts her face towards him and closes those lovely green eyes. The smoke alarm is flashing wildly now.

Then I hear footsteps. The shiny orb of the kitchen door handle is rotating slowly in the gloom.

'Ollie?' The kitchen door flings open. Cecille stands there in her short satin dressing gown, hands on her hips. 'Iz everything OK?'

Thirty

Unsettled by the near-miss kiss, I helicopter off, moving directly up and out, and spend the night in the wonderful peaty wetness of Queen's Wood, only coming back home as the streets begin to smell of cooking bacon and lumps of Sunday newspapers thump on to doormats. And who do I see? I see Jenny, hiking up the road, slipping backwards in her sandals up the hill, carrying her swim bag. She hesitates outside Ollie's door and takes a deep breath, as if summoning courage for something that is not just municipal swimming.

'Jenny!' Freddie barrels into her arms. He is already wearing his red swimming goggles. 'You going to walk upside down today?'

'No chance!' She kneels down and peers directly into his goggles, as if looking through a telescope. 'I've had my hair tinted. I don't want to look like Shrek again.'

'Smoky bacon?' The highlight of any swimming trip for Freddie has always been putting coins in the vending machine, watching the spirals rotate and that shiny packet of Walkers falling magically into the black tray.

'If you swim a length.'

Ollie steps out of the kitchen into the hall, stifling a yawn. His face lights up when he sees her. 'You look criminally well after the party last night.'

'Croissants and Nurofen.'

Ollie tussles his floppy dark hair, runs his finger through his bison beard. He looks like he hasn't slept. 'Come on, coffee.' He pulls her by the hand towards the kitchen.

'Allo,' interrupts Cecille.

How long has Cecille been standing on the stairs? She wears a navy silk dressing gown that gapes open over her pert décolletage. The same one she wore last night. The one that foiled the near-miss kiss. I think I owe this dressing gown.

'Morning, Cecille,' says Jenny, trying and failing not to stare at the décolletage. 'How are you?'

'Very, very well.' Cecille flicks her eyes coquettishly at Ollie, head poised, one hand on the banister in a cinematic manner.

Freddie is pulling on Jenny's hand. 'Come on, Jenny, let's go. Let's go swimming.'

'OK.'

'What about coffee?' Ollie looks disappointed.

'Best to beat the crowds,' Jenny says quickly.

'Oh.' Ollie rubs his eyes. 'I'm going back to bed then.'

'I cook fry-up first,' purrs Cecille, pulling the belt tight on her dressing gown, showing off her slim waist.

He grins. 'Cecille, you're an angel.'

Whoa! Who's the angel here?

'Have a good breakfast,' Jenny says tightly, as she rushes out of the house with Freddie, a great spume of emotion trailing behind her, thick and white as an aeroplane trail. I get caught up in its tailwind, spun in its vortex as we hurtle towards the door, and I am sucked in, in, inwards into Jenny. Suddenly I'm somewhere very red, pulsating. It's like being inside a small red tent at dawn. Ba boom ba boom. It's a heart alright. And I tell you what, Sam isn't in it.

Thirty-one

The rap on the car window made her jump.

Jenny squinted into the dirty Camden sunshine. The first thing she saw was the hand. A tiny dolphin tattoo on the wrist. Her eyes zipped from hand to face, a beautiful face wearing large white sunglasses. She froze. It was the woman from the white Fiat, the one who looked like Sophie but seen up close was patently *not* Sophie. She had the same thick dark hair. The same oval-shaped face. But she was most definitely not Sophie. Well, of course she wasn't.

'Sorry, I didn't mean to startle you,' the woman was saying. She had a soft, lilting voice, well spoken.

Jenny opened the car door warily, heart starting to pound. 'Can I help you?'

The woman's eyes glittered. 'I hope so,' she said, sounding just a little bit crazed. 'I do hope so.'

Oh God, a nut. Camden was full of them. She'd got a nut on her tail. A nut who looked like Sophie. Wanting to get away, she got out of the car and locked the door, in case the nut was hoping to nick the car. She conceded that the woman was a surprisingly well-turned-out nut. Maybe it was someone normal who had had a breakdown? Someone who'd bought lots of nice clothes before she lost the plot. 'Excuse me,' she said in her polite nut-avoidant voice, stepping past her to the sunny pavement and edging closer to the safety of her flat.

'I just need to talk to you, if you don't mind.' The woman began walking next to her.

Jenny felt properly uncomfortable now. What did this woman want from her?

She put a hand on Jenny's arm. 'Please, Sophie.'

The blood drained from her head. It took a few moments to collect herself. 'What? What did you just call me?'

'Your name is Sophie, isn't it?' The woman squinted in the sunlight, less sure now.

'No, no it isn't.'

The woman looked puzzled. 'Really? Sorry. I . . . I . . .'

'Why did you think I was called Sophie?'

The woman looked down at the ground. 'I got confused.' She stopped, looked up, her brown eyes panicky. 'It's just, Sam,' she blurted. 'I know Sam. There was something . . .'

Jenny's stomach knotted. 'Sam?'

The woman narrowed her eyes. 'You're his girlfriend?'

Jenny didn't answer immediately, not taking her eyes off the woman's face. 'Fiancée.'

'Fiancée?' The woman's face fell. She started walking backwards. 'Right, right.'

'Wait! Why do you want to know? Hang on a minute,' Jenny called out as the woman turned on her blue heel and started to walk away, glossy dark hair swinging behind her.

Thirty-two

'She looks like Sophie?' Sam exhaled tusks of smoke from his nostrils. It scarved up towards the speaker in the ceiling, trembled by the bass of the Kaiser Chiefs.

'A dead ringer.' Jenny sat on the cold black granite worktop. For a moment she felt like she was perching on the edge of a building, ready to jump off.

'Don't be weird, babes. Sounds like a Camden loon to me.' He flicked his ash into his favourite fifties blue glass ashtray.

'Sam, she thought my name was *Sophie*. How freaky is that?' She leapt off the worktop. 'She said she knew you.'

She noticed that he'd paled a little beneath his weekend stubble. Aware of her scrutinising him, he turned and started fiddling with a foil packet of coffee, letting his cigarette burn down. 'I told you, babes, you need to chill out.'

'I am chilled out!' she gabbled, spitting in an unladylike fashion across the kitchen. 'Sam, she asked if my name was Sophie. Why would she ask that?'

He picked up his fag, shifted behind a veil of smoke, glancing up at her sideways. 'A white Fiat, you say?'

'A white Fiat. And she had a tattoo!' she said, suddenly

remembering. 'A little dolphin on her wrist, poking out from under her watchstrap.' He closed his eyes and pinched the skin at the top of his nose very tightly. 'You know who it is, don't you? You do. Tell me.'

'Dominique.'

'And who the hell is *Dominique?*'

Sam drew his hands across his jaw, as if even the memory of her exhausted him. 'She always was a bit Looney Tunes.'

'You've never mentioned her before!'

Sam crossed his arms. 'Haven't I? Well, I guess I wouldn't. It was no big deal.'

OK, she had never been one of those women who demanded a detailed biography and score out of ten for every ex. But still. Who the hell was Dominique? And what would he give her out of ten?

'It was before you. Obviously.'

'When?'

'I can't give you the precise calendar dates, I'm afraid.'

'When, Sam?' She was shaking now.

He reached for her hand. 'Look, Jenny, there were quite a few women before you. I've never pretended there weren't.'

'So she was a fling, just a fling?'

He nodded. 'A fling.'

She looked away from him, eyes blurring with tears. 'I suspect you meant more to her.'

'Come on, darling. We're getting married in a few weeks. Let's forget about the past.' He touched her jaw lightly, drawing her towards him. 'I love you. You have no reason to worry about other women.' He put her hand to his lips and kissed it. 'Don't get in such a blimmin' flap about everything.'

241

'But why did she think I was called Sophie?' She couldn't let this one go, she just couldn't.

'Maybe she got confused?' Giving up on the bodily contact approach, he spooned some coffee beans into the grinder and flicked the switch. 'Sophie is a common enough name.'

She leaned back against the wall, spent. She was no longer sure of anything. The grinder sounded like her own brain, reducing all certainties to pulp. They were silent for a few moments while he made coffee. She watched him and wondered.

'Hey, what do you reckon about Mum's idea of having the local brass band welcome people into the marquee from the church?' he said, pouring the coffee into two little cups.

'What?' She could still see Dominique, those intense brown eyes peering in through her car window, searching for answers in her own face.

'A brass band.'

'God, I don't know.'

'I like a brass band.'

'I hate brass bands.'

'You'd make Mum very happy if you said yes. Here you go. Coffee.'

'I don't want coffee.'

'OK, I get the mood you're in. I won't mention Mum's Morris Dancing suggestion.'

'Please don't.'

He took a sip, winced slightly. 'Mum was also asking about the wedding dress.'

'Sam, she gave me a hard time about it last month,' she

said, remembering the dreadful meeting, the day of Suze's party. 'I don't need it again. I will get the wedding dress. I'm not going to walk down the aisle naked.'

'Shame.' He smiled. 'Actually, sweetheart, she's asked me to ask you whether you want her to go shopping with you. For the dress.'

'No!' She caught herself, took a deep breath. 'Sorry, that's very kind of her, but no.'

'I'm trying to be understanding here.' He put his coffee cup down, eyes flashing dangerously blue. 'But are you waiting for Sophie to reappear and go shopping with you or something?'

Maybe she was. Maybe that's what it was.

'Babes, it ain't going to happen.'

'I'll get it soon,' she said tightly.

'I think everyone would feel better if you did.' He pulled a strand of hair off her face and tucked it behind her ear. His fingers smelled of Marlboro Lights. She didn't like it. 'By the way, Mum and Dad are coming over for brunch on Sunday. Perhaps you could think what kind of food we need to get in? Mackerel? I rather like a bit of mackerel of a morning.'

'I take Freddie swimming on Sunday mornings.' She hated mackerel. She struggled with oily fish. They were oily.

Sam stirred more sugar into his coffee with an angry vigour. 'Maybe Ollie could take his own kid swimming now?'

'It's our thing.'

He looked up. 'Is that wise?'

'What do you mean, *wise*?'

'Freddie's getting attached to you, Jenny.' His voice became soft and remedial. 'Look, I know you've pulled back from Ollie a bit since Cecille arrived.' He threw back his head and drained his cup. 'But not really from Freddie.'

'Of course I haven't bloody well pulled back from Freddie!'

'You're not going to be able to continue being as hands-on as you have been, are you? Not when we're married.'

'I don't see what difference me being married makes. I'm there for as long as he needs me, Sam.'

Something hardened in his eyes. 'Then it's a life sentence.'

She stared at him in disbelief. 'I *love* Freddie, Sam. Don't you get it? I love him because he's lovable, but also because he's Sophie's boy. I will always be there for him. And I don't care if that's a life sentence. I bloody well hope it will be.'

Sam broke off a corner of a bagel left over from breakfast and took a bite, chucked the rest of it on the side, never taking his eyes off her face. It was funny the way he was looking at her. 'You'll feel different when you have your own kids, that's what Mum says.'

'I don't see it's any of her business.'

He didn't speak for a very long time. 'This is about Ollie, isn't it?'

'No!' How to explain that whenever Ollie was in the room, the room seemed brighter? That was all it was.

'The Hugh Hefner of N10.'

'Don't be ridiculous.'

A vein pulsed on his temple. 'Did you ever think about how it made me look at that terrible party you cattle-prodded me into going to, when you were locked in deep, whispery conversation with Ollie and I'm standing there like a bloody eejit . . .'

She spoke carefully. 'I was just aware that it was his first party without Soph. I wanted to make sure he was OK.'

He turned to face her and she felt pinned by his gaze, like it had skewered her there. 'Is there something you want to tell me?'

She closed her eyes. If she kept them shut maybe this would all go away. But Sam was still there when she opened them. Yes, yes, she knew that beneath the bluster Sam was hurting, jealous even, and that she should be doing more to placate him, convince him that Ollie meant nothing and that she was all Sam's, heart, soul, body, forever and ever. Why wasn't she? Couldn't she?

She squeezed her eyes shut again and saw a flicker book of images on the black of her lids: Sophie's gummy smile; Sophie throwing her head back doing The Honk; her crooked body lying in the road: her yellow knickers; Dominique's dolphin tattoo; Sam tearing off a bit of bagel, looking at her in a way he had never looked at her before. She couldn't process any of it. It was all part of a strange algorithm she didn't understand. 'I'm taking a shower.'

She stripped off her clothes and gazed at her naked body in the mirror – in the unflattering bathroom lighting she looked pale, soggy and fleshy, rather like a scallop – then got into the shower, turning it to its hottest so that it was on the very threshold of burning her skin. She stood there for an hour, the hot water pouring down her head, over her eyes, into her ears, trying to wash it all away.

When she re-emerged, Sam had gone out. Thank goodness. She peered out of the window, took three deep yogic breaths, which made her feel slightly dizzy. Jolted by a hoot from the street below, she opened her eyes to see some school children pointing up at her and laughing. She was still wrapped in a bath towel! She fled to the sofa and stared blankly into the spotless, expensively furnished sitting room, Sam's coffee cup still on the side, his cigarette stub in the ashtray. Her skin was cool now, hair frizzing at the ends as it dried. Traffic rumbled outside, the kitchen tap dripped, and for a powerful, lucid moment she felt like her life was unravelling, there and then, unspooling like loo paper rolling across the American walnut floor. Soon it would be everywhere, sheets and sheets of it, blown about by the wind. And as it was impossible to roll loo paper back neatly on to its cardboard tube, it would be impossible to put her life back as it was, too.

If she went on like this Sam would dump her. After being engaged for so long, to lose him now would be like queuing all night on the pavement to buy a ticket to Wimbledon's centre court, only to turn around and go home the moment her name was called. Yes, he'd dump her. Or, just as bad, no, worse, he'd nuke her friendship with Ollie, impose some kind of Ollie purdah. Then she wouldn't see Freddie either. Oh God. Unimaginable. She needed to do something, something persuasive, placating and symbolic.

And fast.

Thirty-three

Four days later, Jenny stood anxiously, shifting from the sweaty insole of one tan gladiator sandal to the other on Tottenham Court Road, rather doubting her flash of genius. Could this really be the solution to the Ollie versus Sam problem? The bridge across the boiling waters? Well, she hadn't had any better ideas. And she needed to move on. She needed to stop thinking about the letters she'd discovered in Sophie's drawer. Stop thinking about Dominique. Ollie. The entire bad-thought disco in her head. Sam was right. She needed to chill right out. Grief had knocked her off course. It was time to get back on track. This was a start.

Twelve-thirty. Jenny checked her phone in case he'd sent a message. Nothing. Maybe he'd blown her out. She'd pretty much forced him into it, after all, flexed the power of bridal entitlement like a bicep. She would give him five more minutes. Two more. One more, just in case. Until the lights changed. The pavement began to swell with office workers on their lunch break. Although it was blustery, it was hot, making her grateful that she'd slathered on the deodorant as well as having got herself fully waxed and plucked. Today,

247

special reinforcements would be necessary. One more light change.

Just as she turned to go, defeated, there he was, waving, walking up the street in a slim-cut black suit, white trainers, his floppy dark hair alive in the wind, more vivid than anyone else, like he was in high definition colour and everyone else was in black and white. I'm always going to remember this moment, him walking up the street in his black suit. I'm going to remember it forever, she thought.

She kept her thoughts to herself.

'Am I late?'

'I was just early,' she said, even though he was late.

As they started to walk down Oxford Street, Jenny became very aware of the wind, of the way it was blowing her blue dress flat against her body, showing everything, bust, belly, swell of pubic bone.

'Pretty dress,' Ollie said, giving her a sidelong glance.

She swung her big handbag over her torso shyly. 'Thanks.'

'I've brought supplies.' He rummaged in his trouser pocket and pulled out a packet of Haribo. 'I'd have brought harder drugs but I fear your disapproval.'

Jenny laughed. 'I can't believe I'm making you do this.'

'Nor can I.'

She'd already told him why she'd asked. It was quite simple. Easy to explain. He was here because Sophie wasn't. That was the reason. He understood that. She understood that. By taking Ollie wedding dress shopping she was placing him firmly in the role of Gay Best Friend. This would clarify the relationship for all of them and stop her life unspooling. He could be gay! He could be gay and musical and sexy, like

Rufus Wainwright. They must all completely forget that he was heterosexual.

Selfridges. Ollie pushed open the heavy glass doors, stood aside to let her through into the hungry scrum of the handbag department – who were all these women feeling so rich in the middle of a recession? – before they jostled their way towards the huge escalators that cut through the fabric of the building like a giant zipper. Jenny held on tightly to the rubber handrail. She hadn't been to a big department store since Soph died. The glass, the chrome, the lights and noise were overwhelming. As if sensing her discomfort, Ollie put his hand on the small of her back. It burned a palm shape through the thin cotton of her dress.

He leaned over her from the step below, resting his chin on her shoulder. 'Now, so I know, Jen, are we going white or off-white or something more radical?'

'Off-white. A lady at John Lewis said it was softer on the "mature bride's complexion".' His mouth was centimetres from hers. He was too close. She moved up a step on the escalator.

'She actually said that? I'm scared now.' He smiled at her. 'But do *you* want off-white?'

'I don't know what I want. And I should warn you now that I have to battle my inner Dolly Parton, Ollie. I'm always drawn to the most hideous dress in the shop. Your job is to stop me buying something that should not be seen outside Nashville.'

'I may not.' His breath was on the back of her neck. For a moment she thought she smelled everything she loved in it – coffee, fresh air, sleep, sex – then she caught herself and mentally shut her nostrils. 'I may let you go rhinestone yet.'

They burst into the bridal suite, the groomed staff eyeing them curiously, discreetly. Perhaps they were wondering about the handsome man with her, who he was, why he was there. If he was gay. She caught sight of Ollie's face in the white ornate mirror on the wall opposite and started at the familiarity of it, almost as if she'd inadvertently caught a glimpse of her own reflection.

'How can I help you?' A headmistressy shop assistant with a name badge – 'Penny' – approached them, beaming. Her teeth were so white they looked almost blue, as though they were under UV light at an eighties disco.

'I'm looking for a dress.' State the bleeding obvious. 'A wedding dress.' Even worse. She could feel Ollie smiling next to her, shifting from trainer to trainer at the inherent weirdness of the occasion.

'Well, you have come to the right place.' Penny waited for Ollie and Jenny to laugh. They laughed. 'What sort of gown are you looking for?'

Something about the word gown. It made her feel old and musty, or someone about to be admitted to surgery in a hospital ward.

The shop assistant raised a questioning eyebrow.

'Modern?' Ollie offered.

Jenny nodded gratefully. 'Yes, yes, modern!'

'Modern gowns for the modern bride,' repeated Penny with rehearsed enthusiasm. 'If you'd like to follow me.' Like school children in a lingerie department, she led them giggling to a rack of serious dresses, all lined up like different mismatching sections of one long, billowing curtain. She could feel her heart start to slam. Just the sight of the dresses made her anxious. They were all so forbiddingly romantic. And she was so . . . so . . . prosaic somehow. Sophie used to be able to wear frills and flounces and look like Kate Bush. Whereas if Jenny so much as went near a lace hem she looked like one of those mad women who wander around Portobello market mumbling about the summer of 1974 and how the area was better before the bankers moved in.

'Like?' said Ollie, picking a cream column off the rail. 'Not like?'

'Like,' nodded Jenny, trying to work out if like was love. No, not love.

'Do let me know if you'd like me to put any of them in the dressing room,' exuded Penny, block heels wedged in the deep pile carpet. She'd smelled a sale and clearly wasn't going anywhere.

'This is cute,' Jenny muttered, fingering some intricate pearl beadwork around the neckline of a dress.

Penny was there in a flash. 'Stunning! I'll put it in the dressing room. What is your size?'

She felt embarrassed to be revealing such information in front of Ollie. 'A size twelve?' She knew she shouldn't have stated it as a question.

Penny gave her a quick once over. 'I'll put a couple of fourteens in there too, shall I? The sizing varies so much from dress to dress.'

Jenny blushed again, hating the thought that Ollie would think she was trying to pretend she was slimmer than she was. Which of course she had been. 'I'll let you know if we need any more help, thanks.'

Penny stepped backwards with comic servility just as a twentysomething blonde and her equally livid blonde mother giggled into the bridal suite. Something about their excitability gave Jenny a pang of longing for a feeling she didn't yet have. She would soon. Yes, she would. As soon as she had her dress. Obviously, the dress was key. You couldn't be a bridezilla without a bridal gown.

'This rocks.' Ollie held up a long oyster-coloured dress with a pale blue sash around the waist.

She fingered the frilly sleeves. 'A bit Grayson Perry?'

'You've ruined it for me now.' He flicked it away on its hanger, making a metallic whoosh sound on the tracks. 'This one?' He held up a long white dress with barely any embellishment.

She cocked her head on its side. 'Gorgeous. And yet. No sparkle.'

'You're right. The girl must have sparkle.'

He was silent for a few moments, and when she next looked up at him she could see that something had changed. He looked quite different to how he'd looked a moment ago. He was frowning into the rack of dresses with a strange, distant look in his eyes. Oh God. He was staring at a fifties-style dress, a dress just like Sophie's wedding dress.

Sophie's had been a vintage dress, cinched in tight at the waist, the skirt flouncing out as if hooped, filled with layer upon layer of petticoat, so that she looked like a Degas ballerina when she leaned forward. Most keenly, Jenny remembered the morning of the wedding, its intimacy, the excitement. It was just her, Sophie and a make-up artist with pea-green eyes called Lottie in a little boutique hotel with lilac upholstery. Jenny could still hear the hiss of the glasses of champagne and smell the basket full of untouched toast and croissants, a freshly showered Sophie sitting on a stool in her white hotel dressing gown, nervous and happy, her river of dark, freshly washed hair falling down her back.

She had watched, awestruck, as Sophie had got more beautiful with each stage of the prep process: hair dried and curled, make-up applied, diamonds clipped to her ears, blue lace garter snapped to her thigh, flower behind the ear. Sophie had worn a red flower behind her ear that day. Jenny had helped Lottie wire it, pin it in, holding the spare pins between her front teeth. She remembered wondering what it must feel like to be so blessed. Never in her wildest dreams would it have occurred to her that Sophie would be dead seven years later. Or that she'd be here choosing a wedding dress with Sophie's groom.

She felt a wave of guilt. In her haste and selfishness to convince Sam of the platonic nature of her relationship with Ollie, she'd not considered Ollie's feelings. She put the dress she was holding back on the hanger. 'Let's go, Ol.'

'But we haven't found your dress.'

'I can get my dress another time.'

'This is the time.' He slipped his arm around her waist. She felt the cuff of his suit against her skin. 'I want to help you, Jenny. I really do.'

She blinked back unexpected tears. There was a part of her longing for him not to facilitate any of it. Longing for him to stop the wedding, to tell her it was too much too soon. To tell her to stop being such a bloody div, and lead her away some place dark and quiet until the feelings that were mashing up her head abated. 'You're sure?'

'Sure. You need to try this shit on.'

Penny appeared by their side. Jenny tried to ignore her.

'I hate trying stuff on.'

She could hear the shop assistant tutting beneath her breath.

'How many weeks until the wedding?'

'Four.'

Penny gasped, before whipping their choice of dresses away to the dressing room with a stagey kick of the heels.

It didn't take long for the changing room to whiff of sweat as she struggled into dresses, out of dresses. And yes, annoyingly, the shop assistant was right. In two dresses out of three she was a fourteen. She couldn't help but dislike those dresses. She yanked on the size twelve off-white column number, plain apart from a sash bow studded with crystal – just the right amount of twinkle? – and emerged self-consciously from the changing room, not knowing how to dangle her arms, aware of her corset-fortressed bosom spilling over the neckline. 'This one?'

At first Ollie didn't say anything. He just stared.

'You don't like it?' She pulled up the dress to hide her cleavage. She looked like an extra from *Blackadder*.

'You look beautiful.'

Jenny blushed. Had she found The One?

'But . . .'

There was a but! She deflated.

'It doesn't show off your shoulders.'

'My shoulders?' Jenny had never noticed her shoulders.

No one had ever noticed her shoulders. It was like noticing her elbows. Her shoulders were entirely unremarkable.

'Try on the one with the cut-away sleeves.'

'You're not meant to do cut-away sleeves over the age of thirty-five.'

'Says who?'

'I don't know, the fashionistas. Women who know about these things.'

'I think we know what Sophie would say.'

'Bollocks to that.' She leapt back into the dressing room and eyed the sleeveless dress combatively. It looked heavy and overly worked, the kind of dress that would look *stunning*, as Penny might say, on the sylph-like twenty-something with the waist-length blond hair in the next-door cubicle. Plus it was size fourteen. It was harder to get into than the others. Penny had to lower it down over her face like a piece of armour. A sharp tug on the inner corset lost her a lungful of breath. Then there were dozens of pearl buttons that ran up the spine, each one requiring the fingers of an elf to fasten.

'Almost there!' Jenny called out to Ollie through the curtains, as Penny fastened the last button. 'Don't run off to the pub just yet.'

'Stunning,' sighed Penny, standing back, hand at her throat.

Jenny stole a glance at herself in the changing room mirror. The dress made her look different in some way she didn't quite understand.

'Come on,' Ollie called from the other side of the curtain.

She yanked back the edge of the curtain. Penny gave her

a little push on her flank, as if nudging a horse from its box, and she nearly fell out of the dressing room. Under his gaze she could feel herself sweating. 'Too much?'

'Look at yourself in the mirror.' Ollie held her by the shoulders and swivelled her round to face the long, gilt mirror. 'Do you realise how beautiful you look, Jenny?'

She caught her breath. It felt like the corset had just been yanked tighter.

'I think you should wear dresses like this every day.' He walked over to her and kissed her on the cheek. 'Sam's going to want to rip the thing off.'

'Truly stunning,' said Penny, hand still at her throat.

'It's the one, Jen.'

She looked at her reflection again. Now that Ollie had given the dress his seal of approval, she loved it too. It was *the* dress! It was an amazing dress!

'Sold?'

Jenny swallowed hard. 'Sold.'

So why did her hand shake so badly as she handed over her credit card at the till? Penny grabbed one end of the card to take it. Jenny didn't let it go. Penny pulled. Jenny still didn't let go. Her mind had started to whir with one word. Dominique. Dominique. Dominique. Why was it repeating on her now? She'd done her best to put it behind her and believe Sam's explanation. She thought she'd put it to bed.

'May I?' Penny said tersely, strengthening her grip on the card.

'You alright, Jenny?' whispered Ollie, giving her a funny look.

'It's so much money. I'll only wear it once.' *Dominique. Dominique. Dominique.*

'Would you like to take a moment?' Penny gave her mirthless, tight smile, releasing her fingers from the credit card. 'Perhaps you'd like to sit down.'

'Jenny, you more than anyone deserve a beautiful dress.' Ollie put an arm around her shoulder. 'Don't worry about the money. Don't you love it?'

She could taste the salt of tears in the back of her throat. 'Yes, but . . .'

'If you wouldn't mind moving aside a little,' said Penny, irritated now, 'I will serve the next customer while you . . . make your mind up, thank you.'

The mother and daughter pair stood behind them, the mother clutching a flamboyant white feather headdress. They were still giggling.

'Stop,' said Ollie suddenly. Everyone turned to look at him. He dug into his back pocket. 'I will pay for the dress.'

'No! Don't be ridiculous. You absolutely can't pay for the dress,' protested Jenny, mortified at the turn of events.

'I want to.'

'It's not the money . . .' she began, suddenly not quite knowing what it was.

'Shh. My call.'

Penny's hand shot up like a piston to grab Ollie's credit card. As she shoved it determinedly into the card machine, she looked up at Jenny and winked. 'It's your lucky day.'

Thirty-four

'Ollie *bought* the wedding dress?' Sam is saying, hands gripping the steering wheel so hard his knuckles are white. He doesn't look happy, not at all. From up here, somewhere near the car's padded ceiling, I can see a vein pulsate on the top of his shaved head. Feel sorry for Jenny now.

'Yeah.' Jenny squeezes her lower lip with her fingers. She has Heathrow's lost luggage depot around her eyes. She doesn't look happy either. And she should do because the dress that Ollie bought her really is beautiful. When Jenny unzipped it from its cover last night I settled on its folds like a moth, absolutely still on its silk. She spent the best part of an hour just staring at that dress, walking around it, viewing it from different angles, like someone in a gallery puzzling over a painting.

'Is there anything that the guy *can't* do? No wonder half the women in north London are wanking off about him.' He gives her a sidelong, confused glance as he says this. Like he can't quite work out what's going on. He senses a shift in her, I think, sniffs it like a wolf in a changing wind, but he

258

can't identify it. To be perfectly honest, nor can I. What's going on with my Jenny?

'He's just gay enough!' Jenny says brightly, sounding slightly rehearsed.

Sam doesn't smile. He slams the horn at a van driver. 'Yeah, yeah. Sophie probably cut his balls off.'

Jenny rolls her eyes and looks despondently out of the window. Sense this conversation is not going to plan.

'That's the problem with good-looking women.' He spits out the word 'women'. 'I see them in my office all the time. They castrate their husbands, thinking it's what they want, but the moment he submits to her she runs off with her personal trainer.'

Jenny is gazing out of the window, not listening, her wide blue eyes elsewhere. 'It's beautiful, Sam.'

'Sounds it. You two, out shopping.'

She turns to him and grins. 'I'm talking about the dress.'

Natch.

Sam pulls up outside Tash's house. 'That'll be twenty quid, Miss Vale.'

'Will a kiss do?' She bends over to kiss him.

'A snog, thank you.' He holds Jenny's pretty round face in his hands, thrusts his tongue into her mouth. It's a short, sharp snog, like the mating of two small amphibian animals.

'Gosh,' laughs Jenny, hopping out of the car and away from that long, hot tongue pretty bloody quickly. 'I shouldn't be too long. It's just a catch-up meeting with the girls. Hey, you shooting straight home?'

'Where else do you think I'd be going?' he says, suddenly defensive, face slamming shut like the car door.

Temper, Sam. *Temper.*

In a small monochrome flat not far from St Albans, a woman is preparing for Sam's arrival. She is zipping up a black dress. Beneath the dress is lingerie, black with pink velvet trim. It matches. She is lighting a scented candle – 'Invigorating Gingerlily' – which illuminates the heart-shaped contours of her face. She sinks into her rose-pink sofa, waggles her heel-shod foot back and forth, back and forth, slapping the sole against her skin, and waits. She doesn't know that she has a fleck of red lipstick on her front tooth. There is something terribly vulnerable about this fleck, the flaw in her make-up.

The distance between her and Sam narrows and narrows until there are just a few clouds between them, five miles, a street, a paved drive. He pulls up, steps out of the car, shoves his blue shirt into the back of his jeans where it's ruched up. He has a panel of sweat on the back of his shirt in the shape of a crucifix. He knocks three times, not softly.

She opens the door wide, face full of hope and lipstick. 'Hey.'

'What the fuck do you think you're doing?'

Thirty-five

'Crisis!' Suze declared with rather too much relish for Jenny's liking. She'd been hoping for a good nose around Tash's flat and a gossipy catch-up; instead it seemed she'd walked into one of the Government's emergency Cobra meetings.

'Will someone tell me what's going on?'

'There are rumours, Jenny. Rumours.'

For one dreadful moment she thought they might be inferring something about the wedding dress. She hadn't thought how it might look. 'What? What is it?'

'On Saturday night a friend of a friend of a friend saw Ollie out drinking with one of his mates at The Royal Oak.' Suze waited for her words to sink in.

Jenny felt a sense of relief. It had nothing to do with her. 'This is bad?'

'There was *a lot* of drinking,' added Lydia, pausing for effect. 'And laughing.'

'It must be stopped,' Liz said in a German accent. 'Immediately.'

Jenny laughed.

'Liz!' said Tash crossly. 'This is serious.'

Jenny straightened her smile. 'Was the drinking out of control?' She remembered Sam's comment about them all being addicted to Ollie's grief and felt a little uneasy.

'Well, they ended up in Chicken Cottage. You don't end up in Chicken Cottage unless you're trolleyed,' said Liz.

'Sorry, I'm not with you. What's the big deal?'

'You tell her,' mouthed Tash to Suze. Tash's eyes flashed dangerously.

'Jenny, I'll cut to the chase. There was talk of a woman . . .' began Suze, wincing slightly as she said the word 'woman'.

Jenny felt the hairs on her arms prickle. 'A woman?'

'This friend of a friend . . .'

'. . . of a friend,' added Liz waspishly.

'. . . heard Ollie talking about how he had . . . feelings for this woman.' Suze stopped. 'Well, sexual comments were made.'

So it had happened. He'd moved on. Jenny clamped her hand over her mouth. 'Fuck.'

'Yes, that word was mentioned,' said Liz with a glint in her eye.

'It's too soon,' said Lydia, her eyes filling with the inevitable tears. 'He's far, far too vulnerable.'

Jenny felt a wave of nausea whoosh over her. She was struggling to hold it together now and wanted so badly to dart out of that door and run down the hill, back into the crowded anonymous fug of the city.

'What the hell shall we do?' asked Tash.

Breathe. That's what *she* must do. Breathe. Jenny took a deep breath and gagged on her sip of wine. 'I guess it was going to happen,' she managed to blurt out.

Suze touched Jenny's hand with her soft, pudgy fingers. 'It's more complicated than that. We think we know who the woman is.'

Her heart started to thump in her chest. 'Who?'

'Cecille.' Suze spoke as if the answer pained her. 'Cecille.'

'*Cecille!*' Jenny sat bolt upright on the chair. 'Cecille?'

'Now do you see why we're concerned, Jenny?' said Lydia quietly, eyeing her with renewed curiosity, as if her reaction had given something away.

'He'll get hurt,' said Liz knowingly, nibbling her way around a Kettle Chip. 'Or Freddie will. Let's face it, it's unlikely to end prettily.'

'We think someone needs to speak to Cecille,' said Tash firmly. 'You . . .'

'Ollie would go nuts if we interfered,' said Jenny quickly, remembering Cecille's face when she was caught looking for the letters. Oh, the superiority of youth.

'I told you. We can't just wade in there, Tashie,' Liz agreed. 'It's none of our business.'

Tash flicked her hair crossly. 'Makes me want to flipping hurl,' she said, summing up the general feeling in Jenny's own digestive tract.

'We've put so much effort into helping him through this. To see all our hard work fall away because of some little French *minx*!' Lydia's eyes watered again. 'It's too much to bear.'

'I'm afraid I can't say anything to Cecille,' said Jenny. 'She'll only tell Ollie anyway.'

'Can you at least find out if it's true, Jenny?' Tash said through a mouthful of chewed fingernails. 'From Ollie then?'

'It may be a way of stopping the gossip,' added Suze.

'Gossip?' Jenny's sinking feeling sank lower. 'Who else knows?'

Liz laughed. 'The school gate is a-*blaze*, Jenny. Clinton and Lewinsky had nothing on this story.'

'Look, I think we at least need to let him know what the other parents are saying, before things . . . blow up,' Suze persisted. '*I'd* want to know. Wouldn't you, Jenny?'

'I could tell him—' began Lydia.

'I think it would be best coming from Jenny,' interrupted Liz. 'Jenny's closest. Plus she's got a sane, rational head on her shoulders. She'll be able to keep the conversation as unemotional as possible.'

'Thanks! And I wouldn't?' said Lydia.

'*No*,' said Liz, Tash and Suze in unison. 'You wouldn't!'

Jenny pushed her nails into her palms. Get a grip, she told herself. Ollie is not yours. He is not Sophie's. Sophie is dead. You are about to get married. Ollie is free. He can do what the hell he likes. He can even marry an au pair.

'Jenny?' Suze asked, looking at her strangely over the neck of the wine bottle. 'Are you OK?'

'Oh, Jenny.' Liz put an arm around her shoulder, just as horrifying, unstoppable tears started to bubble up. 'Oh, Jenny, you're really not OK, are you?'

Thirty-six

I watch her pad slowly out of my bedroom, naked but for Ollie's big blue shirt. The dimple on her left buttock smiles at me. She has long, tanned legs. Her lips are bee stung from kissing. Her skin is rashy on her neck where his beard has been. So are her upper thighs. She walks past Freddie's room, where Freddie, my poor darling Freddie, stirs in his bed. I hover a few feet from the carpet outside the bedroom door. I dance round her. She is oblivious.

I did not see it happen. I chose not to. But I did see the warning signs, her twirling her hair around her index finger while leaning across the table, the way she rearranged her top so it showed more cleavage. I saw how after every glass of wine – four and counting – she moved closer to him, found ways to casually touch him, a knock of knee against knee, feather fingertips on his arm. I witnessed the small wrap of white powder and the two thin lines racked out on her Chanel compact mirror.

The kiss was hungry and urgent. Panting, grabbing at each other, they bundled up the stairs, heading for the privacy of the bedroom. Ollie had the presence of mind to wedge a chair against the door, presumably to stop Freddie joining them. Cecille is out for the evening. That was the last thing I saw, that chair. I sucked myself through the keyhole pretty damn fast. And I waited, guarding Freddie's room while they did it, wondering where he was touching her, if she felt different to me. Wondering if he was thinking of me at all, even a little bit, or if, as is more likely, he was lost in the sensual tangle of limbs and skin and that luscious glade of hair.

I twist round the corner to peek into the bedroom. Ollie is lying there, spread-eagled on the white sheet, panting and naked, spent. There is something glistening on his cheek. He turns over and buries his head into the pillow. His tears make me feel better.

'Ollie?' She is pushing open the bedroom door. 'Are you alright?'

He says nothing, head still embedded in the pillow.

She starts to look vulnerable and hurt. I feel for her now. 'Shall I go?'

He sits up, squints at her standing there in the puddle of hall light. 'Sorry, I'm so sorry.'

She reaches for her top, pulls it down over her head. 'Forget about it.'

'You are lovely. It's just that I can't . . . sorry.'

'Stop apologising. I understand.' She doesn't look like she understands. She looks rejected. Dressed, she hovers for a moment, waits for him to tell her to stay, and when he doesn't she slings her handbag over her shoulder. 'See you.'

'I'm truly sorry.'

Thirty-seven

The sky was milky blue, the air swaying with midges and barbecue smoke. Through the gap in the fence at the bottom of the garden Jenny could see a slice of London in its filmy bowl, the Gherkin, the wheel, the buildings that somehow reminded her she was in London, but, up here in Muswell Hill, elementally separate from it too. Her body had that pleasant post-swim feeling, which meant getting out of her deckchair anytime soon was inconceivable. Ollie was lain out on a towel on the grass beside her, skin darkening piratically in the sun, an old spliff stub in an ashtray next to him, a big bag of Kettle Chips open at his elbow. He had his eyes closed, which should have made things easier, but didn't. Yes, she was failing spectacularly in her appointed role of romantic interrogator. How could she possibly ask him about Cecille when the ingénue was roaming the house in a denim mini skirt and slogan T-shirt reading, 'The Answer's Yes!'.

Ollie opened one eye, looking at her dozily. 'Still in love with the dress?'

'Yes, of course.' She picked up a peppery blade of grass

and chewed it, omitting to tell him that every time she looked at the dress she burst into tears. It wasn't the dress's fault. It had done nothing but hang there and look beautiful.

'Can I see you in it?' Freddie slung his wiry arms around her neck from behind, pinning her into her deckchair. She could smell the chlorine on his skin.

'No one can see it.'

Freddie's arms loosened. 'But Daddy saw it.'

'Ah, but he came shopping with me.' And he's my gay best friend, she informed herself privately.

Freddie let go of her neck, picked up a small plastic bat and started hitting the orange Swingball hard around its pole. 'Mummy used to take me shopping. She said I was the best shopper.' He whacked the ball really hard. 'I don't see why I can't see the dress.'

'It's bad luck to show people your wedding dress before you get married, Freddie, that's all,' said Ollie, yawning. The sun caught a shade of amber in his otherwise black beard. He really was absolutely gorgeous. Catching herself staring, she looked away quickly.

Freddie threw the bat down on the grass. 'Bad luck?'

'Yeah, bad luck.'

'Don't show me the dress then!' Freddie looked panicked. 'I don't want you to have bad luck, too.'

'Oh, Freddie . . .'

Ollie pulled him on to his knee, rested his chin on his shoulder. 'Hey, hey. It's not really bad luck, Fred, just an old wives' tale.'

'What's an old wives' tale?' he asked quietly.

'Like a fairy story.'

'Oh.' Freddie frowned, looking from Jenny to Ollie and back again, uncertain. 'And fairy stories don't happen, do they?'

'No, fairy stories don't happen, Freddie,' said Ollie quietly, pushing his nose into Freddie's neck.

Jenny's phone started to ring. Sam. She rummaged in her stripy blue 'summer' bag – Soph would surely be impressed at this seasonal rotation – and flicked it to voicemail. 'Guys, I've got to get back for Sunday lunch. Great swim, Freddie. I reckon you'll be doing a whole length next week.' She'd ask him another time. Or not.

'Thanks, Jen. Look, I'll drive you back.' Ollie stood up and brushed grass seeds off his baggy cargo shorts, shoved his feet into pink flip flops. 'Cecille's here, somewhere.'

She froze at the mention of Cecille's name. Looking back at the house she caught a glimpse of her behind the glass doors, a swish of hair over a bare shoulder.

'Freddie, you want to watch *Deadly 60* with Cecille while I drive Jenny back?'

Freddie's bottom lip pouted. 'I want to watch *Deadly 60* with Jenny.'

'Really, Ollie, you don't need to drive me back.'

'I want to drive you home.' He flicked his aviator shades down over his eyes, making him look instantly rock star. 'I want to talk to you.'

Ollie leaned forwards over the steering wheel, resting on it, as they sat stationary in the street. 'Are you going to tell me why you're acting so weird?'

Jenny stared determinedly out of the window at the

splashes of sun on the vivid green trees that lined the avenue. 'I'm not acting weird.'

'You won't look at me.'

Jenny turned, to make a point of looking at him. 'I'm just tired from the swimming.' She smiled. 'And I'm looking at you.'

He raised a black, devilish eyebrow. 'You forget that I actually know you quite well now. It's been the surprise ace of being widowed.'

'OK.' She felt the heat rise in her cheeks. She was going to have to do this. Deep breath. 'Ollie . . .'

His eyes danced with amusement. 'Yes, my darling Jenny.'

'I feel so embarrassed saying this, and I'm not sure I even should be saying it so please don't be cross with me . . .'

He frowned, took his sunglasses off. 'Ominous.'

'There's been, er, gossip.' God, this was awful. Why the hell had they made her be the one to interrogate him? Lydia should have done it.

He laughed. 'Gossip?'

'At the school gates. About you and . . .'

'Fuck.' He turned the key in the ignition, stepped too hard on the gas. He wasn't laughing now. For a moment no one spoke. 'Tash is the soul of discretion then.'

'I don't think it was her that said anything.'

'So who else is going to spill the beans?' He slammed the horn hard at a white van. 'As far as I was aware it was only me and Tash in the bedroom, or has Suze got a lens trained on the house?'

Tash? *Tash?* In his bedroom? Had she misheard him?

Was Tash the woman Ollie had been talking about in the pub? Not Cecille. Tash! Oh God. She covered her mouth with her hand, sure she was about to hurl out of the window.

They drove along in awkward silence. This was it, she decided. This was the end of their long, unexpected journey that had started when Sophie died. Yes, she'd been a channel for his grief. A conduit to Sophie, to the past. Now he didn't need her. And this was good. Her work was done. He pulled up on her street. She reached for the car door handle, unable to look at him as her eyes were prickling with tears. 'So is it serious?'

'What do you think?'

'No idea.' She suddenly wished she had long dark hair like Tash. Or Sophie. Or Dominique. That she wasn't mousy with green highlights. That she didn't have thighs that rubbed together. That she wasn't a woman whose signature colour was navy.

'I know what you're thinking, Jenny.'

Thank God he didn't.

'But it just happened. Tash turned up with a bit of coke.'

She snorted. 'Helpful.'

'In a really funny way it was. Just getting off my head.' He stopped, frowning, his dark eyes melting into that faraway blackness that was making her heart flip in her chest. 'I'm dreading seeing her at the school gates. Shit, Jenny, does everyone know?'

'I don't think anyone knows about Tash.'

'What do you mean?'

The conversation was beginning to take on a surreal edge. 'The rumours were about Cecille, actually.'

Ollie slapped his forehead and laughed. 'Do you mean that you didn't know about Tash?'

'No, I didn't.'

'Can you keep a secret?' He put a hand on her knee, looked up at her boyishly, appealingly. She wanted to slap the grin off his face. 'Please?'

'Of course. Look, I've got to go, Ollie.'

'Do you hate me now?'

'A little bit.'

His eyes darkened. 'I haven't forgotten Sophie, Jenny.'

Jenny bit down on her lip very hard to stop herself crying. She couldn't look at him. She hated him. How could he? How?

'It wasn't perfect. You seem to think me and Soph were completely perfect. Everyone thinks that. It doesn't help.' He pulled at his beard, his features strained to the point of contortion. 'Maybe this is my way of reminding myself that we weren't. Then I don't have to feel like I've lost absolutely everything that will ever be good in my life.'

'Oh, Ol.' He was breaking her heart now. 'I understand that. But you don't need to do *this*.'

'She was bored, Jenny. Sophie was bored.'

Jenny looked down. She thought of the hidden stash of letters and once again wondered what they were and where they were. If they held the key to this.

'She wanted another baby,' he said quietly, his voice breaking.

'Yeah, I know. I found her maternity stuff in the chest of drawers.'

'I think maybe she blamed me for that. You know, on a subconscious level.'

'She didn't. She really didn't.'

'You know the worst thing, Jenny?' It felt like the world had shrunk down to just them, just them sitting in the car. 'That it felt good. The coke. The sex. It made me feel alive.'

Jenny closed her eyes. She didn't want to hear this. Yet she needed to hear it. She needed to come to her senses and cement the dissolving boundaries.

'And I don't know how it can be possible to miss someone so much, ache for them every minute of every fucking day, and yet still find pleasure in someone else. My brain can't compute it.'

'Where was Cecille when . . . this happened?'

'Out.'

'Right.' It was then she realised she had her hands over her ears like a child.

'You're judging me.'

'I'm not judging you.'

'It's just sex, Jenny.'

'You don't have to justify yourself to me, Ollie. You really don't.'

'I feel like I do.'

'Well, you don't.' She put one foot on the pavement, stepped up and into the bright sunlight, which no longer felt warm and bucolic but dehydrating and dirty.

'It was soul-searchingly shit afterwards. For the record.'

'I don't keep a record.'

'Jenny . . .' He wouldn't let her go. He wanted something. She couldn't give it. He reached out to her. His skin sizzled on hers. 'You OK? I'm concerned about you.'

'Me?'

'Yeah, you.'

'Tired, you know.'

'Wedding stuff?'

'Think so,' she replied tersely.

'Jenny, it'll be fine. Totally fine. Everyone is rooting for you two.'

She kissed and inhaled him. 'Stay out of trouble.'

It was only as she stood on the sunny pavement, watching the silver bullet of his car recede into the distance, that she realised Ollie hadn't actually denied any involvement with Cecille.

Thirty-eight

Whoa! Is there something I don't know here? If I thought Jenny was looking doolally before, she is looking positively *deranged* today, wild-eyed, foot pressed hard on the gas, shooting north like a boy racer. She spins down Fortis Green, does a loud, screechy turn into one of the avenues, making me bounce like a ball in the back. I expect her to stop outside number thirty-three – what has Ollie done? – but no, she's turning right. She's screeching to a halt outside Tash's house. Oooh, this could be interesting.

'Hey, this is a lovely surprise,' says Tash, answering the door, looking puzzled. She smells of roses – Jo Malone – and is naked beneath a long grey cashmere dressing gown that has no visible moth holes. There is not one pube on her entire body. She is as smooth as an egg. I wonder if he liked that.

Jenny storms right past her. Half-Jenny, half-juggernaut, she's a heavy load vehicle intent on destruction. I'm scared, and I'm the ghost.

'Excuse me,' says Tash, half-joking, stepping back.

'I know about Ollie, Tash,' Jenny hisses, releasing the demolition ball. 'I *know*.'

It's like she's speaking for me here. Great!

'Look, Jenny,' stutters Tash, cheeks flaming, 'it . . . it was just one night. I don't know how it happened.'

'Bollocks!' Jenny grips the back of a chair, like she is about to pick it up and throw it across the room. Tash looks worried. (It's a Hans Wegner.)

Tash's exposed tanned décolletage rises and falls more quickly now. You can almost hear her brain whirring, trying to think of a way out. But there's nowhere to turn. Jenny has her by the vajazzles.

'Cocaine! What the fuck were you *thinking*?'

'You're not going to tell the others, are you?'

Jenny is not moved. She turns away from Tash, like she can't bear to look at her any more, stares out of the window at next-door's mossy green drainpipe, hot air tusking from her nostrils. 'I might do.'

'Please, Jenny.'

'Fuck off.'

Woo! Go Jenny!

'Don't be such a bitch!'

'*Bitch?*' says Jenny, turning away from the drainpipe to face her slowly. 'Bitch? *You* are the bitch, Tash.'

Tash's face hardens now.

Even I wonder if Jenny might have overstepped the mark.

'What's your fucking problem, Jenny?'

'That you've been pushing cocaine and sex on Sophie's husband!' Jenny is shouting properly now. I haven't heard her shout properly for years. She's got some lungs on her.

'He's not her husband. Sophie's *dead.*'

'Hardly!'

276

Tash narrows her eyes. 'You know what, Jenny? You sound jealous.'

Jenny starts. 'Don't be ridiculous.'

'Is this what it's all been about?' Tash can see she's hit a soft spot and goes in for the kill. 'Jenny the ringmaster. Jenny, Ollie's confidante. Have you ever reflected on your own motivations, Jenny?'

'I am about to get married,' Jenny utters in pale-faced defence.

Tash rolls her eyes. 'As if that has any bearing on it.'

'Fuck you, Tash.'

Tash's eyes narrow to dark glossy slits. 'You think you're so perfect, don't you, Jenny?'

She's getting nasty now.

'Look, I was Sophie's best friend. That's all. I don't pretend to be anything else. I didn't apply for any post. Suze just asked me to help, you all did.'

'Best friend?' Tash smiles. It is not a nice smile. 'I'm not sure I'd count Sophie as my best friend if I were you.'

Jenny's hands fist at her sides. A sinewy muscle on her neck swells and twitches. 'What are you talking about?'

Tash looks lost for words, like she's unsure how to follow up. Then she smirks. She is suddenly no longer beautiful. 'You've got no idea, have you?'

There is a rumble like thunder in the distance. I'm not sure if it's a train or something far worse hurtling towards us on the tracks.

'About what?'

'Nothing,' she says quietly, pulling her dressing gown tight over her slim body. 'Nothing.'

'Tell me.'

'Look, Sophie told me about Sam's roving eye.' She wrinkles her nose in faux empathy. 'Hardly a best friend's discretion,' she scoffs.

Shit! It's something far worse.

'Roving eye?' Jenny's hands are shaking. She pales. 'She said that to you?'

Oh God. It was just school mum drinks chat. I told them, I think it was at Suze's one night, that I had a best mate who was waiting to get married to someone with a wandering eye and wondering what I should say or if I should say anything. We ummed and ahhed and drank and debated the ethics of interfering in friends' relationships like the panel of *Loose Women*. What you should say, what you shouldn't, how it's best to stay out of it and let matters run their course. Drunken, silly stuff, in which we asked ourselves what Jennifer Aniston would do. That was the end of it. Or so I thought. I didn't imagine anyone would remember the conversation. Or that they'd ever get to know Jenny.

'You're full of bullshit.' Jenny shakes her head, refusing to believe it. 'You're unbelievable.'

'What about Dominique then?'

Jenny gets a shade paler. 'Dominique?' Her voice is very quiet, little more than a whisper.

Tash presses her fingers into the lids of her closed eyes and winces. 'Look, Jenny, I don't know how we got here. I like you. I really do. This is all a bad look. I'm really sorry. Can we make peace?'

Jenny slumps against the table, the rage from earlier

evaporated. 'You can't say that and just expect me to forget you said it.'

'It's no big deal. It's in the past, Jenny. I'm sorry I ever mentioned it. I really am.'

'You know Dominique?' Jenny whispers hoarsely.

'Oh, from years ago. She's a sister of someone I used to work with.'

Something shifts in Jenny's face. She's made the connection.

'From my marketing days.'

Jenny stands up straight, urgent. 'You have a number?'

'A number?' Tash looks flustered. 'Er, no.'

'Please, Tash. This is important.'

Tash hesitates. 'I'll have a pop at tracking down her number if you agree not to tell the others about me and Ollie.'

Thirty-nine

It is eight-thirty pm. Freddie's light is off, but the burnished evening sunlight is seeping through the sides of his blackout blinds and he is sitting up in bed, twisting the limbs of Buzz Lightyear. He lifts Buzz in front of him and addresses him sternly. 'Mum, do you remember that Joe kid in my class?'

Whoa! I am Buzz now. I am a Space Ranger. Excited by my transformation and the possibility that we may finally be able to communicate via the third party of a clairvoyant toy, I try to make Buzz do something, for the laser to flash on his arm. Needless to say, it doesn't. 'Yes, of course I remember, darling,' I say. Buzz's mouth doesn't open. Freddie doesn't seem to care.

'Joe jacked my Ben Ten ruler that Granny gave me.'

'Have you told the teacher?'

Freddie purses his lips thoughtfully. Is he receiving me? He is silent for a moment, head cocked to one side like he is listening.

'OK, I'll speak to the teacher,' he says.

Explode with joy! How mad is that? A proper conversation. Or is it just that he is *my* boy still? That the glorious six years we spent together was enough to cement me – and my love – in his bone marrow. He knows what I would say to him because he still knows his mother.

'To infinity and beyond,' whispers Freddie, flying Buzz up into the air and whirling him around his bed, his wings clipping the blobs of Blu Tack on the walls.

You see, while everything else is going greyer as the weeks pass, Freddie's resilience gets ever brighter. He is sad and he misses me and he talks to me and he opens the memory book that Jenny made and brushes photographs of me with his little fingers. And sometimes he sleeps with my old nightie pressed into his nose. But this is OK. I believe he will be OK. I really do. While I know that problems may manifest themselves later, probably in his teenage years when he hates me for deserting him and being so stupid as to step out into the road drunk, right now he is my little warrior. He still smiles and laughs and plays. He has a solid hidden ore of happiness buried deep inside.

I watch over him until morning. I watch over him as he sings a song in the year two assembly about rainforests. I bob against the ceiling like a balloon, buoyant with pride, anxious he'll screw up. But he sings his heart out, gazing fearlessly at the audience, some of whom, feeling the poignancy of my absence, wipe away tears with their sleeves while holding up their camera phones. His voice, the wonderful voice he gets from Ollie, is clear and pure, life itself. He finishes the song. Applause erupts. I am a shower of sparks, a berserk Catherine wheel that has come loose from the monkey bars on the gym wall. Ollie and Jenny are watching too, sitting four rows from the back, clapping wildly. And we are all united in one thing: our love for Freddie.

After the assembly, Joe returns the stolen ruler.

Leaving Freddie to bask in the triumphant return of the stolen goods, I leave the sweaty, echoey hall with the huddle of proud parents. Ollie shoots off to the studio, while Liz and Jenny break ranks with the other 2Bers – how they manage to escape Suze's clutches I have no idea – and skank off for coffee. It's incongruous seeing Jenny in my old haunts, on the coffee mum circuit. She looks far more comfortable than I'd ever have given her credit for. I feel a wave of guilt for having compartmentalised my life so brutally.

The cafés on the broadway are cluttered with children and huddles of Fortismere pupils with their dog-eared paperbacks and iPods, the girls in thigh-skimming floral tea dresses, the boys flicking their long, lanky hair out of their eyes. Liz and Jenny squeeze on to a little round table on the pavement and order cake. Liz is wearing a billowy orange dress which clashes brilliantly with the scarlet tips in her hair that poke out beneath her seventies-style Fedora. Jenny is wearing navy.

'Hey, it's good to catch up after all this time,' says Liz cheerfully, her cheeks chipmunked with brownie. 'More coffee?'

'Lovely.'

Liz shoves the plate of brownies towards her. 'Please finish them off. I'm a stone heavier than I was last year. If I carry on like this they'll have to winch me out of my bedroom through the ceiling using a crane.'

Jenny obliges. There is a lull in the conversation. They

people-watch. A teenager bounces past on chunky neon trainers. An elderly lady totters by licking a Fab ice lolly with a lap dog under her arm. There's a flotilla of prams as a baby massage group spill out of their session.

'I feel quite the fugitive,' laughs Liz. 'Breaking ranks.' She leans back in her chair, lifts her face to the sunshine and closes her eyes. Jenny rests her chin in her hand and gazes at the pavement, her face clouded by thoughts.

Liz opens one eye and peeks at her. 'So you're geared up for the wedding?'

'Yeah, yeah.' Jenny's face shadows. I'm finding it harder and harder to read. Something funny happens to her face when she talks about the wedding.

'Do you need a hand with anything?'

'That's very sweet of you, but no. Future mother-in-law is very much on the case.'

'Ah, I see,' smiles Liz, eyeing Jenny more watchfully. 'Nervous?'

Jenny stiffens, puts her cake fork down. 'Yeah, guess that's what it must be.'

Liz smiles kindly. 'It's normal to have wobbles, Jenny.'

Hmmm.

'I had *huge* wobbles.' Liz ruffles her hair, depositing a brownie crumb in its rosy thatch. 'But it was a dream on the day, a total dream. And we had the best bonk afterwards!'

Jenny laughs and blushes, then she looks pensive.

Liz sees it too. 'You're not having second thoughts, are you?'

Jenny bites down hard on her lower lip. How I wish she would talk! Liz is a sane woman. She'd understand. Tell her!

'Jenny?' Liz looks more concerned now. She's on the scent. 'There's no one else muddying the waters here, is there?'

'No!' Jenny practically ejects herself from her rattan café seat. 'It's just that marriage is such a big step. Bigger than I thought. I know that sounds deeply immature.'

'It doesn't, not at all.' Liz hesitates, unsure how to push the conversation forward. 'It must be hard, you know, losing Sophie and . . . well, spending so much time with Ollie.'

'Ollie hasn't got anything to do with this,' Jenny retorts.

Liz twiddles a spike of scarlet hair, not taking her eyes off Jenny's strained face. 'Sometimes feelings can be confusing, that's all.' She looks away wistfully. And I wonder if she's thinking of her ex, Riley. The one she finally defriended on Facebook this morning, and by doing so deleted all the past mooning and embraced her lovely present. 'There's not one woman alive who hasn't been confused about who she loves at some point in her life.'

'I don't know what you're talking about, Liz, sorry.' (I'm not quite sure where she's going with this either.) She bends down and picks up her handbag. 'Sadly, I've really got to get back to work.'

'Me too.' Liz stabs the last bit of brownie with her fork. She looks up and smiles cheerfully. 'But you know what, Jenny? It's not over till the fat lady sings. Remember that.'

Forty

Jenny's heart leapt when the phone rang. Could it be Tash with Dominique's details, finally? It had been two weeks since the showdown in Tash's house and she still hadn't given anything to her. It was almost impossible not to say anything to Sam, to go on as normal. But she didn't want to say anything until she had the facts, if there were facts, if Tash wasn't making mischief, which was the most likely scenario. She wasn't going to handgrenade her relationship for nothing. She picked up the phone. 'Hello?'

'Jennifer.' Her mother was the only person in the world who called her Jennifer.

'Oh, Mum. Hi. Yes, yes, I'm really well, things are great. I'm at work right now, though. Yes, I know it's the weekend.' She'd taken on extra work so she didn't have to think too much, or spend too much time with Sam. 'I know, I know, it's just that I've got this massive manuscript.' Explanations were fruitless. For as long as she worked at home her mother would not believe that she was actually working. Work was something you went to. It was something that required a pencil skirt and a commute and a KitKat at eleven am. 'How's things, Mum?'

Her mother paused, cleared her throat, the throat clearance giving Jenny a taster of the answer. 'I'm worried, Jennifer.'

Not this. Not again. 'The wedding is all under control. Promise,' she said, in what she hoped was the reassuring voice of a calm, organised bride rather than one who was trying to sleuth into the past life of her fiancé and who went to bed every night and had weird dreams about her dead best friend's husband.

'Your father's concerned.'

'Look, Mum, the marquee is going up in ten days' time.' As she spoke it was like listening to badly dubbed telly, as if there was a time lag and it wasn't her speaking. 'I have shoes! Lovely white shoes. I have a wedding dress! I will have my hair coloured at the weekend. I will not look like Shrek, OK. Everything, I promise, has been crossed off the list. Do not fret,' she said, wondering how long she could keep up the wedding prattle before her brain seized up. It was as if the whole subject was too big and complicated for her to process, the nuptial equivalent of quantum physics.

Her mother did one of her tight little coughs. 'I have no doubt that Penelope will have organised everything expertly, down to the last napkin ring.'

Jenny felt a wave of sympathy for her mother, who understandably felt usurped.

'Don't you want more of a say, love?'

'I've had my say, Mum.' Yes, she'd let the details ride over her. And Penelope had such fixed ideas. She really did care about whether the guests should have little net pockets filled with pink almonds.

Her mother sniffed. 'I just think the Vales should be more involved, that's all.'

'How about I ask Penelope if there's anything you can sink your teeth into? She's coming over for dinner tonight.'

'But don't say anything, Jennifer. I don't want to cause an at-mos-*phere*.' There was nothing her mother hated more than atmosphere.

'I'll have a run through Sam's spreadsheet later and phone you tomorrow with an update.' The word update always sounded impressive and efficient. 'Right, let's speak soon . . .'

'Don't "update" me, Jennifer.'

'Sorry.'

'Darling, you sound down, very down.'

'I'm not down. Just a bit tired.'

'Why are you tired?'

'I don't know. Work, I guess.'

'You need to stop working. Working doesn't suit brides.'

'I'm committed. I need to get it all done before the honeymoon.'

'Oooh, any idea where . . . ?'

She glanced up at Sam, who was engrossed with his iPhone. 'No. Sam is proving very good at keeping secrets.'

The moment she hung up, her own mobile started vibrating on the kitchen table.

'Like living in a bloody call centre,' complained Sam, lighting a cigarette and blowing smoke out of the open window.

Once the phone call was finished, she sat down next to

Sam, wondering how to break it to him. 'That was Ollie in New York.'

'I know that. You were using your girlie talk-to-Ollie voice.'

She ignored this. 'Freddie's got chicken pox.'

'Tell him not to pick.'

'Actually he's really sick, Sam.' She hesitated, unsure how to sell this one. 'He's been calling for me.'

Sam flexed his bare right bicep, prodded it, checking its muscle tone. 'And?'

'I've got to go to Muswell Hill.'

He fingered the bulge of his bicep with his left hand. 'Not tonight?'

'Ollie wouldn't ask unless he was worried, Sam.'

'My parents are coming to dinner any minute to run through the wedding. The chicken is in the oven. And you want to run off?'

Trying to placate him, she stroked his shoulders, smoothing over the little black dots where the hair was growing back after his shoulder wax. 'We saw your parents last week.' Every bloody week! 'And Freddie really is sick. I kind of have to do this.'

'He's got chicken pox not cholera, babes. You do not *have* to do this. Anyway, what's going on with the French bird? Where's she?'

She started a little at the mention of Cecille. She'd been trying to make herself forget about Cecille. It was best just to deny her existence. 'She's struggling a bit apparently. I may have to stay the night, I'm afraid.'

A low growl came from the back of his throat, which

may or may not have had something to do with the cigarette.

'It'll only be one night.' She reasserted her shoulder stroking. 'Ollie's back tomorrow.'

Sam stood up, flicking her hand away. 'This is about you, not Freddie. Can we at least be honest about that?'

'*Honest?*' The word Dominique hissed on the tip of her tongue. 'I tell you what, Sam—' she began, only to be interrupted by the doorbell and Penelope's shrill voice rising from the street through the open window.

Forty-one

Cecille appeared at the door of number thirty-three looking dishevelled, her normally smooth dark hair frizzed, a large white shirt sloppily tucked into her brown leather belt. She looked like a teen on a bender, and for once, genuinely pleased to see Jenny. 'Thanks for coming,' she said breathlessly.

'Has Freddie still got a temperature?' She had phoned her mother back for advice – much to her mother's delight – which amounted to a bottle of Calpol and a bottle of pink calamine lotion.

She bustled into the hall with her medical supplies, a little part of her hoping that in some small way, her stepping into the crisis like this, taking control, might right the humiliation of being discovered poking around Ollie's chest of drawers for those letters. It might make things less embarrassing for everyone.

'You go and have a cup of tea or something, Cecille. I'll take over,' she said, dropping her overnight bag in the hall and leaping up the stairs.

Freddie was a pathetic spotty mess, dozing on his bed.

She put her hand on his forehead. Hot. Where was the thermometer? Was this it? She picked up a plastic probe from the bedside table. It took a moment or two for her to work out which orifice it was designed for. She chanced sticking it in his ear. Thirty-nine degrees. She scrambled into her handbag and Googled kids' temperatures on her iPhone. OK, yes, hot. She must definitely wake him up and give him medicine.

'Freddie, Freddie, sweetie,' she said, wobbling his shoulder gently.

He groaned and turned over in the bed.

'Freddie.'

'Mummy.'

'Freddie, it's me, Jenny.'

'Want Mummy,' he muttered, eyes still shut.

'It's Jenny. It's OK.'

He opened one eye very slowly. 'Jenny?' He looked puzzled, taking a moment to get his bearings. 'Are you going to stay with me?'

'I'm here now.'

'Promise?' he said, blinking back the tears and trying to be brave.

'I'll stay until Daddy gets home. Now I'm going to give you some medicine.' She poured a spoonful out, spilling pink, sticky liquid all over his Spiderman duvet cover as she did so. Using a bit of loo roll she carefully dabbed the calamine lotion over his raw skin so that he looked like he'd been dunked in strawberry ice cream. She cupped his little hand in hers when he tried to scratch. 'Try not to.'

Freddie began to cry quietly. 'It hurts.'

'It won't hurt soon. The medicine will kick in. Medicine is great stuff.' Jenny slipped off her shoes and lay down next to him. 'Shall I read you a story? Then we can think about stories, not itching.'

He shook his head.

'Not even pirates?' Surely pirates would work.

He shook his head again.

'Tintin?'

'Tell me things about Mummy.' He dropped his head on her chest. It was a comforting weight, griddle hot where his skin touched hers. 'Did Mummy get sick, too?'

'Now that's a good question. Because you know what? Mummy was the least ill person I knew.'

Freddie smiled.

'She got sick like you when she was a little girl. She had mumps and chicken pox and stuff. Everyone does, I'm afraid. But when she was grown up, she was ridiculously healthy. I don't ever remember her with a cold. She must have had colds, I guess, but nothing ever stopped her. She didn't moan about anything like that. Not even when she was pregnant. You know, Freddie, the night before you were born, she was dancing!'

He smiled sleepily. 'Dancing?'

'There was a big thirtieth birthday party, an old friend of ours from university. Most pregnant women about to give birth don't go to parties, Freddie. They sit there with their feet up in front of the telly, moaning. But Mummy *insisted* on going. She hated missing a party. And she was convinced that you were going to arrive late anyway.'

He looked puzzled. 'Arrive late for what?'

'The date the doctors said you'd come out of Mummy's tummy. It's called a due date.' She smiled, remembering it all, Sophie's fecund magnificence. 'I'll never forget her dancing that night. She was *enormous*. And she was wearing this red dress and dancing with bare feet because her feet had swollen up and she couldn't fit into any shoes.'

'So she danced me out of her tummy?'

Jenny laughed. 'Yes, I guess she did.'

He lowered his lids dreamily. 'I loved it when Mummy danced.'

'Everyone loved it when your mummy danced. She always looked so happy dancing, and that made other people feel happy, too.'

'So did I pop out on the dance floor then? Like I was on *Strictly*.'

'Nearly! She made it to the hospital in time. Just. You came out about six hours later.'

'And then what did she do?' He scratched his leg. Again Jenny cupped his hand, held it firm to stop the scratching until the itch subsided.

'Daddy wrapped you in a blanket and Mummy cuddled and fed you.'

'Were you there, Jenny?'

'I was fetching your mummy a cup of tea from the hospital café at the moment you were born. I saw you when you were about ten minutes old, though.'

Freddie smiled. 'You were almost there then?'

'Almost.' This seemed to please him. Jenny ran her fingers through his sweaty fringe, remembering seeing Freddie for the first time, how shocked she'd been at his red raw tininess, his rabbit weight. She'd fallen in love with him immediately, completely.

Freddie yawned. 'What was I like?'

'Very tiny, very beautiful. And you looked just like Mummy when you were born. Dark hair, little pin curls, Mummy's nose.'

He frowned. 'I wasn't dancing?'

'You were a bit too young to dance. You just wobbled your head.'

'I'd like to see you dance, Jenny.'

'Me? Dance?' She shook her head and smiled at the thought. 'I am, sadly, a truly terrible dancer. Two left feet.'

'If you had two left feet, one would be a right foot.'

She curled a bit of hair behind his ear as his eyes shut. 'Clever socks.'

Cecille snapped open a can of Coke and sat down at the dining table with a sigh. 'I so worried.'

'He's asleep. Temperature's down. Please don't worry any more.' Jenny sat down opposite her at the kitchen table, admiring the way Cecille's fine-boned hands circled the Coke can. Was it Cecille's tiredness that was bestowing her with such a louche Gallic sexiness this evening? Or maybe it was something to do with the insouciantly unbuttoned man's shirt. Yes, a man's shirt. Shit. Was it Ollie's?

Cecille folded back one of the cuffs that was falling down over her hand, as if sensing Jenny's gaze.

'So you think Ollie will get back tonight?' She dragged her eyes away from the shirt.

'Very late,' Cecille said, glancing up at the clock. 'If

plane's on time.' She tipped back her head, sipped her Coke.

Jenny calculated that there was about an hour to kill before she could reasonably go to bed without appearing rude. She didn't relish the idea of hanging out with Cecille, and cursed herself for having forgotten her book in her hurried packing. Perhaps she would phone Sam, yes, that's what she would do. He would still be eating the roast chicken and probably wouldn't pick up, but it was an opportunity to leave a contrite message without getting sucked into further conflict. 'I'll go and dump my bag and make a call.' She hesitated. 'Er, where should I sleep, Cecille?'

'I put you in room next to Freddie's,' she said authoritatively, the mistress of the house. 'You will have bad night, Jenny, I'm afraid. Freddie wake up a lot last night. Five, six times.'

'Oh, poor thing.'

'Yes, I know. Very hard.' Cecille yawned, exposing pink tonsils. 'I'm not used to it.'

Jenny still couldn't take her eyes off the shirt. She definitely recognised the blue-striped lining inside the up-turned cuffs. Had Cecille just found the shirt in the washing basket and mistakenly thrown it on?

'First I will make something to eat. What you like?'

'Don't go to any bother, really. Toast. Cereal is fine.'

Cecille wrinkled her nose at the idea of toast or cereal for supper. 'I make steak.'

Her heart sank at the thought of sharing a proper sit-down meal with Cecille. Cecille wearing Ollie's shirt. 'Please don't cook on my account.'

She returned to the kitchen after phoning Sam to find

Cecille chucking a fist of butter into the frying pan. She fried two steaks for an alarmingly brief moment, before sliding them on to the white plates in a pool of blood, alongside some buttered French beans. Yikes. The steak was practically mooing.

'Hope you like,' Cecille said cheerily.

'Wow. This looks . . . amazing,' she attempted. 'At your age I couldn't cook at all.'

Cecille giggled, chuffed. 'Beer? Wine?'

'A small glass of white would be lovely, thanks.'

'May I have some wine?' Cecille asked, suddenly bashful.

'You don't have to ask me, Cecille.' She felt herself warming to the girl, wanting to connect with her. An ill child stirred up a lot of emotion. And yes, it was sweet, and responsible, of her to ask if she could have a drink. There was no sign of the catty superiority she'd seen that time with the letters. The rumours about Cecille were clearly absolute tosh. The gossip mill gone into overdrive. 'You're off duty now. I'm here. Have a glass of wine.'

Cecille poured out two glasses of wine, disappointingly small as politely requested.

'Cheers,' Cecille said, lifting her glass.

'Cheers,' said Jenny, digging into the bleeding meat. How ridiculous that it had taken Freddie getting chicken pox for her to have a proper conversation with Cecille after all this time, she told herself. 'You are doing an excellent job, Cecille, by all accounts.'

Cecille frowned and stopped chewing. 'What accounts?'

'Ollie. The mothers I know at school. Me,' she smiled. 'For what it's worth.'

Cecille shook her head and looked glum. 'Not the other mothers, Jenny. The mothers don't like me.'

'Oh. Why do you say that?' She shifted uneasily on her chair.

'They look at me . . .' She narrowed and hardened her eyes. '. . . like *zat*.'

'Oh no. Really?' Then she remembered the slate-hard stare Tash had given her not so long ago.

'They jealous,' Cecille declared matter of factly, slicing a neat cube out of her steak.

Jenny spluttered into her wine. 'Jealous?'

'About Ollie.'

Something tightened in Jenny's chest. Damn it, Cecille was probably right.

'They want him, you know.'

Jenny smiled at the sweet adolescence of the word 'want'. 'Like who?'

'Lydia.'

'*Lydia?*' She dropped her knife and it clattered to the table.

Cecille glanced behind her as if to check no one was listening. 'Lydia tried to kiss Ollie, Jenny.'

'I think you might have muddled up—'

'It was late, Jenny,' Cecille interrupted. She dropped her voice to a whisper, as if telling a ghost story. 'It is weekend. After party. Suze's party. You remember?'

She nodded. Suze's party. The night Lydia and George had that terrible row. She leaned forward, not wanting to miss a word. 'I remember.'

'They think I asleep. But I not. I not asleep. I come

downstairs and I see Lydia like this . . .' She pursed her lips, closed her eyes. 'They only stop because I come downstairs.'

Jenny covered her mouth with her hand. Not another one.

'And not just Lydia. Tash! Tash left *bra* here, here in house!'

In her mind's eye, Jenny suddenly saw lots of bras, dozens, hundreds, different shapes and sizes, all belonging to different women, floating through the house like an army of Zeppelins, through the hall, across the landing, into Ollie's bedroom.

'You see now?' appealed Cecille, desperate that her point was not being lost in translation. 'They are all jealous of me. Me, living here with Ollie. That is why they are so . . . cold.'

'I guess everyone is very protective of Ollie,' she attempted, still reeling from the revelation about Lydia. Lydia! 'They were good friends of Sophie's.'

'Sophie. Sophie. Everything always about Sophie,' sighed Cecille, resting her chin on her hands like a cherub. 'So . . . so *frustrating*!' She gave Jenny a sidelong look, as if trying to work out whether to trust her. 'I just want Ollie to be happy,' she added quietly. 'He can't be happy when he live in past, Jenny.'

'He needs time.'

'That is what I tell myself. Just wait, wait, Cecille, I say.' She wrapped her small hands tightly around the stem of the wine glass with a heave of sadness. 'But very, very hard.'

Jenny stared at her silently for a moment, becoming aware of a disturbing undertow to the conversation. It could have just been a turn of phrase, but it did appear that Cecille was attached to Ollie in a way that was not *strictly* within the terms of her contract. 'Cecille,' she ventured gently. 'Ollie is on his own. He's very handsome. Well, um, I hope I'm not speaking out of turn, but I could imagine it might be easy to develop . . .' She felt the heat rise on her own cheeks as she spoke and tried to cover them with her palms.

'He is amazing man, Jenny. He makes me laugh.' Cecille's eyes glazed over dreamily. 'And I love the way he plays guitar. He is like . . . like poet!'

'Cecille . . .'

She looked up defiantly. 'I *love* him, Jenny!'

Oh God. Jenny squeezed her eyes shut. 'Don't say that. Please don't say that.'

'He is first man I love.' She put a hand against her heart, her face glowing. 'But this love, this love hurts a lot. I didn't know love hurt so much.'

'Oh, Cecille. You need someone your own age. Ollie is grieving. He is just not . . . not available.'

'Oh no, Jenny, he loves me too,' she said matter of factly.

She heard a loud rushing in her ears. Then the long extended screech of bus brakes. The room started to sink away from her. She slumped her head into her hands. Why wouldn't he fall in love with Cecille? She was lovely. And beautiful. It all made a sickening kind of sense. He'd rebounded into the open arms of youth, someone with whom he had no past, no baggage, someone who didn't look at him and see the missing black shape where Sophie should be, like a figure scratched out of a photograph.

'You are only one who understand, who knows him well like I do. Tell me what to do, Jenny. Please tell me what to do,' Cecille begged. 'I try *everything* to understand him. Everything! I try to understand Sophie, too. Every little thing about her. What he loved about her. What he—'

She got it then. 'Cecille,' Jenny said suddenly, seizing the moment by the scruff of the neck. 'I do understand, I really do.'

'You do?' Cecille's shoulders dropped, unburdened.

'I do,' she said in a soft, maternal voice. 'And I also understand now why you took Sophie's letters from Ollie's chest of drawers.' Cecille stared down at the table. 'You did take them, didn't you, Cecille?'

Forty-two

In the shadowy gloom of the guest bedroom the letter still shone asbestos-white in Jenny's trembling hands. She had folded the other letters, placed them carefully back in the box, the ones from starstruck admirers going back years. But not this crumpled tormentor. Flicking on the sidelight, she pulled it out of its envelope, smoothed it over her bent knee, making herself go through the horrors all over again, until it finally sank in. No matter that it made her feel faint, that reading it was like giving blood.

Sophie,
I am writing to apologise for my brashness, both at the party and since. You were right to reject me, then and now. But it seems to me that what is right and what feels right are two different things. I suspect that is why you came to meet me late last week, wearing that sexy red dress which is now imprinted in my mind forever. (Did anyone ever tell you you have dancer's legs?) It's hard to believe that you met me just to rebuke me so seductively. My lawyer's brain cannot

help but wonder if you came because you couldn't not. And did you really need to meet me for a long walk in the park to tell me – again! – to back off, or suggest that 'let's be friends' lunch by the river? I think not.

Sophie, ultimately I do not want to feel this way any more than you do – life is complicated enough – but I cannot help it. The question is, can you? Your court, babes.

Sam.

The postmark? Almost two years old. At that point she and Sam would have been madly in love, freshly in love. Wouldn't they? Oh God. What party? There had been so many parties in the early days. Had he made a pass at Sophie? He must have. But why hadn't Sophie told her? *Why?* The betrayal winded her again. It made all thoughts about Dominique pale into insignificance. She was strong. She could take anything, even her best friend dying. But she wasn't sure she could take this.

Rage boiled up against Sophie. Wasn't Ollie enough? And why had she kept the letter? Was she planning to show her one day? If so, she'd left it pretty damn late. Too many questions. She started to sob. Even in the best case scenario – Sophie had repeatedly told Sam to fuck off – there had been secrets where she would once have sworn on her life that there was nothing but confidences. And why the hell did she wear the red dress to meet Sam? She knew the dress. The vintage one. With the slit up the side. It was Sophie's favourite. And walks? Lunch by the river?

But the worst bit, worst by far, was that Sam had wanted

Sophie, not her. How stupid to believe that Sam had picked her out from the ark of gorgeous women and said, 'You. You're the one, Jenny. The others don't do anything for me.' It was all flooding back now. The things she'd ignored. The way Sam used to stare at Sophie. The way they sometimes held each other's glances a little too long. The intimacy of their conversational shorthand. The way he always seemed angry with Sophie for no apparent reason. Was it the anger of a man who couldn't have her? Or had he? She spun further into the vortex. There was no way out of it.

Curling on to her side in a foetal position, she wiped the tears and snot away with the back of her hand and shoved the letter under her pillow. She must hide it, she realised. Ollie must not see it. Clearly he had never read it, of that she was sure. He would have pulped Sam if he had, all hell would have broken loose. No, Ollie had been in the dark, just like her. And now he couldn't know. Not after everything he'd been through.

A bang from downstairs. The front door? She flicked off the sidelight quickly as the sound of something heavy dropped to the ground. A bag? Coughing. She knew that cough. Ollie was home. She tensed, coiled, a buzz of excitement overtaking her misery. Do not say anything about the letter, she told herself firmly. Say nothing. Scared she wouldn't be able to keep her mouth shut, she decided feigning sleep was the best policy.

Eyes squeezed tight, she listened to the soft scuff of his feet on the stairs, the wooden floorboards, the creak of Freddie's door opening. There was silence for a few moments, then footsteps again, the creaky closing of Freddie's door, the heartstopping opening of hers. Through the filigree of her wet lashes, she could see his floppy-haired figure silhouetted in the doorway. The mattress depressed as he sat down on the edge of the bed. She wished she'd not decided to pretend to be asleep now. She wanted to sit up and lick his face like a puppy. He was a survivor like her. He was . . . he was everything, the only light in the greyness.

'Jenny,' he whispered, placing a hand gently on her shoulder. She caught the smell of aeroplane on his clothes. 'Are you awake?'

She lay there rigid.

'Jenny?'

Her eyes pinged open. The sight of him sitting there was still a shock. She'd been anticipating him in her head all night, and here he was. Warm, human, smelling of aeroplane and chewing gum. 'Ollie.'

'Sorry, did I wake you?' In the gloom she could just see his eyes were smiling, like he knew she'd been faking sleep. A strand of dark hair curled over one of his eyes and she longed to nudge it gently aside with her fingers so she could drink in the whole of his face at once. In his presence, the terrors of the night – the past, the betrayal – began to fade and take on a surreal, blurred edge, like something that had happened long, long ago. There was no one else she wanted sitting on her bed, she realised. Not even Sophie.

'You are a star, Jen. Thank you so much for coming over.' Ollie's breathing was a soft, animate thing in the darkness.

'No problem.'

'Have you got a cold?'

'Yeah,' she sniffed.

The bed sheets crumpled as he moved closer, the curve of his back sinking into the curl of her stomach. They fitted together perfectly. Like he'd been ergonomically designed for her. They lay like this in the darkness for a moment, their breathing synchronising slowly. 'I don't know what I'd do without you, Jen.'

'I'd do anything.' The words twanged in the darkness. She wished they'd sounded less sexual. She was very grateful for the dark. 'To help, you know.'

'I know.' He had a smile in his voice now. 'Cecille OK?'

Cecille. Her name spoken out loud spiked the intimacy.

'She's been sweet.'

'Good, good.'

'But she's in love with you.' It shot out before she could help herself.

He paused for an eternity. 'I know.'

'She's too young, Ollie.'

'She's twenty.'

She bit hard on her lower lip. There was nowhere else in the universe she'd rather *not* be now. Anyone other than Ollie she'd want sitting on the side of her bed.

'You're angry.'

'Imagine how you'd feel if you sent your daughter to a foreign country to work for a family . . .' She turned on to her side away from him and stared at the black wall, convincing no one. 'Oh, what do I know? Do what you bloody well want.'

He surprised her by tucking a strand of her hair behind her ear.

305

'Nothing happened, Jen.' His breath was warm on her bare shoulder. 'But tell me, how long am I meant to live like a monk?'

'I don't know.' All she knew was that her life was plummeting downwards. And she was going to smash into the ground. Everyone in the world was in love with Sophie. Even her own fiancé. Sophie had eclipsed her, even in death.

'I played by the rules. But when did life ever play by the rules?'

'So I guess that's why you fucked Tash, then. And what about Lydia? Are you going to do her, too?' She was still talking to the wall and hated the way she sounded so stiff and bitter.

'I just want to be free,' he said, so softly she could barely hear him. 'Free.'

'You are flipping free!'

He was silent for a long time. 'I am not.'

She was the person strapping him to his past. She was the ballast who must be shed. She must get up tomorrow morning and walk away and not come back. Let him get on with his life. He must be free of the past. Of Sophie. Of her. And she must be free of the whole damn lot of Sophie-in-her-red-dress worshippers.

'Jen.' He slipped one hand on to her waist, making her take a sharp intake of breath, and pulled her over so she could face him. His eyes were luminous. 'I couldn't bear it if you despised me, you of all people.'

She sniffed tearfully then, unable to hold back the tears.

'Hey, baby, what's the matter?' His voice was full of such tenderness it made her cry harder. And he'd called her baby.

She hated it when Sam called her baby. She loved it that Ollie had just called her baby. 'What's the matter?'

'I . . . I . . . I don't know. I guess I've been getting too close to you, to Freddie, to everything up here.' She wiped away the tears crossly on the back of her hand, arching her body away from his confusing touch. There was an intimacy in the darkness of the hour that filled the room with too much possibility. Even the letter under the pillow. Despite the horrors it contained, it was oddly liberating. There was nothing that life could throw at her now. 'I was Sophie's best friend. Not yours. Sometimes I forget that.'

He stared at her intently. 'But things have changed, haven't they?'

She heard her heart pounding in her ears and slowly became aware of something in the room, something thrilling and unutterable.

'I didn't know you before, not how I know you now. You and I, we're not who we were, Jenny.'

The city rumbled distantly outside the window, yet it felt as though she and Ollie were the only still point, the very centre of the city, the most vital bit of it, and that everything rippled out from them.

'You and Sophie were an impenetrable little world when you were together.' His voice broke now. 'I would not have been surprised had you backed off after she died. Lots of her friends have, you know, slunk away like I never knew them. They look at me like I'm a bad omen.'

'People just don't know how to react.'

'No, it's not that. It was Sophie who drew them into our orbit, her dazzle, her drama . . .' He stopped and frowned.

307

'But you, *you*,' he said more urgently. 'Since she's gone you have got bigger and bigger, brighter and brighter. It's like you've come into focus. Sorry, I can't explain it.' He sank his head down, resting his forehead on her shoulder. 'I'm not making any fucking sense.'

But he was making perfect sense. And the darkness of the bedroom was suddenly buzzing and alive, like the darkness around a bonfire on a summer's night.

'I feel like I've got to know you for the first time. I feel . . .' He hesitated, his voice lumpen. '. . . that if you weren't in my life, in Freddie's life, it would be a terrible, terrible thing. That's all.'

He hugged her tighter. Instinctively, she reached for his head, threading her fingers through his forest of black hair, losing them there, realising as she did how she'd longed to do this. He took her other hand and sucked the tips of her fingers, one, then the other, another, and with each kiss she felt a tidal tug towards him.

'I know what I want to do and I know I shouldn't.'

'Don't,' croaked Jenny hoarsely, wishing he would.

He ran his fingers along her jaw line. 'You are so beautiful.'

Beautiful? Beautiful! His words fluttered around her head like butterflies. And at that moment, for the first time in many months, years, she actually felt beautiful. A long, soft sigh came from deep within her, as if she were exhaling a breath that she'd been unaware she'd been holding.

'I've come to see you as mine, just a little bit. I so rarely see you with Sam, it's quite easy for me to delude myself. I can't get my head around the fact that you're about to get married.'

Married. *That* no longer made sense.

He wiped a tear off her cheek with the pad of his thumb. 'In another life we could . . .'

'Please don't, Ollie.' Sophie had been dead eight months. Eight!

'I'm sorry. I'm so sorry. I'm lost, Jen. I'm a fucking mess.'

His mouth was inevitable then. He tasted like cigarettes and old coffee and tears. His beard rasped deliciously against her cheek. His soft lips moved down her face, buried into her neck, and the scent and feel of him filled her world completely.

'No. We can't, Ollie,' she finally managed, gasping for breath.

His lips moved reluctantly away from hers. 'You're right. We can't.' He fell back on the pillow, stared up at the ceiling, breathing heavily. She didn't speak. He didn't speak. There was nothing left to say. The rightness and the wrongness were irresolvable. Slowly his lids began to close and his breath found the long, drawn-out rhythm of the jetlagged. She lay there, awake, heart slamming – the letter beneath her, Ollie beside her – fevered with longing and self-disgust. Soon there was a pink glow at the crack in the curtains. Dawn was breaking. And with it, a terrifying new day.

Forty-three

What the hell's been going on? I take a mini break and everything goes tits up at number thirty-three! Obviously I had no idea that poor little Freddie had chicken pox or I wouldn't have gone on my weekender. I feel horribly negligent, an Asbo angel. I only went because after my recent solitary in Ollie's trainer I was yearning for fresh air. I caught a keen south-easterly from the street's highest chimney – number fifteen's wonky one – and hung on to it as it picked up speed, bouncing over rooftops and electricity pylons, until I clipped the canopy of Highgate Woods. What can I say? Joyous. I was more air than anything else, a shape only, a balloon without its rubber skin. I could freefall with no fear, spin round and round the uppermost branches of the trees, elastic as a teenage Russian gymnast, then rest for a while in a blackbird's nest alongside twigs, feathers and a scrap of Snickers wrapper. I need to rest more and more now. Getting old.

It's not just London's air pollution levels – soaring now in this sticky summer – I am definitely getting fainter, a footprint on the beach. In the heady early days of my afterlife

I was able to slice through time like a hot knife through butter. But now it feels as if the air is thick and viscous. I seem to get stuck in it, like one of those crumbs that are impossible to remove from the golden syrup tin.

Anyway, I'm back from my treetop weekender now. And something has clearly happened in my absence. Freddie is spotty, obviously, but over the worst. It's Ollie I'm worried about. He is subdued and has been staring out of the window for hours. The house itself feels altered too in some way that I can't put my finger on, like it might have subsided a millimetre or two into the ground, or is leaning a teeny bit sideways. I don't know. It just doesn't feel like it did. Not like the number thirty-three of old.

I check in on Jenny, too, and discover she is in an even worse state. There's a dissonance in that horrible sterile-lux Camden flat, crackling, hissing, like a melting nuclear reactor. The atmosphere is so poisonous I have to limit my exposure. It's just as well Sam has stropped off to the country with his parents. Imagine he'd be freaked to see Jenny like this, crying like a baby in the bath. Worried about her, really worried about her now, I stay close, dangling from a leather tassel on her bag, wondering where we are marching to and with such demented purpose. Which is how I find myself here, in Starbucks, Great Portland Street, stuck to the air vent above the coffee machine like a bit of chewing gum.

Not crying now, Jenny has got a face as long as Lyle Lovett's. Her eyes are still pink. Her hands are shaking. She's checking her watch. Nibbling a finger. Checking her watch again. Has she been stood up? She takes the last swig of her coffee. Picks up her handbag off the floor.

311

She's been stood up.

Then the glass doors swish open. A rash crawls up Jenny's collarbone.

A woman walks in. She looks around. She sees Jenny and starts. The woman's hair is pulled back into a ponytail, like mine used to be on bad hair days. She is dressed in a nude dress, bright yellow ballet flats. 'Jenny?'

'Dominique?'

Oh my God. Dominique. I'm settling into my front row seat here.

'I'm sorry I'm so late.' Dominique smiles nervously, scrapes the chair across the floor.

'I hope you didn't mind me emailing. Tash said . . .' Jenny falters, as if unsure whether she's allowed to declare her source. She can't take her eyes off Dominique's face. 'Can I get you a coffee?'

'No, thanks, I've got to be somewhere pretty soon.' There is tension around Dominique's mouth, which purses, like it's got a drawstring inside.

'I needed to meet you properly,' says Jenny finally, twisting her fingers together in her lap angularly like crab claws. 'There's been a lot of stuff . . .' She blows out air, collects herself. 'Between me and Sam. So many unanswered questions. I need to know what's going on, that's all. I'm not looking to blame anyone.'

Dominique shifts on her chair. She's already regretting coming. 'Look, to be perfectly frank, Jenny, I always thought that one day me and Sam would get back together.'

'Back together?'

'I wondered if he was with anyone, what his situation

was, so I tracked him down.' She looks at the table. 'I realise this all must sound a bit bunny boiler. I didn't mean to freak you out. Sorry.'

'You must have liked him a lot.'

Dominique glances up. 'I thought we'd marry, actually.'

Jenny closes her eyes, bracing herself. It's bigger. It's bigger than she thought. 'When were you two together?'

'Summer, two years ago,' Dominique says, in the definite manner of a woman who's been counting the hours ever since.

'Two years ago?' Jenny repeats in a whisper, her hand crushed over her mouth, paling.

Two years ago! Then we're talking around about the time he made a pass at me, too. The little turd.

'We overlapped?' Dominique looks down guiltily as she speaks, like she may not have been entirely ignorant of the fact.

'We did.' Jenny shakes her head in disbelief. 'Jesus.'

Yes, we *all* did.

The two women stare at each other across the round, dark wooden table, me from the air conditioning vent. An irritated Starbucks barista sweeps Jenny's empty cup off the table.

'I better go.' Dominique, clutching her large red tote, stands up to leave.

'One more question.' The clatter in the café seems to quieten for the inevitable. 'Why did you think I was called Sophie?'

Dominique hesitates, wondering what the right thing is to say. The mouth purses again.

I wait. Jenny waits. Her left knee jumps up and down inside her trouser leg. 'Did you know there was someone else?'

'Look,' Dominique says, defensive now. 'All I knew was that he'd got this ... this *thing*, some stupid schoolboy crush, unreciprocated, on some woman. Sophie, her name was Sophie.'

'Unreciprocated?' Jenny asks in a scared whisper. 'You're sure?'

'Yes, unreciprocated, definitely,' she answers firmly. 'That was what was so totally frustrating about the whole situation.' Dominique speaks faster, harder, like aggrieved exes do. 'He said I reminded him of her. That I was like her, but ... but better.' She shakes her head and laughs hollowly. 'I thought if I hung in there ... I can't believe how stupid this is making me sound. I'm not that woman, not the woman you must think I am, Jenny. He was just one of those men, you know, who turn you into someone you're not. Do you know what I mean?'

Jenny nods. She knows exactly what she means. And so do I.

Dominique leaves quickly, with a worried backward glance, wondering what she's done. I flatten against the ceiling, desperate to be human again, desperate to wrap my arms around Jenny and hug her and kiss her and tell her it is going to be alright, and that he had a silly, stupid crush on me but she was always the woman he really loved, that it was just my vanity he flattered, that it never went anywhere because I would never do that. I didn't act faultlessly. I'm a flirt, a tease, an erotic fantasist, but I'm not a traitorous friend. Instead I have to watch helplessly as my dear friend finally breaks, there and then, in the middle of Starbucks, oblivious to the people staring. She sobs noisily until a barista brings her a tissue, then steers her firmly by the elbow out of the door to the crowded street.

Forty-four

'Have you lost your fucking *mind*?' Sam shouted, kicking his weekend bag that he'd dropped to the floor. 'I've just got back from a marquee meeting on site. We can't possibly cancel the wedding.'

Jenny held on to a steel ridge of chair for support. If only she could think straight. But she'd been crying for so long her brain had gone smeary. She could not think. She could not breathe. All she knew was that if she put on that wedding dress it would be the most dishonest thing she'd ever done. 'I'm sorry, Sam.'

His face sagged and aged. He finally realised she meant it. 'Jenny, please.' He lowered his voice so that it sounded almost like a threat. 'I am trying to protect you from yourself. You are angry. You are hurt. Understood. I apologise. I will apologise until the day I die. I am in your debt, OK? Whatever it takes. I'll do whatever it takes, Jenny, to make you realise that it was nothing, absolutely *nothing*.' He swiped the letter angrily off the table. 'I don't know why the silly bitch kept it!'

'Maybe she was going to show me?' All night she'd been

thinking of the times that Sophie had tried to talk to her about something: the *it* in that to-do list Ollie had found months ago.

'Come on. She probably kept it because she enjoyed it. I bet she kept all her love letters, didn't she?'

'Sam . . .' This was a way out. It was her way out and she was going to grab the bucking bronco by the horns and hold on tight.

'She was never happy unless every last man in the room was drooling after her. She fucking loved it.' His face paled with repressed anger. 'Do you remember her at parties, dancing? Dancing in those stupid sequiny dresses. Look at me! Look at me! She may as well have written that across her forehead in red lipstick.'

Her instinct was to leap to Sophie's defence. Not this time. 'It doesn't change anything.' There was a calmness and conviction to her voice that surprised her. 'It's too late, Sam.'

'I'd say *this* was a bit fucking late actually, Jenny. Would you just snap out of it?' He tried and failed to smile. 'Please, Jenny?' he asked, more desperate now. 'You want to throw this away? All this?' he said, gesturing around him, as if the flat itself was something she couldn't possibly give up.

I hate this flat, she thought. I hate its hi-tech hardness. When I have my own place I'm going to have knitted patchwork cushions and an old wooden work surface stained with tea and a radio with a big fat dial that I can turn. 'You fucked around with Dominique, too.' She blinked back tears. 'And I was so in love with you.'

He groaned. 'I really, really tried to get her to back off, stop stirring things up. I even asked Tash to have a word

317

with her, Jenny. I did everything I could to protect you. You've got to believe that.'

She turned away from him, still hurt that he'd crept into her Muswell Hill world and taken the confidence of one of her new friends, used it to his advantage. He used everyone to his advantage. 'It makes it worse.'

He dropped his head into his hands. 'I don't understand.'

'Why did you want to set a date, Sam? After all that foot dragging. That's what I don't understand.'

He looked up at her with red, hurt eyes. 'Because I loved you. Because . . .'

'Why?'

'Sophie's death. It made me focus. I'd lost her . . .' He stumbled on his words before he realised what he'd said.

Something twisted in her stomach. 'You mean it was all over and there was nothing left to play for?'

'No, it made me feel I'd been given a second chance. When she was alive I lived in fear of her saying something to you, fucking everything up. It hung over me, my own stupidity. When she died . . .' He shook his head.

'You thought you'd got away with it?'

He was silent for a moment. 'I'm sorry.' He shook his head. 'I couldn't help the way I felt about the others. I love you.'

Others! How many were there? She couldn't listen to this. 'None of this makes sense to me any more. Don't you see?' she shouted. 'It just doesn't make sense to me!'

'If it made sense before, it can make sense again,' he pleaded. 'We have a connection. We always have done. The good times, think of the good times, babes. Me, you, Soph and Ollie, the picnics, the parties, that lovely weekend on the narrow boat in Oxford, do you remember?'

That hot summer's weekend. The gentle sway of the boat. She clearly remembered Ollie and Sophie sitting on the roof, Ollie licking ice cream off the tip of Sophie's nose, while she watched from the deck, thinking that if she had ice cream on her nose, Sam would make a hand gesture for her to remove it, or pass her a tissue. She remembered thinking on that boat that only beautiful people like Sophie got loved like Sophie was loved. That plainer women like herself shouldn't expect so much. She now also realised that Sam had probably spent the whole weekend ogling Sophie in her bikini. 'Sam, it's over.'

His hands fisted at his sides and for one terrible moment Jenny thought he might hit her. 'I smell a rat here. This is all too convenient, isn't it? Isn't it?' he hissed. 'If you really loved me, you'd believe me.'

Jenny shut her eyes. He was right. She knew he was right. Ollie's kiss had changed everything. It would have changed everything even if Dominique and the letter had never come to light. It had set her on fire in a way she never thought possible. However sickening and shameful her feelings, there was no going back. She'd rather be single forever than marry someone she didn't feel that with. It was the *grrr*. The *grrr* that Sophie used to talk about. It had happened to her.

'Listen, Jenny, you have two choices. You stand here right now and tell me like a grown up what the problem really is, and we might, we just might, be able to avert total fucking disaster. Or you watch your world implode from within very, very shortly.'

'I don't think I love you any more.' A final cut. Let it bleed.

'Bitch.'

'I'm sorry,' she said, beginning to sob, the certainty of a few moments ago fraying at the edges with guilt.

'This is about Ollie, isn't it? You think I was the one with the game plan. When all along it was you, waiting to step in there.' Sam laughed hollowly. 'Jenny, do you honestly think that Ollie would want *you*?'

She took a sharp breath.

'You poor, poor deluded woman.'

Legs shaking, she fled the kitchen, ran to the bedroom and started stuffing her clothes into a holdall. Sam didn't try to stop her. Her life packed up surprisingly small. A capsule life packed into a capsule bag. She walked back into the kitchen to say goodbye. He was sitting at the kitchen table, face flattened against the glass, crying. It was the first time Jenny had ever seen him cry.

'Sam, I'm so sorry.'

'Fuck you.'

She hesitated for one moment at the front door, then, closing it behind her for the last time, she stepped into the grimy Camden sunshine.

Forty-five

When the carriage clock on her parents' mantelpiece hit
eleven am, the exact time she would have been getting
married three weeks ago, Jenny still got goosebumps. And
so the calendar marched on, every date an echo of another
life that was so almost hers, the stuff scribbled out in her
diary. They would be back from honeymoon now. Would
she have stopped taking the pill? Might she even be pregnant?

No, she didn't want that. But she didn't want this either.
Living with her parents. The smell of the chicken farm in her
nostrils. Aged thirty-six. With shingles.

The shingles were her hair shirt. Sam's friends and family
certainly thought she was the devil incarnate. Her own
friends and family had decided that she'd lost the plot. Only
Liz had emailed repeatedly to wish her love and luck and
'whatever else you need right now', reassuring her that any
decision she made was the right decision because she'd made
it. Jenny was immeasurably grateful for Liz's lone, sane
voice.

Yes, it *was* her decision, therefore it had to be the right
one, she reminded herself during the most wretched moments

– in plentiful supply in the small hours – or days like today, when she'd finished a manuscript too soon and the empty hours she needed to fill rolled away in front of her like the pen on her parents' maddeningly slanted desk. Even her hair was wretched, a mass of tinder-dry frizz. She couldn't control her life. She couldn't control her hair.

'Shouldn't you think about getting dressed?' Her mother burst into her bedroom. She never knocked. 'You'd feel better if you got dressed, Jennifer. Here, love, nice cup of tea.'

'Thanks, Mum.' Jenny scratched the base of her shingled back, realising now how much torment poor Freddie had gone through with his chicken pox.

'Don't scratch. You don't want scars on top of everything else.'

It was an uncomfortable paradox that the more she was in need of her mother – and what would she have done without her dear mother in the last few weeks? – the more her mother irritated. Sometimes, quite irrationally, she thought she might actually detest her mother. Then she'd catch herself and realise that the only person she detested was herself, that she was merely projecting on to her mother in the manner of a selfish, angsty teenager, and she'd feel a wave of shame for her own ingratitude, followed by an urge to bury herself in her mother's bosom like a sobbing toddler. She picked up her tea, followed her mother's beanbag figure into the sitting room, and sat down heavily in the foamy scatter cushions, next to the John Lewis pot pourri that would forever more be the Proustian perfume of this whole disastrous episode.

'Try and put your best foot forward and cheer up a little bit, love,' said her mother kindly, perching awkwardly on the corner of an armchair, not sure where to position herself around her daughter's grief. 'I know it's hard. But we all have to take responsibility for our decisions. Not let them eat us up.'

Jenny suspected that her mother really thought that most women in their mid thirties might have chosen to believe their fiancé's protest of innocence, whatever the damning evidence to the contrary. Sometimes she was almost tempted to confide in her about Ollie, to help Mum understand. But she always bottled it. How could she explain she'd fallen in love with her dead friend's husband?

Hers was a betrayal so deep, so corrosive that she could not bear to look at her own face in the mirror, let alone share it with anyone. Yes, she could live with herself for jilting Sam so close to the altar. He would, she was absolutely sure, meet someone else fully deserving of him and be completely fine. But falling in love with Ollie? It didn't matter what Sophie had hidden from her, what she had felt or done, falling in love with Ollie was still unforgivable. Sophie was the girl who had shared her cheese with her the first night at university, the only 'it' girl who ever thought Jenny worth bothering with and who made her laugh and laugh until her gusset was damp.

Sophie's betrayal was quietly buried beneath the soil in Highgate cemetery. Her own betrayal was still alive. The hunger of that kiss haunted her. Sometimes she'd wake in a panic in the night, sitting bolt upright on the pillows of her old childhood bedroom, sweating, panting, convinced that

Sophie had witnessed the kiss, too. That she wasn't dead after all. For once the thought of Sophie alive was no longer comforting.

During the day, it was easier to train her mind. She would tell herself that the kiss – the peculiar *rightness* of the kiss – between her and Ollie had been nothing but a symptom of grief, a clumsy grope for human comfort. But then the yearning for him would spring from her body like a trap and there was nothing she could do about it. He was there when she woke every morning, his hand in her hair, those dark, heartbroken eyes searching hers. And that tug, tug between her thighs.

He had phoned a few times since she'd fled for Kent. She hadn't answered the calls, dreading that he would assume that the kiss had had something to do with the whole runaway bride episode, which, of course, it had. So she responded with perfunctory texts and emails, and made occasional journeys to London to see Freddie, who was busier now, more sucked up in school, play dates, football, moving away from the black smoking crater of last January. She liaised with Cecille, who would frequently come and collect Freddie from a place in town so that she, Jenny, could ostensibly get straight back on the train, but really to avoid Ollie. She never dared ask Cecille how he was.

Avoidance was the name of the game.

Helpfully, the wedding guest list provided a concise record of everyone she must avoid at all costs. Buyers of wedding presents. Witnesses to the shame of the rom com gone wrong. While many of them – the ones who would be seated on the right-hand side of the church, Sam's side – had communicated their judgement with a thunderous silence, those on her side were still foraging for explanations. But she did not want to have to explain herself. She could not.

'Are there any practical things I could give you a hand with, love?' asked her mother, disturbing her thoughts. 'Did I tell you that all the wedding gifts have gone back now? Dad's sorted it.'

'That's great. Thanks so much.'

'What about the wedding dress, love?'

'Sam's probably burned it and scattered the ashes in the toilet.'

'Oh don't say that. I was hoping Ollie might get a refund. Have you asked him what he wants to—'

'No.'

Her mother gave her a sharp look. 'Well I think you should, Jennifer. It was so generous of him. Everyone's lost out here, you know.'

'I know, sorry.' Of course no one had ever got round to booking wedding insurance, and so the bills for the marquee, the caterers, the oompah band had all rolled in. 'I'll pay you all back eventually, Mum, I promise.'

'I know you will.' Her mother's voice softened. The tip of her nose pinked as it always did when crying or sneezing was imminent. 'I just want to see you happy again, that's all.'

Jenny pulled her mouth into a smile shape.

Her mother wasn't convinced. 'I really think you should go and see a friend, Jennifer. I know you feel humiliated and want to lick your wounds, but a girlfriend is the world's best tonic. Marj has pulled me through some really tough times.

And Sally. Sally was a saint when me and your dad were rocky.'

'I've got you and Dad and Bobster.'

Hearing his name, the dog jumped up, wagging his stinky tail against her face. 'Why don't you take Bobster for a walk, Jennifer? It's a lovely day out there. It would get you out of the house and it would make one old canine very happy.'

'OK.' Anything to bring the conversation to a close. She drained her tea, stood up.

'And Jennifer?'

'Yes, Mum.'

'You do know that you can stay here as long as you like, don't you? There's no rush.'

'Thank you, Mum. But I'll only be here until the end of the month, latest. Come on, Bobster. Walkies.'

Four months later she was still there, gazing out of the window at the strings of coloured Christmas lights draped over the Post Office in the distance, the smell of chicken shit in her nostrils. She was relieved that her parents had gone out to do the nativity churchy thing on their own. This gave her time to think and check and double check the details of her forthcoming escape. She had a one-way ticket to New York. She would leave on January the sixth. The anniversary of Sophie's death. That seemed fitting somehow. Sophie had gone over to the other side on that day. She'd cross the Atlantic.

Some people might have dropped to their knees in a church and asked God what to do. She'd dropped to her knees in the vegetable patch and asked Dolly Parton. Dolly, the guru of heartbreak and mistakes in love, the mistress of picking yourself up and dusting yourself down. She'd asked. And she was answered, in a Tennessee drawl. *Move somewhere else, honey. Start over. And don't get mud under your fingernails.*

She'd spent weeks Googling New York apartment share ads on Craig's List and visualising herself sitting in diners tapping at her laptop, drinking macchiatos. In New York she wouldn't be looked upon as a freak for being thirty-six and single. No, there in the city of reinvention, anything was possible. She might even wear yellow. She could Skype Freddie regularly. He could come and stay. She could be eccentric, the New York spinster that took him to see weird movies and art shows and filled him with memories of the Staten Island ferry and Coney Island and the roller disco in Central Park. Maybe she'd live at the Chelsea Hotel.

She gazed across the frozen field – its frosting was slowly beginning to melt in the winter sunshine – and wondered if Sophie would follow her.

Shortly after Sophie had died, she'd worried that she could no longer quite remember what Sophie looked like. But now the opposite was true. Sophie was sticking close, too close. That honk of laugh would ring in her head as she walked Bobster along the quiet country lanes. Sometimes she swore she could feel Sophie's warm breath on her hand. Or she'd look out across a field and for a moment she'd see Sophie dancing, sylph-like, barefoot, her thick, dark hair fanning out around her, her hands weaving the air, exuberant and beautiful. And she'd forgive her anything then, anything at all.

Something was rubbing against her ankle. She looked down, grinned. Bobster was doing what he always did so expertly, dragging her back from the past into the present with stinky licks that smelled of canned venison.

She ruffled him behind the ears. 'Come on. Yes, yes, I know. Time for your walk.' Pulling on her anorak – all she ever wore was anorak, jeans, fleece and wellies now; it made getting dressed in the morning so much easier – she peered out of the window to check for rain. The sun was hidden behind a grey cloud shaped like a giant boulder, and the sky below it had gone rice pudding yellow. Christmas trees twinkled in the leaded windows of the huddle of new-build houses.

The front door clicked shut behind her. Bobster yelped. Seeing that he'd got caught up in his lead, she bent down to untangle his foot, instantly feeling the cold damp of the ground seep through the knee of her jeans. 'There, Houdini.'

A loud growl of engine startled them both. She looked up to see a VW van reversing into her parents' small gravel drive. It braked noisily.

'Excuse me,' she began, about to start the this-is-not-actually-a-public-carpark speech, before tumbling backwards in shock.

Forty-six

'Smell that air!' Suze pushed her briar of hair through the car window and sniffed. 'Bloody lovely.'

There was a scuffle in the back of the van, a series of shouts, small palms pressed against the windows. The vehicle juddered on its wheels.

'Flora, stop hitting Ludo!'

'He's stolen my raisins. Evil raisin stealer. I hate you!'

'Now look what you've done!'

'Ludo! I'm at my wits' end.'

'Get out. Ow. That's my foot.'

Jenny watched, speechless, as Liz appeared, trailing a child. Then Tash's legs, one then the other. She smiled shyly, as if unsure of her reception, and looked relieved when Jenny smiled back. Then Lydia, bundled in metres of cashmere and a cutesy white bobble hat. More children. More noise. She blinked, unable to take the surreal sight in.

'Found you at last.' Suze put an arm around her shoulder and squeezed.

Jenny was speechless. She no longer had the social skills. Still, no one seemed to mind, all leaping up and kissing her at once. It was delightful and horrifying in its unexpectedness.

Liz reached for her hand and held it tight. 'Bloody good to see you, Jenny.'

'God, you too!' She only realised quite how much she'd missed Liz now that she was here. 'But . . .' She shook her head in amazement, laughing. 'How on earth did you know where I was?' They all began to talk at once.

'Ollie dug your folks' address out of Sophie's address book, duh.'

'If you won't come to Muswell Hill, Muswell Hill will come to you.'

'We're the persistent friend equivalent of Japanese knotweed.'

'Does all countryside smell of farts, Mummy?'

'Aren't you going to ask us in for tea? I'd kill for tea.'

'Hurry up, I'm bursting to pee,' said Lydia, hopping from one leg to the other.

It was then that Jenny noticed Lydia's tummy, its perfect convexity swelling like an egg from between the folds of beige cashmere.

Lydia grinned and patted it. 'Six months! A happy accident.'

'Bloody hell! Congratulations,' said Jenny. It had been decades since she last saw them. 'Come in, come in.'

Inside her parents' not-big-enough house, she distracted the children with a scratchy *Star Wars* video and the seasonal tin of Roses. It was harder to know what to do with their mothers. 'Drink?' Feeling a little gauche and unused to company, she rummaged through the drinks cabinet.

It consisted of a sticky and unfashionable mix of super-market whiskies and yellow liqueurs. 'Sorry, no wine. Anyone stomach sherry? It's that or strawberry liqueur from duty free.'

'Sherry, lovely!' they all chimed, then winced as they took their first sip.

Suze raised her glass. 'Happy Christmas, Jenny!'

'Happy Christmas. Now will someone tell me what the hell you're all doing here?'

'We could ask you the same question,' said Liz, peering out of the window.

'You might as well have emigrated to Alaska,' said Tash, looking out the window and surveying the scrub of field with an undisguised look of horror.

Jenny smiled, pleased that she felt no animosity towards Tash, that the scene in Tash's kitchen felt like it had happened three thousand years ago. And Tash smiled back, knowing she was forgiven. 'Probably would have been more going on,' Jenny said.

'God, you *are* brave,' sighed Lydia. 'Having the guts to run for freedom days before your wedding.'

Oh how she wished that was the case, rather than the sad, shameful retreat it had begun to feel like. She looked down at the floor. 'Hardly.'

'What on earth happened?' demanded Suze, leaning forward over the dining table so that her breasts swelled across the polished dark wood.

'Suze, I'm sure Jenny will tell us, if and when she's ready,' Liz said protectively. 'You don't have to say anything, Jenny. We're just all horribly nosy, as you know.'

'The honest answer is . . . well . . .' No, it wouldn't come. Honesty failed her.

'No matter,' said Liz, helping her out of the tight spot. 'Tell us when you're ready, Jenny.'

She smiled gratefully at Liz. 'Seriously, have you just come to say hi? I am very, very touched. I don't deserve it at all.'

'Actually there is another agenda.' Suze sat up straight, switching into meeting mode. For a moment it was like being back in Suze's kitchen.

'Oh. Things are OK?' she asked.

'Well, Help Ollie more or less disbanded after you left. Cecille was, I suppose, doing a good enough job,' Suze said reluctantly.

'Great.' She was relieved to hear that. All was OK.

'But I fear we are needed again,' declared Suze.

Jenny felt the blood drain from her face. 'Oh no. Is Freddie OK?'

Liz put a hand on hers. 'Freddie's fine.'

'Ollie?'

'Ollie is less good,' said Suze, exchanging glances with Liz. 'Despite all our best efforts.'

'We've done what we can, Jenny,' said Lydia, her eyes beginning to well dangerously. 'We ordered his Christmas tree, helped decorate it, gave him a list of the "it" toys in year three, put in the Christmas Ocado order . . .'

'He was baked about three million mince pies by the local ladies,' laughed Liz. 'As you can imagine.'

Jenny smiled. She could imagine.

'He had *so* many offers for Christmas,' sighed Suze,

reaching for another chocolate. 'I'd say pretty much everyone on the street has invited him for lunch, or for tea, or something Christmassy since school broke up. I even bought them stockings, just in case.'

'Oh no. Don't tell me he's on his own for Christmas. Where's Cecille?'

'Gone home to France.' She raised an eyebrow. 'And not coming back. She's got a new Italian boyfriend and is following him to Milan like a lovesick puppy.'

Jenny felt a shot of relief. 'But his mum . . .'

'He muttered something to Brigid about going up to his folks' house up north. That was last week. But there's no sign of any movement. He's still at number thirty-three as we speak. I've had a few peeks at the house . . .' said Suze.

'In other words she's been stalking him,' said Liz matter of factly, peeling the colourful wrapper from another chocolate.

Suze ignored her. 'And I see no sign of imminent departure, Jenny. No sign at all. None of us can bear to see him so miserable. And no one, least of all poor Ollie and Freddie, should be alone for Christmas.'

'Tell her about the incident,' said Lydia, sniffing hard now. 'Sorry, ladies.' She waved her hands in front of her face. 'Hormones.'

'What incident?' She feared the worst. Ollie felt very close all of a sudden. She'd pushed him as far back in her mind as she could and now there he was again. She could feel him, smell him, peel the memory of him back like a clementine.

Suze cleared her throat. 'He did agree to one drink, last week. And he got very, very drunk.'

'So drunk he ended up in Chicken Cottage,' added Tash, 'with Posh Brigid.'

Posh Brigid! Oh God. Another. She didn't want to hear. She knew it was only a matter of time before Ollie met someone, but she didn't want to hear it from someone else. She didn't want the indignity of failing to look happy for him.

As if reading her mind, Liz put a hand on her arm. 'Nothing like that, Jenny. No funny business. Brigid is very happily married.'

'He got very, very pissed. And he started crying.'

'Oh no.' Thrown back into her chair with the horror of it all, Jenny started to bite her fingernails. 'Christmas without Soph was always going to be hard. Poor Ollie.'

'It's not just Sophie he's missing,' said Liz gently.

There was a crashing silence, broken only by the plaintive cry of Obi-Wan Kenobi. She felt all their eyes burning into her.

'He misses *you*, Jenny,' said Tash, with an openness that Jenny had never seen before. 'He told Brigid. He misses you desperately, darling.'

Jenny's throat contracted and closed. She couldn't breathe.

'I think you disappearing like this . . .' Suze tried to choose her words carefully. 'Not to lay on the guilt, but he's been really struggling these last few months.' She hesitated. 'Did you not think . . .'

Jenny bit down on her lip. She could not possibly explain. Never. Her feelings for Ollie were her own dark, dirty secret.

'We know you've been going through your own shit,' Liz

said kindly. 'And it must be horrible for you, it must feel like your world has fallen apart.'

'I'm fine.'

'You don't look fine,' said Lydia quickly.

The tears came then. There was no stopping them. Suze immediately pressed her into the fleshy mound of her bosom. A small child's fingers pressed the last Roses' Caramel Keg into her hand. Another dabbed her cheek with tissues.

'Let it all out, Jen,' said Suze, slapping her hard on the back, as if she were trying to burp her. 'Let it all out.'

'Oh God, you've set me off now, too,' wailed Lydia.

'Oh no, Lydia's started!' howled Liz. 'Hit the flood sirens!'

Jenny snorted with laughter through her tears. As she emerged gasping for breath from the group hug – friends who may never be as dear as Sophie, but who had become real friends all the same – she felt different. Like a heavy bag had been picked off her back. Girlfriends were a tonic. Her mother, for once, was right.

'It's snowing!' yelled Ludo. The children jumped up from the floor and pressed their noses against the cold window, entranced as snow whirled in eddies over the field. 'Sick, man. Sick.'

Jenny was not sure whether it was something to do with the snow, or the hug, or the fact that Ludo reminded her so unbearably of Freddie at that moment, but forty minutes later, against her better judgement, she found herself scrawling a note on her parents' telephone pad and picking her car keys off the duck hook on the wall.

Forty-seven

I've been dead for almost a year. Since dying, Freddie has lost two baby teeth, jumped from a size ten foot to a twelve, and grown two inches. He has six chicken pox scars on his stomach where he scratched. He is, like, totally over Beyblades and into the canoeing game on the Wii. He has a crush on Ani, a Sri Lankan beauty in year four. He has learned six handy new swear words to toss about in the playground when necessary, and wants to watch *X Factor* instead of *Deadly 60* or *Strictly*.

Ollie, meanwhile, has gone grey, gained and lost a beard, shed fourteen pounds, worked his way through the entire *Mad Men* box set twice, and no longer listens to Tibetan monks chanting for light background muzak. He doesn't wank over my knickers either. The boiler is up for its yearly service, which he'll undoubtedly forget. The smoke alarm batteries are almost dead, and he'll forget to replace them, too. Against all the odds Ping Pong and my potted palm appear to have survived.

My grave is covered in a crisp crust of snow today, the first Christmas snow we've had in decades, ruining all the bookies' coffers. There is a gothic shoot of vivid green ivy fingering my gravestone. Over the last year there have been bluebells growing beside it, daisies, dandelions, layers of mulching autumn leaves alive with beetles and bugs, and, on more than one occasion, a pregnant badger. The mound of earth that duvets my coffin no longer has that morbid, freshly-dug-up-vegetable-patch look either. See. I've almost settled in.

And yet.

I'm still here, aren't I? Not in a dank patch of cemetery but curled beside the rows of Christmas cards on the mantelpiece above the hissing log fire, like Ping Pong's elderly, dozy grandma. No, I'm certainly not what I was. I am smaller, weaker, grey as a cup of old tea. As in life, as in death, it seems: we're all only going one way and there's nowt anyone can do about it. On the other hand, I do sometimes wonder if I am fading because I am fading from the lives of those I love. There are very few obvious traces of me left now. No scent of my perfume, none of my pubes rolling on the bathroom floor. My voice has been deleted from the answer machine. The clothing catalogues have stopped falling through the door. My email account no longer exists. There has been a settlement with the bus company stored away for when Freddie's older. (I want him to spend it sensibly on lost weekends at music festivals, Italian leather shoes and whisking beautiful girls to Paris. I want him to feast on life itself.) I am fragments of memory now, photographs on the wall, footage on the video camera, an echo in Freddie's beautiful features, his sweet tooth, his bubbly laugh, the glistening ore of love in his heart. And this is OK. I tell myself this is OK. This is enough.

What is far less OK is the fact that I have not been able to alter the fates of those I leave behind. My pitiful lack of supernatural powers has rendered me totally hopeless as either matchmaker or kybosher of weddings; I'm afraid I can claim none of the credit for Sam and Jenny's torching. It makes me sad that Ollie and Freddie will spend their first Christmas alone. And probably their next, too.

The lack of a woman at number thirty-three is obvious. This is a house craving oestrogen, or at the very least someone who cares about the removal of the sticky Lucozade-like substance in the hinge of the loo seat. It's very much a male domain now, more den than home. There are no beauty products or periodphernalia in the bathroom cabinet, no stashes of toffee ice cream, a scarcity of puddings full stop. I fear that the Christmas pud will never make a reappearance in this house, Ollie and Freddie much preferring chocolate biscuit cake. The Christmas tree is up though, next to the mountain bikes scuffing the pale wall in the sitting room with their rubber handlebars. The tree is smaller than last year's – I always was a sucker for a big Disney tree – and has been decorated by Freddie and Suze's kids, a gaudy riot of multi-coloured tinsel and plastic balls. (My tasteful wooden angels and pinecones are collecting dust in a box in the loft.) Paper chains made by Freddie at school dangle perilously over the fire. A tin of uneaten mince pies languishes in the cereal cupboard. The fridge is full of beer and Parma ham and sausages and cracked hard Cheddar. Needless to say, upstairs there is a *vast* amount of empty closet space.

With some effort I extricate myself from my warm nest

beside the Christmas cards on the mantelpiece and wheezily thread myself through the banisters to check on Freddie. My beautiful boy is on the computer in the study playing 'Dom from Canberra' and 'Brad7 from Milwaukee' on a Mathletics game, yelping with delight when he wins, his pupils dilating with pleasure. I leave him absorbed in his game and slide back down the banisters to be close to Ollie who is dozing on the sofa, scraps of cashew nut dust powdering his old sweater. (Who will buy him a new cashmere sweater for Christmas? I always bought him a cashmere sweater for Christmas.) His lips part a bit, his eyes move rapidly beneath their lids, like he's dreaming. The news is rolling on the telly but it is on mute. On the coffee table a bottle of nettle ale is half-drunk, alongside a pile of studio CDs, out-of-date newspapers and one of Freddie's socks. I settle beside him, warming myself on the edge of his thigh, my husband the host. And it is only then that I sense somebody outside the house: the slip of snow under a sole, the melting of a snowflake on a hot cheek.

The doorbell rings. There is a power surge in the house.

Ollie keeps on dozing. Wake up! Wake up, darling! I wham against his side, making as much impression as a baby duck's feather tickling the steel hull of a ship. He sleeps on, still as a moth. The doorbell rings again. The shadow is moving from one foot to the other. The shadow is a familiar shape. And it is walking backwards, receding.

No, the shadow has stopped. It is turning. It is walking back up the path, faster this time. One more quick, sharp ring. Ollie opens a bloodshot eye. He scratches his balls. His brain catches up with his ears and he staggers down the hall towards the door, shedding cashew crumbs. He opens the front door. His face lights up, like all his Christmasses have come at once.

'Hi,' Jenny says. There is snow on the tips of her dark lashes, like tiny white pom poms.

He stares at her in silence, grinning like a loon.

She smiles shyly. 'Er, can I come in?'

They are in the hallway now and the air between them is sparking, ticking, as if we're in a forest of electricity pylons. She flicks snow off her hair. A flake lands on his neck, melting instantly.

'You look different.'

He rubs his hand over his jaw. 'I shaved the Bin Laden.'

'Ah.' She laughs, blushes.

They are in the middle of the sitting room now, lit by the firefly glow of the fairy lights. Jenny doesn't realise that she has a long tail of green tinsel stuck to the bottom of her snowy boot.

'You disappeared,' says Ollie, still staring at her weirdly. He is pulsing with a strange, pent-up energy that is familiar to me but hard to identify.

She looks down at the floor. 'Sorry.'

His eyes don't leave her face. Like he's scared it might go somewhere if he looks away for even a second. 'I missed you, Jen.'

A bittersweet possibility begins to dawn. Could they? *Would* they? Have I been . . . ? Oh my God, have I ignored what was under my nose all this time? I consider the match for all of two milliseconds and I'm flooded, for the first time since I died, with a delirious cascading rush of hope.

Jenny smiles twitchily, like she could just as easily cry. 'I'm sorry for being such a crap friend.' I can see her backing away. 'I really am, Ol.'

I want to fill her heart and tell her it's OK. There is no other woman on planet earth I'd rather replaced me at number thirty-three. You even helped me choose the living room wallpaper! You have legacy here. Oh, Jenny. Look after my boys. Take them, hold them close, and make them eat some broccoli.

'I'm going to New York in the new year,' she says, unable to meet his eye. 'I didn't want to leave without saying goodbye properly.'

Ollie looks stricken. 'New York?'

'I need to start again.'

Oh, Jenny, darling Jenny. Please don't screw up, not this time. Everything is at stake. *Everything*.

'New York is so far away.'

'That's kind of the point.'

'You can start anywhere, Jen.' He takes her hands in his. 'Stay with me.'

She stares at their entwined hands. 'I can't,' she says in a whisper. She's beginning to shake like a leaf. 'You are . . . you are Sophie's husband.'

Jenny, Jenny, I am dead as a dead parrot! Ceased to be! I must do something. I must. Using my last reserves of flagging energy, I whirl dementedly round and round her head, trying to make her see me or sense me or whatever it takes to make her realise that here is her chance. This is it.

In my usual grand paranormal style, nothing happens.

'Please listen to me.' I see it in his eyes then, his love for her. He is no longer mine. Our love has been recycled. Haringey Council would approve.

She pulls away from him. 'Don't, Ol.'

I whirl again, frenzied now, desperate. The future is slipping away, the last grain of sand through my clay-cold fingers.

Jenny steps backwards, touches her forehead. 'Oh.'

'You alright?'

She looks puzzled. 'Yes . . . Yes, I think so.' She closes her eyes, fingers still on her forehead.

Freaky. Did I just do that? I do it again, harder this time. Her eyes squeeze shut. 'Oh,' she says, touching her forehead again.

I did it! I only bloody well did it! I can commune with more than hamsters and smoke alarms.

'Here, sit down.' Concerned, he reaches for her, steadies her with his hands. She perches on the arm of the sofa.

'Give me one minute then you can go again, OK? You can go to New York. Go where you damn well want. Just hear me out, please?'

Jenny nods. There's still a chance. Relief tunnels out of me, long and light, like a last breath.

Ollie's brows knit together and he speaks slowly and carefully. 'I love Sophie from the bottom of my heart, Jenny. I miss her every day.'

'Me too,' croaks Jenny. She puts her hand down on the sofa to steady herself and accidentally presses the remote control lying on a cushion. Music starts to pour out of the speakers, filling the room with something twangy, bluegrass.

'But she has gone, Jen. And losing you for all these

months felt like another huge loss, and I've missed you, missed you so much.' His eyes darken. 'Freddie keeps asking after you.'

She gulps. 'I'm sorry.'

The music rises and falls around them. Harmonica. Guitar.

'I know that I'm a car crash.' He smiles at her so tenderly that it makes me want to weep. 'And I know that any sane woman would run for the hills, but I *love* you, Jenny, I love you not only because Sophie loved you and she would want me to love you too, but because when you are with me it feels like the world is not such a crap place. You take me to a different place to the one I am in. Does that make sense?'

She bites her lip, shakes her head. 'You fucked Tash.'

'I wished it was you.'

Jenny drops her head into her hands.

'Sophie would want us to be together, I know she would. Of all her friends, she adored you, Jenny. She completely adored you. You were like a sister to her.'

'Even weirder.'

'Sophie liked weird. When did she ever play by the rules?'

Jenny smiles and swallows, trying not to cry.

'We loved each other totally, but it wasn't perfect, Jenny. And it did not need to be perfect, nothing needs to be perfect . . . just enough.'

She looks at him with such longing then, I wonder if she's about to lurch forward and take a bite out of his arm.

'You must not see us, me and Sophie, as something that is, was, unattainable, unrepeatable. God, it's so hard to explain.' He shuts his wonderful gypsy eyes, presses his fingers against them. 'It's just that . . . I think you're totally wonderful. That's all. Please say something, Jenny.'

Jenny doesn't say anything. Instead she looks up and she starts to smile, a big, wide smile like a beam of light.

'Come here, you.' He stands up, pulling her with him, slides his arms around her waist, rests his chin on her shoulder, and slowly, falteringly, like teenagers at their first school disco, they start to sway to the music. Jenny is stiff and shy at first, but as the song progresses she relaxes, lets her body be led by his. And there they are, dancing in the living room lit by fairy lights, stepping on each other's toes, the green string of tinsel still stuck to the sole of her shoe.

The track finishes.

Snow is swirling in whirlpool flurries outside the window. It's a strange backdrop, like it's just the two of them in one of those toy snow globes. They are looking at each other in astonishment, as if they can't quite believe the feelings whooshing up inside them.

Then it happens.

The power of the kiss flings me hard against the ceiling. My husband's sad blue body turns pink as she breathes life into his lungs, softly sucking the last bit of it out of me. Like a sweet passed between the mouths of lovers. They are kissing and kissing. The music starts up again. He laughs, and a new song begins.